VOSTOK STATION

J.D. HUFF

SEVERED PRESS
Hobart Tasmania

VOSTOK STATION

CHAPTER ONE

Professor Hamlin had absolutely no idea what a momentous shift his life was about to undergo, or how swiftly this dramatic change was going to happen. Quite the contrary. As far as he was aware, everything was under control and going very much as planned.

He strode briskly down the wide, empty hall, thinking of the papers sitting in a neat pile on his desk. They were his focus now, but only for a short time–assuming he could find the necessary motivation to wade through them. Once they were marked, he would have an entire semester of research to savor and enjoy. He noted the clicking of his heels on the terrazzo floor as the retort echoed crisply down the empty hall. The sound had always appealed to him for some reason. Maybe a little more so at this exact moment, with the positive mood he was in, as he savored the transition from his busiest term to the appeal of working out of the classroom. No more students; no more teaching; no more daily deadlines for the associated preparatory work. That line of thought led him to almost regurgitate the words of a song from back in the day that reflected a similar sentiment—no more teachers, no more books, no more something, something–Alice Cooper, or Pink Floyd, or something along those lines. He wasn't motivated to chase after the tune as it flitted through his memory and disappeared just as quickly. In either case, a truly wonderful scenario, he concluded.

This project would have him living in a temporary camp on the edge of the Likouala Swamp in the Democratic Republic of Congo. It was the largest area of its kind in the world. The region was still rather undeveloped, which was a rare and desirable bonus. For him, as a biologist, this constituted a dream come true. His focus would be to establish a foundation of data based on current levels of life, both in and out of the water. This, in turn, would be used to set up an environmental conservation program before any development encroaching on the area could do irreversible damage. With the blessings of the local government and the United Nations Environmental Sustainability Council, the research was set to proceed smoothly. He was passionate about the work. When it was completed, the results should help to sustain a vulnerable ecosystem indefinitely. He hoped to spend the rest of his career writing and lecturing about it.

And all of that could be accomplished even if he didn't find evidence of dinosaurs. They supposedly still existed there, according to several pseudo-scientific wacko web sites and anti-evolution organizations. He knew they were all crazy. He also knew that William Buckland dined on puppies, Jack Parsons like to dance naked around a fire in his garden, and Nikola Tesla fell head over heels in love with a pigeon. In science, crazy didn't necessarily mean stupid or wrong. Besides, he liked to keep all his options open. Verified evidence of a prehistoric creature would put his name in all the science books. In research terms, he would be a rock star.

He would miss Deborah terribly, of course. There was time for one more round of berating her into tagging along for part or all of the expedition. Surely she could continue to progress through her thesis while there. Besides, he would be available for consulting purposes if the need arose. At the very least, she could fly in for a couple visits while the work was progressing. Love was an amazing thing, but four months was a long time to be apart. He really didn't think she could hold out that long.

"Sir?" The voice was necessarily loud in order to be heard above all the other noise.

Hamlin snapped awake and immediately felt the pains that came from sleeping in an unnatural position for too long. The hum of the plane's propeller driven engines left no doubt as to where he was. At least they were still in the air. There had been some doubt about the wisdom of flying in these weather conditions. He rolled his head in order to work out some of the kinks.

"You had asked us to wake you before landing, correct? We'll be there in a few minutes. There's some blowing snow and a bit of a crosswind, so it might get a little dicey."

"I did. Thanks. And thanks for the warning. That gives me time to brace myself *and* throw up."

The co–pilot smiled and started back toward the cockpit.

"There's twenty bucks in it for you if we make it down in one piece." He had to yell to have any hope of being heard in the noisy plane. He got an over-the-shoulder look in response.

"Don't worry about it, sir. This plane was designed to land in any condition or terrain. We'll be fine."

The plane had also been designed primarily to carry cargo and was anything but comfortable.

"I should warn you," Hamlin said, taking advantage of the fact that he had captured someone's attention temporarily, "in the event of a crash, I probably won't die well. There'll be crying and yelling, begging and pleading. And I'll likely soil myself. We have to think about the rescue workers. They would be quite traumatized by my remains." Hamlin grimaced. What rescue workers? They were over Antarctica.

"Just relax, sir. We'll be on the ground in no time."

Hamlin grunted as he changed his position for one that would hopefully, but not likely, be more comfortable. "I know we'll be on the ground. Gravity takes care of that. That's inevitable. It's the condition we'll be in that concerns me." By now the co–pilot was gone. He transitioned from public ranting to a monologue without audience. He wondered exactly how cold it was going to be down there. "*Safely* on the ground. You left out the word safely. The way you said it could mean something like 'splattered all over the place.' That would still technically qualify as being on the ground."

The plane banked rather sharply, or so it seemed to him. What kind of pilot would take a job flying this type of route anyway? The best of the best? Or maybe these were pilots who liked a challenge. The co-pilot certainly talked and looked like he had a military background. That might be good. Maybe he graduated from Top Gun. The C-130 was a military plane, after all. Why hadn't he taken the time to resolve these questions before getting airborne?

There was a small porthole for viewing, which he stumbled toward in the false hope he could make out the landing site. Everything was grey and incoherent. They were probably flying through a blizzard. They could have been upside down for all he could tell–another unsettling thought. If he did see anything, it might be disconcerting anyway. Shouldn't he be fastening his security belt? He shuffled back to his seat and grabbed the strap, fumbling to get it properly latched. He fancied that the plane changed from a level course of flight to a downward descent. That meant the moment of truth was fast approaching.

The craft creaked and groaned, seeming to be making a show of how it was laboring against the laws of physics. That brought visions of a fiery wreck into his mind. The descent that had been initially smooth was now disrupted by several sudden sharp bumps.

"Think positive thoughts, old man." The flight smoothed out once again. "Good, that's good." Suddenly the plane banked sharply and simultaneously felt like it was driving over a rough set of railroad tracks. "Oh, that's really *not* good." His stomach decided to join in the protest.

Would he suffer if the plane plowed into the ice below, or would it all be over quickly? His hands gripped the mesh that lined the seat and he wished for something more stable. It was a totally delusional thought, however. His hand strength would affect no change to the outcome if they plowed into the ground. He heard and felt the landing gear drop and lock into position. The next movement was easy even for him to interpret. It was the wheels coming into contact with the ground. There were bumps from the runway but not as bad as he had feared they would be. He could now feel the plane slowing down. "Oh, thank God." He started to fumble with his seatbelt. They hadn't come to a complete stop, but he figured if the airplane police wanted to hustle him back to civilization for forty lashes with a wet noodle, then let them do it. He wandered over to the window again and was rewarded with a brief glimpse of a light somewhere in the distance. He started to pick up his meager luggage and organize it by the door.

His office door was ajar. Unusual but not alarming. He pushed against it with the palm of his right hand and it opened smoothly. He entered this familiar place without hesitation or reservation. Sitting in the solitary chair against the far wall was a young lady. She stood as he noticed her.

"Can I help you?"

She extended her hand and he shook it in reflex. She looked to be around twenty—no doubt a student.

"I apologize for showing up unexpectedly. I tried to call earlier but couldn't get an answer."

Hamlin walked behind the massive walnut abomination that was his desk and sat. "No problem. We were short staffed today. What can I do for you, miss...?"

"Lillian Cooper."

Hamlin forced himself back into the moment despite all the other thoughts swirling around his head that threatened to distract him.

"Oh, wait a minute. I do know you. I had you as a student last semester, correct?"

She smiled, revealing a mouth full of perfect teeth. "That's right. Introductory Ecology. I carried a B average."

"Yes you did. Which begs the question, why are you here now? Surely it's a little late to complain about your grade."

"Oh no. I got the grade I deserved. I liked the course but knew it wasn't the direction I was going. I could have applied myself more."

"Well, B is a good grade for someone who isn't really trying. Maybe you missed your true calling. Nonetheless, we've now circled back to my original question. What is it that brings you into my office today?"

She fidgeted before answering. "I guess you're pretty busy."

He waved his hand toward a stack of papers. "I have a lot of marking to do. Excuse me if I seem abrupt."

"I understand." She seemed to be in deep thought. "I'm not sure where to begin."

Hamlin furrowed his eyebrows. "You're not doing some sort of marketing research or anything of the sort, are you? Did Professor Johnston put you up to this? If so, I'm afraid I'm going to disappoint you."

She seemed to set herself in some semblance of order. With the previous uncertainty swept aside, she leaned slightly forward and made solid eye contact.

"I'm not here for myself. I'm here for my boyfriend. He's in your class this semester."

Hamlin didn't care for where this was going.

"Oh? And who would that be?"

"Mark Gallagher. Do you know him?"

He knew him. Mark was a bright enough kid but spent too much time having fun. With girls, booze, and the kind of partying that only happens when you're away from home distracting him, classes just got in the way. He was hopelessly behind in his grades.

"If Mark wanted to discuss his progress in my class, he should have come in person. I'm afraid I can't discuss his status with anyone but him."

Her facial response turned sour. "Look, Mark thinks he is really close to making it in your class. If he does well on the exam, he feels that he'll probably pass the course. And he really needs it. If he fails, he either drops out or starts over again next year."

The professor shook his head. "Why didn't he think of that sooner? It's not like he isn't smart enough. All he had to do was apply himself. A little bit of effort on his part and this all could have been avoided."

"But if he fails, it's a whole year wasted!" She was getting emotional now, her big eyes a little teary. She was a cute one, there was no doubt there. But she was just enough on the plus side of a perfect figure that Hamlin couldn't imagine that she was going to have a serious, long-term connection with Mr. Popular, unless he was underestimating the ethical component to his part of this relationship. Or maybe he was getting cynical in his old age.

"And so what did you think you could do? Come in here and convince me to violate every moral I have by changing his grade? Should I pass him because it bothers you that he's not doing well? Is that what you expected to happen? Because if so, you were very much mistaken." Hamlin was getting pissed.

"If he fails or drops out, I'll probably never see him again!" At this, she started with genuine sobs.

Hamlin nodded. *"And there it is. Well, that's no surprise. I suspected that was what this was all about. I suppose he told you he loves you but if he fails it will tear your relationship apart. He's just using you–surely you can see that. And, by the way, there was never any chance that this little scheme of yours was going to work, just so you know. It's not even particularly well thought out, but I'll give you the benefit of the doubt and attribute that to him. I'm afraid I'm going to have to ask you to leave. This is totally inappropriate and a complete waste of my time and yours."*

She sniffed and nodded slowly. *"I guess you're right. I'm sorry to have bothered you."* She stood awkwardly.

"Don't let a casual relationship dictate your life. You can be or do anything you want. If this character cares about you, he'll find a way to overcome his mistakes without putting you or your passion for each other in harm's way."

She had no immediate response.

"I'll mark him on the merit of his efforts, just the same as everyone else. After that, it's up to him. I wish him well, as I do for all my students, but quite frankly, statistics prove that a large portion of first year students will drop out for one reason or another. Hard work puts the odds in favor of success, and that's a lesson he needs to learn. Correct?"

She stared silently. *"I'll do anything to help him pass. Anything."*

Hamlin really didn't care for the insinuation. *"Look, this conversation has gone as far as I'm going to allow. He can deal with his own problems. You're a smart girl. Focus on your career and on making good decisions. Good day, Miss Cooper."*

She followed his lead and stood up. She turned without another word and exited into the hall.

"I don't know how you can be so smart and so gullible all at the same time," he said after her, although she could no longer hear. He picked up the phone from its receiver. The moment it was in his hand, a tall distinguished looking man walked in through the still open door.

"Oh, I'm sorry." He dropped his voice to a whisper. *"Didn't know you were on the phone."*

Hamlin put it back in its cradle.

"I'm not. Good timing. Besides, I was just going to give Deborah a ring to let her know I'd be home a little late. No big deal. How are things, Brian?"

The two men had a long and pleasant conversation. Both were feeling good about the end of the semester.

"Why the pile of papers on the desk, Francis? Did your assistants stage a wildcat walk-out?"

"No, not at all. Some of these are my potential doctoral candidates. I want to mark them myself."

"Oh, very good. I understand. Say, I should get out of your way and let you get some work accomplished. Listen, once this is settled and before you leave the country, why don't you and Deb come over for a nice barbeque on the back deck? We can drink too much wine and sit in the hot tub until we wrinkle."

Hamlin laughed. "We're already wrinkled, you old goat. Why exacerbate the issue?"

"Because we'll be too drunk to care. Think about it. I'll call you early next week and set something up."

"Great. I'll mention it tonight. Say hello to Carol for me."

"I will. Good night, Ham. And good luck with your marking."

"You should be wishing good luck to my students. They need it more than I do."

And then Hamlin was alone. He looked at the time. He was discouraged to realize that his enthusiasm for marking had completely dissipated. Unfortunately, the work still had to be done. Once he got started, it always seemed to go better. He decided to pick up a cheap bottle of wine, maybe some nice flowers, and surprise Deborah when he went home. Hopefully that would make up for being late.

"I trust you enjoyed the flight, Doctor Hamlin?"

Francis sought after and then shook the pilot's hand. "Thank you for getting us down in one piece. I think I owe you twenty bucks."

He looked confused. "Is there a new fee I didn't know about?"

Hamlin smiled. "It was more like a bribe I made with your co-pilot."

Now he smiled in understanding. "That's all right. You can keep your money. It's our job, and besides that, we do have a vested interest in landing safely."

The side door opened and the man who entered was wearing the biggest parka that Hamlin had ever seen. It looked less like he was wearing it and more like the coat was in the latter stages of devouring its occupant. A gust of absolutely frigid air preceded him.

"Doctor Francis Hamlin, I presume."

"Who else? Do you mean to say that you actually get people who show up here accidentally? You must be Doctor Sokolov."

He bowed slightly. "At your service. I would shake your hand, but these mitts are a chore to remove. You brought lots of warm clothing, I hope."

Hamlin looked down at his bags. "More than enough for winter in New England."

Sokolov grinned. He was a small man despite the additional size added by the coat. "New England is not a fair representation of our weather. You will find winter in Antarctica different from anything you have ever experienced before. But, based on your profile, I think we will have some extra things that should fit you nicely should that become necessary. If you are ready for your first taste of winter as we know it, then I will invite you to follow me. If you can't manage everything, I'll send someone out for the rest of your things."

Francis prepared to disembark. "I can manage. Never liked tipping, you see. I'd rather be self-sufficient, so I've learned to carry a load."

He stepped outside and took a deep breath. That was his first mistake.

"Are you all right, Doctor?" Sokolov asked as Hamlin worked out of a coughing fit.

Francis waved him away. "Yes, of course. I'm fine." His words bore no association to how he felt. The frigid air actually seemed to burn as he breathed it in. His eyes immediately watered up and impaired his vision to a significant extent. His ears already felt frostbitten.

"Then let's get you inside quickly. This way, Doctor, if you please."

There was no arguing that suggestion. As his eyes cleared, Francis was surprised at the layout of the camp. "This is it? Or is there more I can't see from here?" It was dark outside, the gloom broken only by several anemic lights mounted on the outside wall of a handful of dilapidated buildings.

"We have a few outlying buildings, Doctor, but this is the main portion of the camp. Our quarters are in the structure just ahead."

The decrepit edifice looked like the Saturday morning shelter used by the manager of a garbage dump. "We all live in there?"

"Put your mind at ease, Doctor. There are only fourteen of us here for the winter months. Everyone has their own space. You will not find it crowded."

The entry door looked suspiciously like it could have been dragged out of a dumpster. Sokolov wasted no time in swinging it open and ushering Francis inside. The first thing he noticed was the heat. The second was a smell that he was sure he had never experienced before and therefore could not immediately categorize. Finally, he became aware of the crowd of people that were forming a wall in front of him. In this room, about the twice the size of his kitchen back home, the entire staff of the station had gathered.

"Welcome, Dr. Hamlin." This from a burly, bearded man with just a subtle trace of Russian in his accent. Many other voices of welcome blended into a pleasant murmur.

Sokolov raised his hands. "Please, everyone. Let the good doctor step inside. Don't smother him in his first moments."

The murmur now subsided to various gentle apologies.

"That's all right. I've never been this popular before," Francis said as he addressed the group. "I might get to like it."

"Why don't you drop your bags here for now, Doctor? I believe we have some excellent vodka opened for this occasion. There has to be some advantage to being on a Russian station, after all. We will escort you to your quarters once you have been properly welcomed in accordance to our customs. You are not, I hope, someone who believes in total abstinence?"

Francis grinned at his thought. "That is a character trait which I cannot lay claim to."

This caused a murmur of general agreement.

"Very well, then. Doctor Sayansky, would you do the honors?"

"My pleasure." The voice belonged to a tall woman who immediately struck Hamlin as being rather good looking. There were some minor deviations from what was normally considered attractive, Hamlin thought in an abstract manner, but he couldn't exactly put his finger on why he thought that. Her sort, dark hair could have used the services of a fine stylist and her current wardrobe was bland and utilitarian. That was more the fault of *where* she was as opposed to *who* she was, to be fair. She probably wasn't going to be on the cover of any fashion magazines, but he could imagine that she had accumulated a number of suitors in her day. Somehow *cute* was the word that jumped into his mind. She also did a fine job of bartending.

Glasses were quickly filled and passed around. Francis noted that few of them matched, and none would be considered proper drinking vessels in most of the places where he would imbibe. However, the plastic cup with faded flowers on it that was pressed into his hand was doing a fine job of holding the cold, clear liquid.

The large, bearded man raised his glass and the room grew silent.

"Poyekhali!" His voice was deep and booming. The exclamation meant nothing to Hamlin, but the toast was received with smiles and nods of agreement.

"Sorry, I don't speak Russian. What does that mean?"

Sokolov put his hand on Francis's shoulder. "Nothing eloquent or full of deep meaning, I'm afraid. Loosely translated, it means 'let's get started.'"

Francis actually laughed at that. "The perfect toast!" He tipped his glass and drained it in a single swallow. "Wow! Now that's good vodka. Say, have we picked the designated driver for the evening?"

A bright-eyed younger looking man with a slight lisp addressed him. "Don't worry. We'll make sure you end up in your bed if you can't make it there yourself. We've all used that service once or twice."

Sokolov was the only one not nodding. "Let us not forget the work that lies ahead of us. Don't damage Dr. Hamlin too severely on his inaugural evening."

"Francis, please. Call me Francis. We're all peers."

The tall woman playing the role of bartender raised the bottle in her hand. "Another round!"

There was no argument.

Accomplishing such a small amount of marking would throw his planned production off for the rest of the week. It would take some effort to dismiss that aspect of his day–a touch of obsessive compulsive disorder made changes to his schedule seem unusually disconcerting. The side effects of this day were manifesting themselves physically by now. He was growing perceptively weary as he strode along.

Normally, the walk home through his quiet neighborhood was something he enjoyed, but today he just wanted to get there. He also wanted to see Deborah and have a nice, long talk. It was way past supper and he hadn't eaten since early that morning. Maybe that was a contributing factor to how bad he felt. Perhaps she had cooked him something nice; that would be a sufficient remedy.

With that optimistic thought, he made a right angle turn and stepped onto the sidewalk that ran along the perimeter of his driveway. Halfway up, he stopped. The garage door was open and Deborah's car was gone. Terrific. It was Murphy's Law in action—anything that could go wrong, would. He couldn't recall that she had plans for the evening, but then again he hadn't been thinking all that clearly. Hopefully she'd be back shortly. He decided to enter the house through the garage since it was open anyway. Why not save a few steps?

He went inside, put his briefcase on the hall table, and turned toward the kitchen. He knew immediately that something wasn't right, but it took a moment for the notion to manifest itself clearly. There was a lot of stuff missing. Deborah's stuff.

"What the hell?" He walked in a daze toward the kitchen. There, as if in fulfillment of a bad dream, lay a single sheet of white paper in the middle of the table. He hesitated before picking it up; unconsciously acknowledging that it could be the harbinger of his doom. He lifted it mechanically and couldn't stop himself from reading it.

"Dear Francis. I think the time has finally come. Thank you for all the great memories, for being so kind and affectionate, and for all the career advice. You really are a great person. I hope we'll still be friends. I'll call you when you get back from the Congo. Maybe we can have lunch or something.

All the best. Love Deb."

He stared in morbid horror at the sheet. What the fuck?

She was on speed dial and he pushed it without any other cognitive thought.

"Hello?" She sounded bright and bubbly.

"What the fuck?" It wasn't the thing to say, but he had lost his mind. At first all he could hear in response was road noise.

"Oh Francis, don't tell me you're going to pretend that this is a surprise. Please don't make this messy and ugly. Just let me go."

His mind was completely gone. "Why?" It was all he had for a comeback.

"Seriously?" The calm response was evaporating. "Francis, you're seventeen years older than me. We never talked about this being a long-term thing. I thought we were on the same page. You were just what I needed at the time, but I've got to finish following my own path. You go to Africa, and I go back home to figure out what's next for me."

He tried to process and couldn't. "I...love you. I thought you were staying."

"Look, I care about you deeply, but I'm not going to participate in this melodramatic bull crap. Go overseas, do what you love, get famous and all of that stuff. Write books, go on a speaking tour...finish your plan for the rest of your life. And I'm going to do the same for me. Don't make our last conversation an emotional, delusional sob-fest. I want to remember you fondly until the day I die. Don't make that impossible by what you say in the next thirty seconds. Be strong and do what you need to do. Call me when you get back."

Incredibly, the phone clicked and the line went dead. He stared at it like he had never held a phone before and had no idea what it was. He looked up at his house, which no longer felt like a home, as if he was seeing it for the first time. It was somehow foreign now. He was a stranger in his own life. What had just happened? After standing there for an undetermined period of time, he moved listlessly toward the only thing that called out to him. Unfortunately, it was the liquor cabinet.

CHAPTER TWO

Hamlin woke slowly as was his custom. Even in the earliest stages of consciousness, he could sense that something was amiss.

"Oh, crap." His head was full of explosions and broken glass. He had a blurry, fleeting vision of vodka in a plastic cup. "Ow. What have I done?" The broken glass was trying to get out through his eyes. A thought came to him. He was in Antarctica. That startled him fully awake. His eyes flickered open apprehensively. The room he was in was quite dark. He was at a loss as to what to do next. If he chose to sit up and got nauseated, he didn't even know where the washroom was. He didn't want to puke in somebody's closet by mistake. He decided to lay still and do a thorough physical analysis before trying to get upright.

"Shit, why didn't I drink beer?" He didn't even know if they had beer. He could remember meeting everybody from the station, but faces and names were pretty scrambled up in his mind. Was it morning? Had he overslept or was everybody still in bed? He listened and heard nothing but the outside wind moaning through the wall. It then occurred to him that there could be someone else in the room. Probably not, though. It was too quiet.

Did the room have windows? Should there be light coming in? Was that bacon he smelled? The questions came quickly and without any particular structure. Yes, after a moment of delicate sniffing, he was convinced that it was, in fact, bacon that he smelled faintly. His room door slowly opened and a bar of soft light stretched across the floor.

"Doctor, are you awake?"

The voice was gentle and understanding. Francis considered ignoring the question, but to be fair, his current condition was nobody's fault but his own. His punishment would be to force himself into action under extreme physical duress.

"Yeah, I'm awake."

There was a moment of blessed silence and then, "Breakfast is ready if you want to come out."

Breakfast was not going to happen for Francis on this fine day. He forced himself to speak again. "Maybe some coffee or juice."

"Good. We shall see you at the table then."

Francis was already regretting the decision to get up. "Okay." He lay back and immediately fell into a deep sleep.

An undetermined period of time passed before Francis woke once again. He sensed he wasn't alone.

"It seems you are awake again. Very good. We missed you at breakfast."

That prissy voice was quickly becoming familiar.

"Good morning, Doctor Sokolov. Or, at least I'm assuming it's morning." He grunted as he tried to shift positions. "Sorry about the no-show. Vodka isn't my usual drink of choice when I have to work the next day."

"That's quite all right. If anything, it is to be expected. Drinking vodka with a group of Russians is, at best, a dangerous endeavor. I had them leave you some fruit and tea before they dispersed. If you would be so good as to rise now, I'll direct you to the washroom. Perhaps you can regain some stature with the group by getting on your feet before lunch."

Francis slowly and carefully swung his feet out from under the covers and came into contact with the cold floor. His thoughts were still rather incoherent. How did they get fruit down here? Frozen? Of course. And why not? Everything else apparently was. "Let's not talk about lunch. A glass of ice water might be nice, though."

"Ice and water we can manage in any quantity. There is a fine robe on the wall hook to your right. You will need it. Our idea of room temperature is more like seventeen degrees; it may take you a week or two to adjust."

Francis put on the heavy robe. It felt good compared to the cold inside air. "You're not talking Fahrenheit, I hope?"

"Centigrade, my dear doctor. The conversion is simplicity itself. You'll be addicted to the metric system by the time you leave. If you would be so good as to enter through the door on your right, you will find the men's washroom facility."

"Great. Give me a few minutes, would you?"

He bowed slightly. "As you wish. I have a little debriefing prepared which I can present while you sip your tea."

Francis felt only slightly better than when he first woke up, but any improvement was welcome. "Sounds great."

He made it through the rudimentary washroom routine without throwing up, considered it a victory, and then proceeded to the kitchen.

"Excellent, Doctor. I took the liberty of pouring both orange juice and tea. There is milk and sugar on the table as well, should you desire."

Francis sat at the old wooden table which looked like it belonged under a bridge with some hobo's life possessions piled on it. He released a long sigh. "How is it you have milk?"

Sokolov smiled. "It is powdered but still quite serviceable."

"I'm going to move slowly. I may start by sipping some juice."

"Very good. While we are waiting for your constitution to stabilize, let's get you up to speed on our little operation here. Tell me, Doctor, what do you know about Antarctica?"

Francis took a delicate sip. "It's cold. You don't get sunlight in the winter months. And it's the only continent that doesn't have a Wal-Mart. That's about it. This opportunity only recently presented itself and I really didn't have much time to do research."

Sokolov nodded. "I see. As such, Doctor, if you would be so good as to lend me your ear, I shall attempt to improve your knowledge of your new, temporary home. There are many extraordinary features about this part of the world that you will find interesting. For example, you say that it is cold. Did you know that the average summer temperature is about $-30\,°C$?"

Francis looked up painfully. "Did you say summer?"

"Yes. Winter temperatures average about $-65\,°C$. The lowest reliably measured temperature on Earth was $-89.2\,°C$. It was recorded here in Vostok on July of 1983. That translated to $-129°F$."

"My God! Can people survive in that?"

"No. At that temperature, a deep breath can freeze your teeth and the lining of your lungs. Frostbite would be virtually instantaneous. Even with our best outdoor gear, you could only survive for extremely brief periods of time."

"Wow. Can any kind of animal or plant life survive in that?"

"Very few things can, but as you will discover, this makes Vostok a very healthy place. The only germs surviving here would be the ones you brought in with you. Also, you asked if it was morning. Antarctica is the only continent that has no time zone. Everything is subjective. We use Moscow time for the sake of structure. Therefore, it is currently late morning. There are other features that I'm confident will surprise you."

Sokolov seemed to be enjoying himself. "There is an almost total lack of moisture in the air. This is, in fact, the driest place on Earth. All the snow and ice you see are deceiving; it took thousands upon thousands of years to accumulate. Also, you can't immediately tell, but we are nearly 3,500 meters above sea level. That means that there is a noticeable lack of oxygen. Any physical activity will drain your lungs quickly. But you will adapt to that as well as to the cold, at least to some degree.

"And finally, perhaps most impressive of all, the polar night lasts for approximately 130 days, including 80 continuous days of complete darkness."

Francis finished a sip. "I didn't see any of that on the travel brochure. You make it sound great, though."

Sokolov smiled. "You have a tendency to make fun of stressful things. Let me be perfectly and entirely frank while giving you a somber warning that I hope will help you to walk through the acclimatization period. It is perfectly normal and completely expected to experience a variety of symptoms when first arriving in Antarctica. They should pass within a week or two. They could include such pleasantries as headaches, ear pains, nose bleeds, eye twitches, a sudden rise in blood pressure, loss of sleep, vomiting, reduced appetite, joint and muscle pain, arthritic pain, and weight loss averaging around 3 to 12 kilograms."

"Kind of like a health spa. Here's a pointer from me to you. Vodka doesn't seem to help. It may, in fact, hasten some of those symptoms, at least based on my current experience."

"You are learning already. To be completely truthful, the amount of alcohol consumed here is higher than what would be considered average in most places, but over indulge at your own peril. We are a working station and will expect you to perform your duties on a daily basis. There isn't much point to taking time off–after all, there is nowhere to go and few things to do. Experience has taught us that leisure time can actually bring on bouts of depression. It is preferable to keep busy while here at Vostok. That is our official credo, as you will learn."

Francis continued his judicious consumption of liquid. He unintentionally made a show out of rubbing the sleep from his eyes. "If the station ever decides to hire a publicity director, you may want to polish up some of the main points. Having said that, what exactly *is* the appeal of this place? There must be something that attracts people. I understand there is a waiting list to come here."

"Yes, Doctor, that is absolutely true. To be solicited as you were is quite rare. The appeal of Vostok is the research, you see. It is the chance to be part of a discovery that could, in some way, change the world. And we may be on the verge of that right now. Do you know what kind of work we primarily do here, Doctor?"

Francis tried not to speak too loudly. The inside of his head was echoing like an empty warehouse. "Yeah. You are doing core samples of the ice. It's very thick and was laid down many years ago. It gives you an eye to the past. Right?"

"Correct, my good doctor. We have measured a variety of environmental factors, arguably from as far as back as four hundred-thousand years ago. The results are truly fascinating. But we are predominately involved in something a little different right now."

Francis grunted as his stomach turned over. "Really? Should I be excited or filled with dread?"

Sokolov looked puzzled. "Why in the world would you be filled with dread? I'm afraid I don't understand."

"I don't know. This whole talk you're giving me just seems, in some ways, reminiscent of the introduction to a horror movie. Frankenstein probably thought his research was interesting as well."

Sokolov remained emotionless for a moment, working out how he should react. Then he chuckled just a little. "Really, Doctor, the comparison is in no way appropriate. We are not trying to create anything new or monstrous. We are, however, very pleased and excited to have an opportunity to examine and analyze something totally unique. Something pre-existing but never seen by civilized man before. Who knows what secrets lie hidden beneath our very feet–and more importantly, what the knowledge of them can mean to the evolution of modern technology. Science, medicine, history, even economics for that matter–all may be transformed by what we find in this frozen little corner of the world. That is what drives us to be here and to tolerate the isolation, cold, and other negative aspects of this spartan existence. Who knows, Doctor? Perhaps school children will read your name from a textbook in the not too distant future; which I mention in case that sort of thing appeals to you."

Francis risked another sip of tea. It didn't actually taste that bad. "It doesn't. I would prefer to be wealthy and anonymous. So far you haven't indicated that either are a likelihood. And textbooks are quickly becoming obsolete. Not to change the subject too abruptly, but this tea is rather good. I thought all things Russian tended to lean toward mediocrity."

Sokolov frowned for a brief instant. "You are too kind. The tea tastes good because of the water I brewed it with. We melt ice from core samples that are not of interest because they are from a timeline that we have already analyzed. This water is from a time when modern man did not even exist, nor was there pollution of any kind. It is entirely pristine, you see."

Hamlin shifted his position as if it had become uncomfortable. In point of fact, it had. "So what is there to analyze besides ice? Why do you need a microbiologist so desperately in this lifeless place?"

"That is indeed the crux of the matter. Let me explain. Several years ago, space based technology allowed a scan of Antarctica that confirmed something startling and once totally unexpected. Under this station lies a lake, which has been named after the station itself. We have extended our drilling aspirations to include eventual access to the lake water itself."

Francis stared incredulously. "Lake? What do you mean? If you mean a large body of frozen water, then surprise, that's the same as an ice sheet."

Sokolov looked slightly smug. "Not at all. Lake Vostok, one of the ten largest lakes in the world, is beneath nearly four kilometers of ice under our current position. And let me assure you, it is as liquid as the waves that lap the beach along the Jersey shore."

For the first time, Francis started to forget his self-induced physical malady. "How is that possible? Why wouldn't it just freeze solid under there? Is it saline?"

"No, Doctor, it is not. The exact answer to your question is, as of yet, not totally known. One aspect is pressure–sitting under several kilometers of ice creates a tremendous amount of pressure. We think this is a factor. Also, there appears to be an elaborate labyrinth of interconnecting channels that allows the water to move from one place to another. Perhaps that movement also contributes to keeping the water in liquid form. There may also be a geothermal component to this mystery. At any rate, and more to the point, we need a microbiologist because we are about to break through and gain access to the lake itself. Then there will be much analysis to be done. It is possible, if not likely, that some form of life exists down there in the cold waters."

Francis felt an intrigue that was undeniable. "Life deep under the ice. Now that's interesting."

"Yes, Doctor–life that has been separated from the surface world for perhaps millions of years. Imagine that appearing under the lens of your microscope!"

It was a fascinating scenario. "When do you expect to actually break through?"

Sokolov paused for some dramatic effect. "It is not possible to be absolutely precise in our estimations. As you can perhaps imagine, things go wrong in this climate. People get tired quickly and machinery tends to break down in the extreme cold. Having said that, however, a best case scenario would see us breaking through later today." It was like placing a bomb, and the diminutive man looked for a reaction as it went off in Hamlin's mind.

Francis ran a hand through his hair. "Great. And I picked last night to get shitfaced. Sorry."

Sokolov raised his eyebrows. "Sorry for what? The drinking or the profanity?"

"Retrospectively, both. Listen, can I get a quick shower and then check out your lab facilities? I'd like to be ready when the first sample comes in."

"Excellent! Your enthusiasm confirms that you were the correct choice for this research. I would be most happy to direct you to the showers, then to give you the tour of the area in which you will be working for the next few months. The housing may be lacking in aesthetics, but the equipment is top notch. I think you will be pleased."

"Cool. Literally. Speaking of temperatures, you do have hot water here I hope?"

"My good doctor, I do not think many people could or would tolerate a cold shower after exposure to Vostok's frigid temperatures. There is plenty of hot water. Feel free to indulge."

Under the false hope that he could accumulate enough residual heat to keep himself comfortable once he went outside, he did just that.

"Are you absolutely certain?" The chancellor frowned in disapproval.

Hamlin sighed deeply. "Yes. I'm sorry Richard, but I'd be absolutely no good to the expedition."

"Hmm." The white-haired man tapped his index finger on the top of his desk. "This really was tailor made for you. Another opportunity like it will be very hard to find."

"I know." Hamlin stared blankly at the ceiling. "I feel like I've had my life scraped back to the bare bones. It's like starting over again in every way. I must confess, I feel lost."

The chancellor grunted as he readjusted his seating position. "Be that as it may, you still need a plan for living your life. If you don't go to Africa, then what will you do? I'm not sure I'd recommend a sabbatical for someone in your position. It may be therapeutic to have a focus and keep busy. Have you given any thought to what will take the place of going to the Congo?"

"I still have my krill research. I could work on putting it together. I believe it still has some validity."

The chancellor nodded. "Good. That's a start. You can use any of our facilities. I could even offer you funding for an assistant if required."

Hamlin shook his head. "I think not; at least not now. Let me get back into this on my own and establish a good work pattern. Once I get my feet under myself, perhaps I'll be ready to inject some extra life into this project. It will also depend on how my theories mesh with the preliminary data. I'll keep you posted."

Hamlin seemed quite ensconced in this line of thinking. All other options had apparently been lined up against a wall and executed.

"Very well, then. Do keep me apprised of how the work is proceeding."

Francis stood to leave. "I will, Richard. Thanks for your understanding."

And so the first brick was laid in the repair of what had once been a complete foundation. At the end of it all, Hamlin hoped he would have a life once again. He certainly wasn't there yet.

They drove to the research lab in a tracked vehicle, which Sokolov referred to as a 'cat.' Francis didn't get why that name was appropriate for this boxy, lumbering machine, but neither did he care. He was starting to notice a slight closed-in feeling that he just couldn't shake. He figured this was an altogether bad place to get cabin fever. It wasn't hard to imagine why the people here immersed themselves into their work. At least the vehicle offered some shelter from the cold. That was something to appreciate. And he only felt slightly like throwing up. Everything was coming up roses.

They stopped in front of yet another building that failed to impress. Francis couldn't reconcile how research this important, funded by an entire nation in a manner somewhat akin to the space program at NASA, could operate out of structures that could be used as props in a sci-fi movie wasteland.

"Follow me, Doctor."

No further urging was needed. Avoiding the frigid Antarctic temperatures was one of the most effective motivators that Francis had ever encountered. He sped through the open door.

Once inside, his goggles immediately fogged over to the extent that he was temporarily blind. He removed them so he could at least have a blurry view of the room.

"Welcome, Doctor Hamlin."

Francis recognized a face from the previous nights' festivities. The man was young, constantly grinning, and sporting a gap-toothed dental structure that was the most memorable feature of his face.

"Hi. Sorry, I seem to have some self-induced memory lapses. I can't recall your name."

Again the grin. "I think I may have, in a small way, contributed to your condition. I'm Doctor Konstantine. I'm looking forward to working with you." He seemed to have a very slight lisp, which Francis found to be fascinating and entertaining all at once.

He pondered one of life's most recent mysteries that was now staring him in the face. "Why aren't you hung over? I remember you doing shots...vaguely."

"That's like asking an Olympic runner why he isn't sore after a race. Training is the key. I'm a fine tuned drinking machine."

Sokolov didn't like the direction the conversation had taken. "Surely you can think of more appropriate topics to discuss. Something related to this research, for example."

"Right. Of course. Perhaps I can bring Doctor Hamlin up to speed on where we are and how we got here in terms of our most recent discoveries."

Francis tried to help the young man out. "That's a great idea. I can't think of a better place to start."

This seemed to sit better with Sokolov. "Very good. I'm off to the drilling site. Hopefully I'll have some new and very exciting samples for you soon. Try to get yourselves and the lab prepared in the meantime."

He opened the door and quickly disappeared through it. The atmosphere of the lab seemed to change immediately.

"Is that guy as much of a dick as I think he is, or is that my hangover talking?"

"Oh, Sokolov is fine. He really holds this whole operation together." As Konstantine said this, he wrote *THE ROOM IS BUGGED* on a sheet of paper and held it up for perusal.

Francis was shocked and couldn't imagine that it was so, but still managed to play along. "Sorry. I should be more respectful. I think the adjustment to being here is putting me on edge. That and the hangover. I meant no offense."

Konstantine gave him the okay sign. "No apology necessary. We're all comrades now, my friend."

"Sure. So, can we talk about what you've been doing here?"

"Absolutely." This response seemed more genuine. "So far it's been focused primarily on chemical analysis designed to give us a reading of what the atmosphere was doing when the layers of ice were formed. We've looked at everything from ozone to oxygen and everything else you can imagine. It's interesting but so far nothing that we didn't really anticipate. These Lake Vostok samples could change that, though."

"So we might actually see some life-forms that are truly new to modern man?"

"Oh yes. That's the big thing. Water in liquid form always has the ability to sustain life in some capacity. We're all jealous that you come in here as a newbie and perhaps get to do something on your first day that many researchers have been dreaming about for years. But we're all part of the team, so we'll be excited and ready to live the thrill vicariously through the emotional response that you're sure to have when it happens. So make sure you have an emotional response."

"Like what? Break down and weep?"

He grinned his funny grin. "No. Do something American! You know, pump your fists and scream *we're number one,* smash a piece of furniture, or take a drink of something rare and expensive and then spit it out. Sheesh, you should know this. You're not secretly Canadian are you? I only ask because my internet research indicates that you would be boring if you were. We need unbridled enthusiasm. That and lots of vodka. And we have the vodka already."

"I'm enthusiastic about the vodka–or at least I was until I woke up this morning. Does that count?"

"It's a good start, I have to admit. We can use that as a foundation and work up from there."

Francis decided to cooperate. "So is there a chair or stool that I can smash for practice?"

"Yes, that's better. Now you're getting in the right spirit. Hey, do you want to see your actual workspace? Maybe you can do some organizing before the samples start coming in. You probably should set up your files and get familiarized with our storage system. If you would be so good as to follow me to the other end of the counter, I'll get this tour started."

"Do I get access to some kind of computer?"

Konstantine nodded. "Of course. There's a laptop charging over in the corner. It's all yours."

Francis gave the machine a good look. At least the equipment seemed to be in good order. If he could take the work seriously, maybe he would have some chance of getting through this work term without going stir crazy.

"Francis, come in. Please." The chancellor extended a hand.

Hamlin took it and gave it a shake. It was what was expected, after all. "I was surprised by your call," he replied. "I haven't got much more to report since our last meeting. All I can say is that things are moving along."

"That's not why I called you in."

"Oh? What's up, Richard? Pulling my funding? Revoking my tenure?"

He chuckled. "No, Francis. Academic tenure is a difficult thing to take away. And besides, why would I even try? You're one of the best biologists I've ever met."

Hamlin frowned. "Then why am I here?" He wasn't ready to invest a lot of time into friendly, casual interaction just yet.

The chancellor leaned forward before responding.

"How are you, Francis? Are things going well?"

"That depends, I suppose. What are you talking about, exactly?"

"I'm talking about you. Francis Hamlin, the person. How is your life proceeding these days?"

Hamlin didn't care for the discussion, but this man was his friend as well as his boss. He shrugged. "It's fine. I'm eating and sleeping. I work, effectively I think, at least five days a week. No suicide attempts. I suppose I'm drinking more than I should. I try not to change my clothes in front of the picture window without shutting the blinds first. Why, what have you heard?"

"Any social outings?"

"Certainly. Lots of them. Buying groceries counts as a social outing, correct?"

"Have you had any women in your house over the past month?"

"Absolutely. My cleaning lady comes once per week, just like clockwork."

"I see. Any plans to get away? Maybe a week or two on a sandy beach with lots of tanned ladies in two piece bathing suits?"

Hamlin grunted in response. "Look, Richard, I appreciate your concern, but I'm a grown man. For better or worse, I have to be responsible for and take care of myself. And I'm fine. Fine as wine. Or I will be. It's coming. Every day, in every way, I'm getting better and better."

"Very good. This was never meant to be an inquisition anyway. I actually had another reason for calling you in."

"No, I will not consider chemical castration as an option, even though that would eliminate a lot of my long-term problems."

"It's about a job offer."

"Are you firing me?" Francis responded.

The chancellor smiled. "For the second time, no. This is a temporary research assignment. They require a biologist on very short notice."

Hamlin frowned. "I turned down the Congo work, remember? Are you willing to turn your back on my exciting krill research so quickly— because I'm not."

"They asked for you specifically."

That was a surprise. "Oh? Someone I know?"

The chancellor slid a folder across the top of his desk.

"Not exactly. One of your past students who's working in Volgograd recommended you to someone in the Russian government when he became aware of the need. Have a look."

"The Russians asked for me? How utterly weird is that?" Francis was incredulous. He ignored the folder and the papers in it.

"They maintain a research station in Antarctica," the chancellor continued. "Something exciting is about to happen and their biologist was just diagnosed with Malignant Fibrous Histiocytoma. He's on a plane back to Moscow to get treatment and they're short staffed. The window for flying in there is about to close for the winter due to the severe weather, so they need a replacement almost immediately."

"You've got to be kidding. This entire scenario is bizarre. Why would anyone, yourself included, think that I would have any interest in this...especially now. I'm looking for quiet consistency in my life until I can patch it back together. This doesn't qualify."

"Don't be too sure. It pays really well, the research is very exciting, and the research station itself is isolated to the point that you won't have to worry about any peripheral social interaction. There's nothing but really meaningful research to do. No distractions. Just peace and quiet."

Francis reached doubtfully for the folder. "I can have a quick look, but this really doesn't appeal to me in the slightest."

"They need a very quick answer. If you say no, then they have to really move to get somebody else in time. Call me tonight and let me know one way or another. I'll pass your answer along."

"Fine. Can I be dismissed now?"

"Francis, we all want you to get back on your feet and find complete happiness in both your career and your life. Maybe this would be therapeutic for you. A least give it some thought before turning it down."

Hamlin rose to go. "If you'll excuse me, I have to look up how to say no in Russian."

"I'll expect your call."

Hamlin left.

CHAPTER THREE

When the outside door flew open, Francis actually jumped out of his seat. He had been setting up his laptop as best he could.

"You know," he said as he turned toward the door, "if I have a heart attack, you're going to be short one researcher for the rest of the winter."

Sokolov approached with a tube in his hand. "Do you have any idea what this is?"

"A Farah Faucett poster, I hope. I always liked that hair thing she had going on."

"This ice was actual liquid some ninety minutes ago when we drew it from Lake Vostok. May I present our first sample for your analytic pleasure."

Francis was truly impressed. He reached out and took the tube reverently. "Really? I thought you were probably exaggerating when you said it might come today."

Sokolov was in the process of removing his parka. "I would, with your permission, like to stay and watch your first impressions as you start your analysis. This is very exciting."

Francis shrugged. "Sure, I mean, it's your lab, right? No problem." He looked around with a slightly bewildered expression on his face. "Do you care where I start? I'm not familiar with your methods."

"I'm confident your procedures will do fine. Please proceed."

Francis looked at the long metal tube now lying on the table. Konstantine came to his rescue. "Why don't you partially extract the core first? I'll be happy to assist. The storeroom is through this door; we'll do it in there. The room stays at outside temperature so nothing will thaw out. Our other samples are in there, so we'll label this one before we extract it. The tubes and the ice all look the same once they're in there, you know."

The sample was labeled and then removed to the storage room. In there, the ice was partially removed and a small sample cut out. The core was then covered in a plastic sheath and inserted into the storage rack.

"Normally the ice samples remain frozen even while we look at them. That means working in the cold. Since this was originally in liquid form, and we may be dealing with life forms that cannot survive long in the ice, we can thaw it and examine it back in the heated portion of the lab."

Hamlin was already cold from the short period of time they had just spent in the storage facility.

"Sounds good. Let's get back in there."

Francis soon had a drop of water under a slide, ready for viewing. He started at low magnification. After several moments, it seemed apparent that there wasn't anything large enough to be seen.

"I can see a reaction, my good doctor. What do you see?"

Francis concentrated before responding. "Would you expect this water to be turbid?"

"We're not certain. There appears to be some current but we don't know how much or its impact on the bottom sediment. Why do you ask?"

"I can't see anything. It looks perfectly clear. But, that's at low magnification." He adjusted the microscope again. "Okay, let's see. Hmm, nothing swimming around here either. Can I ask the method by which this sample was obtained?"

Sokolov immediately nodded. "Yes, we use a hot water method of boring. We haven't actually pierced into the Lake but stopped several meters short. The pressure of the lake water pushes it through minute cracks and fissures into the borehole, where it freezes fairly quickly. We then extract the sample."

"Okay, good." He pushed his chair away from the counter. "So this came from the extreme surface of the lake. Perhaps there would be a more concentrated amount of life at the bottom. At any rate, it's possible that I need some dye in order to find what I'm looking for. Can I ask you to be patient while I take care of this?"

"Of course. If I was to bring you some coffee and sandwiches, would you consider working later?"

What else was there to do? Francis had no other plans and wasn't up to another night of vodka shots. He consented.

Hamlin had been sitting at his kitchen table for two hours. He was torturing himself with the deafening silence of the house and recent, powerful memories of Deborah. How had he so misread her and their relationship? The scotch in his tumbler had been swirled incessantly but he hadn't taken as much as a sip from it.

Antarctica. Complete isolation. Nothing but meaningful research.
Penance.

"So, at the end of it all, perhaps that's what this is. A chance for some self-flagellation. Is that what I need?"

He mulled the notion over in his head. Maybe he needed some punishment for the as of yet unrecognized mistakes he had made, which no doubt led him to this apocalyptic break down of what had been his life. Maybe the hidden overlord who resided in his unconscious mind would release him from loathing and pity if he punished himself voluntarily with academic solitary confinement. Maybe. He knew he had to make a decision now, regardless of the direction he chose.

"Oh, damn it all to hell." He picked up his phone and dialed.

Several hours had gone by, but Hamlin couldn't really be sure about the passage of time. He had noticed that there was a shortage of clocks in this place. He was now on his sixth slide from the sample. The mood in the room was about to change dramatically.

"Wait a minute. Here we go. What are you?"

Sokolov was on his feet in an instant. "What have you found?"

Francis was still observing as calmly as possible. "It's alive and moving whatever it is. I'm at high magnification, so it's pretty small. If I had to make a quick guess, I'd say it was bacteria of some sort. There isn't a heavy concentration, but I can definitely see one little bastard splashing around in there."

Sokolov rubbed his hands together. "Excellent, Doctor. Capture the image, if you please. I can hardly wait to see it."

He nodded without looking up. "Okay, no problem. Then I'll see what else is lurking in here."

"Doctor Konstantine is an expert on bacteria, so we will give him an opportunity to get involved as well. When you have finished with that slide, he can have his turn at analysis."

Francis was pumped with the discovery. He wanted to prepare more slides and go for the big one–protozoa. They were single celled creatures that in many ways shared the same traits as larger, more complex animals. If he could find one, it would be relatively quick and easy to determine if it was a never before seen species. Konstantine didn't have to wait long for the slide. Sokolov focused his attention on the study of the bacteria. Peace and quiet settled back over the lab. That suited Francis just fine.

They were late for supper but the rest of the staff hadn't yet dispersed from the dining area. All of them were eager to hear about the discoveries of life from the Lake Vostok samples. Sokolov had cautioned Hamlin and his research partner about saying anything speculative. As long as they stuck to the facts, he had no issue with sharing the information. Francis wasn't keen on censorship, expressed or implied. He spoke openly to the gathering and his candour earned him respectful glances from the group.

"So you actually saw life which may be unique to our modern world. How extraordinary." Francis recognized the tall woman with the cute face from the previous evening, although the memory was somewhat imperfect. He saw her in his mind as being just slightly distorted, as if through a double-pane window with vodka injected between the gaps.

"Just bacteria so far, but that's a good sign. Wherever one type of life exists, you can count on there being others. Virtually all life relies on some sort of symbiotic relationship. There are microscopic creatures that eat bacteria."

She frowned. "Eats bacteria? I didn't realize that was possible."

"Oh yes. It actually forms the basis of most food chains. Many protozoa are capable of eating them. It's fascinating, really." He was having a hard time eating his own meal while talking to and being observed by the entire crew. He pushed his plate away and then took a long drink of reconstituted orange juice and ice. "There are bacteria that actually consume crude oil. They are used in clean-up operations. Protozoa won't eat oil, but they will eat the bacteria that eat the oil. It's truly amazing."

"Ladies and gentlemen," Sokolov interjected, "may I suggest that we disperse somewhat. Last night wasn't exactly restful for the good doctor, so let's not add to his weariness by being thoughtless of his condition."

The group murmured its agreement and several members immediately walked out of the room.

"Perhaps we can set up rotating visits of the lab so you can all get a personal feel of what is being done there." Sokolov assumed the role of a benevolent overlord easily. "That might be a more appropriate time to have your questions answered. We could start as soon as tomorrow if there is sufficient interest."

Francis was willing to bet that Sokolov himself had every intention of being present during these tours he had offered and would ensure that no matter which questions were asked, too much information would not be given out, inadvertently or intentionally.

"You really haven't been given a proper tour of the facility yet. Could I interest you in one?"

Francis smiled at the tall woman. "I'd be delighted. Unfortunately, if we've been properly introduced, I don't recall the moment."

"I suppose not. I'm Vladlena Sayanski. Call me Lena."

"Charmed. My friends call me Ham–Fran was never appealing to me."

She raised an eyebrow. "I'm not sure I will use that. It seems somehow juvenile to me. You shall be Francis to me for now." She hooked her arm in his and led him astray.

The tour took eleven minutes in total. It started with the sleeping areas and ended with the boiler room. The overall impression was still one of surprise for Francis at how slummy everything looked. It was functional and obviously well maintained, but everything looked cheap and old. This seemed to get under his skin for some reason. He decided that he would make it his mission to formulate a clear picture of why this was so.

"Francis, I am going to make a suggestion now. I would like you to come into the boiler room with me and make it part of the tour."

"Why? Don't tell me you have cutting edge technology in there. Or maybe that is the only part of this station that looks like the Taj Majal?"

She gave him a smile. "No, none of those things." Her voice dropped to a husky whisper. "It is the only truly warm environment here, and it is the only place that tends to afford some privacy in these tight quarters."

"I see. Do you want to have a frank discussion?" Her intentions were unclear to him.

Her eyes took on a sleepy, seductive look. "My dear doctor, what I want is to undress in front of you and then teach you something about Russian women. Then I want to find out if what I have heard about American men is true."

Francis was almost but not quite speechless. "What's that?"

She checked the hall and made sure it was empty. She leaned forward, put her head close to his, and gently bit his ear. "Do you have an enormous penis? Is it like they say?"

He was able to formulate a response. "My pride won't let me say no."

"Then perhaps you could enlighten me. That is, if you think it is a good idea."

As it turned out, he did.

Francis entered his bedroom in much better condition than the previous night. At worst, he just simply felt tired.

His small but private room was an anomaly. There was only one other single and that was Sokolov's room. He appreciated the privacy. Eventually he planned to put some personal touches to the decorum, but for now he was exhausted and only wanted to sleep. It came quickly, which was itself a major blessing, but before morning, in the deeper reaches of his subconscious, he had a vivid and terrifying dream. After it played out, it faded into the background behind his retrievable memories.

He immediately began to snore.

His work the following day was much anticipated. Hamlin could hardly wait to prepare more slides and start the search for prehistoric, albeit microscopic, life. It didn't take long for his discoveries to start piling up.

Sokolov stopped by to check on his progress about two hours after he started. "Anything to report, Doctor? Are you still progressing successfully?"

He smiled at Sokolov despite his reservations about the man. "Oh yes. This time I've found some viruses. They look unfamiliar, but that's not really my specialty so I'll reserve final judgment. But it's all good. So far, if you forced me to summarize, I would say the frequency of life is definitely less than, say, in the open ocean, but it's there nonetheless. I'm still holding out hope for something like an amoeba or paramecium. I've got a long way to go to work through this sample."

"I am no expert, Doctor. Should we all be using breathing apparatus? We would have no natural immunity to something that is seeing the light of day for the first time in many millennia."

Francis shook his head. "Unlikely. Water-borne viruses would probably not be at home with us. Nor could they jump through the air to get to us. I'm probably the only one really at risk and I'm being careful. I suppose the boring crew should take some precautions if there's any chance of being splashed. I wouldn't want them to stop working, though."

"The water freezes long before reaching the surface, so that shouldn't be of any concern. We are going to make a decision later today regarding boring through the last few meters and probing into the actual lake itself. We will be supplying you with more interesting samples today at any rate. Perhaps that will contribute to your success."

"Awesome. Bring it on. You know, if you loosened up your *no drinking in the lab* policy, I might be inclined to work longer hours."

"Of course you are joking, Doctor. I appreciate your sense of humor. Keep working on that sample—I'll have more for you soon."

Sokolov made his way back outside.

"So you really found some viruses in the sample?" Konstantine had been keeping tabs on his progress, but Francis apparently hadn't uttered the word *virus* until Sokolov came in. "Should we be wearing masks for protection?"

"Like I just said—no, that's not necessary. The kind of virus found in this environment wouldn't be transmittable to humans. You're safe."

Konstantine digested his response. "How can you make that conclusion if this virus hasn't been seen before?"

It was a fair question. "Its environment tells us. It likes to live in water, under pressure, in complete darkness, and in extremely cold temperatures. Our bodies are warm, no increased environmental pressure, and exposed to light frequently. And how would it get transmitted? If we don't consume it in some manner, it couldn't infect us anyway."

"Forgive me, but I'm a scientist too. Couldn't it be absorbed through contact with the skin? Does it become airborne when the water evaporates? I mean, we really don't know, do we?"

"How could a virus survive in that environment for eons if it was primarily in need of a warm-bodied host? Surely that would have been evolved out of the species even if it ever did exist."

"Your argument is persuasive. I feel safer."

"Of course, alcohol is a wonderful disinfectant if you really want to stack the deck in your favor." Hamlin pulled out a small metal flask from his top desk drawer.

"Staying healthy should be a top priority down here," Konstantine agreed.

Francis took a swig and winced. "What happens if you do get sick? Do you have any medical facilities at all? Or could you get evacuated by plane or snowmobiled to the nearest station? Or do you just get thrown into the nearest snow bank until spring?"

Konstantine seemed strangely amused by Hamlin's apparent fear of medical emergencies. "We have Kuvayev, an actual medical doctor, on staff here. We also have some basic diagnostic equipment and a good supply of commonly needed medications. You shouldn't worry. But don't count on being evacuated. We're all committed for the winter now. Nothing can fly in this cold. Jet fuel turns to jelly in the lines. You just barely made it. "

"Wait a minute. What if you cut your hand off or develop pneumonia?"

"That changes nothing. You cannot leave now, regardless of your physical condition."

Francis thought it through for a minute. "What kind of communication do we have here?"

"You mean with the outside world? Not much. No phones, no internet. We have a shortwave radio, but as a rule only Sokolov uses it."

Francis wasn't sure if he felt liberated or horrified. He decided to turn his focus back to his work.

When the evening meal had been consumed, Francis was informed that a movie would be viewed in the common area. He, as newest member of the team, would have the privilege of selecting what would be shown. When he got to the room, he was directed to a cardboard box with a blend of Russian DVDs in it. He didn't recognize any titles and wasn't encouraged by the amateurish illustrations on the cases. He looked at the television itself and was surprised and encouraged to see that it was a Sony.

"Hold on for a second." He walked over to the television and then spun it around. "Well, look at this. You've got a port here for a memory stick. Just wait a minute–I'll be right back."

He returned from his room with a small plastic object in his hand. "Prepare to be amazed, my Russian friends." He inserted the stick and picked up the remote.

"You brought movies on that key?" The burley bearded man was Doctor Kuvayev. He was the surgeon/MD. "Are these American movies?"

Francis couldn't keep the smile off his face. "You bet your ass." He noticed Sokolov watching him intently. "Umm, is this okay? Do you mind?"

Sokolov waved his hand dismissively. "Proceed, Doctor. Have your fun. This should be less damaging to your productivity tomorrow than a night of drinking vodka."

Kuvayev approached with a look of fascination on his face. "You have American action movies perhaps?"

Another voice called out, "What about something scary—like a werewolf?"

His tall friend with the provocative voice said, "Romance, maybe? Something to make me cry?"

The menu appeared on the screen. He had a pretty good selection. "Sorry, no romance on here. I do have action and I do have scary. What's your preference?"

"You choose," someone immediately suggested. Francis paused for a moment.

"You can't beat Bruce Willis." He selected *Live Free or Die Hard* for its humor and action, along with some decent special effects.

He had never seen an audience sit so quietly or watch so intensely. They laughed at the jokes, gasped at the explosions, and nodded in agreement with the hero's interpretation of the situation he found himself in. At the end of it all, they gave the movie a standing ovation.

"That was awesome!" Konstantine blurted. 'Do you have more?"

"Oh yes. If we show some restraint and watch one weekly, I can get us through the entire winter without any repeats."

Kuvayev poked the person sitting beside him and did a terrible interpretation of the main character. "*I was out of bullets.*" The scene he referred to was fresh in everyone's memory. The two laughed raucously.

To Hamlin's surprise, Sokolov had stayed to watch from beginning to end. He now shook his head slightly. "No wonder you Americans are fascinated with guns and violence. Hollywood presents it like it's coated in chocolate. Good guys shooting the bad guys. It is an over-simplification of a complex issue with far reaching social implications."

"Kicking them down an elevator shaft is also a popular option," Hamlin said. "You have to diversify or risk losing the audience."

"Good night to both you and your sense of humor, Doctor Hamlin." Sokolov turned and walked casually away. The rest of the audience was much more enthusiastic. Francis finally left for his room, enjoying the good feeling that he had introduced them to the kind of quality movie that democracy, limited censorship, and big budgets could produce. He was seriously considering one of his all-time favorites for the next time. Watching them react to *Caddyshack* would be a highlight of his entire stay. As he strolled down the hall, he couldn't help but notice that Doctor Sayanski was making no attempt to conceal the fact that she was following him.

"Could I interest you in some company, Doctor?"

Several other researchers could see and hear her clearly.

"Uh, sure. Are you certain this is really okay?"

"You are surprisingly shy. We are all adults here. And we all tested clean before we came. Nobody minds or cares what we do. So yes, I am certain it is okay."

Francis reached for his door. "I see. What happens in Vostok stays in Vostok."

The look on her face revealed that she didn't understand in the slightest why he had said that. He felt it would be tedious to explain. And he was tired. If something was going to happen, it better happen fast. "Come in, please."

She did. "What's wrong, Francis? Is this too easy for you? Should I put up a fight? I can role play if you wish."

He filed that away for future reference. "That won't be necessary, I'm sure. I just didn't realize that Russian women took the initiative. Perhaps Siberia has some promise as a tourist destination after all."

"No more jokes. Take off your clothes and get in bed."
He did just that.

It was the first 'morning' that Hamlin actually felt like breakfast.

"That is a good sign," Kuvayev said, and he was an actual medical doctor. "In this cold, you need many more calories. You can eat all you want. Don't worry about your diet."

"I never do." Hamlin didn't know exactly how it came to pass, but someone had cooked up a fair imitation of bacon and eggs. He was really piling up his plate. He wished he had thought to bring some decent coffee with him. Everyone here seemed to be fixated on drinking tea. At least they had instant.

Sokolov came walking in, wearing a rather sporty black turtleneck sweater. He had a huge smile plastered across his face.

"Doctors Hamlin and Konstantine–I'm sure you'll be interested to know, as will the rest of you for that matter, we've decided to bore into the lake itself today. I have just confirmed it. With luck, you should have samples from the bottom of the lake within a short time. What do you think about that?"

Hamlin was just setting down his heaping plate. He looked at Konstantine. "This is when I should be breaking some furniture, correct?"

Konstantine seemed a little alarmed about the funny look Sokolov gave him and didn't immediately reply.

"I must say, Dr. Hamlin," Sokolov said, "that my ability to sense and comprehend western humor has been put to the test since your arrival. I shall assume that you are sharing some sort of joke."

Hamlin sat and looked with satisfaction at his food. "I am. The truth is that your news is very exciting. I might soon get to view what amounts to a microscopic equivalent of a dinosaur. And that's pretty cool."

Sokolov picked out the needed requirements for a cup of tea. Hamlin couldn't remember ever seeing him eat.

"Although you are not designated as a marine biologist per se, I understand you have done previous research on ocean based life. Is this not so, Doctor?"

Hamlin was busy shoveling scrambled eggs into his mouth. He waited for them to relocate before attempting a reply.

"That is true. I did some research on krill. I was in the process of dusting it off and polishing it up when my chancellor made me aware of this opportunity."

"And what is the central theme of this research, if I may ask."

Hamlin was chewing again. He decided to risk communicating with a mouth that was only partially empty in the interest of speeding up the process.

"I was interested in the correlation between krill numbers and the population of other marine life, transient apex predators in particular."

"I see. And was *Euphausia superba* the species of primary interest to you?"

Hamlin was surprised and impressed. "Yes. That is the predominant species in terms of numbers, so naturally it has the biggest impact."

"Quite so. And interestingly enough, most of your research data was collected in the waters not far from the continent on which we now sit, correct?" Sokolov dropped a tea bag into his steaming mug.

"Yes sir. That was one cold boat ride, I can tell you that."

"And yet, here you are. It would almost seem that Antarctica has been calling out to you."

Hamlin hadn't looked at it that way. This trip had appeared out of the blue. Coming here of all places hadn't been on his mind at all prior to that.

"I suppose you could interpret it that way. You'd be wrong, of course. Keep in mind that I was scheduled to go to Africa to do research based primarily on lizards and amphibians before this slightly less than tropical alternative landed on my plate."

Now Sokolov was staring. "Then how in the world do you explain why you decided to come here instead?"

Francis really wanted to finish off his food.

"I flipped a coin."

Sokolov took a preliminary sip of his tea. "I see. Apparently, I have exceeded the limit for probing questions. Fair enough. Do try to keep your LDL cholesterol levels below where they would be considered hazardous, my good doctor." He stood, took his tea, and walked out.

CHAPTER FOUR

The research was interesting, Hamlin couldn't deny that. For the next few days, the excitement level slowly waned as the drilling team ran into some mechanical issues in reaching into the actual lake itself. Nothing new appeared under his microscope. Work became somewhat routine. And then the first big storm hit.

Gale force winds put so much snow in the air that visibility was restricted to several feet. There was a very real risk of getting lost, even if you took just a few steps outside. Once you were disoriented, you were in deep trouble. With the added wind chill, survival time in this cold amounted to a few minutes only. And there was no way for a rescue attempt. Your footsteps would be almost instantly erased, and the would-be rescuers would have no more ability to see than the person who was lost.

Ropes had been strung around the outside of the base so it was possible to get from building to building by following them carefully, hand over hand. It someone did venture out, they knew that the number one rule was to never let go of the rope. Ever. For any reason.

Since GPS technology was available here, it was possible to run the Cat to the outlying buildings. But at the height of the storm, with winds in excess of fifty miles per hour, the risk just became too great. So for two days, they all stayed in their quarters. Hamlin quickly recognized the onset of boredom and knew how dangerous that could be down here. After fighting off several panic attacks, he decided to organize a Texas Hold 'em tournament.

The cards were faded and no one was really familiar with the game, but most knew the basics of poker and all were eager for a distraction. It turned into quite a spectacle. Imaginary fortunes were won and lost, tempers flared, cards were tossed, and accusations made. Even Sokolov played for a while before excusing himself for some unknown but important activity that required his immediate attention elsewhere.

The first day of isolation was almost over before the novelty of poker wore off. This left relatively little time for indulging in vodka based refreshments, a definite plus in terms of the condition they were going to be in the following morning.

Day two presented a fresh set of challenges in terms of entertainment. Hamlin broke with his original ration of digital movies and presented The Lord of the Rings trilogy (the extended version) followed later in the day by a couple "B" movies featuring sharks, piranhas, and a ridiculous amount of cleavage (not necessarily in that order). That combined with microwave popcorn, vodka, and cheap Russian cigarettes (in designated areas only) got them through the day.

It was a relief to discover that day three found the storm abating to the point where work could progress as normal. Francis couldn't wait to get back to the lab.

He processed slide samples with a smile on his face. He had discovered a total of six different types of bacteria since starting his work, along with several viruses. That alone could get his name mentioned in the scientific studies presented to future scientists. Beyond that, he was starting to entertain the idea that he could be involved in winning a Nobel Prize. Delusional thinking, perhaps–but he allowed it because of the cheap thrill it gave him. It made a nice offset to the emotional drag of realizing that he was stuck here for the next three months or so, no matter what else happened. He would go back to civilization with a new set of coping skills if nothing else.

It was mid-afternoon Moscow time when Sokolov entered the lab carrying a new sample. Hamlin looked over as he came through the doorway and noticed his smile. If it extended any further, his face would be in danger of splitting in half.

"What have we here?" Francis asked. "Your face gives you away, Sokolov. No wonder you're only a mediocre poker player."

The smile didn't waiver.

"This is it, my dear doctor. The culmination of nearly three decades of work and research." He extended the core sample like he was offering a Fabergé egg.

"A bit delicate, is it?" He accepted the tube.

"This sample could contain life never before seen. Who knows what wonders are now held in your hands? A little respect is not out of order, in my opinion."

Hamlin knew Sokolov was right. It boggled his mind when he really thought about it.

"Only one way to find out. Let's have a good look at this bad boy. Give me a few minutes to prep a sample. I assume you'll be staying to see this for yourself."

Sokolov nodded. "Wild horses could not drag me away, Doctor. Please proceed."

Hamlin started to walk toward the workbench he would use. "So you can't get it to the surface in liquid form, I see."

"Quite true. By the time the sample reaches the surface, it is frozen hard. But I suspect the short amount of time would not be fatal to most life forms that survive in the frigid temperatures of Vostok."

Francis nodded. "A reasonable theory. I'll soon put it to the test." He pulled the core sample part way out of the tube. He noticed with his unaided eyes that the coloration was different.

"The water must be turbid," he observed. "This sample has suspended particulate in it. I assume it's organic."

Sokolov stepped closer. "How exciting. Doctor Konstantine, perhaps you could assist in order to move this along."

Hamlin waved him off. "I don't think it would help. Not at this point, anyway. If we were working from multiple samples, maybe. Let me slog through this one myself. This won't take long."

Sokolov maintained a degree of poise. "Very well. Please continue. I shall refrain from any further interruptions."

But he was unable to keep his word. As Francis proceeded to prep the first slide, he noticed a faint, high-pitched beep. Sokolov reached into his pocket and withdrew a small device furtively.

"That is most interesting and unfortunate. I'm afraid I must leave you at this key moment. Rest assured I will return as soon as possible. If you would be so kind, Doctor, as to file any digital photos immediately, I will review them from my office. Perhaps you could flag anything exciting or noteworthy by putting the file name in red."

Hamlin wondered how something that timely and important could come out of nowhere at an Antarctic research station, but kept his thoughts to himself.

"Certainly. I will do just as you have requested."

"Excellent," Sokolov replied. "Then I shall bid you a temporary farewell." He zipped up his monster parka and disappeared out the door.

Francis smiled and shook his head, but refrained from saying anything controversial or derogatory. Since learning that the lab might be wired for sound monitoring, he had gradually been learning to keep his tongue and choose his words carefully.

"That was unusual," he said. Surely that choice of wording was safe enough.

Konstantine was grinning like a lunatic but chose not to reply.

"Anyway, here we go. First sample of the good stuff." Hamlin walked carefully to his workstation.

Konstantine stopped what he was doing, stood, and walked over beside him.

"I hope you don't mind. Perhaps close proximity will make me feel like I'm part of this."

"No problem as far as I'm concerned," Hamlin said. "Maybe you can get some weird, quasi-scientific osmosis thing going. I'm happy to share."

It was not lost on him that this moment could change mankind's knowledge and understanding of the past. He was trying to focus on doing his job. With the slide in place, he looked through the microscope at low magnification.

Konstantine leaned closer. "See anything yet?"

Hamlin looked carefully. "I do. So far, it looks like standard organic crud. They must have jammed the probe right into the seabed and stirred things up. There's a lot of stuff in here."

"Stuff?"

"Sorry, I apologize for being so technical. I should have said 'shit.' Looks like clay and rotting organic matter, maybe algae residue or something similar. It's quite typical for a Benthos layer, if we use the oceans as a standard for measurement."

Konstantine nodded. "We weren't really hoping for typical results. We were hoping for something new and different."

"I know," Hamlin said. "Something never seen before by the eyes of man. Let's turn up the magnification and see what's happening up close and personal."

He looked for some time without comment.

Konstantine was getting restless.

"Well? What do you see?"

"Hmm. Well, numbers of life, including bacteria and viruses, are way lower than you would expect in the open ocean, but that's no surprise. They are there, just in way smaller numbers. There doesn't appear to be any phytoplankton. Again, that's no surprise, as the sunlight doesn't reach to these depths. The phytoplankton form a base food source for other life, so without them, naturally we would expected fewer life forms, at least in terms of the overall concentration. Now, here's the interesting part. I see some protozoa."

Now Konstantine was getting excited. "Really? Is it something you recognize?"

Hamlin continued to watch the miniature life forms swimming about. "I'm not sure. It's very similar to the Phylum Mastigophora that you would find anywhere from a puddle to the middle of the ocean. But I think, maybe, this one is a little different. Yes, if I had to guess right at this moment, I would say we just found our first new species of protozoa. Here, have a look. Then I'll photograph the little bugger and see what else is in this sample. I believe it's the heavy tail that sets it apart. That is one unique flagella, no doubt about it."

Konstantine took over the microscope eagerly. "So, is this the tiny dinosaur you had talked about?"

Hamlin laughed. "You remember that line, do you? I really need to come up with some new material. In a matter of speaking, yes. And who knows–perhaps millions of years ago a t-rex might have slurped up some of these while slaking his thirst. At any rate, we just took a giant stride toward a Nobel Prize, in my humble opinion. This is a moment likely to have profound long-term implications to the entire field of science. And this is just the beginning. How can we possibly imagine the changes that these miniature marvels will have on knowledge and subsequent technology? It's like Neil Armstrong stepping on the surface of the moon. Now, if you'll pardon me for a moment, I have to pee."

Konstantine smiled at the sudden turn and contrast in the conversation. "Maybe I will assist you for the rest of the day, if you don't mind. It makes me feels like I am part of this."

"As long as you're not referring to the peeing part," Hamlin said over his shoulder. "You help me, then that way if I screw something up, I can blame you."

"God bless America. I am learning so much from you."

"Stick with me, kid. You'll go places."

"Not for the next four months," Konstantine said with his own attempt at humor.

The kidding soon dissipated and the serious work resumed. Hamlin was starting to feel good about the decision to come here for the first time. These were extraordinary findings.

They all toasted the day's success after supper, and Hamlin began to wonder what the effect of four months of excessive vodka consumption was going to have on his liver. He had discovered two other unknown species from the same sample. The potential importance left him almost breathless whenever he contemplated it. Sokolov joined them for the meal, offering no further explanation for his disappearance. What he did offer was lavish praise for the accomplishments they had made. He also announced that there was some ice cream available to add to the celebration. It was American, and unbeknownst to Francis, it had hitched a ride with him when he flew in, along with some other, as of yet, unrevealed treats. It was Chocolate-Chip Cookie Dough and was very well received. Burning off calories trying to keep warm gave people an appetite for sweets.

Hamlin marveled at the ecstatic expressions and audible moaning caused by the frozen indulgence.

"So tell me, Doctor," Sokolov said, "why do you have such an interesting but cryptic expression on your face?"

"You don't miss much," he replied.

"My dear doctor, there isn't all that much to miss. I'm afraid the only skill I can lay claim to is that I am conscious. Are you telling me that you weren't thinking of anything special?"

"I was thinking that if I could have any one of these people in America for a week, they'd never want to return to Russia again. Just look at what that ice cream is doing to them."

"Indeed. But it is not as if Russia has no appeal. The people are unique and interesting, the land is diverse and beautiful, and we make virtually everything that you do. And some of it is better. Don't be too arrogant, Doctor Hamlin. We do very well on our own. Perhaps a better challenge would be for you to come to Russia for a week. Then you would be better suited to make a diagnosis about how desirable our country really is alongside yours or any other."

Francis sensed that he had hit a nerve. "I'm sorry. Perhaps it is more this place than Russia that has put them in a frame of mind where they can be so easily and profoundly impressed by something as simple as ice cream."

"I believe, as you Americans are prone to say, that you are onto something. Wait until you've been here two months. I daresay I could finagle you into running naked through the snow for a Big Mac meal and an evening of live streaming NFL football."

"Hey, I'm there already."

"Of course you are. And so, once again, I run headlong into your exuberant sense of humor. With regrets, I'm afraid I must return to my room. There are people in Moscow who are extremely interested in your progress and who I must keep appraised. You are all to be commended. Until tomorrow, then." He made a partial bow and then walked out of the room.

Hamlin was surprised to find he couldn't suppress a massive yawn. He pushed his chair back away from the table. It would be early to bed tonight. He was exhausted.

"Good night, boys and girls. See you all tomorrow."

And with that, he shuffled off to his room.

He should have been asleep by now. But when his room door swung slowly open, he was wide-awake. Thinking about the discoveries he had made that day had so far kept him from being able to relax and disengage his mind. He was just at the point of being frustrated.

"Francis?" It was Lena's husky voice. That was no surprise by this time. The surprise was that she wasn't alone. A second, more robust figure was right behind her. He couldn't see any great detail because of the low light.

Francis sat up, clutching his comforter. "I'm sorry. I wasn't planning on entertaining any company."

Lena moved into the room. "You don't have to entertain us." Her voice was dropping to a whisper. "We are here to entertain you."

This was a little too much. Hamlin felt like he was on overload. "Look, it's late. I need some sleep, and I don't even know your friend. This is starting to feel weird. Very weird, actually."

"Oh, you haven't been introduced yet? This is Zoya Grekov."

"How do you do," she said formally, also whispering.

He had seen her around, but wasn't sure what her specific job was. He thought she worked at one of the drilling outposts, but that was just a guess.

Hamlin wasn't sure how to respond. "I'm fine, thank you. I'm just, um, feeling a little uncomfortable."

He looked the other way and saw to his further discomfort that Lena was in the very final stages of undressing. She finished and unceremoniously climbed under the comforter.

"Are you crazy?"

She demurred with sleepy eyes and a soft voice. "I think not. But you can be the judge."

He wasn't sure what his options were in terms of opting out of what was already one of the weirdest nights of his life.

"At least I won't be cold," he conceded.

Lena kissed his ear. "No, you will not."

Once again, breakfast seemed awesome to Francis. He must have been burning more calories than he realized, because he was absolutely starving. Everything smelled and tasted great. He sat beside Doctor Kuvayev and immediately started to dig in.

"Where's Sokolov?" he asked with his mouth only partially empty.

Kuvayev was also busy with his fork. "He left early. I think he was going to the drilling site."

"I see. Lots of excitement there, I suppose."

"Too much, I think. The water apparently shot back through one of the boreholes and erupted like a geyser inside the shed. This was a surprise as it usually freezes quite quickly."

"Did anyone get hurt?" Francis asked.

Kuvayev shook his head. He was the resident medical doctor, so he would know. "Just wet and cold. Everyone is fine. But now they have water frozen all over the drilling site, which somehow needs to be cleaned away. I think Sokolov is leading the charge to get the cleanup done. And then they have to figure out what went wrong so it won't happen again."

"Well, that's just fine from my point of view. I can get caught up on the samples I already have waiting for me." He resumed eating and contemplated the activities from the previous night. If Antarctica had any laws governing decency, he was confident that he had broken most of them. Now he had both excessive drinking and lewd and lascivious behavior on the list of bad habits he was picking up. What would Deborah think? His initial reluctance had been banished by gentle encouragement. He had accepted the invitation to participate in several acts that had never been on his agenda before. But they seemed like a good idea at the time. A very good idea, to be precise.

How had his standards been corrupted so quickly and easily? He needed a good rationalization, and quick. He settled upon categorizing the bad habits as coping methods for adjusting to the psychological and physical demands of being here. That seemed plausible enough. At this rate, he figured that he might as well take up smoking. Was it possible that any of these Russians had smuggled some pot in with them?

Konstantine strode over. "No Cat ride this morning, Doctor. Would you care to walk over to the lab with me instead?"

"Oh, yes. Of course. Just a moment." He threw the last few forkfuls in his mouth, then stood and carried his plates to the sink. "Right. Let's suit up. Discovery awaits."

Putting on outside clothes in Antarctica was more of a process and took more time than in other less frigid climates. When they stepped outside, Hamlin was pleased to note there was virtually no wind. Their feet crunched loudly in the snow as they walked along. He looked up and saw a perfectly clear sky. There were so many layers of stars visible; it was as if there was no darkness in the sky whatsoever.

"Beautiful morning, is it not?" Konstantine observed, despite the fact that they were in absolute darkness.

"Wow. Indeed it is. Almost makes you wonder why nobody has put an observatory down here."

"There is an excellent facility in Mauna Kea. Would you rather be in Hawaii or here?"

Francis laughed. He managed not to choke on the cold air and silently congratulated himself. "I guess that answers the question. Well put."

They trudged along noisily.

"You know," Konstantine said, "this is really the only place where we can talk openly."

Hamlin raised an eyebrow. Where was he going with this?

"I'm not going to talk about last night, if that's what you are interested in," Hamlin said preemptively.

It was Konstantine's turn to laugh. "I saw Lena and her friend go into your room. I have a good idea of what happened already."

"I see. Apparently discretion is an unknown commodity down here. Then I'm afraid I'm fresh out of secrets or controversial information. Sorry."

They both continued walking.

"Of course, you are right. We should continue to concentrate on our work."

More crunching.

"There isn't much point in being coy, Konstantine. If there's something on your mind, spill it. Or is it that you're not yet sure if you can trust me either?"

Again, only the sound of walking.

"No, no. I trust you. You were right. I...just, ah, want to hear about last night."

"Envelope please. Ladies and gentlemen, the award for *worst liar ever* goes to..."

"What?" His confusion was genuine enough.

"Look," Francis replied, "you've got nothing to worry about with me. This was a last second decision and I didn't have any contacts with anybody here prior to stepping off the plane. I'm not part of any hidden agenda. If you want to get something off your chest, fine. If not, let's enjoy the walk. Paranoid delusions aren't really my cup of tea. And speaking of that, how about you make me one of those when we get to the lab?"

"Are you married?"

It was a sudden and unusual turn to the conversation.

"No."

"Do you have a girlfriend?"

That one stung a little bit. "I used to."

"Any children?"

"Again, no."

"Are your parents alive?"

"They both passed away," Hamlin said. "This is an uplifting line of conversation."

"I could have correctly guessed the answers before posing the questions. You are like the rest of us, then. No close family members at home. Only Kuvayev, the medical doctor has children and a spouse."

Francis thought he was starting to see the point of this. "Ah, conspiracy theorist, eh? Look, they probably like unattached people because we're not pining for our loved ones back home. This is like spending a stint on the space station. If you're not able to let go of your previous life while you're here, you'll be curled up in a corner drooling before this is all over. It makes perfect sense."

"It makes it easier if we somehow don't come back. Fewer people to ask questions."

This was the first time anybody had been so morose about being here. Either Konstantine was losing his grip, or a subtle undercurrent of mistrust was showing itself for the first time.

"I see. So have you evidence of people disappearing down here, never to be seen again?" The question was asked mostly in jest.

"Yes."

That was disconcerting. Hamlin could see the lab approaching in the distance. "Look, it's too cold to finish this conversation before we get inside. This is all very interesting, yet terrifying. Perhaps we should plan to resume this dialogue during our next walk."

Konstantine was silent in response. Hamlin couldn't see his facial expression because of the huge hood that covered his head.

"And don't forget that tea, right?" Francis added. He was relieved when Konstantine answered in his usual tone of voice.

"I could make you iced tea. We have lots of that."

"No thank you," Hamlin said. "Something hot would be more appropriate right now." It would be a relief to get back inside. He needed shelter from the cold and the sinister insinuations. The research gave him enough to think about. He was glad to refocus.

CHAPTER FIVE

Sokolov didn't appear until late afternoon. Francis had actually been thinking about packing it in for the day and facing the cold walk back. At least now there was a chance that they could hitch a ride.

"You look like you've had a long day," Hamlin noted. It was the first time he had seen Sokolov look at all disheveled.

He simply nodded in agreement. "Yes, Doctor. It has indeed been a long day. But at the end of it all, we accomplished a great deal. We should be back to taking samples sometime tomorrow. And that, given the condition of the site just several hours ago, is quite an achievement. May I inquire as to whether or not you two are ready for a ride back to our quarters? I fear I am ready to bring the working portion of this day to an end."

Hamlin gestured him over. "Before we go, let me show you something that might make you feel better."

Sokolov was immediately interested. "Another discovery, Dr. Hamlin? Something exciting, perhaps?"

Francis smiled and waved Sokolov toward the microscope.

"Perhaps. Have a look and judge for yourself."

Sokolov worked the focusing knob. It didn't take long. "Oh my. Look at that robust little beast. He's still rather frisky, I would say. Have you identified it yet?"

"Not certain, but I'd say crustacean and I'd also say new species."

Sokolov pulled away. Hamlin was beaming.

"Excellent, Doctor. This is extraordinary. To think that there are some who speculate that this water has been isolated for over thirty million years. It makes you wonder about this little fellow and his family history. It is astonishing to contemplate the possibilities. Have you catalogued it yet?"

"Everything is done. And you should find some excellent photos on the server."

Sokolov actually rubbed his hands together in anticipation. "Outstanding. I shall endeavor to synchronize with our satellite at the earliest possible moment and share this data with my colleagues. You are about to excite a lot of people who tend toward being blasé about most things. Congratulations, Doctor."

"The work is its own reward," he replied. "That and the Nobel Prize that I'm going to get when we return."

Sokolov smiled. "If you would be so good as to share some of the credit, then I think I would be most satisfied with that result. Why don't you consider that motivation for pushing ahead with your research? Who knows what you might find tomorrow?"

"That's what keeps me up at night." That and boinking the two female members of the crew, a thought which was best left unsaid, he figured. He turned off the light on the microscope. "If you could give me five minutes to clean up, I'll be ready to accept that offer of a ride. How about you, Konstantine?"

"Yes, five minutes would let me get ready. A ride sounds good."

"Awesome." Francis was sincere when he said it. He really wanted to avoid the cold. He also wanted to avoid prolonging the conversation they had started on the walk over. Riding was much more suitable.

Supper was centered around a large tray of fried chicken. There were also biscuits, mixed vegetables, and brown beans. Francis ate like a lumberjack. He felt better noting that the others were doing the same. When apple pie came out for dessert, he had no problem finding room to put away a large slice. A friend had once told him that dessert went into a separate stomach. It was a theory he readily accepted. The fact that the pie had been frozen and reheated made absolutely no difference. It was simply delicious.

As the meal was breaking up, Sokolov stood and held up his hand. The room immediately quieted down.

"My friends and colleagues," he said as loudly as he could without actually yelling, "I believe the time has come to reconnect somewhat with the outside world."

Hamlin had no idea what that meant. Sokolov pulled a sheet of paper out of his pocket and straightened out the creases.

"Our newest addition, Doctor Hamlin, has now been with us approximately two weeks–the rest of us appreciably longer than that. I thought you might enjoy some of the headlines that summarize what has been happening back in civilization since we arrived here. Do you agree?"

There was an eruption of applause, punctuated by someone who knew how to use their fingers to create a piercing whistle.

"Very good. Settle now, please. Let me proceed." He cleared his throat in anticipation.

"From the New York Times, the headline says, 'Federal Government Headed Toward Possible Shutdown.' Really, Dr. Hamlin, you Americans create more problems than you solve with your boundless democracy. At any rate, I shall refrain from any further commentary on the matter. That one was for you.

Where was he getting this stuff, Hamlin wondered. Maybe it had come in with him on the plane and was being revealed just now.

"From Sweden, the Aftonbladet, the headline screams, 'Researchers Certain That Mammoth Will Yield DNA.' Complete rubbish, but even if true, it pales in comparison to what we are doing here."

This was met with more cheering.

"Now, from the London Daily Mail, 'Miley Cyrus Says Women Should Masturbate Every Day.' Do I need to offer comment on the effects of decadent western living? I think not."

There was laughing and snorting from the crowd.

"More along the same lines from the National Inquirer, 'Bill Caught in Teenage Sex Ring.' I should imagine none of us need a surname to know whom this is referring to. Thanks once again to our American friends for providing such excellent entertainment fodder.

"From the Toronto Star, and I kid you not, 'Marijuana Issue Sent to Joint Committee.' Where have all the good editors gone?

"From Reuters, 'I'm Not From Another Planet says Ronaldo After Loss.' That is perhaps for the experts to decide. Let's see, what else? Closer to home, perhaps.

"From the Moscow Times, 'New Approach to Ruble Crisis Seen in Russian Central Bank Reshuffle.' It would appear our savings and our future are both stable and secure. Good, good.

"From Pravda, 'Russia, China and India Building new Multipolar World Order.' Once again, my apologies, Dr. Hamlin. Perhaps we should have kept you shielded from the inevitable decline of your society on the world stage. One more, perhaps. Something with some humor. Ah, yes.

"From the Examiner, 'Homicide Victims Rarely Talk to Police.' Indeed! Once again, the shortage of capable editors is apparent.

"In summary, all of you should imagine the dramatic impact that you will have on headlines around the world when they find out what we are doing down here. This work of yours is critically important. Here, in this little corner of the world, with this handful of people, research is proceeding that will eclipse anything else that will transpire all around this crazy world during our time in this place. And this is our time. And each of you is an important part of this work. So enjoy your evening and rest well. Tomorrow is another day."

The exercise seemed to have amused the crowd, Hamlin noted, but in his case, it just made him homesick for all the good comedians back in America.

"Dr. Hamlin?" The deep voice of Doctor Kuvayev brought him back to reality.

"Yes," Francis replied. "I seem to have drifted off there a bit. What can I do for you?"

"We need one more person for a game or two of darts. Are you interested?"

This was a pleasant surprise. "Yes, that sounds fine. I haven't played for a long time, mind you, but I always enjoyed the sport."

A smile went across Kuvayev's bearded face. "Perhaps we will play for rubles, Doctor. Did you bring your wallet?"

"Sorry, I was told not to bring cash or valuables. Now I know why. Where is this dartboard, anyway? I don't recall seeing one."

"It is on the wall in the laundry room. We can wash our clothes and play at the same time."

"Excellent. I assume you'll still be wearing something. If so, lead on. I shall try not to embarrass myself too severely."

"I was joking about the rubles, of course. We only play for fun."

Hamlin was on his feet. "In the interest of preserving my delicately balanced mental state, fun it is."

For the next two days, research proceeded in a more routine manner. Sokolov had been wrong in his estimate for returning the drilling site back to service. The heating unit shut off during the night as melting water dripped into it. Everything refroze and they had to start cleaning and drying all over again. With the entire area encrusted in ice, even getting the air heated seemed to take longer than normal.

At the end of the second day, Hamlin noticed Dr. Kuvayev returning with the crew from the drilling site. When he asked him about it during the meal, Kuvayev almost seemed angry. But then his countenance softened. He blew out a long stream of air.

"Sorry, Doctor," he replied in his deep voice. "I was deep in thought. You pulled me out of it."

Hamlin was content to return to his food. "I did not mean to intrude. I should have read your expression better."

He dismissed the explanation with the wave of a big hand. "Not at all. It's just that, even though I am a medical doctor, I am primarily a researcher here. I get stressed when my services are required to deal with injury or illness."

By now the meal was in large part over, and the dull drone of multiple conversations drowned out their words so no one else could hear but the two of them. Still, with politics and emotional stability to take into account, he pondered the wisdom of pursuing this any further. Perhaps just one small step.

"I see. Did someone get injured at the drilling site?"

He shook his head. "No. Well, to be accurate, one of the men pinched his finger while attaching a large chain to an even larger sprocket. It is a painful injury, but nothing serious. My concern is that one of them seems to be coming down with a virus of some sort. I'm going to recommend bed rest for him tomorrow and keep an eye on his condition. It is almost certainly not serious, but in these close quarters, things tend to get passed around rather easily."

"I thought," Hamlin said, "that germs couldn't live down here in this cold."

"Technically, they can't. This was probably already in his system. Perhaps the shock of being doused with freezing cold water weakened his immune response and the pathogen was able to overwhelm him that way. At any rate, some rest and acetaminophen should take care of it nicely."

"Very good. Then I shall leave you to your meal. Sorry to interrupt." He pushed his chair away from the table and took his dirty dishes to the counter.

As this was movie night, Hamlin had some minor prep work to do. He chose an old Clint Eastwood comedy/action movie in which Clint co-starred with an orangutan. As had been the case with most of his presentations, it was a hit with the audience. While he found himself smiling and occasionally chuckling, his peers roared at the funny parts and yelled with gusto during the action scenes. This success always made him feel like a bit of a hero. When it was over, he was sure to get his hand shaken, his back slapped, and other possible rewards if Lena and/or her friend had anything to say about it. No wonder Hollywood held such an addictive attraction to so many.

On this night, he was glad when it ended and the crowd broke up. Once again, the climate and mental fatigue brought on by the concentration he needed to do his work left him tired and ready for some sleep. He slipped away and was soon under the covers. He wondered if his sleeping patterns would be this consistent and successful when he returned home. Here, he had no problem falling and staying asleep. This night was no exception. He snored a little once he had dropped off, but no one was there to document or report on this phenomenon, so he would never know. Later, in the early hours, he dreamt of Deborah.

Sokolov appeared sometime around mid-morning at the lab. He politely inquired about their progress and then suggested that they both work together on some of the larger specimens that had been found in the lake water. He asked if there was any likelihood that a species of krill would be discovered. He was also interested in the specifics of the diet that these newfound creatures had. Hamlin thought the requests seemed a little odd and disjointed, but since they hadn't had any new samples for several days now, he was happy to fill his agenda by doing some tests. Running out of work would have been disastrous.

"So, Konstantine," Hamlin said, "how many people are here exactly?"

"Fourteen including you."

"That seems right. Have I met them all?"

"Certainly. We all live in the same quarters. I suspect if you put your mind to it, you could probably come up with all of their names."

Francis refocused on a drop of water at low resolution.

"I doubt that. It's not like trying to remember Smith or Jones, after all. Your names tend to be tedious and intimidating."

Konstantine looked up from his microscope. "I hadn't really given it any thought. You don't have long names in America?"

"We do, of course, but I think the frequency is much lower. We have a lot of family names like Hill, Brown, and Reed. You get the occasional tongue twister, but they tend to be more contemporary in origin. The lengthier names were recently dragged over from Europe somewhere. My theory is that when many of our ancestors came over to the New World originally, they took the opportunity to change and simplify the family name right after getting off the boat. Therefore, Hoffenmeister became Hoff, or eventually some other abbreviated variant thereof. It was like a filtering system for names."

"Where did your name originate, Doctor?"

"Aha, you shouldn't have asked. I know the answer. Now you'll have to listen to my spiel. Hamlin is English, but of French pre-10th century origins, being originally introduced at the Conquest of 1066. How's that for detail? It is derived from the Norman personal name 'Hamon,' itself a variant of the early Germanic word 'haim,' meaning home. I've done some research, you see. It would seem that the melting pot gets smaller the further back one goes, but so do the chances of successfully finding anything."

"Impressive. I don't know my family background beyond the stories my grandmother told me."

"Hmm. I have some general idea of the origins of the Russian population, but you may not view it as flattering. Perhaps we should venture off into another line of conversation."

Konstantine looked up. "How can it be that bad?"

"Imagine a boatload of Vikings engaging in what they consider to be free trade of commodities and culture in the St. Petersburg region in perhaps the eighth century. This consists of such concepts as introductory arson, stabbing as a population control method, and the benefits of semen deposits for village women, men, and slower farm animals. Hence, we see the beginning of the gene pool from which your ancestry was drawn."

"Are you kidding?"

"I'm going to go with a yes, I do believe I am."

Konstantine laughed. "You were right. Let's talk about something else."

"All right. What interests you?"

"I don't know. You choose."

Hamlin pondered. "I have no idea what your background is. How about this? What is your favorite album of all time?"

Konstantine didn't hesitate. "I like 'Rivers and Bridges' by Mashina Vremeni."

That stumped Hamlin. "Really? Is that a person or group?"

"It's a group."

"I see." He really didn't. "I find it hard, personally, to select only one when there are so many awesome albums, especially from the seventies and eighties. If forced to do so, I would be entirely subjective in my decision making process and say 'The Wall' by Pink Floyd."

Konstantine looked up and frowned. "Why is Floyd pink?"

"He's not. It's a group, not a person."

"I see." He really didn't.

Hamlin rolled his neck around to work out some kinks. "This isn't going anywhere. We need a topic with more common ground. Or...say, what are the chances of us getting a radio for out here? You need to listen to some Pink Floyd. You'd be addicted to it in no time."

"I don't think we have one. There are no stations to listen to, after all."

"That is a stumper," Francis conceded. "But more concerning is the fact that this entire line of conversation is starting to sound like a first date. Hold on now, I may have thought of something. As a resolution, I have a suggestion. I have Pink Floyd on a memory stick. I currently have in front of me a serviceable computer that accepts memory sticks. I propose that I insert the stick, find the appropriate file, and then we can resume our research while listening to *Comfortably Numb* et al. What do you say, Konstantine?"

He smiled. "I say that rock music will rot my brain."

"This from a man who drinks vodka from a straw. I'll keep it low and you can interject with a *cease and desist* order whenever you deem necessary. Acceptable?"

"Acceptable."

The rest of the day slid by with a musical accompaniment.

CHAPTER SIX

With his accelerated metabolism acting as a moderating influence on his culinary standards, supper was entirely acceptable. Francis then enjoyed casual conversation with several people in close proximity at the dinner table, and caught Lena smiling at him in a blatantly suggestive manner from across the room. All in all, a fine evening. At this point, he resigned himself to the fact that if he didn't do laundry, he would be wearing soiled clothing in the very near future.

The laundry room was situated awkwardly near the end of the hall that led away from the dining area. One had to walk past the kitchen, past a seldom used research room, past the boiler room and several storage rooms before finally reaching the cramped room that always smelled like laundry soap. There was only one washer and one dryer, so timing was everything. Hamlin had found that the first person to arrive after supper got the lion's share of the available time, so he made sure he was the initial person to lay claim to the room. He threw his load in, gave it the prescribed amount of detergent, pushed the regular cycle button, and set things in motion. The wash cycle would take about fifty minutes, so he planned to return to his room and break out one of the novels he had brought with him. He had been saving them, not wanting to read through them in the first few days but rather savor the anticipation for a while. He turned to see Lena blocking the doorway; an unexpected but not altogether unpleasant obstacle to his plan.

"Hello, Doctor."

Even her voice was having an immediate effect on him now. Hamlin would have sworn that she was more attractive than when he first arrived. He recalled some joke about natives taking the ugliest woman in the village along when they went hunting. Once she started looking good, it was time to return.

"I guess it's time for me to return," Hamlin said as he walked slowly towards her. He immediately slipped his right hand under her sweater and enjoyed the soft warmth of her skin. This seemed to distract her from any concerns about his incoherent opening statement.

"Doctor, please. You're too forward for me."

His hand remained under her top. "You're the one interrupting my laundry routine. You should have heeded the standard protocols of clothes washing.

"Please, don't take advantage of my innocence," she gasped softly.

Hamlin smirked. He thought that this role playing game was quite good. Not exactly Shakespearian, but then again, that wasn't the sort of performance they were about to enjoy. A sharp crash came from the dining hall. Somebody must have dropped a plate. That temporarily broke the spell. It did not, however, immediately motivate him to release his grasp.

"Say, Lena, doesn't this seem a little bit too...public for this sort of thing? There are usually at least three or four people doing laundry every night. Therefore, I feel safe in saying that we're probably going to get interrupted. With my luck, I'm sure it would happen at the worst possible time."

She reached back with her one hand and grabbed the doorknob. She then pushed him slowly back into the room. Her voice was still low and suggestive. "You don't mean that they could catch us doing...you know. Surely not that."

Once the door was pulled shut, she turned and looked over her shoulder.

"What have we here? Oh, a latch. Just one moment." She hooked it shut. "Now, you were telling me about my mistake. What is that you want to do to me, my overlord?"

Francis was trying to slip back into character. "Silence, you. Only talk when I give you permission. That's the way it's done in America."

"I find that hard to believe," she replied with a smile.

He bent down until his lips just brushed against hers. "Would you believe me if I gave you my word?"

A thunderous crash startled them both. Lena actually screamed just a little bit. They pulled apart and looked around for the source.

"What was that?" Lena had been scared back into reality.

"I don't know." Francis stared at the wall where the sound seemed to originate. He couldn't imagine what could have generated a sound that loud. His heart was pounding. "What's on the other side?"

"We call it the medical room. There's almost nothing in there. We never use it."

Another crash vibrated through the wall. It was accompanied by a hideous shriek.

Lena had a look of absolute terror. She reached for the latch on the door.

"Come on. Let's get out of here. We must tell the others."

Francis was seriously shaken by this totally unexpected turn of events. He was unable to imagine what could possibly be the source of the ruckus.

"Great idea," he said. "Let's get back to the dining hall." He was desperate to fulfill his safety in numbers yearning. All the intuition he possessed was telling him that something was very wrong. He clung to enough control to restrain himself from pushing Lena out of his way.

Another thunderous crash, this time sharper, perhaps mechanical in nature, assaulted their ears. It sounded like someone had thrown a piece of furniture into the wall. It was followed by another terrible scream.

She fumbled with the latch, then flung the door open and stumbled into the hall. Hamlin was one small step behind her. Most faces in the dining hall were now turned toward them. Sokolov appeared as they ran back down the hall.

"Doctors, if you would be so good as to keep the physical aspect of your relationship in check to the point where you're not destroying our station, we would greatly appreciate it."

Lena pointed toward the end of the hall. "There's something in the medical room. We heard crashes and screaming."

Sokolov immediately assumed a grim expression. "Dr. Kuvayev! Come here at once."

A chair scraped and the big man rose up. "What is it?"

Sokolov waved him over. "I'll explain in the hall. The rest of you should go to your sleeping quarters, just as a precaution until I give the all-clear. Dr. Hamlin, would you be as good as to accompany us? Dr. Sayanski, please join the others in returning to your room."

Kuvayev arrived, and the three of them started down the hall.

Hamlin was anxious for information.

"What the hell is going on down there? Do you know?"

"Let us walk a little further down the hall before engaging in conversation, if you please," Sokolov insisted.

They walked until they drew even with the laundry room. Sokolov stopped and looked toward the last door in the hall.

A horrible, inhuman scream pierced their ears. The door crashed as something slammed into it violently.

It was Kuvayev's turn to look grim. "Pechkin is in there."

Sokolov nodded. "Yes."

Hamlin almost felt ill. Something was very wrong here. "Is he all right? Is he being attacked?"

Kuvayev's eyes were wide and unsure. "He is in there by himself."

Sokolov turned toward Kuvayev. "Perhaps some tranquilizer is in order. Would you be so kind, Doctor?"

"Yes, of course. I'll be right back."

"Here, Doctor. This supply room right here should have some stored in it. If you please."

"Certainly."

An animal-like roar echoed down the hall. Hamlin felt like a character in a horror story.

"What is happening in there?" Hamlin asked. "Who is Pechkin?"

Sokolov resigned himself to the necessity of sharing some information.

"Yegor Pechkin works on the drilling crew. He started feeling ill yesterday. We had him resting in the medical room, trying to keep him isolated to the point where the virus wouldn't spread."

"He has a virus?"

"Doctor Kuvayev believes so, and he is our resident physician. This behavior, however, is quite unexpected."

"Then why did you immediately suggest a tranquilizer?"

Sokolov sighed. "There are no large animals in Antarctica that could break in and make this kind of ruckus. He is in there alone. I am concerned about his safety, but ours as well. His actions sound quite violent, wouldn't you agree?"

Kuvayev returned with a syringe in his big hand. "Here we go."

Sokolov surveyed it critically. "What dosage do you propose?"

"Twenty milligrams benzodiazepine. Does that sound right?"

Sokolov dismissed the question. "You're the doctor. How fast will that work?"

Another crash at the door.

"Not instantly, if that's what you mean."

"Very well. It's what we have. Let's try to determine what is happening without opening the door, if possible."

"How do you propose to do that?" Francis asked doubtfully.

Sokolov stepped toward the door. "Let's ask him."

It took some effort for Hamlin to walk right up to it. He wasn't feeling comfortable at all.

"Yegor Pechkin! Yegor, are you all right? It's Doctor Sokolov."

Silence was the only response.

"Yegor, we're here to help you. Can you hear me?"

Again, not so much as a whisper.

"Do you think he might be unconscious? Perhaps he has injured himself."

Sokolov considered this. "Perhaps."

"Is the door somehow locked from the outside?" Hamlin asked. "Couldn't he just open it and get out anytime?"

"Yes. It begs the question; why hasn't he?" Sokolov weighed their options. As if on impulse, he suddenly reached out and knocked loudly on the door.

From in the room came the sound of furniture being thrown violently against the wall. Francis was really uncomfortable to know that the door wasn't secured at all. Just simply shut.

"The bed is the only thing in there," Kuvayev said in awe. "How could he be throwing it around like that?"

Hamlin nodded. "Good question."

Sokolov looked more subdued than either of the others had ever seen.

"The pertinent question before us is–do we open this door and engage him, or not?"

"He could die or do very serious bodily harm to himself if we don't intervene," Kuvayev observed. "If he hasn't already."

"But what would he do to us if we do open that door?" Hamlin asked. He just didn't feel like he knew enough to make a good decision one way or the other.

"I am concerned that he won't engage us in dialogue," Sokolov said.

"Or can't," Hamlin expanded.

"Look," Kuvayev said. "I am bigger and heavier than Pechkin. I could rush in, grab him, and pin his arms. One of you take this needle. Just jam it into his thigh or shoulder–anywhere really, keeping the skeletal structure in mind. Pump it into him, and then we run back into the hall and shut the door. It won't take long for this stuff to knock him out."

Hamlin found he was still skeptical. "And then what? He's going to wake up again sooner or later. What if he's the same way?"

"Do we have any restraints?" Sokolov asked.

Kuvayev nodded his head. "Yes. We'll have to get him on the gurney."

Hamlin was even more horrified. "Why would you have restraints here?"

"It was a question, Doctor. Nothing more. It's not that unusual. They could serve a multitude of perfectly normal purposes. Desperate times call for desperate measures." Sokolov sighed in anticipation of the inevitable. "If you have another suggestion, this would be the optimal time to present it."

Francis actually did a quick mental check. The shelves in his idea store were empty. One thought suddenly appeared.

"Should we get more help? Perhaps several other people in case this is more difficult than we imagine."

Kuvayev had no response.

"It is my responsibility to oversee and maintain this facility. We are currently cut off from civilization and simply must survive on our own until closer to spring when the weather starts to improve. My concern is that we put more people at risk if we bring them down here. And there is another factor to consider, as well."

Hamlin had no idea what that might be.

"What are you talking about?" he asked.

A dull thud came from the room. It was much less fierce than the others had been.

"Mental and emotional health are absolutely critical to our survival," Sokolov answered. "It is no different than the isolation of being on the space station. Extensive psychological testing is done on every astronaut. If any one of us was to lose the ability to cope with the isolation and other stress factors of being here, the entire station would suffer greatly. And there would be little to nothing that we could do about it. At best, we would strive to ensure that the emotional malady didn't spread to other members of our party. The affected person could easy suffer permanent damage before they could be returned to society for treatment. That is why we tolerate any number of mildly aberrant forms of behavior that can act as distractions and stress relievers. You would hardly imagine that I find it desirable to have two of my researchers having intercourse or doing God knows what in the laundry room while the rest of the team sits only a few feet away down the hall. But I would warrant a guess that you were not feeling stressed about being here while you were enjoying your little romp."

"That's true. At least until the crashing started."

"If we expose more of our precious group to the possible but as of yet unknown horrors that lay waiting beyond this door, we could do permanent and devastating damage to the emotional state of this entire station. That must be avoided at all costs. That is why I sent them as far away as possible. And, my good doctors, that is why we may have to alter our story as to what happened here when this is all over."

Hamlin was immediately offended. "You mean lie?"

"Yes, Doctor, I mean lie." Sokolov sighed. "Look, why do you think I asked you out of all the others to come with us to help deal with this situation?"

Hamlin shrugged. "I'm more expendable?"

Sokolov had to smile despite their circumstances. "Not in the slightest. We wouldn't have bothered to find you and fly you here if your presence wasn't essential to our work. No, Doctor, in you I see a strong and emotionally stable person. I felt you could handle this stress better than any of the others."

Hamlin was shocked. "Are you kidding? I wouldn't have even considered coming here if I hadn't been an emotional wreck. I had totally lost my focus and my life was a mess. Otherwise I'd be in a nice, hot climate doing research I love and hopefully spending the nights in my tent with the woman who I thought was going to be my life partner. I definitely wouldn't be here."

"Really, Doctor? Do you remember the list of side effects I quoted you when you first arrived? You've exhibited almost none of them. You made friends, or at least acquaintances, from the moment you walked in the door. You engage in virtually every activity available to us, but you are not obsessed or addicted to any of them. You utilize your sense of humor as a buffer against almost any kind of confrontation or issue. You have engaged in sexual behavior with at least two of our other members, yet you seem to have no possessiveness or paranoia regarding the other aspects of your relationship with them. You are, no doubt, the most stable person here. That is why I chose you, and that is why I don't think the others could handle really bad news–if that is in fact what we find in here."

Francis had been standing there long enough.

"Come on. Let's do this. I'm ready."

"You take the needle, then," Kuvayev said, extending his hand toward Hamlin.

Sokolov tried to read his reaction. "Are you comfortable with this, Doctor? The injection is an essential part of our plan."

Hamlin nodded. "Yes. I can do it. Give it to me."

"Very well. I shall open the door once you two are in place. Kuvayev, you enter first and try to hold Pechkin still. Hamlin will then inject him. We will then exit the room and wait for the drug to take effect. While we are waiting, we can formulate a plan on how to deal with him, based on what we find when we walk in. Are we ready?"

The other two stepped in front of the door.

Sokolov grabbed the handle. He made eye contact, nodded, then threw the door open.

Kuvayev entered first, Hamlin pushed right up against him to keep as close as possible.

They stopped immediately upon entering. The stench of urine and feces assaulted their noses. There was no light, even when Francis flipped the switch. The sound of labored breathing came from the far corner of the room.

"Pechkin?" Kuvayev spoke softly, slowly.

More labored breathing. As his eyes adjusted to the gloom, Hamlin could barely make out the outline of a figure crouched in the corner. Details were lacking, but he appeared to be naked and covered with dark smears. If the smell meant anything, Hamlin already knew what they consisted of.

"It's me. Kuvayev."

Still no discernible response. The figure was definitely staring at them. The breathing was fast, like someone who had just been running.

"We're here to help." The words were still said slowly and softly.

Still no response. Hamlin decided to risk some conversation.

"He's going to be hard to reach with this needle while he's crouched down like that."

Kuvayev nodded. "He's going to be hard for me to grab, as well."

Sokolov was in the doorway, holding his sleeves over his face as best he could.

Francis figured anything less than a full HAZMAT suit wouldn't be enough. He looked at Kuvayev, then back to the figure in the corner.

"What now?"

"Let's move closer," Kuvayev said. "Stay right behind me. We'll go nice and slow and read his reaction to us. Maybe I can get him to stand up. It would be a good start."

"I'm with you. Nice and easy now."

The big man took a single step. The noisy breathing continued unchanged.

"Yegor. We're here to help you."

The breathing stopped. Completely. The room was silent.

They were so close together that Hamlin could feel Kuvayev stiffen noticeably.

"Pechkin?" This time was question was loud and urgent.

Sokolov leaned further into the room. "What's happening?"

"Damn!" Kuvayev walked toward the now silent man. He reached down to touch him, Francis lagging behind. The sick man leapt to his feet and roared–a deafening sound that was more like a beast than a human being. He grabbed Kuvayev and then appeared to reach in and bite him. Kuvayev screamed and grappled with the delirious man. He was thrown across the room like a rag doll. After hitting the wall hard, he slumped to the ground.

Hamlin was now unprotected and close enough to reach out and touch Pechkin with his hand.

Pechkin stood there, breathing hard and fast but not moving. He seemed to be looking at Sokolov in the doorway. Hamlin was sure he was mistaken, but he thought he could feel the heat coming off Pechkin's naked body. But that would be impossible. Hamlin didn't move a muscle, trying to become part of the wall.

Pechkin suddenly lunged for the doorway. Sokolov screamed and slammed the door shut with just an instant to spare. The crazed man howled and slammed into the door. The crash was significant but the door held. This seemed to be as far as Pechkin was prepared to go with his reaction.

And then came the breathing. No other sounds of movement were apparent. Hamlin was alone in complete darkness with this deranged person.

He warned himself not to panic. He stood perfectly still, not making a single sound. Would Sokolov go for help? What kind of condition was Kuvayev in? He was the resident medical doctor! How would they survive without him? Then he remembered the syringe in his hand.

Sokolov stood outside the door, thinking furiously. He needed to do something and fast. But what? Which course of action would best serve the long-term needs of the station?

The man on the other side of the door screeched. It slammed and then there were several other crashing sounds around the room. What had just happened? Sokolov grimaced but held his ground.

The room grew deceptively quiet once again. Sokolov thought he heard moaning several times, but couldn't be certain. Stress made time passage seem slow. He remained frozen in place. None of the others had left their room as far as he could tell. That was good.

A full minute ticked by. Then two. Nothing seemed to be happening. After five minutes of quiet, Sokolov decided that it was time to act, regardless of consequences. He reached for the door handle and then slowly turned it.

The stress of swinging the door slowly open was tremendous. Sokolov moved it slowly, eyes trying to make out details in the room that might tip him off as to what had just transpired. He was also looking for movement.

There! In the center of the room, Pechkin stood silently. His head swiveled ever so slowly until he stared directly at Sokolov. He opened his mouth and a wheezing sound came out. It was almost like he was trying to speak. Sokolov took a big risk and stepped just a little farther into the room.

"What is it, Pechkin? I can hear you."

His mouth worked slowly. Open, shut. Open, shut.

Where were the other two? After allowing his eyes time to work, he saw Kuvayev along the side-wall crumpled, and what appeared to be Hamlin in the back corner, lying on top of what used to be a bed.

"Pechkin?"

The sick man fell over sideways with a thud and lay motionless on the floor.

CHAPTER SEVEN

Hamlin regained consciousness only to find himself in the same hellhole. Now there was some light. The hallway door was open and there was Sokolov standing in the room. How was that possible? It was then he saw Pechkin motionless on the floor. He then decided to disengage himself from whatever he was entangled in.

"Doctor Hamlin!" Sokolov rushed over and gave him assistance. "Are you all right?"

Francis winced as he moved. "I think so. My right side is pretty sore."

He was able to regain his footing and hold the upright position.

Sokolov hesitated. "We have much to do and I don't know how much time we have."

Hamlin was beginning to wonder if he hadn't hurt a rib. Perhaps it was even broken. "Well, Pechkin should be docile for some time, if that helps."

"You were able to inject him?" Sokolov asked.

"Yes. At first he didn't even seem to notice. That allowed me to empty the syringe. Then he whacked me pretty good. I don't even remember landing on whatever this is."

"Excellent, Doctor! Excellent! So, now we have a possibly injured comrade and a very sick comrade who is at least temporarily incapacitated. I must confess; I am not quite certain how to proceed. I'm afraid this contingency isn't in any of the training manuals. Do you have any suggestions?"

"Let's get Kuvayev out of here first. We can assess his condition and try to figure out what kind of treatment, if any, he needs. Over and above any personal feelings the crew has for the man, we definitely don't want to lose our only real medical doctor."

"What about Pechkin?" Sokolov said.

"He apparently can't figure out to open a closed door in his current state. I say we rescue Kuvayev, close Pechkin in here, and get some assistance from the others."

Sokolov looked like he had been punched in the stomach.

"Look," Hamlin said, "I understand the theory behind the propaganda and misinformation. But there's no way we're going to be able to do this ourselves, and there's no way you can keep this a secret, even if we both try. Let's grab Kuvayev and get him and us out of this horrible environment."

Sokolov conceded. "Very well. You take one side, I'll take the other."

Hamlin nearly screamed while lifting and carrying Kuvayev out of the room. It put a lot of stress on his sore side. But it had to be done. After a bit more cajoling, Sokolov gave in and released the rest of the staff to give them assistance. There was universal horror and revulsion, but after the initial shock, everyone rolled up their sleeves and got to work.

Kuvayev regained consciousness shortly after being removed from the room. He had clearly suffered a concussion despite his insistence that he was able to get up and help. He finally agreed to twenty-four hours of bed rest.

One of the unused storage rooms was hastily converted into a medical/confinement room. Pechkin was strapped down on a gurney and wheeled into it. There really were no other options. Cleaning him up was a terrible chore. Four crew members spent nearly an hour removing feces and blood, then treating a myriad of minor wounds. All of them were astonished at the damage he had done to the room. The other surprise was his body temperature. He was roasting.

When a thermometer was finally located, he topped out at forty-one point seven Celsius. Hamlin had to insist on a conversion to imperial measure in order for that number to make any sense to him. It translated to one hundred and seven Fahrenheit. When consulted, Kuvayev became greatly distressed. He immediately subscribed medication to bring it down.

"This level of hyperpyrexia is almost always fatal. We need to bring it down right now. Someone will have to watch him constantly until it is under control. Don't be surprised if he goes into a convulsion."

Hamlin was still participating despite his sore side. He decided that nothing was broken. "What else can we do?" he asked. "Especially if he convulses."

"Strip him naked. Apply cool, wet towels. Blow a fan on him. Open a window. Anything that would make you feel cool should help to bring down his temperature as well."

Francis went to get some towels. He passed two crewmembers that had located Hazmat suits and were on their way to clean up the room where the attack had happened. He silently wished them luck. They would need it.

It was late into the night. Some of the crew had gone to bed–many were still too wound up for sleeping. Hamlin accompanied Sokolov in to check on Pechkin. Most of their efforts had all centered around bringing down his temperature.

He lay on the gurney, still strapped in tight. All of his clothing had been removed except for his underwear. As they approached him, it was clear that he was still not well.

His eyes opened, and he strained against the straps. He moaned and thrashed as much as he could.

Hamlin was shocked at what he was observing.

"Are you seeing this? His skin looks like a glazed carrot."

Indeed, his skin glistened from sweat, and was an unnatural reddish-orange color. The heat was pouring off him.

"Has anyone taken his temperature lately?" Francis asked. "He feels like I could fry an egg on his midsection. No wonder he's delirious and agitated. The surprise is that he's still conscious at all."

Sokolov, in a move that seemed totally uncharacteristic for him, reached out his hand and actually touched Pechkin's shoulder. He withdrew immediately after making contact.

"Good heavens. If he gets any hotter, he's going to melt the plastic coating off the frame. I'll consult with Doctor Kuvayev and get some more medication for poor Pechkin. Give me a moment, if you would."

Hamlin couldn't tear his eyes away from the ailing man. Pechkin's mouth opened wide, and he started to breath loudly. Each breath sounded to Francis like Pechkin was saying, "awww…awww." It was creepy and disconcerting. But everything about this evening fell under that heading. He continued to emit the same sound over and over.

Sokolov returned, a needle in his hand. He stared at it as if unsure of how to procedure.

"My dear Doctor Hamlin, would you be as kind as to inject our unhealthy comrade? You do have some recent experience."

Hamlin reached out and took the syringe. His mother had been diabetic toward the end of her life. He knew about giving shots.

"That's fine, Doctor. I don't mind doing it. As a matter of fact, I'd love to help this poor fellow in any way I can."

With Pechkin effectively restrained, it didn't take long to administer the medication. Unfortunately, there was no immediate effect.

Sokolov assessed Hamlin openly.

"You've had a very long and stressful day, Doctor. Would you consider a mild sedative to assist you in falling asleep?"

He shook his head in response. "If everything is under control in here, I think I'll try to find someone who would be willing to share a drink or two with me. I believe that will help me to relax as much as anything."

"Very well. I may have a quick nap and then I shall check in on Pechkin and see how he is progressing. I do believe if he could shake this fever, he would return to normal quite quickly."

Hamlin had his doubts. This kind of temperature would probably cause permanent damage of some kind–neurological in all likelihood. And this virus, if that was in fact what it was, was unlike anything that Francis had ever heard of. He had doubts of them being able to control it with the limited medical supplies they had available.

"If you need me, you know how to find me."

Sokolov gave a smile that actually seemed predominantly genuine. "Good night, Doctor. I shall see you in the morning."

Hamlin went into the dining hall and was happy to see Lena. He walked over to where she was talking with two of the other crewmembers.

"Mind if I sit down?"

Lena smiled. "No, of course not. Please."

The two across the table said something briefly in Russian, then stood up, stretched, and headed toward the sleeping quarters.

"Was it something I said?"

Her face became serious. She was slow in answering. "You are spending too much time with Sokolov. Why did he chose you tonight and send the rest of us to our rooms?"

The question was blunt. Hamlin could sense she was very serious about this.

"I don't know. It surprised me as much as anybody. Based on what I experienced, I would have been more than happy to trade with any of the rest of the staff. It was hell in there. I wasn't even certain that I was going to live through it at one point. So what do they think, I'm KGB or part of some secret conspiracy?"

"Perhaps." She was still serious.

"Let's see, how do I maneuver out of this? Here, see what being chosen did for me." Hamlin raised his shirt and revealed his side where he had landed after being thrown by Pechkin.

"Oh my God. That looks terrible."

His move had revealed a massive, purple bruise. There was a small cut that was still bleeding just slightly to top it all off.

"Well, that's funny because it feels great."

Now she smiled. "I'm sorry. Is there anything I can do to improve your condition?"

"Sure. Pain pills and some antibiotic cream should help."

"I have direct access to neither. You should have asked your new friend, our little overseer. Perhaps, with all this night has thrown at us, it would be a good idea to go to bed and get some sleep."

So much for the vodka, he though regretfully. In fact, Hamlin was feeling sleep overtake him even in the short time that he had been sitting there.

"I agree. I'm exhausted. I'll see you in the morning then."

"Good night, Francis. Sleep tight."

Oh, I'll be tight all right, Hamlin thought to himself. *By morning, I probably won't be able to move.* He shuffled off toward his room. This day had been long enough.

He woke several times during the night because of the pain in his side. When he finally crawled out of bed, he was surprised to see what time it was. He had slept in and nobody had bothered to wake him. This deviation of the normal schedule was puzzling. Perhaps it was a reward in recognition of what happened the previous night.

The dining hall still contained most of the crew. Only three seemed to be eating; the rest were sitting around in small groups, talking quietly. Most of them looked up when he entered the room. The majority didn't maintain eye contact for long.

Konstantine waved him over to where he was sitting with one of the drilling crew. Thankful, Hamlin wasted no time getting to the indicated chair. Somehow sitting down made him feel assimilated into the group. The other Russian remained when he sat down–an improvement over last night's experience with Lena.

"Good morning, Konstantine. A bit of a sober atmosphere, I would say. Why isn't anybody following the schedule?"

Konstantine for once maintained a perfectly serious expression.

"Pechkin died during the night." He spoke in a whisper.

"What! Oh no." A million questions and scenarios started swirling around in his head.

"Apparently he passed in the early hours. Sokolov went in to check on him and he was gone."

Francis could do nothing but stare for a moment. Finally, he collected his thoughts to a degree.

"What now? Has this ever happened here before?"

Konstantine shook his head. "There have been many deaths in Antarctica, but not at this station."

Hamlin pondered the implications.

"So, there is some sort of protocol for this?"

"I'm sure there is. Don't ask me for details, though. All I know now is that we have the morning off."

Sokolov entered the room and most conversations immediately ceased. He started to walk toward the table where Hamlin was seated.

Hamlin cursed silently. If the crew was having second thoughts about how trustworthy he was, this would only make things worse. Sure enough, Sokolov went directly to him.

"Doctor Hamlin. Were you able to get any sleep?"

"Yes, of course. Some, at any rate."

"Very good. Certainly you've heard about the tragic passing of our colleague during the night. I was wondering if we could have a word. In private. Could you come with me, please?"

It was the worst-case scenario as far as relationships with the crew was concerned. Persona non grata for the next three months. They would have him pegged as a traitor or stoolie or teacher's pet...or something like that.

"Of course." What else could he say? He pushed his chair away from the table.

"Follow me, please."

As he pushed the chair back under the table, he made brief eye contact with Lena. The pleasant expression he was accustomed to had been replaced with a very somber one. He hoped it was due to the circumstances, not a growing distrust that she had of him. That was when he realized that everyone else in the room had the same expression.

Hamlin found himself in Sokolov's room for the first time. It was quite a bit larger than his own. There were a significant number of books, binders, and folders on the shelves. A conglomeration of radio and computer equipment sat on a counter in the corner. A huge desk was the centerpiece of the space. The remainder of the room was nondescript.

"Doctor Hamlin, I'm afraid things have not gone well during the night. I need your help. Difficult decisions have to be made and immediately acted upon."

"Yes, I understand that, at least in theory. But why me? Every time you center me out in this crisis, the rest of the crew suspects me of some sort of conspiracy or perhaps at least collaboration in a plot against them. I don't even know you. I have no interest in your agenda, if in fact you have one. Why can't you pick one of your own countrymen to help you? If you keep this up, no one will be willing to speak to me again for the next three months."

Sokolov's expression didn't change. "My dear doctor, I am sorry for your personal dislike for confrontation. However, I have more serious matters to resolve. If you don't help me, we may not have three months in which to be uncomfortable with our relationships. I ask you because you don't loathe me or harbor the desire to see me fail. It is another advantage to having one brand new, neutral crew member at the station."

"I suppose you need someone to help with preparing Pechkin."

Sokolov hesitated before answering.

"Yes. But it is worse than you know."

"He's dead, right?" Hamlin said. "How could it get any worse?"

"Doctor Kuvayev is running a fever as we speak."

Francis was stunned. "What!"

Sokolov nodded perceptively.

"Is it...the virus?"

"I have no way of knowing for certain. I think we have to assume that it is, circumstances being what they are. The good news is that I have given him some medication and it seems to be in check right now. He doesn't feel that bad, and he is perfectly calm and cognitive. But he is terrified. And frankly, so am I. If we had trouble controlling Pechkin, a rather slightly built man, how would we manage Kuvayev, who is a large, powerful individual? Again, I'm afraid some difficult decisions must be made. And quite frankly, the crew will not like them."

Hamlin felt a cold chill creeping up his spine.

"What are you talking about? What do you propose we do?"

"First of all, Dr. Kuvayev needs to be immediately restrained."

"You intend to strap him down like we did with Pechkin?"

"Precisely. I spoke to him about it and he is in full agreement. We need to do it now before his condition worsens. You see, we are not completely certain how fast Pechkin declined. It is not outside the realm of possibility that this condition takes hold very quickly. But as I said, the doctor is popular and well respected. The crew will bristle at the idea of him being restrained while he is, for all intents and purposes, outwardly healthy. We will look very bad as we walk through the dining hall toward his room with the straps in our hands."

Hamlin could imagine it.

"I think as long as he is in agreement, the staff will go along with it."

"How will they know? We must keep him in isolation as much as possible. We don't know if this is the same virus, but if it is, then he has contracted it quite quickly and easily."

"Airborne transmission?"

Sokolov shrugged. "He was also bitten, if you recall."

"Oh my God. You're right." Hamlin cogitated briefly. "Look, there's an eight hundred pound gorilla in the room we need to address."

Sokolov understood the premise but not the specific implication of the analogy. "What do you mean?"

"I mean the origin of this contagion, whatever it is. Kuvayev originally speculated that it may have already been present in Pechkin before it manifested itself. Based on the unique and severe manner in which it presented itself, I have strong doubts about that analysis."

Sokolov didn't look happy about the direction the conversation had taken. "What then, may I ask, is your theory, Doctor? Keep in mind, of course, that you have no medical training."

"I'm not sure I need it for this diagnosis. It seems rather obvious."

"You might just as well forego any fanfare and simply enlighten me," Sokolov said.

"He was exposed to the water from Lake Vostok when it backed up and shot through the drilling rig. I would speculate that he got some splashed into his mouth or eyes. The virus was present in the water and had direct access to his entire system at this point. Neither Pechkin nor any of the rest of us would have any natural resistance to it. And so it ran amok and caused great physical damage, the end results of which we now know."

"No one else that was splashed has shown any symptoms, but I suppose there could be a plethora of viable explanations for that. You yourself have been working in close contact with the water and have shown no ill effects."

"I didn't drink it or splash it on myself."

"So your theory revolves around direct contact for transmission. As such, poor Kuvayev has possibly contracted it through the same method."

Hamlin nodded. "I assume the bite punctured his skin?"

"Yes, it was quite deep, as a matter of fact."

"Damn."

"Yes," Sokolov said. "I suppose the only redeeming quality to your prognosis, if it is correct, is that we should be easily able to contain it. No direct contact, no further spread."

Hamlin sighed. "Yeah. That's it. It doesn't help Kuvayev, regardless."

"And that is a best case scenario based on an unproven theory. There is still one more unpleasant piece of business, unfortunately."

"Carrying Pechkin's body out in front of everybody?"

"No. Worse than that I'm afraid."

Hamlin drew a blank.

"What is it, then?"

"Disposal. We can't just store his body as we usually would. He is infected with what could possibly be a highly contagious disease. Your theory about the spread of it is only that–a theory. We can't take the chance that you're wrong. We can't return him back home to his family, exposing civilization to this thing, and we can't keep him here."

Sokolov paused while the implications sank in.

"What do you propose?" Hamlin asked.

"Cremation. We have the means to do it. Again, I doubt it will be popular with the crew."

"There's a crematorium here?"

"No," Sokolov said. "It will be nothing so dignified. We'll have to construct a pyre out of pallets and other waste wood. There are several old tires we can position at the base. Then we soak everything with diesel fuel and light it up. It should work. The worst scenario would be for the body to partially survive the first attempt, which would force us to go through the process a second time."

Hamlin envisioned it. He was repulsed. "Can't we put him in one of the outer buildings that is no longer used? We can cover him up tightly, and you can alert the team that comes to retrieve him so they can be properly prepared for safe transport of the body. He'll stay secure through the winter, and I think it's safe to say that nobody will go in there in the meantime. Perhaps some testing should be done on this virus or whatever it is, anyway. Otherwise, research in Antarctica may no longer be viable. If you think about it, when word of this gets out, the whole world will be shaken."

Sokolov stared. "The results of this conundrum could be life or death for all of us. We really have no proof at this point how it is transported from person to person. If it is airborne, many of us have already been exposed. We should consider some sort of isolation, at least temporarily. I'm just not sure how to make that happen in a manner that wouldn't tip our hand and panic the others."

Hamlin came to a decision.

"Listen to me. We can't act like we're above the rest of them in all of this. They have to know. They have to be part of it. They have to participate. If you insist on being furtive and clandestine with every move, then of course they'll be suspicious. Why wouldn't they? What's the point of hiding or even sugar coating what's happening here? These are all smart, educated people. They're going to figure it out anyway!"

"What choices do we have?" Sokolov asked.

"Let me talk to them. Right now. Trust me when I tell you that if there is any lack of information, they're just going to imagine the worst. I would bet the farm they have done that already. Let's tell them everything so we can gain back their trust and support, at least to some degree. They all expect you to be sneaky about this. Let's pleasantly surprise them. This is an emergency. We need them. We need them all."

Sokolov shook his head. "I fear a mutiny of sorts if we shock them with the truth."

"That's exactly why they need to be included. They need to be a part of this, starting right now. That will build some semblance of trust. Let's get them on board."

Sokolov turned away and looked at nothing in particular while he thought about the proposal.

"The fate of every life here depends on my decision. Don't make me regret this, Doctor."

"All right, everyone, let me have your attention please," Hamlin said loudly.

A thought occurred to him and he turned to Sokolov.

"Does everyone speak English?"

Sokolov shook his head. "Yes. But some of the drilling crew have only a very basic understanding of the language."

"Should we, considering the importance of the moment, speak to them bilingually?"

"It's conceivable."

"Can you translate for them?"

"I can. As such, however, please try to keep your remarks as concise as possible."

"Okay. I'll try."

The group had pushed two tables together and all sat together. Hamlin pulled a chair over from another table and then stood upon it.

"Let me have your attention, please."

"Pozvol'te mne imet' vashe vnimaniye pozhaluysta."

A hush fell over the crowd.

"We are in a serious situation."

"My nakhodimsya v ser'yeznoy situatsii."

"We need to work together."

"My dolzhny rabotat' vmeste."

"There's no easy way to say this. For those who don't know, Pechkin died last night."

"Tam net prostoy sposob skazat', chto eto . Dlya tekh, kto ne znayet , Pechkin umer proshloy noch'yu."

Hamlin collected his thoughts. The room was absolutely silent. "We must prepare and remove him. We will need your help."

"My dolzhny podgotovit' i udalit' yego. My nuzhdayemsya v vashey pomoshchi."

"We have another serious matter to attend to. Doctor Kuvayev has shown signs of a fever."

"U nas yest' yeshche odin ser'yeznyy vopros , chtoby prisutstvovat' na . Doktor Kuvayev pokazal priznaki likhoradki."

Various crew members were looking at each other now, but so far no one had spoken.

"We need to give him the best medical attention we can. But we also must try to maintain some isolation to prevent further spread."

"My dolzhny dat' yemu luchshiy vrachu my mozhem. No my takzhe dolzhny popytat'sya sokhranit' nekotoruyu izolyatsiyu dlya predotvrashcheniya dal'neyshego rasprostraneniya."

"We need your help, desperately."

"Nam nuzhna vasha pomoshch."

"Please. Let's work together."

"Pozhaluysta. Davayte rabotat' vmeste."

"Okay, let me think. Wait a minute," Hamlin said, and then added, "Don't translate that."

The ones who spoke English smiled slightly at his stumble.

"There is one more unpleasant task. Kuvayev needs to be restrained. He has agreed to this."

"Sushchestvuyet yeshche odin nepriyatnyy zadachey. Kuvayev neobkhodimo sderzhivat'. On soglasilsya na eto."

At this, there were several soft murmurs for the first time since he started addressing them.

"This unexpected emergency has caught us all by surprise. But, my friends, we can work together and resolve this matter."

"Etot neozhidannyy avariynyy poymal nas vsekh vrasplokh. No , druz'ya moi, my mozhem rabotat' vmeste i reshit' etot vopros."

"I have nothing more to say. Thank you all for your friendship and support."

"YA ne imeyu nichego bol'she, chtoby skazat'. Spasibo vam vsem za vashu druzhbu i podderzhku. I tak zakanchivayetsya razglagol'stvovaniya o nashem bezumnom amerikanskogo tovarishcha."

Hamlin suspected that there was something extra in that last statement. A few of the crew smirked a little.

"Have you finished?" Sokolov asked.

"Yes. Thanks. To everyone. It wasn't as inspirational as I wanted it to be." What Hamlin was really thinking was how much his words sounded like propaganda despite his desire to accomplish the opposite.

Konstantine spoke. "You did fine. What do you want us to do now?"

Lena spoke from the far corner of the table. "How can we help?"

"How do we proceed from here, Doctor?" Sokolov asked.

The day was just getting started, but he felt weary already.

"I think I'm ready to let you take over. Or at the very least we should start working as a team right now."

"Very well. The two immediate items on our agenda are tending to both of our comrades." Sokolov hesitated before continuing. "Does anyone feel like helping to secure Dr. Kuvayev? You are free to consult with him about this manner before proceeding, if you wish. Those who will be coming into contact with our two comrades will need to wear respiratory protection. This is available in the storage room down the hall."

In the spirit of cooperation, volunteers stepped forward and the tasks at hand began. The training they had all received before coming here along with the professional makeup of the staff combined to prevent any wholesale panic. Apparently there was still sufficient trust in Sokolov's ability to see them through this to keep them calm under duress. In regards to the ailing doctor, Hamlin didn't help with the strapping, but he did venture in and have a conversation with Kuvayev. If the only actual medical doctor became incoherent, somebody needed to have an idea on how to react in terms of administering medication. Kuvayev was happy for the company and the conversation. Clearly he was very stressed about his possible future physical deterioration. He left explicit instructions on how he wanted to be treated if his condition became similar to Pechkin. Hamlin reluctantly agreed to his wishes. He hoped the worst-case contingency would simply never occur.

CHAPTER EIGHT

Lunch was late. That was because everyone wanted to finish what had to be done before stopping. It had been a long morning.

Kuvayev was now strapped down securely. He was clearly uncomfortable, and various crew members had ignored the possible health risks to put on respirators and take turns staying with him and responding to his various requests for water and other adjustments to aid with his comfort. Hamlin had insisted that special effort and attention had gone into cleaning and maintaining the bite wound. The skin around it had a nasty red color and some swelling was evident. So far, the fever had been kept in check by medication. They still had other options if necessary, such as stripping off his clothes, cooling the room itself, and applying cold compresses.

Pechkin was removed and placed in one of the outlying sheds. The cold would do a good job of preserving his body. He had been well wrapped by several members of the drilling crew who had known him best. It had been a sad and touching procession as he was somberly transported to his temporary resting place.

Eating was performed as if it was a task. There were conversations, but they were subdued and encapsulated. Sokolov actually asked the crew what they wanted to do for the afternoon. The proposition of returning to a normal work schedule was offered but not insisted upon. For most, it was an easy decision. The only members of the crew that didn't eagerly accept the opportunity were the two who agreed to stay and provide constant attention and monitoring for Dr. Kuvayev. A list of emergency contacts was established in the event that his condition started to deteriorate.

Hamlin was more than happy to be back in the lab. His main hope for the remainder of the day was to work quietly without interruption–a desire spurred by the fact that he was on the emergency list for Kuvayev. The old adage of *no news is good news* had never been so strongly applicable.

After consultation with Sokolov, he had decided to forego any new research on the actual lake water samples, at least for now. There were too many unanswered questions about the origin of the virus that was now plaguing them. He worked, with caution and all protocols for safety firmly in place, on some of the older samples taken from the ice itself.

The drilling crew kept busy trying to design a mechanism that would prevent any further backflow through the borehole from creating another geyser in their enclosure. Even if they could divert the flow of lake water through a sluice of some sort and direct it outside, they felt the likelihood of toxic exposure would be greatly reduced. They could then resume the task of drilling for more samples. No one at the station wanted to shut down just to spend months looking at the wall and twiddling their thumbs while waiting for the weather to become suitable for incoming flights to resume.

The afternoon expired with no ill effects, and Hamlin was dressing for the ride back to the crew quarters before Konstantine could control himself no longer and asked the big question.

"Do you think Kuvayev will be all right?"

The question hung in the air like a bad odor left in an elevator by a flatulent but anonymous rider. Should he answer honestly or with optimism which amounted to a sort of propaganda?

"I don't know," Francis replied, opting for honesty. "But nobody came to get me, so I would presume that means he has gone through the afternoon in good shape. If that's the case, it is a very good sign. Poor Pechkin deteriorated very quickly. Perhaps the extra attention and medical assistance that Kuvayev is enjoying with allow his immune system to ward this off."

The conversation was left at that. To agree seemed like blatant pandering and to disagree felt like condemning a friend, which didn't leave a lot to talk about. Very few conversations here revolved around the weather. *So, I heard it's going to be cold today...really, that's surprising, what about tomorrow...?*

The sound of the approaching Cat was welcome news. Following in Konstantine's example, Hamlin immediately asked about Kuvayev's condition.

Sokolov hesitated before answering. Francis supposed it was the ingrained tendency to withhold and control the flow of information that restricted his ability to just blurt out the answer.

"He is battling heroically. His temperature continues to climb, but we have been successful in keeping it somewhat in check. Currently, he is around one hundred and two degrees (which Sokolov now presented in Fahrenheit so Hamlin could understand its significance). This is quite warm, but he is still relatively comfortable and quite lucid. He is drinking a lot of fluids and completely cooperating with all of our efforts to assist him. I don't think he is entirely at ease with the notion that we felt his clothing should be temporarily removed, however."

Both of his passengers smiled at that thought.

"It is strange to me how a person could be facing such a serious threat and still prioritize their appearance to the point where it is their primary concern. I would be surprised if any fashion models or photographers stop by the station to have a look at him. I suppose self-image is a big part of the human psyche, however."

Hamlin cogitated. "I read a Stephen King book where one of the main characters is impressed by another's ability to fight while naked. Perhaps Kuvayev simply wants his armor on for this battle. Maybe being naked makes him feel more vulnerable."

Konstantine nodded in agreement. "Maybe it makes him feel like his enemy has already struck the first blow."

"Your attempts at psychology notwithstanding," Sokolov said, "it is still necessary for him to be in this condition to assist with temperature control. Might I suggest that you don't engage the crew in a conversation about the right and wrong aspects of being undressed. Let's not open the door to any dissention. Cooperation was the platform you campaigned on, Doctor Hamlin, if my memory is correct."

"Indeed it was, and still is. We'll keep our talk in a totally supportive direction."

That seemed to pacify Sokolov somewhat.

"Very good. Then let's go and check on the condition of our comrade."

Supper was somewhat better than lunch. Kuvayev ate a small amount of soup that was made especially for him, even though he had to be fed by a crew member due to the restraints. His relatively good condition at this late point in the day helped keep everyone's spirits higher. Most put on respiratory protection and took the opportunity to go in and visit briefly, wishing him well and promising to visit again in the morning. The human contact seemed to help him keep his outlook positive. Sokolov reviewed and confirmed the regiment for meds and other attention for Kuvayev before crew members started heading to bed. A rotation was set up so that someone would be monitoring him all night. Hamlin took the two until four shift, a decidedly unpopular time frame. It could possibly help him gain back some respect and trust from the crew, he figured. In a worst-case scenario, he could always steal a quick nap later on in the lab. Konstantine wouldn't tell.

Getting to sleep once he was in bed was another matter. Hamlin tossed and turned, and finally determined that no position was comfortable. He resigned himself to simply staring at the ceiling. When he finally drifted off, he had bizarre and dark dreams with themes of death and disease. Pechkin haunted him, always lurking in some dark corner, naked and smeared, gaping and gasping, turning slowly to look at him with milky eyes. He would roar, Hamlin would scream in response and then he would awaken, heart pounding and terrified, looking about his room wide-eyed to make sure he was alone. After his second bout with Pechkin, Francis cursed himself for not stashing some vodka in his room. When his alarm went off at one-fifty, Hamlin was exhausted. At least there would be no dreams for the next two hours.

He was not happy about Kuvayev's condition when he got to his room. Although uncovered and in front of a pedestal fan, his temperature had climbed to one hundred four. Hamlin grilled the crew member he was replacing but was told convincingly that Kuvayev's medication was maxed out. They were running out of options. It was up to his immune system now.

"How was he the last time he woke up?"

The lanky man whose name escaped Hamlin almost removed his respirator prematurely, but caught himself just in time. "He's been sleeping for the past hour or so. He was still talking before he nodded off. But his sentences were short and he was tiring out easily."

The mask Francis wore was already hot and uncomfortable. The room was cool though.

"What about the room temperature? Can we drop it more?"

He shrugged. "It is fourteen degrees Celsius now. Sokolov said to consult him before going any lower. We don't want frozen pipes or for Kuvayev to catch pneumonia on top of whatever this is."

"Logical on both accounts. All right, I'll keep a close eye on him. You'd better get some sleep."

The man moved toward the door. "You look like you could use some yourself."

Hamlin smiled under his mask. "I feel worse than I look."

"I doubt that." The door closed, bringing the conversation to an end.

Hamlin turned his attention back to the big man strapped on the gurney.

"Hang in there, Kuvayev. You can beat this thing."

The words didn't sound inspirational. It was all he had.

"Damn. I wish there was something I could actually do to help you."

He looked around the room. Maybe there was something here that they had forgotten. He saw a small pile of rags on the counter by the sink. Perhaps if he soaked one in cold water, he could lay it on Kuvayev's forehead. That might help a little. Surely it couldn't hurt. And it would give him something to do, even if only for a few minutes. Without distraction, the next two hours could last a very long time.

Sokolov arrived at four. He looked as fresh and proper as always. Francis felt like death warmed over.

"How is our comrade faring in his good fight?"

"He just hit one hundred and five. It's been creeping up slowly since I got here. But he's been quiet. So far he's been sleeping through it."

Concern was evident in Sokolov's eyes. "I really don't want him to go any higher. Under the circumstances, I wish we could chance another dose of medication. Regardless, I can manage by myself, I'm sure. Perhaps you should return to bed and get some rest. I would be willing to be lenient with your starting time at the lab today. Why don't you turn off your alarm and sleep in a little longer?"

Hamlin was grateful for the offer. "I might just do that."

The gurney rattled loudly. They both spun around, eyes wide and expectant. Kuvayev appeared to be sleeping, his face and body glistening with sweat.

"What was that?" Hamlin asked. He tried to sound calm.

"Perhaps just a twitch," Sokolov said. "It wouldn't be unusual for someone with a high fever."

They stood with their eyes locked on the ailing doctor. Nothing else happened.

"I guess you're right."

"Of course I am. Stop worrying, Doctor." Sokolov reached over and removed the cloth from Kuvayev's forehead. "I'm afraid this is no longer helpful. I'll run some cool water through it and reapply. Go to bed, Dr. Hamlin. Perhaps morning will bring good news about our friend here."

"I sure hope so." Francis felt a fresh wave of weariness wash over him. "I'm off, then. You know where to find me if you should need assistance."

"Good night, Doctor; at least for what remains of it. Pleasant dreams."

Hamlin walked to the door. No dreams at all was his current goal. Just sleep and nothing else.

The gurney shook again. Francis stopped and walked back into the room. He stared, transfixed, waiting for the source to become evident. He didn't have to wait long.

Kuvayev, eyes still closed and for all appearances still asleep, suddenly arched his back and bucked against the restraints.

"Damn it!" Hamlin exclaimed. "Is he having a seizure?"

Sokolov approached carefully. "As bad as that would be, I think it preferable to the issues that plagued Pechkin. Keep a close eye on him while I get this cloth cooled off. I don't know what else we can do."

Kuvayev's breathing had changed. Now he was taking in rapid, shallows gasps of air.

"Something's happening. I would bet his heart rate just spiked."

Sokolov wet down the cloth with purpose, then strode back and applied it to Kuvayev's forehead. No sooner had he done so than the sick man's eyes opened wide.

"Good Lord!" Sokolov jumped back before he could stop his reaction. He calmed himself and approached again.

"Dr. Kuvayev? How are you feeling? I'm afraid you startled me somewhat."

The doctor's eyes rolled around with no real purpose. His mouth gaped open but no words came out.

Sokolov leaned in. "Doctor, can you hear me? It's Sokolov. We're here to take care of you. Is there anything you would like?"

No further response was apparent.

"Can you hear me?"

The eyes sought, then lost, then reacquired Sokolov's face.

"Uh." It was a short, gasping moan.

"What is it? I don't understand."

His jawed worked and the eyes started to wander again.

"Uhh. Uhh."

His back arched again and he strained against the restraints. His eyes bulged and the veins in his neck and arms popped against the pressure he was applying. The heavy straps creaked under the stress.

"He can't break these straps, can he?" Hamlin asked, suddenly concerned. He remembered the strength that Pechkin had when he lost his senses. Kuvayev was a much larger man.

Kuvayev continued to strain. His mouth opened wide and he let loose with a horrible scream.

Both men cringed and moved away from him.

"This isn't good. He's going over, just like Pechkin." Hamlin couldn't tear his eyes off the straining prisoner.

"What about the tranquilizer?" Sokolov said. "It worked with Pechkin."

"Yes, but he died before coming out of it."

Finally Kuvayev stopped pushing against the constraints and slumped back down. He continued to gulp short, shallow breaths.

"He is strapped down," Hamlin replied. "As unpleasant as he is when he's incoherent like this, maybe for his sake we should let him continue. Perhaps it will work itself out after a while. The fever can't last forever. He has several advantages over Pechkin because we knew more about what to expect and adjusted his treatment accordingly."

Sokolov considered his suggestion. "We don't want him loose. Remember how difficult and dangerous it was to inject Pechkin."

Yes, I remember you slamming the door and trapping me in the room with him, Hamlin wanted to say. He didn't.

"How much pressure can those straps hold?" he asked.

Sokolov had to think. "I believe in the vicinity of two thousand kilograms."

"Okay. Then regardless of how hard he tries, there is simply no way he can generate that kind of pressure. I say let's just leave him."

"He could injure himself while trying to escape his bondage."

Hamlin had already thought of that. "Which is still preferable to death induced by the tranquilizer, wouldn't you say?"

"Yes, I suppose you're right. Well, this should provide me with a very interesting shift. I feel, probably for the first time, that I might be getting too old for this."

"Do you really need to be in here? Unless he's due for medication or the fever starts to break, what can you do for him anyway? Why not slip in, say, once every thirty minutes or so? He might even rest better with nobody in here to catch his attention."

Sokolov shook his head. "No, I prefer to stay in here with him. I can at least monitor what he is doing. In another hour I might be convinced to give him more medication for the fever. I fear any sooner might result in liver damage."

"What about an anticonvulsant? There is some valproic acid here in storage."

"My good doctor, how is it that a microbiologist has such a detailed knowledge of medications and human physiology? I must say, I am both impressed and confused."

Hamlin smiled for the first time in what seemed like eons. "I don't. Kuvayev suggested it to me before his symptoms became so severe. He didn't know if it would work, but he felt we should consider it."

"I shall take it under advisement. At this point, I'm not sure that the convulsions are persistent or problematic. Go to bed, Dr. Hamlin. You'll be no good to me if you don't get some rest."

He turned toward the door for the second time, risking one last glance at Kuvayev. He didn't look good.

"Be careful. I'll see you after I get some sleep."

This time, despite the turmoil of his shift, Hamlin fell asleep almost immediately. There were no dreams to contend with. He slept so soundly that when he awoke, he had no semblance of an idea of how long he had been out. It even took a few seconds for his brain to reboot and remember what his circumstances were. He rolled over and looked at his alarm. It was after nine.

He shuffled out into the hallway and turned toward the dining hall. He was thankful for the extra rest, but uncomfortable with the missing structure. Schedules are what made the world go around, as far as he was concerned. Without them, everyone would be a sort of hippy, searching for peace as a cover story while in fact accomplishing nothing as their lives drifted away. Or something like that.

Once again, most crew members were present despite the relatively late hour. Faces looked haggard and listless. Once fully in the hall, he knew immediately why. He could hear Kuvayev screaming and banging.

He sat with the nearest grouping. They barely acknowledged his arrival.

"Who's in there with him?" No point in being coy about it. Small talk seemed inappropriate.

"Sokolov and Obolensky," a younger man from the drilling crew responded.

Hamlin had to think. Obolensky was a short, stout researcher who focused more on environmental findings, testing samples for obscure clues as to what life here had been like in the past millennia.

"Why Obolensky?"

The man's eye continued to focus on a stain in the porcelain of his coffee mug. "He was on the schedule."

Francis stood up. He was going in. He had to see for himself.

As he reached for the doorknob, a thunderous crash sounded from inside the room. He jumped perceptively. Now what? More bellowing from Kuvayev. He turned the knob and swung the door open.

Somehow the big man had managed to tip the gurney over. It lay on its side while Kuvayev continued to strain and yell.

Hamlin reached for his respirator and quickly slipped it on.

"I'm afraid the atmosphere is lacking in pleasantries," Sokolov said with a raised voice.

Obolensky looked terrified.

"How did he manage that?" Hamlin said, looking at the tipped gurney.

"He is generating a tremendous amount of kinetic energy for being strapped down. When he throws himself, the weight of the gurney doesn't always contain the momentum."

Kuvayev looked even worse than before, lying on the floor, writhing and screaming.

"There are three of us in here now. Should we try to lift him up?"

Sokolov nodded. "Excellent idea, Doctor. Obolensky, why don't you give us a hand and then consider your shift expired."

"Yes, of course." The man answered almost too quickly. From the look on his face, Hamlin guessed that he was counting the seconds until he could get out of the room and away from the howling perversion on the floor.

"May I suggest two at the head, one at the foot," Sokolov said. "And do watch his mouth. He gives every indication that he would bite if given the opportunity. I believe he is capable of removing a finger."

Hamlin didn't need to be told twice. If getting chomped was a possible means of transmission for the virus, he wanted no part of it. He figured that he would rather be on the deck of the Titanic as it sank than in the clutches of Kuvayev in his current state, anyway.

It was an awkward resurrection to say the least, and they nearly dropped him twice as the wheels of the gurney slipped on the floor. But they managed to get him righted, followed closely by a wave of relief from all three.

"Shall we try him against the wall?" Sokolov suggested. "Perhaps that will lend a degree of support, even if only on one side."

It was an easy matter to roll him now that the gurney was on all four wheels. They settled him in, and then Obolensky quickly excused himself.

Kuvayev finally stopped straining and yelling. His breathing was very rapid, however. His skin was a rosy-red color and the heat was radiating off him to a point where Hamlin was certain he was warming the very temperature of the room.

"Have you taken his temp lately?"

"He's been less than cooperative. So the answer is bluntly no. If you wish to try, please proceed."

Hamlin looked at Kuvayev who was gasping air like an Olympic runner at the finish line of a long distance race. He looked like he was about to spontaneously combust.

"I guess not. Would you say he's close to where Pechkin was?"

Sokolov nodded. "Yes." His voice was subdued.

Hamlin focused his eyes on the floor. The gurney had put a small dent in the lime green linoleum when it tipped over. Too bad. They just didn't make it like that anymore.

"Question?" Hamlin said.

It was hard to read people's reactions when their face was primarily covered over.

"Certainly, Doctor, although in my current state I wouldn't vouch for the quality of the response."

"How's everyone else feeling? Any other maladies reported?"

"No," Sokolov answered. "I fear, before you get too excited, that an unfortunate side effect of strapping Kuvayev down so early into his diagnosis is that we have created a very viable reason for the crew to keep their aches and pains to themselves."

"I'm still going to put a check mark in the *no news is good news* box. Every little bit helps."

Sokolov grabbed Hamlin by the shoulder. "His breathing...it's slowing."

Indeed it was. Kuvayev was no longer gasping.

"Hey, maybe he's turning some kind of a corner now. I wonder what his temperature is doing."

"I have a strong feeling that we should give him more time to settle down before we try to take it. But I think the question is valid."

A deathly silence now fell over the room.

Francis found himself leaning forward toward the unfortunate Kuvayev.

"He is still breathing, isn't he?"

Sokolov moved in as well.

"I'm not sure. Try to get a pulse in his wrist."

The request seemed safe enough. Hamlin grabbed it and felt. "I've got nothing."

"Carefully, try his carotid artery. Mind your fingers. Remember how Pechkin went through this before bouncing back so ferociously."

Francis reached in gingerly. The heat felt unnatural and disturbing.

"There's nothing here either. Now what?"

Sokolov seemed to be at a loss.

"Mouth to mouth wouldn't be an option," Hamlin observed.

Sokolov shook his head. "Absolutely not. That would be an open channel for transmission."

Hamlin spun around. "Where are those gloves?" He spied the box.

"What are you going to do?" Sokolov asked.

"I'm not entirely sure." He only took the time to slip on one. He stepped up to the gurney, hesitated, and then slapped Kuvayev on the face.

"Hey! Wake up!" He tried it again. There was no response.

He took a slow step back.

"Any ideas?"

Sokolov stood motionless. "I believe we have implemented everything in our limited arsenal. I truly can't think of anything else to do."

"How long was Pechkin like this when we first went in?"

"Not too long," Sokolov said. "Perhaps the maximum time would have been, what…perhaps a minute?"

Hamlin nodded. "Sounds right to me. Kuvayev is over that now."

The room was silent again. There was a knock at the door.

"Who is it?" Sokolov demanded.

"Is everything all right in there? It got so quiet, we were starting to wonder."

Sokolov seemed uncertain how to proceed.

"Dr. Hamlin, if you would be so good, go out and speak calmly to the crew. I will stay for a few more minutes. If Kuvayev shows any signs of returning to us, I'll let you know immediately."

"This is one of the reasons I resisted my parent's urging to get into medicine. I hate being the bearer of bad news."

"I can do it, if you prefer to stay with Kuvayev."

Francis felt like he was one of the crew now. Surely that meant something. "I'll do it."

"Thank you, Doctor. Regardless of circumstances, I will join you shortly."

Once again, Hamlin found himself addressing the group. He kept it concise and to the point. There wasn't much reaction. Quiet resignation seemed to be the collective response. He had no clue what to do after making his unwelcome announcement. He pulled out a chair and sat. It would have to suffice. It was all he could come up with.

Sokolov joined them ten minutes later. The look on his face was enough to confirm the worst.

"Ladies and gentlemen, I apologize in advance for this next question, but I believe it is essential to ask in order to preserve the viability of our outpost. Do any of you feel sick in any way? Please be honest. The truth is vital."

Now they were all looking at each other. Hamlin couldn't tell if the motivator was suspicion or optimism. No one admitted to having any sort of malady.

"Very good. Please, for all of our sakes, should your condition in any way change, let me know immediately. For now, let us make the assumption that the virus has not spread any further. Getting past that, we once again are faced with the unpleasant task of preparing one of our own for the long, cold sleep that will be their lot until spring. I know Dr.

Kuvayev was well liked and well respected. As such, I am asking for volunteers to assist with getting him ready."

Most of the staff responded immediately–more volunteers than were required. The first three to raise their hands were chosen. Sokolov gave them their marching orders with special emphasis on safety. Once they walked off to face their task, Sokolov's shoulders slumped just a little.

"The rest of you may want breakfast. If not, then tea or some other beverage. At any rate, I am suspending our morning tasks. We will need a crew to move Kuvayev once he has been prepared. Until then, I want to thank you for your strength and perseverance through this ordeal. I truly hope better times are ahead. If you will excuse me, I think I shall freshen up."

As Sokolov walked away, Hamlin realized, to his dismay, that he had no idea what to do with himself. He decided to start with a cup of tea. He returned to the table with the steaming mug cradled between both hands for stability, and as he sat, Lena appeared beside him.

"Is there room for me?"

"Yes. Absolutely. Please sit down."

She sat close beside him.

"Would you like a tea?" Hamlin asked.

She smiled slightly. "No, thank you. I've reached my limit for the morning already."

He picked his up and took a small sip. It was too hot for anything more than that.

She put her hand gently on his leg. "How are you faring, Doctor? Are you all right? You've been in close contact with some of the worst of this."

Hamlin gave it some thought. "Well, let's see. I suppose I would say...sad, tired, discouraged, afraid, confused...and I'm sure I could come up with a more comprehensive list of adjectives if you gave me time. How about you?"

"The same. We all liked Kuvayev. I suppose we all felt safer knowing his vocational skills. I never heard him say a bad word about anybody. He was a good man."

The answer was a bit disjointed, but Hamlin understood.

"So he had a family then?"

She nodded. "Yes. A wife and three children. The youngest is still at home, I believe. This will be very difficult for them."

Hamlin's brain finally felt like it was marginally functional. Or at least he had what seemed to be a cognitive thought.

"Let me ask you something. I should have thought about it long before I came here. Is it typically dangerous down here? Or is this an aberration? Has Antarctica traditionally been a safe place for explorers and researchers?"

"No," she said. "Unfortunately, Antarctica has been a very treacherous place. Many deaths have occurred here. There have been fatalities caused by almost anything you can imagine–fires, explosions, poisonings, animal attacks, exposure…"

"What a minute. You just said animal attacks. I understood that there weren't any large animals living here in Antarctica."

"That is not entirely true. Not if you count what is in the water and under the ice. A research diver was attacked by a leopard seal. It killed her before the other divers could rescue her."

"That's terrible! So how many people have died down here…or do you know?"

"I have heard that it is over two hundred and sixty, but I'm not certain of the exact number."

"Two hundred and sixty! What in God's name has been happening down here?"

She shrugged. "I suspect many of those were the first explorers from years ago. They had little resources and marginal knowledge of what to expect. They probably died from the cold."

Hamlin shook his head. "I shouldn't have asked." He took another small sip of tea.

"Perhaps not." She looked around at nothing in particular. She started to rub his leg. "You know we have probably at least two hours with nothing to do but sit and stare at the ceiling."

"I know. I'm not exactly looking forward to it."

"You were about to do laundry when this all started."

"Hey, if there's a connection, I'll never do laundry again, believe me."

"You were also about to do me, if I remember correctly."

"I remember something along that line," Hamlin said.

"I am confident that I know a way to make the next two hours go by much more pleasantly than just sitting here."

"Lena, I do believe I am about to set a precedent and say no thanks."

She lowered her voice. There was a hum of conversation in the room, and nobody seemed to be paying any particular attention to them. "Are you sure? I know what you like."

Hamlin shook his head and took another sip. "I have no clue how what has just happened here could possibly put you in a place where you're turned on, but it isn't having that effect on me. The only thing I feel like doing in bed is sleeping. Now that sounds like a good way to pass the next couple of hours away."

"Excellent. Then we can cuddle and sleep. I promise to behave."

Hamlin decided not to feel guilty about this encounter regardless of how it turned out. He needed something therapeutic, a badly needed pleasant reprieve from the horrors of the past two days. Falling asleep in her arms sounded pleasant and relaxing. Maybe her presence would keep him from fixating on death and disease.

"As long as you promise to behave." He stood up and she followed suit. He slipped his arm around her shoulder and started walking.

"Of course," she purred as she crossed the fingers on her hand that was hidden behind her back. "Don't worry. Russians are very trustworthy people."

CHAPTER NINE

In the end, she was unable to deliver on her promise. As things unfolded, Hamlin decided that he didn't mind so much after all. How she had learned the things she knew about human sexuality, in a very 'hands on' practical sense, was a mystery to Hamlin. As he lay under his comforter, feeling completely drained in both a physical and emotional sense, it occurred to him that he could have easily lain there and slept for the next two days.

"Darling," he said, "As much as I don't want to, I'm afraid I must disengage myself from the adult theme park that is your body. I need a shower. I'm quite sure I smell like you. Or at least certain parts of you."

Her head lay on his chest and her hand on his stomach. "This is not a complaint, I hope. Your seasonal pass might have to be revoked."

"Not at all. I plan to visit often. I think there are still one or two rides I haven't tried out yet."

"Or perhaps just a nice lunch. We do offer things to eat."

"You are incorrigible." As he struggled to get untangled, he grabbed a handful of her well tousled hair, held her head steady, and kissed her on the forehead. "I'll see you in a few minutes."

She smiled and lay back down in his bed. "Don't worry. I'll let myself out. Unless you want some help washing your back?"

He chose not to respond directly. "Do remember to throw something on before you go strolling back through the mess hall." He closed the door behind himself as he exited the room.

He ran the shower long and hot. By the time he was finished and dressed, he felt relatively human again. It was time to rejoin the others. He just made it in time.

Sokolov was preparing to address the group.

"Very well, then. I believe we are all present and accounted for. First of all, I wish to thank those of you who prepared Doctor Kuvayev. You did an excellent and professional job under the most difficult of circumstances. I appreciate it, the rest of the crew appreciates it, and I'm positive his family and friends back home will greatly appreciate it as well.

"Now we have but one more rather miserable task ahead of us. I need volunteers to move our friend to safekeeping in the outer equipment room. We will lay him temporarily to rest beside Pechkin. Keep in mind that Kuvayev is a big man. His weight will be awkward to manage in the snow. I would like to have four at minimum; perhaps six would be even better. What do you think?"

Everyone in the room tried to volunteer. Sokolov had to choose who to use. Hamlin was thrilled to be one of the six.

"I can see no point in prolonging this. Let's get dressed for outside and move our friend. He cannot stay amongst us any longer."

They were able to wheel Kuvayev on the gurney right out to the door. Considering how big he was, having his body lifted as high as it was made it much easier to get a good hold and lift him to carrying height. Sokolov was right, Hamlin quickly decided. Even with six people, the deceased doctor was heavy and awkward to hold. This was going to be a long walk.

The weather had done them a favor. There was no wind as they moved off the landing and out into the snow. Their feet crunched loudly and their breath formed vapor that looked like exhaust coming out of some big diesel powered machine. There was no talking.

Sokolov walked in front, encouraging them and giving instructions to make minor changes in their direction. Hamlin found himself thinking about the university. That led to a quick recap of his previous life and how unbelievable it was that he now made up part of a funeral procession at the very bottom of the world. How had things changed so dramatically and abruptly? Regardless, this was his new reality, at least for now. So the question became, what would he do and what would his life consist of once he returned home? He had a lot of things to work out. Maybe he should start looking for some answers.

The shed was finally approaching. Hamlin felt like his arms were going to fall off. Sokolov stopped walking and held up his hand for them to do the same.

"Hey," Hamlin said, "I don't want to complain, but I don't think I can hold him much longer."

Sokolov didn't respond, but continued to look at the shed. Hamlin followed his example. He didn't notice it at first, but as his eyes cleared away the blurriness from the extreme cold air, he couldn't help but see. The door to the shed was hanging open.

The others quickly noticed the door. Everyone stood motionless and silent. Sokolov held up a hand in the universal 'stop' position and moved toward the shed. He peered inside, cautiously. Then he moved through the doorway and left their field of view. He reappeared momentarily and waved for them to approach.

"What happened?" Hamlin yelled.

"Bring him in. He's too heavy for you to manage much longer."

They did, all curious as to what they would find but also eager to be relieved of Kuvayev's weight. They laid him down gently under Sokolov's direction and then looked around. The heavy nylon bag, as well as the other material that Pechkin had been encased in, lay torn and strewn around the room.

Hamlin was stunned. "I thought there weren't any large predators down here."

Sokolov stood musing. "There aren't."

"Should we try to find his body?" one of the drillers asked.

Sokolov still didn't seem to have this figured out.

"Let us return to the shelter of our quarters. We can give this further thought from there."

The door, upon closer examination, did have some damage. Two of the crew volunteered to return and make repairs. Everyone's focus was now split between keeping Kuvayev secure and finding out what happened to Pechkin. If it wasn't for the cold, they certainly would have stayed and investigated the site more thoroughly.

Instead, they returned to quarters, tersely passed on the information about Pechkin to the others, and sat down to tea and an impromptu session to determine what had just happened at the shed.

"I am at a loss," Sokolov said. "There are no bears or wolves down here; nothing that would have the size and strength to break into the shed. The door might not look like much, but it is of heavy construction and so are the hinges and the latch."

"What is the largest animal down here?" one of the remaining drillers asked.

"On land? In the vicinity of this station?" Sokolov pondered. "There is really nothing. Penguins would be the largest land predator and they aren't within three hundred miles of this place. They wouldn't be breaking down the door, regardless."

"So what happened? How could you explain it?" Konstantine asked.

"I must apologize, but at the moment I can't."

The room grew silent.

"You've never had an incident like this before?" Hamlin asked. "Never any scratch marks on the doors or bumps in the night?"

Sokolov shook his head. "No. There are no monsters in Vostok. It is too cold, even for them. We are quite alone here."

They all pondered the implications.

"There is one large predator down here. Us."

Hamlin was relieved that one of the original crew said it before he did. No doubt they were all thinking it at this point.

"Of course," Sokolov said. "But I must reject the implication. If it was one of us, then why didn't that person simply open the door to gain access? It wasn't locked. And who among us is strong enough to force it open without acquiring any visible signs of injury or physical duress? Besides, we all know where each other is at all times. It would be impossible to go outside without drawing attention to yourself. And at the end of it all, why would you?"

They all pondered his words. Nobody knew that there was a very subtle sensor on the door that sounded a small alarm in Sokolov's room when it opened.

"I say we should look for him!" one of the drillers exclaimed. "His body can't be far. What will we tell his family if we lose him up here? Let two of us take the Cat and do a search."

It was unusual in Francis' experience for any of the crew to confront Sokolov in any regard, even with a demand such as this. There was obviously a strong emotional attachment motivating them.

Sokolov nodded. "Very well. But I must insist on some parameters. I don't want you driving halfway across the continent. Perhaps we could lay out a simple grid search. The GPS will allow you to follow it easily. One person drives–the other acts as the lookout. If you find anything, call back here to the station before getting out of the Cat. I cannot tolerate any more injuries or accidents. Preservation has taken on new significance. Now, rather than having a volunteer riot, let me choose two of his closest comrades to do the search. Hmm, Barinov and Yedemsky, you two can suit up and go out if you wish. We will draw up a search plan while you prepare."

The grid was based on a one square kilometer area with the station as its center. No one could imagine that it was possible for his body to get moved further than that in the cold, regardless of how it happened. It was an acceptable starting point at any rate.

Zhabin and Kravchuk, the two door repair volunteers, had just returned to the shed. They looked at the door with a technical eye. Exactly what repairs were needed here?

"The hinges are fine," Kravchuk noted. "It is just the latch that is damaged."

Zhabin quickly agreed. "Da. But look at the frame. It has been pushed out here too. We will have to move the mechanism up slightly and put in a new latch."

Kravchuk was silent. His hand found its way onto Zhabin's shoulder. "What is it?"

"It was pushed out from the inside."

Zhabin stood upright. He hadn't previously considered the implications. "That's not possible."

They both spent some a few minutes examining the interior of the shed. Apart from the shredded cover, everything looked normal.

"Look," Zhabin said, "I don't know what happened, but we need to secure this door and we need to do it now. We will be too cold to function if we don't get started. What do you say?"

Kravchuk was still clearly bothered by this disturbing revelation. But he was also aware of the realities of working in extreme cold.

"You're right, of course. Let's get this done. We'll have to report this when we get back."

"To all the others?"

"No." He pulled a small box out of his large pocket and fumbled through it for a suitable screw. "Just Sokolov. He can dispense the message if he chooses."

Kravchuk nodded. "Very well. He gets paid to worry about these things." He looked around furtively. "Let's get this done. I'm starting to feel creeped out."

The Cat was topped up with fuel before the search began. Twenty-five gallons of diesel would keep them going for all the time needed to search the grid. The heater still worked fine, and it was immediately turned to the maximum setting.

As they roared away from the camp, Barinov pulled off his mitts and spread the grid sheet out across his knees.

"Give me a moment, please. Let me plot the coordinates in."

Barinov, the oldest member of the entire crew at fifty-eight, was also the gruffest. The others simply ignored his rough edges. And it could have been worse. He never really lost his temper—it seemed that the continuous venting of frustration and anger kept him in a constant state of mild annoyance, but never anything more serious than that. He was also a marvel when working on the drilling rig. The others found it hard to imagine being functional without him there to help with repairs and to proactively find issues before they became major breakdowns.

"There. That should do it. Let's go."

Yedemsky started the Cat rolling out into the white unknown. The GPS was a lifesaver down here. Even this fine machine couldn't keep them from getting lost without some navigational assistance. A compass made a decent backup instrument, but the electronic screen mounted on the dashboard gave them pinpoint accuracy as they began to search.

"The wind has covered any tracks," Yedemsky observed.

"And why wouldn't it?" Barinov growled. "It blows constantly in this God-forsaken place. Did you bring anything to drink?"

The lanky driver pulled a bottle out of his parka pocket. "Here."

Barinov grabbed it. "You're a good man, Yedemsky; no matter what the others say."

He grunted in response. "Just keep your eyes open. Let's find our friend Pechkin. He's got to be out here somewhere. And I don't want to drive over him."

Barinov took an alarmingly long tug at the clear bottle. "You worry like an old woman. I have eyes like a hawk."

"The vodka will blur your eyes if you keep that up." The comment was made in jest.

Barinov extended the bottle. "Here, have some. It will remind you of home."

Yedemsky shook his head. "It reminds me of the hangovers I have had in this place. Besides, we still have a job to do."

"Fine." Barinov wedged the bottle into a cup holder molded into the console. "So what the hell do you think happened to him?"

"I think Sokolov must be wrong about the animals. I think it was a bear."

The constant creaking of the track on the Cat was a sound they had learned long ago to tune out. It simply meant they were moving and everything was running as it was supposed to.

"Sure. What else could it be? He surely didn't just get up and walk out on his own."

"Da. What else?"

They drove on for a full minute in silence, each man lost in his own thoughts.

"Hey, Barinov—how are you feeling?"

"What?" He turned to stare defiantly at the driver. "What's that supposed to mean?"

"Nothing." Yedemsky stared straight ahead. "It's just that, well, we all got splashed when the rig backed up on us."

"So?"

"So how else did Pechkin get sick like that?"

"How would I know? I'm not a doctor." As a matter of fact, Barinov was one of three people at the station without a doctoral degree of some description. He would have been one of four if Pechkin were still alive.

"I feel fine, in case you're wondering," Yedemsky said.

"Well, I do too. Now stop being such a pussy."

Yedemsky made a small adjustment to their course. "There'll be extra work to do now. We have suffered a twenty percent reduction in our workforce."

"If I recall, Yedemsky, you never did all that much work anyway."

"But if that is true, why would I want to start now?"

"What I meant was," Barinov snapped, "any extra work will likely fall on me to do. So stop bitching."

"Stop bitching, stop bitching," Yedemsky mimicked in an artificially squeaky voice. "Why don't you drive and I'll sit and drink vodka?"

"You told me just now that you didn't want any. Make up your mind."

Yedemsky looked at the paper with the grid sketched out on it. "How long will it take us to cover the whole area?"

Barinov was staring out the window with a look of shocked surprise on his face. He held up a hand.

"Stop!"

Yedemsky obeyed without understanding.

"My God. Look at that."

Yedemsky saw it too. Across the otherwise flawless surface of the snow cut a deep set of tracks.

"They must be fresh," Barinov surmised. "The wind hasn't had time to fill them in yet."

"What made them? The tracks look funny to me."

"Get closer."

Yedemsky moved the Cat over nearer the tracks.

Barinov shook his head. "I can't tell for sure. Hold on."

He pulled his hood up, popped the door, and jumped out.

"Hey," Yedemsky screamed, "Sokolov said to stay in the vehicle!"

Barinov either didn't hear or simply chose to ignore him. He walked right over to the tracks, and then lowered his head to get a really detailed look. He studied them for quite some time before straightening and returning to the Cat. He hopped in and slammed the door shut.

"Well? What are they? Can you tell?"

The crusty old bugger looked almost sick.

"I think it was a man. He appears to be on two legs. And it, ah…"

"What? Tell me!"

"I think…it looked like bare feet."

Yedemsky gaped. "That can't be. You must be wrong."

"Well then go out and look for your own fucking self! I'm telling you what I saw."

"It has to be wrong. He would have frostbite in what…one minute? How could he have gotten this far?"

"Stop asking me these asinine questions!" Barinov barked. "We need to follow them and we need to do it fast! Whoever it was doesn't have much time."

"Yes, of course. As you say."

The cat lurched forward. Yedemsky drove directly alongside of the tracks.

"Visibility is good. Go faster!"

"But who could it be? Except for Pechkin and Kuvayev, everyone was left back at the barracks."

"I don't know!" Barinov shouted. Then, as he settled back down, "Maybe Zhabin or Kravchuk took a bottle with them when they went out to fix the door. Maybe one of them had too much to drink."

Yedemsky doubted that theory for a variety of reasons, but decided not to verbalize any of them.

"What if we are not alone? Is that possible? Could it be someone from one of the other stations?"

Barinov shook his head. "Impossible. There is nobody anywhere near us. And when I say nowhere near, I mean within hundreds, if not thousands of kilometers."

As they travelled, the tracks began to fill with drifting snow.

"Damn! I can't believe they are still going. This is the most incredible thing I have seen in my life."

"Really?" Barinov said. "Then I should show you the tochkas of Moscow. The girls will be able to show you things that will surpass this."

"You are and always will be a pig, Barinov."

"Oh? You know what the Americans call it, don't you? Makin' bacon. Huh?" Barinov flashed tobacco stained teeth.

"Pig. Look out there. A few hundred more meters and the tracks will be gone. What do we do then?"

"Keep going as far and as long as you can. I hate to say it, but I'd better call Sokolov."

"Da." The cat plowed along steadily, making good time.

"Mobile One to base, over."

"Mobile One, this is base."

How had Sokolov reached the radio so quickly?

"We found tracks. We have followed them to the edge of the grid. They are now filled in with snow. How do you want us to proceed? Over."

"What sort of tracks?"

Yedemsky grinned. "He forgot to say 'over.'"

Barinov didn't seem impressed by the attempt at humor. "They appeared to be human. Over."

"Impossible. Everyone is accounted for. Where are they going? Over."

"They are leading away from the camp in a north-west direction. Over."

Now there was silence. When it was finally broken, the message was terse.

"Return to base immediately. Over."

Barinov returned the microphone to the clip that held it in place.

"Well, you heard him. Turn around and return to base."

Yedemsky stared off into the endless white in the direction the tracks had been going.

"Shit." He swung the cat around and began to retrace their journey.

Sokolov escorted the two men from the cat into his room when they returned. Apparently the concept of being open and sharing information was now waning in popularity.

He grilled them over their story several times, but the details never wavered. Finally, he sighed and released them.

Hamlin was considering getting a game of cards started when Sokolov sought him out.

"Excuse me, Doctor. I was wondering if you would be so good as to meet with me in my room. I fear I need help in sorting this all out. Perhaps you would allow me to use you as a sounding board."

"You're in luck. There happens to be an opening in my busy schedule."

"Then follow me, if you please."

Sokolov closed the door behind them after they entered.

"Please, take a seat and get comfortable. I feel the need to break into my private stock. May I offer you a glass of cognac?"

"That sounds more French than Russian. But yes, a change from vodka would be nice at this point."

"It is thirty years old. You will find it more than just nice, if your taste buds are in any way similar to mine."

Sokolov extended a balloon shaped snifter with a golden liquid inside.

"Thank you," Francis said, accepting the glass.

"Have you ever read Doyle?"

The question came out of nowhere and caught Hamlin by surprise.

"Doyle?"

"Yes. Sir Arthur Ignatius Conan Doyle, to be precise." Sokolov bent down and fumbled with a lower drawer in his desk.

"Of course. I loved Sherlock Holmes when I was a boy. I suppose I still do. Or, at least, I would if I made time for reading."

Sokolov pulled out a small but gorgeous wooden box.

"So if I was to say, *this is, I think, a two pipe problem*, you would understand my meaning."

He opened the box and extended it toward him. It was a small humidor.

"You are particularly clever today. *The Hound Of The Baskervilles* was always a favorite of mine."

"There's no pipe, I'm afraid, but these are Cuban. I was led to believe they came from the Castro family's private stock."

After hesitating, Hamlin extended his free hand and carefully selected and removed one of the large cigars. "Good heavens. It's going to take at least two hours to smoke this thing. I'll be sick for a week."

Sokolov dismissed his concerns. "Enjoy until you feel you've had enough. The quality is too high to make you ill. Just puff, don't inhale. I myself find it to be quite soothing."

A box of long wooden matches appeared in Sokolov's hand. He lit one with some flair and then extended it.

"All right. What's the worst that could happen?" Francis drew air through the substantial stogie while slowly twirling it.

"Outstanding, Doctor. I see you have a grasp of the basic principles. Now, as they say, we're in business."

Hamlin took an exploratory puff. It was fine. He was still concerned about the effects on his constitution. He wondered how Sokolov would react to him puking out a ninety-dollar cigar.

Sokolov lit up and then leaned back in his chair. He drew in some smoke and exhaled it with some degree of showmanship.

"Ah, excellent. So, now that we're as comfortable as two gentlemen in Antarctica can be, let us cogitate over our little problem. I am interested in your thoughts and feelings at this juncture, Dr. Hamlin. Without structure or thought to consequence, I would appreciate you sharing your innermost reflections on what has transpired here over the past few days. Don't worry about shocking or offending me. As this is at my invitation, anything you say will not be held against you. We shall consider it a brainstorming session. If you please."

Hamlin swirled his cognac before venturing a sip. Procrastination played a role in his actions.

"Say, this is good. There's a lot going on in there."

"Which is to say that the flavors become more complex and varied over time. You Americans have no regard for formality in how you express yourself. I cannot imagine how liberating that must be."

"Yeah." Hamlin placed the glass on the corner of the desk. Language skills of any sort wouldn't help when discussing the disaster that had befallen them. "Well, let me start by asking you this–has anyone else shown any signs of illness since Kuvayev came down with symptoms?"

"No. Nothing obvious or that anyone is admitting to, at any rate."

"Good. Very good. If, and I suppose this is a very large and important 'if,' we assume that transmission only happens with direct contact with the virus, then we have reached a very important juncture. It seems to me that the crisis is now over. There should be no more new cases. Perhaps what we should be doing is mapping out a plan to get back to our research and reestablish a normal routine to get us through the rest of the winter."

"A very satisfying and optimistic analysis, Doctor. One which I greatly appreciate, to be completely honest." He let out a long sigh. "But I fear there are still some small details that disturb me."

"Such as?"

Sokolov took and puff, toyed with it, and then exhaled. After a moment's hesitation, he picked up his glass and took a sip. Hamlin waited patiently.

"Barinov and Yedemsky just returned and reported from their grid search."

"I saw them."

"It was a disturbing or at least confusing report.'

"Oh? How so?"

"They discovered tracks leading away from our compound."

"And that is unexpected?"

"Remember your orientation, Doctor. There is no wildlife here."

"What kind of tracks, then?"

"They say human."

Hamlin was taken aback.

"Whose?"

Sokolov stared at his cigar, watching the grey smoke rise lazily toward the ceiling.

"That is the question, indeed. At the approximate time these tracks were discovered, all crew members were present or accounted for elsewhere. Or deceased."

"Could they have been made sometime earlier?"

"No. The drifting snow fills in tracks quite rapidly. Admittedly, the wind is light today. But even taking that into account, they wouldn't have been visible if they had been there for any length of time."

"How is that possible?"

Sokolov smiled. "Again, that is the question. Really, Doctor, I'm having second thoughts about your value to me in finding an answer to this."

"Sorry. I'm just working through the initial shock phase."

"There is one other disturbing detail."

"Great. And what would that be?"

"Barinov was of the opinion that the tracks indicated a person walking in bare feet."

Hamlin almost spit out a swallow of cognac. "What! That's impossible."

Sokolov nodded. "Yes. Frostbite would be almost instantaneous. The discomfort would be so severe that no normal person would willingly submit themselves to that kind of torture."

Hamlin pondered the options.

"Is it possible that he was mistaken?"

"I considered that possibility. Neither man is a fool and they both have extensive experience down here. I questioned them at length and they were both consistent and adamant as to the details. Besides, what else could account for what they saw?"

"No wildlife, huh? Any chance they were drinking?"

Sokolov assumed a sour facial expression. "Barinov definitely had vodka on his breath. Yedemsky seemed dry, as far as I could quickly ascertain."

"It has to be a mistake. What other explanation could there be?"

"I agree. What I need is a plausible alternative. Surely the rest of the staff knows about the tracks, probably even now based on how Barinov talks when he's been drinking. How do I assure them that everything is now fine? What do I tell them when they start asking questions?"

Hamlin decided it was time for another puff. "These damn Ph.D's and their inquisitive minds."

"Precisely."

"We have to tell them something."

"No doubt about it."

"Some sort of straw for them to grasp, even if it represents an unlikely theory."

"Any ideas would be appreciated."

"Antarctic fur seals."

"I beg your pardon."

"They live around the perimeter of the continent and nobody is sure of what their winter range is. Therefore, although I would not be an advocate of the theory myself, you cannot discount the possibility that one could venture this far inland. Maybe it is motivated by the same desire as the chicken who crossed the road; trying to get to the other side."

"The other side of what?"

"The continent."

"A most improbable suggestion."

"It only has to be plausible."

"There is no research to disprove it?"

"Not irrefutably."

"Then that should suffice."

"More *could* than *should*."

"But at least it sounds better than an unknown shoeless individual meandering about in the frigid cold."

"Yes." Hamlin had drained his glass by now. "Any chance I could get a refill of your excellent cognac?"

"I believe the chances are quite good."

"I believe," Hamlin said, "that being under the influence of alcohol may not be a bad idea when presenting this theory to the group."

Sokolov froze in place. "Doctor, you are a genius."

"I'd like to agree, but…what?"

"Let's go out and suggest to the group that the appropriate response to the stressful experiences we have just been through would be to drink large quantities of alcohol and make a party out of it. We'll congratulate ourselves on our resilience, we'll toast our fallen comrades, we'll vow to persevere in our work, and we'll casually toss in the seal theory once everyone reaches a point of moderate intoxication."

"Dr. Sokolov, I do believe that after another snifter or two of cognac, that idea will sound very good indeed."

"Your support is invaluable, Doctor." He extended the bottle and refilled the glass, and then repeated the action to his own.

"Cheers," Sokolov said.

"To great ideas," Hamlin responded, thinking just the opposite was more likely to be true.

The party suggestion was a huge hit. Everyone was feeling the need to relieve some accumulated stress. Sokolov surprised everyone, Hamlin included, when he magically presented an unopened case of Irish whiskey. Any semblance of hesitation or moderation quickly evaporated. It made Francis wonder what else he might have up his sleeve.

Before things got too out of control (or the alternative explanation to the tracks in the snow was presented), Sokolov proposed a toast.

"To our fallen comrades. May their memories sustain and inspire us. May our work be a reflection of their determination and professionalism. And may we do them proud here at the very end of the world. Cheers."

Everyone drank.

And drank...

CHAPTER TEN

Hamlin figured he was building up a tolerance to the alcohol. He remembered most of the night's festivities fairly well, and he only felt moderately hung over. He checked his clock and it said seven thirty-eight. How was that possible?

Sokolov had indicated that they could all have the morning off before returning to the normal schedule and duties. After a very brief reflection on the matter, Francis decided to go back to sleep.

He awoke the second time around mid-morning and decided that he better start moving. After a shower and a light breakfast of reconstituted juice, dry toast, and coffee, he felt ready to tackle an afternoon in the lab.

Later, while riding there in the Cat, he couldn't help but discreetly look for tracks in the snow. He saw none.

Sokolov simply dropped them off. Apparently he had other things to do. Hamlin was the one to open the door and step in first. It seemed like weeks since he had been there, and he found himself actually feeling good about returning to some semblance of normality.

"So," Konstantine said as they settled in at their respective workstations, "you are cleared to work on the lake samples, yes?"

Hamlin nodded. "Yes. I have a few new, self-imposed restrictions designed for added safety. But other than that, it will be business as usual."

"Good. I'm glad to hear that." The frequent grin he tended to sport was back. "You know, we used to use the ice from the core samples in our drinks. I suppose that won't be happening again."

Hamlin was ready for a sample. He walked into the storage area and selected one carefully. He would be using more caution going forward.

"I imagine the ice is still pristine. It's the water down below that causes the issues."

"Or maybe the alcohol in the drink kills the germs."

There was something in the statement that stopped Hamlin in his tracks. He had no idea about Pechkin, but Kuvayev didn't drink. Or at least not much. He remembered because it was a definite oddity down here. But no, that didn't make sense either. Kuvayev came into direct contact through the bite he had suffered. A lack of alcohol consumption couldn't have played any role in him getting the disease. Could it?

"Are you okay in there?"

Francis kicked himself back into gear. "All good. Just being more cautious, that's all."

"Can we listen to some of your decadent American music? That might lighten up the mood."

"Absolutely. Glad it's rubbing off on you."

Hamlin decided that a proven winner was called for. He found *Hotel California* on his memory stick. It was just the ticket. Konstantine gave him an immediate thumbs-up. With the background music to soothe them, they both went back to work.

The research was therapy. They both toiled away happily for some time. With the various demands of the work now in the forefront of their minds, even conversation waned to occasional short exchanges. Time passed pleasantly and productively.

Hamlin suddenly looked up from his microscope. He looked around the room, confused.

"What is it?" Konstantine asked.

"I'm not sure. Did you hear something?"

"Not me. I would like some more music, though. It is a little too quiet in here." The Eagles had finished some time ago.

The hairs were standing up on the back of Hamlin's neck. He focused all his senses and came up with nothing unusual. Silence fell back over the lab. A subtle creaking sound came from the far wall.

"What's that?" Hamlin said.

Konstantine swiveled around on his stool as if looking at the wall could provide the answer.

"Probably the wind. I wouldn't have noticed if you hadn't pointed it out."

Francis couldn't understand what his body was reacting to. He stood, stretched with an artificial casual flair, and then walked over to the only window. With suppressed trepidation, he pressed his face against the glass and strained to see out. It was still complete darkness outside. He saw nothing. It was a relief.

"Turn on the outside light it you want to see," Konstantine suggested. "But there's nothing out there anyway. I wouldn't waste a lot of time."

Hamlin weighed his options. He walked over and threw the switch to the 'on' position.

Seeing what he had done, Konstantine got up, stretched, and then met him at the window.

"What are we looking for?"

Francis didn't want to be an alarmist. Besides, he really hadn't experienced anything worth being alarmed about. The low wattage bulb gave a viewable area that was very limited. He couldn't see anything but snow.

"I don't know. Nothing probably."

"Maybe a seal?"

Hamlin grimaced. "Oh, very funny. You liked that, did you?"

Konstantine's smile said that he did. He opened his mouth and said something in passing, but Hamlin heard nothing. His concentration was elsewhere. From under the floor, up through his foot, he felt three distinctive taps. He literally jumped back away from the window.

"What the fuck!"

Konstantine was uncertain how to respond. "What is it? What's wrong?"

"You didn't feel that?"

"Feel what?"

"There's something under the floor. I felt it tapping under there." Like all the buildings in Antarctica, the lab was suspended on posts. Traditional foundations were not feasible on top of the ice. Nobody was pouring a cement wall down here. This created a small, open crawl space under the structure.

Konstantine wanted to grin, sensing a joke in the making, but the contrast of Hamlin's grim expression led him elsewhere.

"What? Just now? Under this floor?"

"Yes! For God's sake Konstantine! Stop responding like someone with a single digit I.Q. I'm serious."

And then it happened again. This time it was two distinctive thumps, loud enough to be heard. Hamlin sought Konstantine's face for confirmation. By his shocked expression, clearly he had heard it too.

"There, you see? What could it be?"

The stocky young man's face slowly softened, and then finally mellowed into a smile.

"It is a joke! What else? Some of the others are trying to fool us." He dropped to his knees and pounded on the floor with his fist. "Hey! Bugger off! We know you're there. I'm telling Sokolov if you don't stop. Come in and see us, you stupid bastards, before you freeze under there."

There was one resounding thud in response. Then it was quiet.

"There, you see. I told you."

Hamlin was horrified. He envisioned some sort of monster breaking up through the floor in response to Konstantine's flippant response. But as they stood waiting, nothing happened.

Before he could stop him, Konstantine strode over and opened the outside door.

"Come on in, dumbasses! At least it's warm where we are. Come on!"

There was no sound; no response at all, just a very cold breeze wafting into the room.

"Close the door, Konstantine." Francis tried not to sound panicked. "You'll freeze us out."

He closed the door. "Lunatics. Do we have a flashlight here? I'm going to go out and kick their frozen asses." He started to rummage through various drawers.

"Don't do that. What would be the point?"

"I want to confirm my theory. Then you and I can plot some revenge before Sokolov comes to pick us up."

Hamlin didn't want to fully reveal how fearful he was becoming.

"Just don't, okay? This is the most work we've done in over forty-eight hours. We really should stay on task."

"Since when did you become such a company man? Or are you giving up on open democracy and embracing the Russian way of doing things?" Konstantine reached into a drawer and extracted a long, black flashlight. "Here we go! Just what the doctors ordered, right?"

A sudden deafening crash made both of them jump. What followed was a rapid-fire series of thumps against the back wall. It sounded like several men hitting it with clubs. It stopped as abruptly as it started. Then came the scream.

It sounded like a man, starting loud and getting higher and higher; the sound of someone being severely burned or slowly crushed. It was so penetrating, so immediate and so real, Francis found himself chilled to the bone. When it stopped, he found himself incapable of doing or saying anything.

"Did you hear that?" Konstantine spoke barely above a whisper.

"Of course I heard it. How could anyone scream so loud?"

"Not just that; listen."

Hamlin heard it too. It was the sound of the Cat approaching.

"Damn, it's Sokolov. Do you think we should warn him?"

"Wait. Let's throw on our coats. Quickly! We can just run out to meet him before he gets out. Hopefully that keeps all of us safe."

"Or sets us up to be ambushed. Shit!" No knowing what else to do, Hamlin joined his working partner in throwing on his outside clothes.

Konstantine was scampering toward the door. "Come on, move! Let's get out of here."

"Wait! Check the window first!" Hamlin urged. Konstantine had gone from one extreme to the other.

"No time!" Konstantine flung the door open. He ran out without as much as a perfunctory glance. Hamlin saw him take several steps successfully and decided upon impulse to follow. He almost forgot to shut the door in his haste. He flung it shut and joined Konstantine in running pell-mell toward the Cat and the perceived safety it may offer.

"Good heavens!" Sokolov said with a smile as they jumped in and slammed the door behind them. "Are you really that anxious to quit for the day?"

He saw the looks on their faces and immediately turned sober. "What is it?"

"There was somebody outside the lab," Hamlin said succinctly.

The lights from the Cat illuminated the front of the building quite well. There were no signs of anyone or anything out of the normal. Sokolov turned so he could see Konstantine in the back seat.

"What are you talking about? When did this happen? How do you know someone was there?"

Konstantine pointed, his expression one of pure horror. "Look there." His voice cracked when he spoke.

"Good Lord," Sokolov gasped.

There, on the edge of the light provided by the idling Cat, appeared a solitary figure. Hamlin, unable to stop himself, strained for a better look. It was Pechkin.

He now stood perfectly motionless, his hair blowing in the frigid wind. He was slightly stooped over for reasons that weren't immediately clear. And he was naked in the ferocious cold.

"How is that possible?" Konstantine whispered in complete revulsion. "He died."

Hamlin was trying to make sense out of it. "Are we absolutely certain he was dead?"

"He had no pulse and wasn't breathing. What other conclusion could there be?" Sokolov said.

"I don't know. Maybe the virus did something to his metabolism to slow it down." Hamlin had no other ideas.

"How do you explain what he is doing now?" Konstantine screeched. "Let's get out of here, just to be safe."

Sokolov hesitated. "What if we could save him? He's alive now."

"How can he not be freezing without any clothes on?" Hamlin asked. As he looked closer, he thought he actually saw little vapors of steam emitted from his uncovered skin.

"Lock your doors, Doctors, if you please."

"Why?" Konstantine gasped. Francis simply complied.

The Cat began to roll ever so slowly closer to Pechkin. He didn't appear to react in any way. Hamlin could see that his skin was a natural healthy orange, not the mottled white and blue you would expect from someone exposed to this cold air. As they got closer, he could see that it was almost a little red. The heat must have been radiating off him in a big way, as the puffs of blowing snow not only melted but seemed to transform to vapor almost immediately after landing on him.

The Cat stopped rolling. Sokolov started to roll down his window.

"I don't think that is a good idea," Hamlin said. Konstantine was too terror stricken to even vocalize his concerns. He actually started to slide up the back of the seat as his feet pushed against the floor in an involuntary attempt to get away.

The pane of glass was only open a couple of inches. Sokolov strained to get his mouth in position.

"Pechkin! Can you understand me? We want to help you."

Pechkin stood motionless, but his mouth began to move. It looked for all the world like he was speaking.

"Can you see this, Dr. Hamlin?" Sokolov asked, ignoring the panicked Konstantine.

Francis, to his chagrin, couldn't find a way to tear his eyes off the stricken man.

"I see it. Is he talking?"

"It would at least appear so. I can't hear him at all—we're still too far away."

"Wait," Hamlin said abruptly. "I don't know what you're thinking, but before you get any closer, keep in mind how strong and wild he was when he first got ill. If he was in his own sound mind, don't you think he would have approached us by now?"

Sokolov seemed uncertain. "Perhaps. But what alternative do we have? Do you propose we drive away and leave a conscious comrade standing naked outside in fifty below zero temperatures? Even if it seems sensible now, how is this going to sound to those back home when this is all over? How is it going to sound to his family?"

Hamlin would have gladly erased his entire memory of this place at this point and transported back to New England to pick up where he had left off. Unfortunately, it wasn't an option.

"What do you want to do? Open the door and let him jump in? Remember what happened to Kuvayev after being bitten."

"Dr. Hamlin, I should think it very unlikely that I will ever forget that. Let me try something a little less hazardous before abandoning poor Pechkin to the unlivable environment of the Antarctic."

He rolled his window back up. The Cat lurched forward toward Pechkin.

"What are you doing?" gasped Konstantine.

"Quiet!"

It was the first time Hamlin had heard Sokolov lose his patience.

He turned the big machine and rolled it just past where Pechkin stood. When he stopped, the machine couldn't have been more than five feet away.

The driver side window that was closest to steaming man opened an inch.

"Quiet, both of you," Sokolov commanded. He shut off the engine. Konstantine made a soft sound, not unlike a man crying.

"Pechkin! We want to help you. Do you understand?"

All was silence. Then the sick man's mouth began to move.

"Pechkin, we want to help you." The words were hissed more than spoken, but they were distinguishable. His voice put a chill through Hamlin. He sounded like some ghoul in a cheap horror flick.

"Yes, that's right," Sokolov yelled.

Silence again, and then...*Pechkin, we want to help you...*the words felt like they were spraying acid on their ears.

"Sokolov," Hamlin said, "shut that window. His breathing is starting to elevate."

"Start the motor!" Konstantine yelled. "Get us out of here!"

Sokolov had apparently reached his limit as well. The Cat shot forward, throwing Hamlin awkwardly. He regained a seating position and looked behind them. It was already too dark to see Pechkin. Hamlin imagined him running after them, wild eyed and screaming. The last thing he wanted was that image stuck in his head.

"See anything?" Konstantine was too frightened to look for himself.

"No, nothing. Just darkness. Thank God."

It was going to be only a two minute ride back to the barracks. Hamlin wished it was longer. If Pechkin was following, he wouldn't be far behind when they got there. The last thing they needed was for him to find his way back and start wandering around where they lived. Sokolov was thinking the same thing. They drove for a full minute before anyone spoke.

"Doctors, bear with me please. I'm going to do a loop here and see if Pechkin is following."

The Cat spun in a surprisingly tight circle. The headlights couldn't reach the lab they had just left. There was no sign of Pechkin.

"Excellent. Let's go home." He straightened it out and resumed their original course.

Konstantine looked at Hamlin with frightened eyes. "Hey, are you planning on doing any sleeping tonight?"

Hamlin hated the thought. "Probably about as much as you, I'm afraid."

Konstantine decided to risk a backwards glance. He lowered his voice to avoid detection from Sokolov.

"I want to go home."

The others were terribly agitated about the news. There was disbelief, horror, sadness, fear, and a variety of other slightly less fervent reactions. The group was split between wanting to go look for Pechkin and wanting to lock all the doors and staying inside to avoid him. After some debate, Sokolov agreed to let a group of men take the Cat, as well as some cords to secure Pechkin with if they found him, and go searching. The rest stayed behind and contemplated the wisdom of putting locks on all the doors. Currently there were none. Crime had never been an issue down here.

Francis took the first opportunity he got to see Sokolov alone in his room.

"Yes, Doctor. What can I do for you now? Or do you have some epiphany that will correct our bizarre situation?"

"No, sorry. Just a couple questions, if I may be so bold."

"Why not? It would seem I've lost all semblance of control here anyway. What is on your mind?"

Hamlin decided to just blurt it out. The door to Sokolov's room was closed as added security.

"Do you have any weapons down here?"

"Weapons?" Sokolov either was, or decided to pretend to be, surprised. "Why would we have weapons down here?"

"That's not a direct answer."

"Weapons would only pose a greater risk to the health and well-being of the crew."

"Another indirect answer."

Sokolov sighed. "Your persistence wouldn't be tolerated under different circumstances. This is an answer that absolutely must not leave this room."

Hamlin contemplated the restriction. "I can live with that."

"I shall take you at your word. There is a hidden cabinet behind my bookshelf that contains a small number of weapons."

"How small?"

"There are two automatic rifles, two handguns, and a meager supply of ammunition. Satisfied?"

"I guess. I just wondered. In my mind, I was putting together a worst case scenario."

"How encouraging. I would surmise by the question that your worst case scenario must get quite bad. Is that all?"

"One more inquiry. Well, this isn't a question exactly. Well, it is, but it's more rhetorical I suppose. At least at this point."

"Spit it out, Doctor."

"What about Kuvayev?"

That earned Hamlin a very sharp look.

"What do you mean?"

"I'm pretty sure you know what I mean. And I'm also sure the others will be thinking about it as well."

Sokolov sounded tired. "Doctor, might I suggest that we deal with the trouble that is directly before us before creating anything new to be concerned about. Besides, I have absolutely no idea how to answer that question. Or perhaps I'm just too tired to begin the lengthy mental odyssey that leads to the closest thing to an answer that I could come up with."

"Fair enough. I appreciate your honesty. I guess I'll go lose some money in a poker game and let you get back to whatever it was that you were doing."

"Thank you, Doctor," Sokolov said. "Let me assure you, I can put any quiet time to good use."

Hamlin opened the door and returned to the common area. It didn't take long to get a game going. Everyone was looking for a distraction from reality more than was typical, even by Vostok standards. Vodka came into play early in the evening. Cigarettes followed closely afterwards. Francis actually had good luck for once, although he was a little hazy on the value of the ruble compared to American dollars. At one point he was up slightly over one thousand rubles, but when he asked if this would be enough money to change his life, the others just laughed.

Lena ended up at the table, drinking and smoking with the best of them. She was also flirting with everybody, which Hamlin was surprised to find quite annoying. That would give him a reason for some self-analysis later. He hoped that he wouldn't notice if she left to spend some quality frolicking time with one of the other crew members. Ignorance might not be bliss, but it definitely could be a mitigating factor. He could always blame it on the booze.

Nobody wanted to go to bed, apparently. Finally Sokolov reminded them that they were still going to put in a concerted effort to get back to a normal work schedule tomorrow. Most took the hint and the game quickly split up. There had been no loud crashes, unexplained banging sounds, or bone-chilling screams all evening. Francis was working very hard internally to convince himself that there was no longer any reason to be worried about Pechkin. Surely there was no reason he shouldn't climb into bed and enjoy a nice, long, peaceful sleep. He wished that the sun would rise and throw some light on this forsaken place. They would all be ridiculously happy when old Sol finally peeked over the horizon. It was a day circled conspicuously on the wall calendar in the common room.

Hamlin finally faced the inevitable and crawled under the covers. He wished he had drunk more vodka. He lay quietly, conceding that the stressful thoughts would soon come and shake his emotions. While he waited, sleep overtook him.

Pechkin, we want to help you
That voice…
Pechkin, we want to help you
Those words…
Help you…
There stood the smoldering, soulless abomination that was once a quiet, unassuming drilling worker who wouldn't hurt a fly. Its wild eyes locked on and gave a preview of the madness that went on behind them. Hamlin did the only thing he was capable of—he screamed. Or at least he tried to scream. All that came out was a strangled squeak. He tried again as Pechkin lunged.

He sat up abruptly in bed, the transition from sleep to consciousness transpiring in a blink. It took a moment for him to find understanding. It had been a dream.

"Shit." He gasped air as his metabolism slowly recovered from the scare.

"Only a dream." Hamlin lay back down and closed his eyes. What a relief. And yet, there was the smallest seed of doubt. He quieted his breathing and listened to the darkness. Outside, the omnipresent wind howled. A faint bar of light was visible under his door, and the soft clink he heard was no doubt another crew member getting a drink. It came as no surprise that he wasn't the only one not sleeping through the night. There were no other sounds.

"Oh, great."

Now all he had to do was get back to sleep.

"Like that's going to happen." His mouth and his mind seemed to be having a good conversation going on between them.

He closed his eyes and realized that he wasn't entirely convinced that Pechkin hadn't somehow broken in to the barracks, then snuck down the hall and hid in his room. Hamlin remembered that some of the crew had installed deadbolts on the outside door. Now if only they would put bars on the windows, he could feel somewhat secure.

The person in the kitchen must have done something to cause a slight bumping sound. Or was it Pechkin tapping on the floor or knocking on the wall? Although Hamlin was sure it wasn't, he was also sure that he wouldn't be getting back to sleep anytime soon. He had a brief, fleeting vision of what the camp in Africa might look like should he have chosen a different path. And then Deborah filled his consciousness. He missed her so badly that he actually felt a passing but sharp physical pain. Why couldn't he think of anything positive?

He resigned himself to some tossing and turning.

CHAPTER ELEVEN

It might have been dark outside, but at least the common area was well lit when Hamlin dragged himself down the hallway for breakfast. He wasn't as hungry as usual, but his mouth was dry. He settled for a bowl of oatmeal and several glasses of orange juice and ice. Halfway through his second glass, as he swirled the ice around to ensure even cooling of the drink, he started to develop some qualms about consuming the frozen water. In his mind, the research about the viruses in Lake Vostok took on new significance.

Konstantine sat down beside him while Hamlin had been daydreaming; he hadn't even noticed. Not until he started talking, at least.

"Well, I bet you can hardly wait to get back to the lab, huh?"

How did he really feel about that? Hamlin decided he wasn't sure. "Look, we have to keep busy," he replied. "And what we're doing is still just as important."

Konstantine leaned in closer and lowered his voice.

"Do you think Pechkin is a zombie?"

"What? No!" He shook his head in disgust. "What would make you even say that?"

Too many heads were turning their way. Hamlin cursed himself for not keeping his voice down.

"I just wondered. I've seen some of the movies, you know. So don't blame me…they are an American invention, right?"

Hamlin shook his head. "No. They originate from Haitian folklore; a side effect of voodoo magic. So get off your high horse, Konstantine."

"Really? That's interesting." He began to eat.

Hamlin immediately started daydreaming again. He made no attempt to control where his mind went or to add any type of structure to his thoughts. He was too tired for the required effort. He meandered into the realm of firearms.

"You know, I used to have a gun once. I sure miss it now."

Konstantine looked up from his sausage and eggs.

"Really? That's awesome. What was it?"

"It was a beautiful thing. The company that made it was Beretta. It was a 9mm semi-automatic handgun. It was gorgeous and deadly. It felt like a real weapon in my hand. So hard and cold and heavy. Mine could hold fifteen rounds—enough to start a war with a third-world country. The Italians made it as sexy as an exotic sports car. I loved it."

"So you got rid of it?"

"Yeah. I went through a real liberal-democrat phase. I decided it was too dangerous and represented an unacceptable way of dealing with issues, no matter how serious they might be."

"And now?"

"I'd pay big money to have it back in my hands."

"Even one thousand rubles?" It was nice to see Konstantine with a grin on his face.

"Okay, tell me smart guy—how much is one thousand rubles anyway? What could I buy in America, or Russia for that matter?"

"Roughly…it's worth about thirty American dollars."

Hamlin shook his head. Now he too had a smile on his face.

"I should have known. All that fuss you guys made, like I could afford a mansion and a private jet."

"You could get a nice pair of boots."

"You know, if I was a woman, that sort of thing would probably appeal to me."

He immediately got swatted on the shoulder. Lena stood behind him.

"That is a particularly prejudiced thing to say. Should we talk about the stereotypical male and his various idiosyncrasies?"

She sat down beside him.

"No, not necessary," Hamlin said. "We're just making conversation. No harm intended."

"No harm intended? I think I will propose that becomes the official credo of this place." She suddenly looked like she realized that those words shouldn't have been uttered. She changed the subject abruptly.

"So, did you get any sleep last night, Francis? You look a little tired around the eyes. Now Konstantine here, on the other hand, looks like he just finished drinking a chocolate milkshake and watching three hours of cartoons."

Konstantine didn't look up from his plate.

"Good morning, Lena," he said.

She put her hand on Hamlin's leg and started to rub it.

"Did I offend you last night?"

Hamlin played dumb. "What? Why?"

She smiled and slid her hand a little higher.

"I thought you looked a bit put out when I was being flirty. Maybe I was wrong."

"Maybe you were." It wasn't much of a response. Her hand was getting dangerously high now.

"I think you were. I think I should find a way to make it up to you."

"Not here and now," he said, pushing her hand away from the danger zone.

Suddenly she showed signs of being offended.

"As you wish." She looked around. "Just as well. I think my crew is ready to get started. Have a good day, Doctor."

"You too."

It was the first small bump in the road between the two of them. Why did he feel so bothered? It wasn't like he didn't already have enough on his mind. He certainly wasn't trolling for additional issues to deal with.

"I don't see Sokolov. Excuse me, Konstantine. I think I'll try to catch him in his room before we leave."

Sokolov's door was open just a crack when Hamlin arrived. Cleary he had visitors. Voices seemed to be arguing in Russian.

"Oh, what the hell?" Hamlin pushed the door open. At the end of the day, he was really an invited guest here. That should earn him some sort of privilege.

"Excuse me," Hamlin said as all heads turned and conversation stopped. And then, stupidly, "Am I interrupting?"

Sokolov took a moment to formulate a suitable response. "Whatever would lead you to think that, doctor? Do come in and join the party."

The remaining members of the mining crew stood around the desk. Looks of frustration were unanimous.

"Arguing over who's going to win the World Series, I suppose."

"Not at all," Sokolov said. He looked as frustrated as the miners. "We have reached a bit of an impasse on how to proceed with our work here. I suppose you'd like to hear about it. Perhaps you could offer your level-headed opinion on how we should move on from here."

"Perhaps you could give me the short version."

Sokolov looked off to the side, as if detaching himself from contact with the others so he could formulate a response in peace.

"Very well. The heart of the matter revolves around Pechkin. These gentlemen, who happen to be his closest confidants, feel that we should suspend all activities and concentrate on finding him. What we do at that point is somewhat hazy, but would be contingent upon his condition at the time. I feel that could easily become a waste of time. Antarctica is, in fact, a continent, and he could be anywhere. If he is still alive, which I view from an incredulous slant, he could have walked miles overnight. If he succumbed to the disease or the environment, then the snow would have drifted over him by now and he would be, for all practical purposes, invisible. That would render any time and effort put into finding him pointless."

"He was alive yesterday," Barinov growled. "If he is in the area of the buildings, which seems to be where he is staying, then it wouldn't be that hard to find him at all. And we should start now! He can't have much time left."

The other miners nodded in agreement.

Barinov put his hands on the desk and leaned toward Sokolov.

"Give us half a day, if nothing else. We'll use the Cat, so we can cover a large area quickly. We'll rig something to subdue and hold him. We'll bring him back if we find him and at least try to treat his disease. We owe him that! What if it was you or me out there? It could have been, you know. And if we fail, then we assume the worst, and go back to work using the new safety protocols."

Sokolov knew he was taking a risk, but felt he had few choices left.

"Your thoughts, Doctor?"

Hamlin didn't have to weigh it out for very long.

"I'm with them. We can afford half a day. If he is still really alive, we have a strong moral, if not legal, obligation to do everything we can to save him. And if either this disease or the environment has dispatched him, or rendered him incapable of rational thought, we need to know that too for our own safety and peace of mind. I don't know about any of you, but I didn't sleep worth a shit last night."

That put smiles on some of the faces.

"You, men, if you do this, need to face the reality that he might never be himself again," Hamlin said. "I saw him at the end, and he was out of his mind. And he was very dangerous, just think about what happened to Kuvayev if you have any doubts about that." Hamlin was a little uncomfortable saying it, but felt it had to be said.

"Very well," Sokolov conceded. "But this is the end. Find him if possible, save him if you can. But after this morning's search is over, I will take matters into my own hands to bring this to an end. I am responsible for both the safety and productivity of this station and both are now in jeopardy in my opinion. Get your supplies, formulate a plan, and go. Get this over with. We're all too stressed to let this continue."

The men nodded solemnly, and then left the room.

"Just what did you mean by that?"

Sokolov looked grim. "Just what I said. If they cannot bring this to a conclusion, good or bad, by searching through the morning, then I'm going out and hunting him down myself. A 7.62x39mm high velocity bullet will put all of this to rest once and for all. Enough with the distraction and sleepless nights."

"You're willing to kill him?"

"No," Sokolov said. "If he is alive in the traditional sense, we will spare no effort to save him."

"But..."

"I don't understand what has happened to him. If he is brain damaged or some sort of resurrected corpse, if you will forgive me, then I will blow what's left of his brains out as a favor both to him and to us."

"You yourself?"

"I have had extensive training with firearms. I was little more than a boy when I fought the last days against the Mujahedeen in Afghanistan. Don't be fooled by the appearance of the prissy little man before you. There are many good reasons why I was chosen to be in charge of this outpost."

As Hamlin looked at the glint in the small man's eyes, he didn't doubt it. "You're right about one thing. We need to get over this and get back to work. There's altogether too much time to think about the unpleasant situation we find ourselves in."

Sokolov raised his right hand and pressed the palm of it against his forehead. He slid the hand slowly up and pushed back his hair.

"Doctor, if you please. I'm certain you can find a way to pass the time productively."

Hamlin turned toward the door. There was a Steig Larsson novel with his name on it back in his room. That would have to do.

The mining crew spent the entire morning driving a circuit around all the buildings. They never saw so much as a hint of Pechkin. They returned discouraged and sullen. This particular ending gave no closure at all. But it was the reality they now had to face.

Hamlin was glad to get into the Cat and head for the lab. Konstantine was quieter than usual; no doubt the experience of the previous day still weighing on his mind. Things got worse for him when they arrived. Before Hamlin exited the machine, Sokolov asked him to stay back.

"Konstantine, please get started on your own. I need to go for a little drive with Dr. Hamlin and have a bit of a talk."

Konstantine was obviously not thrilled, but didn't voice his objections. He hopped out and headed into the lab.

"What's up?" Francis asked.

"We're going for a nice, leisurely drive."

The Cat started to roll, the unavoidable creaking sounds heralding the movement.

"Look, I enjoyed the cognac and cigar, but I'm not putting out if that's what you think."

"Your sense of humor sustains me, Doctor. If you would be so good as to reach very carefully under the seat, you will find a rifle there."

"What?"

He reached (and *very* carefully at that) and found a cold metal object. He withdrew it slowly, not even sure initially what part of the weapon he was holding.

"What the hell am I supposed to do with this?"

"Bring an end to this madness once and for all," Sokolov said. "Either that or take over driving and let me hold the gun."

His voice dropped considerably. "We're hunting Pechkin?"

Sokolov remained resolute. "We're hunting what remains of Pechkin. For the sake of all of us here, we need to put him down."

Hamlin looked the gun over. "I've never shot anything quite like this before."

"But you have fired guns?"

"Yes. I used to own one myself."

"The basic principles are the same. Once you take off the safety, it becomes a simple point and shoot interface. A man sized, unmoving target at close range shouldn't be any problem at all."

Hamlin had doubts. "You wouldn't think so."

"Do you wish to trade spots?"

Even afterward, when he had time to really analyze his thoughts, he had no idea why he answered the way he did.

"No, I'll keep the gun. I can do it if I have to. You keep driving."

"Excellent. Steady on, Doctor. Let's go for some touring."

In the end, it mattered not who held the gun. They had no more success than the mining crew. They never once saw so much as a hint of where Pechkin might be or what kind of condition he might be in. After a couple hours, Hamlin asked to return to the lab. He figured that Konstantine would be a bundle of nerves by now. Reluctantly, Sokolov complied.

As the Cat covered the final few feet and aligned itself perfectly with the entrance to the lab, Hamlin noticed something extremely unnerving in the glow of the headlights. The door was ajar. Grasping wildly at theories that would ultimately result in a happy ending to this unexpected scenario, he wondered if Konstantine had heard their approach and was rolling out the welcome mat in a matter of speaking. There was no sign of him, however.

"What is the meaning of this?" Sokolov said as he opened his door. "Doctor, if you would please pick up the rifle and join me. Perhaps the *just in case* rule would apply here."

Hamlin, reluctantly, did just that. He checked and the safety was off. He was more than happy to follow behind and let someone else go in first. Once Sokolov got in the doorway, he seemed to freeze in place. Seconds ticked by and still no perceptible signs of movement.

"Dr. Sokolov, are you all right?"

His shouldered slumped just a little. "No, I'm afraid not. Perhaps you should take a moment to brace yourself before entering. Actually, I wouldn't find any blame in you simply returning to the Cat while I investigate further."

All of Hamlin's internal warning systems were now going off in a big way. But he simply couldn't walk away without looking. He followed Sokolov into the building, his mind nowhere near prepared for what he was about to see.

His eyes swept to the right upon entering. This was the direction of the work areas. His eyes were wide open, and the grisly scene had every opportunity to imprint itself in his mind and memory–an indelible vision that he would never be completely rid of for the rest of his life.

His first impression was that Konstantine had somehow exploded. Half of the spacious room was literally covered with blood and gore. It was even on the ceiling, contrasting boldly with the otherwise bright, white paint. Konstantine himself, or at least what remained of him, was sprawled on his back across the table along the back of the room. The flesh that was in and around his mid-section had been destroyed to a degree that Francis could see his individual ribs poking up from the center of the carnage. There appeared to be parts of him strewn about in random fashion–a section of an arm was on full display on the linoleum floor. It seemed to be reaching for something. At least from this angle, he couldn't see his face.

There was so much more to assault his senses, but this was when Hamlin made the unconscious decision to run for the door and vomit in the snow. He made a good production out of it, fully losing what remained of his lunch and then throwing in some dry heaves for good measure. When he finally looked up and wiped the tears from his eyes, Sokolov was standing on the porch watching. Hamlin didn't realize that he had dropped the rifle, which Sokolov now cradled.

"My God! That's the most horrible, disgusting thing I've ever seen."

"I agree. And I've been in wars."

Hamlin was nowhere near recovered from the shock. In fact, it hadn't had time to fully manifest itself yet. That would continue for days and weeks.

"What do we do now?"

"I may need some time before I can answer that."

Francis realized that he was starting to shake. It was only partially from the cold.

"Doctor," Sokolov said, "go back into the Cat and get warm. I'm going to walk around the building and look for signs of tracks. I'll rejoin you as soon as I finish."

Barely able to think, Hamlin simply complied. He sat limply, shut the door, and was satisfied to meditate upon the sound of the idling diesel engine. His mind was reacting by trying to shut itself down. He didn't fight it.

Sokolov climbed in behind the wheel.

"Any tracks?"

"There is one set leaving the area, but it is only visible up close to the lab. The wind has filled them in once they get more than a few feet away."

"Pechkin?"

Sokolov hesitated. "I would estimate that these tracks are larger. And they appear to be boots, not bare feet. I'm afraid neither of those things are good news for us."

Hamlin found he was largely incapable of generating a lot of creative thought. His mind was quite muddled.

"What does that mean?"

"It means we are taking a small detour on the way back to the barracks."

The Cat started to roll and Francis tuned out. His mind went fuzzy; a grey haze in place of where his conscious thoughts usually formed. And that was fine. As a result, Sokolov was almost upon the outer storage shed before Hamlin realized where they were going. When it finally caught his attention, he immediately noticed more bad news. The door had been knocked completely off its hinges and lay partially submerged in the snow.

"That was fixed, right?"

"Yes. It was."

The power and violence necessary to rip it out of the frame and off its hinges was readily apparent. The frame itself had suffered great damage; splintered pieces of wood easily visible even from this distance away.

"Did Pechkin do this? Is he really that strong?"

"I think not." Sokolov spoke slowly, as if taking extra time to formulate his words. "If you look carefully, it is apparent that the door was pushed out from the inside."

The nightmare continued to unfold, getting worse with every subsequent revelation.

"You mean..." Hamlin had trouble verbalizing his fear.

"I'll have to go in to know for sure." He grabbed the rifle and then swung his door open.

The frigid air that swept in was all but forgotten in the face of larger concerns. The Cat's door made a solid 'thunk' when it shut, and all that was left for Hamlin to do was watch Sokolov walking cautiously.

Sokolov approached slowly, the rifle held in position for a quick shot. He paused to look at the door before continuing his slow pace toward the entranceway. He was almost in, and he hesitated, standing perfectly still, while all his senses were no doubt on full alert. Sokolov seemed to brace himself, and then he stepped in and out of Hamlin's line of sight.

Now it was Hamlin's senses that were on full alert. He strained to hear any possible sound. He feared screams and gunshots, but the low howl of the wind was all he heard. A full minute went by before Sokolov stepped back out. He seemed to be in good shape, and as if anticipating Hamlin's concern, he gave a quick, dismissive wave. He seemed to be working something out. After standing motionless for a few moments, he finally started walking back toward the Cat.

He was perhaps halfway back, when he stopped, a perplexed look on his face, and turned to look back toward the shed.

Hamlin followed his line of sight. On the edge of the gloom, where the headlights faded to black, a form came into view. The movement drew his eyes toward the charging figure. It wasn't Pechkin.

Kuvayev had gone through the same disturbing transformation. He was running full out, a huge, bearded monstrosity, plowing through the loose surface snow like it wasn't even there. He appeared to have the remnants of a shirt and a pair of boots on. It might have been funny except for the crazy look in his wild eyes, the bulging veins in his neck, and the grotesque bellowing that Hamlin could now here. There was no doubt that he was coming for Sokolov. And there was no doubt he was going to reach the diminutive doctor before he could get to the possible safety of the Cat.

Sokolov had also worked that out. He spun to face the creature of destruction that was bearing down on him and managed to get one shot off before they made contact.

The powerful crack of the rifle's retort was almost comforting. But would it have any impact on the roaring giant?

Kuvayev struck Sokolov without any attempt to slow. The impact sent Sokolov flying through the air, and Kuvayev fell, rolling over several times in the snow until his momentum was spent. Sokolov, to his credit, immediately sprang to his feet and made a run for the Cat.

Kuvayev stumbled back to an upright position, and then seemed to need a moment to process what to do next. He roared like a wild beast and then churned after Sokolov.

It was going to be close. Hamlin slid across the seat and threw the driver's side door open. Sokolov threw himself into the Cat at the same time that Kuvayev reached him. The door slammed partially shut and pinned Sokolov in place. The roaring monster was on the ground, arms and legs churning as he tried to regain his footing. The door suddenly went slack and Sokolov popped into the cab. With adrenalin fueled desperation, he lunged for the door handle and slammed it shut. Kuvayev was now visible, obviously on his feet. He reached for Sokolov but seemed to be a least temporarily stymied by the glass.

"Go!" Hamlin screamed as Sokolov stomped his foot on the accelerator.

The Cat sprang forward, but its course intersected with the wall of the shed. Sokolov spun it at the last possible moment, then let it build up to maximum speed as it diagonalled away.

Kuvayev was in full pursuit, his muscular legs pumping like some mechanical device, plowing without hesitation through the snow. The Cat seemed to be slowly pulling away. That was the first good news Hamlin had experienced in some time.

"Are we losing him?" Sokolov gasped.

"Yes. I think so. I can't actually see him anymore."

The Cat was screaming along, and both of them wondered if that was sustainable. Sokolov decided to slow just slightly.

"My God. I fear have a problem."

Hamlin looked in horror. Sokolov had lost a glove in the melee, and had apparently sustained a bite from Kuvayev in the process. Blood was running down his wrist and dripping on the floorboard. They both had a good idea what that meant.

"You didn't cut it on the edge of the door?"

Sokolov sighed long and hard. "I'm afraid not. To be honest, everything happened so fast that I don`t know exactly how it happened."

They drove in silence. Francis was wracking his brain for an answer.

"Don't panic yet. Let's think this through."

Sokolov stared straight ahead. "I'm afraid your advice has come too late." He turned and looked at Hamlin. "Of all the things that could have happened, I really feel this is the worst. I just…have no idea what to do next."

"Wait, wait. What do we know? What have we learned?"

"We know, or at least very strongly suspect that it can be transmitted through a bite. And I have just sustained a bite."

"Wait a minute. There's a first aid kit in here somewhere. Let me find it. I can clean the bite thoroughly right now. That couldn't hurt. Who knows…maybe we can prevent the spread."

"If you don't mind, I'm going to continue to drive. One encounter with Kuvayev was quite enough."

"I don't mind at all. Wait a second…aha! Here's the kit."

"I can steer with one hand. When you're ready, you may have the other."

Hamlin had the kit open and was quickly rummaging through it.

"All right, let me have it. We'll do this in stages. I'll start by wiping off the blood and having a good look at it."

"Doctor, wait! Make sure you put on gloves or you risk coming into direct contact yourself."

"Hmm, good idea. I don't seem to be thinking as clearly as I should. Here we go."

Francis pulled on the gloves carefully, and then reached for the offered hand. He wiped it with sterile cloth and had a good look.

"Damn. It's definitely a bite. I can see the curvature of his mouth. It's not very deep, though. He must not have had time to give you a good chomp. That might be a good thing. The bite Pechkin gave to Kuvayev was very deep. Brace yourself, doctor; I'm going to disinfect the wound."

"Don't worry about my comfort. Clean it out as much as possible."

Hamlin could feel Sokolov tense up as the disinfectant entered the wound. He grimaced, but didn't make a sound. Francis alternated wiping and disinfecting for some time. When he finished, the wound looked quite clean and bleeding was slowing.

"That looks good. I'm going to put a temporary dressing on it and you should be fine until we get back to the barracks. Try to keep calm and don't let your breathing get elevated."

"Doctor, really. I'm way past that. Being attacked by a giant, crazed lunatic tends to raise one's vital signs."

Hamlin looked out the back window. There was only darkness.

"Do you think he has enough sense to follow the tracks this thing leaves?"

Sokolov was trying to be still while Hamlin applied the dressing. His voice was subdued when he responded.

"After seeing what he can do to a solid door, and what happened with Konstantine, I most sincerely hope not."

One last bit of hope remained to be laid to rest. "Do you think you hit him when you shot?"

He shook his head. "I missed a great opportunity—one that I now regret tremendously."

The Cat continued on its way.

CHAPTER TWELVE

All the remaining crew members were at the barracks when they arrived. The story they brought with them caused quite a stir. The research work was beginning to fade into the background. Survival was becoming the sole focus. The first concern raised from that line of thought was what to do with Sokolov. Kuvayev had agreed to being strapped down. The leader of the site was unwilling to submit to that. After his wound had been exposed, cleaned for the second time, and rewrapped, he spoke in the common area.

"Look," he said, addressing what remained to the crew. "I have no intention of putting anyone in harm's way. If I develop a serious fever in the next week, I believe we all need to be realistic as to what that means. If that should occur, I will take myself to a place where I will pose no threat to any of you. You have my solemn vow on that. I refuse to be tied down. At least let me control my own destiny if the worst case scenario begins to unfold. I do not want to become a walking abomination. I will leave this world with my senses and dignity intact."

There was little reaction from the crew. An uneasy silence had fallen over the room.

"I'm going to put myself on a regiment of antibiotics. Also, I'm going to start immediately with medicinally controlling my body temperature. If any of you have any other suggestions, I would be very thankful to hear them. I must tell you, I have been through a number of harrowing situations, but I've never been scared like this before."

The room continued to be void of sound. A number of people had seemingly found something interesting on the floor that required their immediate attention.

Barinov was the first to speak. "What about Pechkin and Kuvayev? How can we sleep or feel safe as long as they are out there?"

Sokolov nodded slowly. "I tend to agree. We need to find out how to stop them and put them out of their misery. They may be up and about, but I would argue that they really aren't alive in a traditional sense."

Lena cleared her throat. "What if they could be? What if the fever breaks after several days and they revert back to themselves again?"

Sokolov was grim. "Then they will freeze to death before they can get back to shelter. This extreme fever is all that stands between them and being frozen solid. In this temperature, they would last maybe five or ten minutes before succumbing."

"You said Kuvayev knocked that door off its frame?" Barinov asked. "Then what would stop him from doing the same with our door? If anything, it is lighter than the one that was on the shed."

That thought had already flickered through all of their minds.

"I will volunteer to go out after them," Yedemsky said.

"What about Konstantine?" Kravchuk said, speaking for the first time.

Sokolov was clearly hesitant. "What do you all think? I must tell you that I am not entirely certain what to do about him and the outer lab. What are your thoughts?"

"Surely we can't just leave him there!" Zhabin exclaimed.

Hamlin knew they had no idea how bad that scene was nor the condition Konstantine's body was in. He decided to speak.

"There isn't much of him left. Any volunteers for that job better have a very strong constitution. Also, I suspect you need to be prepared to have nightmares for the rest of your life."

That diminished the enthusiasm considerably.

"I could do it," Lena said quietly. "I spent time as a battlefield nurse before getting my doctoral degree. I have seen terrible injuries before."

Sokolov held up his good hand as if to stop her thoughts. "I turned the thermostat way down before I left. He should stay well preserved for a few days. We have time to think about this before deciding what to do. Myself, I think in the name of our health and well-being that we should stay away from the outer lab. I cannot guarantee that the atmosphere is safe, even if you factor out the grisly nature of the scene."

Hamlin had a thought but hesitated from verbalizing it. He saw the lab in his mind being burnt to the ground–a giant funeral pyre that cleansed the scene within it from the face of the earth. That sounded good to him. But that was partially because he had actually seen the horror within and he was having an emotional response.

"I have a suggestion which is also a request," Sokolov said. "The first group to go out; if you would be so kind as to swing past the outer storage shed, I must confess that I dropped my rifle in the skirmish with Kuvayev. It is lying somewhere in the snow, perhaps fifty feet straight out from the entrance. I would love to have it back, if it is not hopelessly buried."

"We have an excellent metal detector in the mining shelter," Barinov replied. "We'll swing past the shed and make a quick attempt to find the gun. If we're not successful, we'll pick up the detector and try again on our way back."

The others were nodding. As the plan came together and actions were plotted, life and hope began to renew within them.

Sokolov held up his hands and looked emotional for the first time since Hamlin had arrived.

"Friends, I must tell you, I have never appreciated you all as much as I do now. Many times I felt like you all relied on me to keep this operation safe and viable. Now I realize that I count on you every bit as much, and in these circumstances, way more, than you count on me. Thank you for your assistance regardless of what form it takes. Let us pull together to find some semblance of hope for ourselves. Surely we deserve that much.

"Now, as far as our immediate plans are concerned–Barinov, I have a rifle for you to take on your expedition. I know you are trained in its use. Be extremely careful out there. Pechkin is very dangerous, but Kuvayev is even more so. He is extremely powerful now that he is under the influence of whatever this is. Do not take any risks. Stay clear of him at all costs. If you want to take a shot, do it from a safe distance if you can. Don't count on a building or the Cat to keep you safe. As comforting as it would be to know that our sick friends have been neutralized, it is paramount that we all stay safe going forward. Our original fourteen is now down to eleven. And let us hope and pray that I will not be taken off that number anytime soon. Each person represents a skill set that we need. So I will say it again–please be careful at all times."

Sokolov went to get the rifle while three of the miners got dressed to go out. There was a quiet hum of talk and activity while this played out. Francis was concerned about how silent the room was going to be once they left. For now, a new era was being ushered in. No longer would research be the focus that gave them structure and purpose from day to day, and even moment to moment. Now simple survival became the nucleus of their existence here. Or much worse than that–waiting for the terror that was out there to find them. They needed a more comprehensive plan that included tasks for all of them. The plan *could* make them safer, and *would* keep them occupied. Both consequences were vital.

Once the men had left, Sokolov again addressed the dwindling crew. Besides him, there were now seven around the table.

"Friends, I wouldn't normally even consider this as an option, but we find ourselves in unusual circumstances. I propose that we arm one person, a volunteer who has the responsibility of defending us should one of the two sick members arrive and try to force their way inside. I have an MP-446 Viking in the very effective 9mm caliber, which I will hand over to the defense of our barracks. Perhaps we could set up a rotation, especially for the night-time hours, so that one person does not have to bear the entire load. I would not expect anyone without some firearms training or experience to volunteer; neither anyone who is uncomfortable handling the weapon in close proximity to your fellow members. I'll get the gun and prepare it while you folks decide who's willing to participate."

Out of all of them, only Lena expressed a desire not to be involved. She had a fear of firearms, she explained. It came from seeing the damage that could be done by a small, high velocity projectile on the battlefield. Nobody ridiculed or criticized her for taking this stance.

Hamlin was glad to volunteer. He was a fan of handguns and missed his old Berretta terribly under these circumstances. It would feel good to hold one in his hands again. No matter what else happened, he would not go quietly into the night while properly armed. Sadistic virus be damned! He was cognizant of ballistics to the point where he knew what a 9mm slug would do. It leveled the playing field quite nicely against a stronger, faster opponent.

Sokolov returned and they set up a rotation between all the volunteers.

The search crew was gone nearly two hours before the sound of the Cat heralded their return. Hamlin wasn't the only one out of the crew that was praying for good news.

They barely got in before being besieged by questions.

"Just a minute!" Barinov yelled.

Hamlin noticed that Kravchuk looked ill. What exactly did that mean?

Barinov held out Sokolov's rifle. "We do have some good news. We found this."

Sokolov retrieved it gratefully. "Excellent work. Thank you, men. Another component of our self-defense plan comes into place."

Hamlin had to ask. The answer was too important.

"What's wrong with Kravchuk? He looks terrible."

Barinov snarled. "As well he should. After some arm twisting, he convinced me to let him have a look in the outer lab."

Kravchuk's skin color was almost grey. He sought, and then made eye contact with Hamlin.

"You were right. I'm going to have nightmares for the rest of my life."

Hamlin had no response. The memory would be more than punishment enough.

"I presume there was no sign of Kuvayev or Pechkin," Sokolov said.

Barinov shook his head. "No. No signs at all. No tracks–nothing. Sorry."

"Now, now," Sokolov soothed. "There is certainly no need to apologize. We all appreciate you going out there and putting yourselves potentially in harm's way for our benefit. We could ask for nothing more."

Barinov and his fellow miners looked like beaten men.

"I could use a nice, hot shower. If you'll excuse me, I think I'll indulge." Barinov shuffled off.

"Very well," Sokolov responded. "As for the rest of you, may I suggest that the last task of the day could be to see if there is any way to reinforce our few windows and the door? The peace of mind that comes from doing it might be invaluable while trying to sleep tonight. I have to go and prepare some medication for myself."

This last statement put a hush over the crowd. Sokolov noticed immediately.

"May I ask for volunteers to take my temperature every few hours from here on in until such a time as when we all agree this matter has been definitively resolved in one manner or another? That helps me and gives some peace of mind to the rest of you, I would assume."

Lena was quick to put up her hand.

"Yes, perfect. Ms. Sayansky has experience in the field of medicine, so there couldn't be a better choice. Now, I shall leave you all to work on a security upgrade. Until later, then."

There was plenty of scrap lumber in a small storage room near the end of the hall. Hamlin had no clue why it was there, but when coupled with an old hand saw and a hammer that looked like a relic from the when Neanderthals roamed the earth, they were able to reinforce all the windows quite well. The doors took a bit more engineering, but they finally came up with a method to secure both the hinges and the lock. And in the end, Sokolov was right. The effort, as well as the result, made everyone feel slightly better.

They had pizza for dinner. Francis was pleasantly surprised at how well it turned out, considering all the ingredients were either frozen or came out of a can. That seemed to bolster everyone's spirits somewhat– or at least everyone but Kravchuk; and Hamlin knew exactly what his problem was. Not the sort of thing food could help.

It was decided that another movie night would be a good way to wrap up the day. Hamlin was careful with what he chose. Nothing dark or scary tonight. He selected *Groundhog Day*, and then did a brief explanation on the premise of the movie before starting it. The reception was quite good, even a fair amount of laughter at the right moments. When the credits started to roll, Hamlin was not looking forward to lying in bed, waiting for whatever dreams may come. But the group dispersed and the end was apparent.

Obolensky was the first to act as security. He had the handgun set on the table within easy reach and also had a pile of Russian magazines which apparently were the night's entertainment. His presence did make Hamlin feel more secure, he decided with some degree of relief. He wondered if Sokolov had anything that could help them sleep. That led him to wonder if Sokolov was going to be around much longer. He then had to contemplate the immediate future for all of them. There were so many negative thoughts. Fortunately, he had 'borrowed' a bottle of vodka, which now awaited his arrival in his room. Maybe sleep would be possible after all. After half a bottle, it was.

When he woke, Hamlin had no idea where he was. When that passed, he realized he had no idea what time it was. Wishing he didn't care, but fearing the worst, he slowly rolled over. The clock said 8:37 and that was a pleasant surprise. He had slept straight through.

He got up as casually as possible, pretending that it was just another day. A shower was high on his agenda, but breakfast and some quick recognizance came first. He sauntered in the common area. Several people were preparing food; three already had plates full and were eating quietly.

Yedemsky had taken over security duties. He was flipping listlessly through the magazines. He also looked tired. Hamlin was surprised that a Russian of all people wouldn't have thought to use vodka as a tranquilizer. He decided to walk over and see him.

"Good morning, Yedemsky. Can I get you anything from the kitchen? Food? Coffee or juice?"

Yedemsky looked up through bloodshot eyes. "No, I already had some stuff when I first got up. Thanks for asking, though."

Hamlin decided to eat next. Then he really wanted to know how Sokolov was feeling. A simple bowl of oatmeal, two pieces of dry toast, and a small coffee got him started. He was surprised to discover he still had some appetite.

"Hey you," Lena said as she slid him beside him. "Get any sleep last night?"

Francis had to smile despite the obvious physical side effects his indulgence from the previous evening was having. "Green Mark Cedar is becoming my favorite vodka and new best friend. How about you?"

She had to think about her answer. "I tossed and turned. Perhaps imagining Konstantine is worse than actually seeing him."

"I wouldn't bet any money on that," Francis replied before taking in a steaming spoonful of oatmeal.

"I'm fighting an uncontrollable urge to ask you to describe the scene to me. Who knew I had such morbid curiosity?"

"I knew you had uncontrollable urges," Hamlin added, taking a risk that she would find his comment funny.

"Hmm. I should have snuck into your room last night and fucked both of us to sleep. That's got to be an improvement on shattered nerves and frequent waking. No matter what your moral compunctions might be about this deviant behavior of mine, Doctor, you've got to admit that this horror we're enduring makes me and what I do look like a Sunday school teacher polishing the ambry in comparison."

"I'm not sure I'd endorse the comparison, but trust me when I tell you that I have no complaints about your behavior since I arrived here. As a matter of fact, I'd like to bring you and a case of this awesome vodka home with me when this is all over. Lena, New England would seem so warm compared to this place, you'd never want to wear clothes again. That should go a long ways toward making the transition fun."

She was giving him a sly grin. "No clothes, huh? I think I am having a bad influence on you, Doctor."

"Well, maybe a G-string, pasties, and stiletto heels on the cool days. I could live with that."

Her smile grew wider. "I guess we wouldn't be going out much. So, tell me, Dr. Hamlin, do you own one of those huge American houses with a big garage for all your cars and a pool in the back?"

"Are you considering my offer?"

She shrugged. "You'll have to work harder to sell it first. Who knows?"

For a brief moment Hamlin was back home, in his living room, sitting in his recliner and watching Lena walk seductively down the stairs. It was his fantasy, a man's fantasy, so of course she was naked. Deborah was for the moment nowhere to be found. He found the whole scenario quite acceptable.

"My dear, I have a very nice house. It has four bedrooms, although God only knows why, a beautiful kitchen, and hardwood flooring throughout. No pool, mind you, but a very nice hot tub on the back deck."

"Ah, a deck. Tell me Francis, do you have a big deck?"

"I thought that was an American joke."

"I have to practice if I'm going there with you."

"I suppose you have a valid point."

It was at this juncture that Sokolov made an appearance. He walked briskly to the kitchen and came back with a coffee in his hands. He sat across from Hamlin and smiled. He was wearing a short-sleeved shirt and that was a first. Francis was surprised that one even existed down here. Even in the summer, it would serve little purpose.

"Good morning, Doctor. Ms. Sayansky, how are you?"

"You seem chipper," Hamlin said, stating the obvious.

"So far, my good doctor, there are no ill effects. Surprisingly, I slept well. I feel fine. No aches, pains or signs of a fever."

"Your shirt gives you a dapper look. Trying to stay cool, I suppose?"

"Yes, and why not? If you recall, Kuvayev responded to some extent to our physical efforts to keep him cool. At any rate, I can't imagine that it could hurt in any way."

"I can't argue against that."

"Perhaps when you finish, Ms. Sayansky, you would consider changing the dressing on my wound. Again, keeping it clean certainly can't hurt."

Hamlin was finding himself relieved that Sokolov seemed so healthy. Maybe they had a chance after all–assuming, at least, that they could stay clear of Pechkin and Kuvayev. Obviously Konstantine wouldn't be reanimating any time soon. Hamlin winced at the very thought and regretted having it.

"Yes, of course. I would be happy to help in any way." Lena gave him a big smile.

"Excellent. Thank you, my dear. Now, I'm going to take my black coffee over a table and talk to Yedemsky for a few moments. He looks a little worse for wear this morning. Excuse me, please."

When he left, an awkward silence fell over them. Hamlin sipped his coffee. Lena leaned in toward him and lowered her voice.

"Do you really think he is all right?"

Hamlin had no idea how to answer that. But, he had to respond in some fashion.

"I don't know. I sure hope and pray that he is. So far, so good."

She didn't seem satisfied with his answer. But then again, Hamlin reasoned, she had been through plenty of government sanctioned bullshit before. She no doubt expected Sokolov to lie through his teeth. Hamlin thought that as manager of the site, Sokolov had been relatively forthcoming so far. But he would have to be watched very closely for the next few days or so. If Sokolov lied about how he felt and nobody else was checking, they could all be in big trouble.

The first activity for the day was to send out hunting parties. Three men–consisting of a driver, a spotter/navigator, and the one responsible for carrying and using the gun–would set out for two-hour patrols. After that, the Cat would undergo a very quick mechanical check and the crew would be spelled off. That way, so their reasoning went, everyone on patrol would always be fresh and alert. The two-way radio would be constantly monitored by someone back at the barracks. The initial search grid was rejected in favor of a course that kept them close to all the various buildings for the camp. This seemed to be an anchor point for the two specters that were currently haunting them. Anything else seemed to be more of a *needle in a haystack* venture anyway, since the two were likely to be in constant motion.

Once the Cat left, Sokolov managed to convince the remaining members that the common area, the large room where they met as a group to eat and hold other activities, was overdue for a good cleaning. They assigned specific tasks, and then went about the business of locating and preparing all the needed supplies. Lena went with Sokolov to change his dressing. When she returned, she had a message for Hamlin.

"He wants to see you in his room."

Hamlin put down the bucket of soapy water he was holding.

"Okay, I guess this can wait."

"We can trade spots," she said. "After you are finished with him, we'll fight over who keeps this job."

"When you say fight, I hope you mean wrestle."

"Grope is a good word."

"At least we're both on the same page. And yes, it is." Hamlin finally managed to pull off his disposable gloves and headed for Sokolov's room.

"Yes, come in, Doctor. And if you wouldn't mind, could you shut the door behind you?"

"Of course." Hamlin tried to be casual and relaxed as he took the seat at the front of the desk.

"Very good. I feel it necessary to verbalize several thoughts, and as you now know, I trust you with these more controversial details. You have proved to be more levelheaded and resourceful than I would have expected. And I believe you are capable of separating yourself from your personal agenda and putting the good of the station first when difficult decisions need to be made."

"Are we facing difficult decisions?" Hamlin was not thrilled with the beginning of the conversation.

"We already have, of course," Sokolov replied. "But it is not beyond probability that more will be coming shortly. I think you and I need to discuss the future of the station if something should happen to me."

Hamlin hated this, but he knew Sokolov was right.

"And what do you think that's going to look like?"

"I think," he said, "that it's going to look like you."

Hamlin winced. "That sounds like a bad idea to me. Why would all these experienced researchers, who have all paid their dues down here, accept a newcomer, and a foreigner at that, as their new overseer?"

Sokolov managed a smile despite the dark composition of their topic.

"I think 'overseer' is a bit strong and outdated, even for Russia. The truth is, your democratic urgings notwithstanding, there will be times when it is absolutely necessary for someone to have the will and ability to make unilateral decisions on behalf of the entire group. Otherwise, anarchy and discord are knocking at your door. These people all have too much history and emotional attachment to each other to do this task impartially. Familiarity breeds contempt. An abundance of casual and friendly contact ensures a lack of sufficient respect for each other to the point where they would not become subservient to the will of anyone else here. Or at least anyone that they know well."

"And that's where I come in."

"In my opinion, yes."

"Great."

"Your leadership skills may be the only hope for these people to ever leave this place alive. I trust you will not take the task lightly."

"Should it ever become necessary. Let's not wave the white flag just yet."

"That goes without saying, of course. But this discussion has to happen now, while we have the opportunity, and I am completely in my own, right mind."

Hamlin shook his head. "You know, this is all Deborah's fault. If she hadn't dumped me like a bag of garbage on the curb, I never would have considered coming here. I'd be doing research in Africa, complaining about the heat and mosquitos. It would sure beat the hell out of this, though."

Sokolov sat quietly for some time before responding. "If you are going to be in charge, to some degree at least, it is time we had a long discussion. I'm going to be forthcoming about details which cannot leave this room. And that restriction will have to continue if anything happens to me. Do you understand?"

"What a mess. Yeah, I understand."

"Your lack of enthusiasm is completely understandable and justified. Having said that, let me start at what I perceive as to be the beginning."

"All right. Let the bombardment begin."

"Please promise me that you will not respond emotionally. Nor will you share any of this with anyone, at any time."

Hamlin frowned. "What possible motivation could there be for me to promise you that?"

"The very survival of this station and the people living here."

"For crying out loud. Fine."

Sokolov broke eye contact, swiveled on his chair, and stared toward the bookcase.

"I have called Moscow over the radio. They are aware of our situation and will send a team in should the weather ever present an opportunity to do so. This is not likely, but it is a straw to grasp."

"That could come in handy."

"All right. What do you need to know? First of all, I suppose I should tell you that the research here has progressed so rapidly and successfully that there really isn't any overwhelming reason to even continue. We can always strive for some new, unexpected revelation–but mostly the motivation is just to keep everybody busy; to add the structure that I know you appreciate, Doctor. Circumstances dictate that we are going to be staying here in Antarctica whether it is now necessary or not."

"Doctor," Hamlin said, "I'm already stunned. What could you possibly mean? What have we discovered that has made the rest of our work virtually obsolete?"

Sokolov continued to stare at the books. "Why, this virus, of course."

Francis felt time grind to a halt.

"What do you mean?" His voice was low, but there was an obvious undercurrent.

"Why do you suppose the American government was willing to fly you down here in the first place?"

"You didn't answer my question."

"You haven't answered mine."

Hamlin felt his blood pressure rising. "Our two countries work cooperatively on projects like this. I just assumed it was a gesture of goodwill."

Sokolov still wasn't making eye contact. "It's not unprecedented."

"What are you insinuating?"

"I am beyond insinuations. We are both looking for answers to a serious problem."

"A serious problem?"

"Look around the world, Dr. Hamlin. How has it changed?"

He had only a glimmer of understanding as to where this was supposed to be going.

"It's changed in many ways. It continues to change almost daily." Francis opted to be purposely evasive.

"World War One, World War Two, Korea, Vietnam, Afghanistan, The Gulf War–these were the wars we fought, sometimes on the same side, sometimes on opposites. The world has always been a violent and dangerous place."

"What's that got to do with Antarctica?"

"We fight different wars now. Our enemies don't mass together on the battlefield–they hide wherever they can. They don't die with honor– they send others to do the dirty work for them. They don't go after strategic targets–they attack the weak and vulnerable. A bus load of school children is a preferable target over a piece of artillery. They won't fight back."

"You're building up to justify something terrible, aren't you?"

Now Sokolov swiveled so that their eyes met.

"Oh yes, there you stand on the moral high ground, feet spread apart and planted firmly. You were slapped in the face on 9/11, and what a horrible thing that was. But you have no idea what it is really like. For all the thousands of miles of border you have, you only share them with two countries. Canada, which would apologize for a single candy wrapper blowing across from their side; and Mexico, with whom you have a decent relationship, and which has more than enough internal problems to ever give credence to the notion of attacking you, even before you compare the size of your respective militaries.

"We share our borders with fourteen different countries, including some that are experiencing great political turmoil. Surely you have heard of our Ukraine issues. Separatists and religious zealots tend to be the most dangerous, because sometimes their ideologies simply border on insanity. You cannot reason with them because they are innately unreasonable. And they don't fight fair. They know they can't win that way, so they fight dirty. And that leaves us with a problem. Here, at the ends of the earth, we may have found a solution."

"You're scaring the hell out of me."

"Imagine it, Doctor. An area over-run with extremists, all of whom would be thrilled to murder your grandmother, best friend, or the mechanic who services your car, for no logical or justifiable reason. They hide while they chuckle with glee over the death and despair they are spreading. And no military can target them when they cannot be found."

"So what do you propose?"

We give the general population in the region a fair warning, and then we expose the bastards to our little virus. We both know what happens after that."

"Are you insane?" Hamlin was starting to feel a little ill.

"Your government is also interested, before you get too high and mighty. That is how and why you came to be here. Just imagine the deterrent value. Leave us alone or get ready for a regional apocalypse."

"So, let me get this straight. You were looking for something like this all along?"

"What else could possibly be down there in Lake Vostok's frigid waters? It is highly unlikely that any higher life forms are there due to the harsh conditions. Your discoveries eclipsed what we had anticipated. And also, as expected, we discovered a virus that modern man has never been exposed to before. Which means, no immunity. And no, originally this station was created to study changes in the environment through analysis of ice cores."

"I feel sick."

"That is the next topic of conversation."

That was equally scary. "Are you feeling ill?"

Sokolov shook his head. "I feel wonderful. Maybe a little stiffness in my neck, but I suspect that is a side effect of Kuvayev crashing into me."

"That's a relief."

"Yes. But that could change. And if it's going to, the transformation should happen soon. I want you to be fully aware of what is going to happen if I develop symptoms comparable to Pechkin and Kuvayev."

"You're a fount of good news."

"You need to know. In that most unfortunate event, I am going to walk out the front door, pace off exactly one hundred meters, then blow my brains out."

Hamlin couldn't even think of a response.

"You need to be able to find my body so you can be certain of my fate. Also, you will want to retrieve the pistol, as it may be a handy tool to have in the midst of all this. That eliminates any fears over my ultimate end. I will not be knocking on your door, reanimated, in the middle of the night. Frankly, I don't really care if you just leave me there. Should you feel compelled to do otherwise, a cremation ceremony would be acceptable. Just be careful handling my remains."

"What about the plane?" Hamlin asked. "If it is by some fluke able to arrive, they are going to take all of us out of here, correct?"

"Of course. There is no conspiracy to cover any of this up. Once it is properly studied and perfected, we'll be bragging to anyone who will listen about how great this discovery is. Why not let our enemies know what they are in for if they continue to be a problem?"

Francis had never felt so dejected. "This is one of those moments when I'm embarrassed to be a human being. Is there anything else?"

"I think not. You've absorbed enough damage to what remains of your coping mechanisms. Let me quickly summarize with some of the good news."

"Good? Did you say good?"

"In some aspects, yes. You will easily have enough food and supplies to sustain you until spring. The station is sufficiently armed to put an end to the Pechkin and Kuvayev problem. There is no reason to risk any further exposure to the lake water, so spread of the disease should stop. Finding ways to keep people busy and in good spirits may be the biggest challenge to face you going forward."

"Let me ask you a question. It's a thought that I've been repressing. How can we be certain that this virus can't be transmitted indirectly?"

"Respiratory?"

Hamlin shrugged. "I'm just asking."

"My question back to you would be if that is true, why isn't everyone showing symptoms by now?"

"I don't know."

"Nor can you control it either way. I suggest you hold on to as few stressful thoughts as possible. And please feel free to join me later for a drink. Perhaps even a cigar. But for now, I have more plans to make. If you could see yourself out, I would be appreciative."

Hamlin stood. "Sure. I have important places to go and important things to do."

"Oh Doctor, before you go, there is just one more thing."

"Yes, of course. You forgot to put the icing on the cake, no doubt."

"Thank you."

"I beg your pardon."

"I appreciate who you are and what you've brought to us down here. I really feel like you are the one person I can truly trust."

Hamlin was caught off guard. "Okay. Well, I'd say you're welcome, but in truth, if I had a way to leave, I'd be out of here so fast you wouldn't believe it."

"As always, I appreciate your candor. Goodbye Doctor."

Hamlin was happy to leave.

CHAPTER THIRTEEN

The kitchen cleaning wasn't done, so Hamlin relieved Lena of his bucket and supplies. It had progressed quite well, however. It had a nice, clean smell. Perhaps a hint of pine in the air?

"So, now you are Sokolov's little assistant. Did he expose himself to you or ask you to bend over and pick something up off the floor?"

"No, and don't be a jerk. I hate it when he calls me in there. I want to blend in, not stand out. Why doesn't he call one of you in when he wants to wax nostalgic about this station?"

"Oh? Is that what he was doing?"

"Amongst other things, yes. He was telling me that Russia has problems back home. Who knew?"

"I might have had some idea."

"Let's concentrate on the work at hand. What's left to be done? I've had enough depressing talk for one day."

"How surprising that American men can be so accommodating and helpful, especially in the kitchen. Perhaps there is some potential for your country. I believe the counters are ready to be washed down."

"That I can manage. Stand back and watch me go."

"Perhaps I will watch you. That is a nice change of pace."

"Awesome. You can regale me with stories of your life to distract me from the tedium of my task."

"Really?" she said. "I thought you would be tired of hearing my voice. What could be left for me to say?"

"Honestly? All of it. We have never really talked. We were either distracted by our physical exertions or you were saying something designed to encourage my efforts. I really don't know the first thing about you."

She looked at Francis and then a strange expression came over her face. Her mouth was frozen in the open position but no words were forthcoming.

"Are you okay or has my awesome physique taken your breath away?"

She smiled a little and the spell was broken. "No, sorry. I just can't get used to all the strange things that I've seen down here. And to think initially I expected it would be very dull."

Her attention was still clearly focused somewhere over his shoulder. Hamlin spun around to take a look. The door to outside hung open pointlessly. As soon as he saw it, he fancied that he could feel the cold air coming in.

"That is weird. But I can fix it. I'll just shut the door. See how effective creative thinking can be?"

He took one step and felt Lena's hand on his shoulder.

"What is it?" Apart from the door, he had seen nothing else amiss. Yedemsky, who was in charge of security, also seemed quite comfortable with the situation. Or so it looked from this distance.

"It was Sokolov. He just walked out."

That didn't set off any alarms. "Okay. Maybe he's coming right back in."

"I hope so, for his sake. He was only wearing that short sleeved black shirt. He'll freeze in a few moments out there."

Now bells and whistles were going off in Hamlin's mind. Big time.

"Really? Just the shirt?"

"Yes. I saw him clearly."

"Wait here." Hamlin started moving toward the door.

A single gunshot cleaved through the soft drone of conversation, exploding in their ears as it echoed through the building. The speed of its assault was stunningly fast and totally unexpected. Everyone jumped. In its wake came the contrast complete silence.

"No, no, no. What have you done?" Hamlin rushed to the door, hesitated only briefly before running outside with only his shirt and pants on. He was careful to choose a straight heading, and counted off paces as he went. He was nowhere near one hundred when he saw Sokolov sprawled on the snow. There had been no time for the drifting powder to cover any of the carnage. There could be no doubt of his fate. The evidence was sprayed in a terribly large and graphic pattern over the otherwise pristine white. If nothing else, the man knew how to handle a firearm. Hamlin wondered why that thought had formed in his mind.

He walked over to where the now former leader of the station lay. He bent over and pulled the pistol out of his limp fingers.

"I guess you weren't feeling so good after all." Tears formed in his eyes and not from the wind. Now he was feeling the cold. "At least this is over for you. I hope you don't end up being the smart one in all of this."

Hamlin couldn't take any more and returned to the barracks. He was shaking violently when he stepped back in. He had everyone's attention now, whether he wanted it or not.

"Are you crazy?" Lena's voice was angry and concerned all at once. "Somebody get him a blanket. And close that door!"

She suddenly exuded authority and people immediately responded.

"Why would you do that? And where is Sokolov?"

"He's dead," Hamlin stammered through quivering lips. "He shot himself."

"What?" The others had all stopped what they were doing. You could have heard a pin drop.

"He told me that if he contracted the disease from Kuvayev's bite, that he would kill himself before he transformed. He told me how and where so that I could find him and so we would all know for certain and not have to speculate. I...I just didn't realize it was going to happen this fast. He told me he was feeling fine."

"Probably not the first and only time he lied," Lena said in a softer voice. She pointed at one of the bystanders. "Get a shot of whiskey. There's some left in the cupboard. Bring it over here."

She took the pistol from Hamlin's hand. He offered no resistance. She observed it carefully.

"It's clean. Good." Another crew member was singled out. "You. Take this. I want two people on guard at all times. And how long until the patrol comes back? Anybody?"

"Another forty-five minutes," Yedemsky said.

"Okay. Let's focus on the task at hand. I'm going to get Hamlin here warmed up. Yedemsky–you and Grebenshchikov keep watch until the patrol returns. We'll figure out a new schedule then. The rest of you, finish cleaning and put all that stuff away." She looked for, and then made eye contact with the Zoya, the only other female in the group. "Zoya, when this is done, pick a volunteer and make something for lunch. We will get through this, friends. Everyone stay calm."

She observed Hamlin as he stood shaking. "As for you, come over here. Let's get you sitting down. Where is that blanket?"

Hamlin found himself drifting off. Things that were happening around him began to softly fade. He transformed back to his classroom at the university. Sights, sounds, even smells made the experience seem almost real. He recalled many of the individual students, their strengths and weaknesses in his courses, and the different personalities. His fondness for teaching returned; the daily opportunity to do or say something that could have a lifelong effect on someone's life. And then the scene was gone–replaced instantly by a vision of Deborah smiling and waving him in as he returned home from work. He heart leapt for joy.

"Francis?"

Lena's voice refocused him on the present. She was offering him a glass with a shot of brown liquid brooding in the bottom of it.

"Here, take this."

He discovered that someone had draped a heavy blanket over his shoulders. He lifted the vessel and drained it in a single gulp. It warmed his throat all the way down.

"I'll take that." She pulled the now empty glass from his hand.

Hamlin looked down and noticed that several scratches and imperfections in the floor lined up by coincidence to form an almost perfect isosceles triangle just to the left of his foot. He was surely losing his mind, he decided.

Lena patted him on the shoulder. "You just stay here and get warm. I'll check in on you in a few minutes."

"Okay," Francis responded. It's all he could come up with. He was making plans to catch the next train out of there.

There wasn't time to deal with his issues, Lena figured. There were simply too many other things to do.

An indeterminate period of time passed before Hamlin snapped out of it. Suddenly things came back into focus. He stood up slowly and then draped the blanket over the back of his chair. He looked around the room to get a feel for what was going on. Only faint, muddy visions remained of what had transpired since he'd found Sokolov.

"There you are. Back with us, are you?" Lena walked over and gave him a quick visual evaluation. "How are you feeling?"

Hamlin had to think about it. "Okay." The truth was more like numb. "What's going on? It seems so quiet."

She thought carefully about how to word her response.

"We're just doing some cleaning up."

Hamlin looked back toward the kitchen. Only Zoya was there and she was obviously cooking something on the big, old stove.

Lena positioned herself directly in his field of vision. She was almost the same height.

"Not that. We are disposing of Sokolov and Konstantine in a good and proper manner. We had to add some dignity and finality to their ultimate fate."

Hamlin was still trying to get his mind to function at normal speed.

"What do you mean?"

She had a very determined look. "We will no longer leave these abominations to lie around and haunt us in various ways. And the outer lab was simply unacceptable to leave in its state. If I may say so, in my opinion, it was also terribly disrespectful to Konstantine, our friend and trustworthy coworker."

"So what are you doing about it?"

"Sokolov has been cleaned and prepared as best we could. They are dropping him off at the lab as we speak. When they are finished, I think it would be good for the entire remaining crew to go out there and watch. We will use the lab as a pyre to remove this blight from our presence. When we are finished, there are but two issues that demand our attention."

"Pechkin and Kuvayev."

She nodded. "Yes. Once they have been dealt with, we will come up with a new, workable agenda for getting through the rest of winter in a productive manner. Surely there are still good and positive things we can accomplish. Do you not think so, Doctor?"

Hamlin couldn't think of anything, but surely she had to be right.

"Yes, of course."

"Find your warmest clothes and get ready. As soon as the Cat returns, we will shuttle people out to the outer lab. It will take several trips, so be prepared."

"Yes. How much time do we have?"

"They should be back any moment now."

"Very well." He shuffled listlessly toward his room.

She was right about being warmly dressed. It was a calm evening, but even then the cold was brutal. In the end, they all huddled together in a tight, little group. Francis was just thankful that he couldn't see inside the room. He already had a lifetime's worth of that memory.

Barinov and Kravchuk volunteered to go in and start the blaze. They soon came out (who would want to linger in that horrible environment?) and joined the others. They all stood in silence waiting for signs of the fire. It took some time. At first, there was nothing. Then all they could see was a soft orange flicker reflecting on the outside door, which they had left ajar to facilitate airflow to feed the flames. The glow grew gradually brighter, and soon the sounds of popping could be heard as the fire began to consume various materials inside the lab. One particularly loud bang was accompanied by the sound of breaking glass. No one cared.

Finally the flames were visible through the open door. Soon they were licking at the wall and upwards toward the roof. Momentum shifted in favor of the inferno as it grew quickly and simply engulfed the building. Flames shot out through holes in the walls and roof. Hamlin could actually feel the heat radiating through the air. All of their faces glowed in the reflection of the now impressive conflagration.

The flames continued to rise higher. When they reached their zenith, Hamlin actually started to feel uncomfortably hot for the first time in weeks. The unstoppable, cleansing power in the flames gave them all a sense of peace. At least a part of the horror would be erased forever. There would be little more than ashes left by the time the fire went out. It finally reached a point where consumable materials were starting to dwindle, and the flames diminished gradually until the show was no longer as impressive. It was clear that it was time to return to the barracks. They all felt a little better–like they had taken control and changed their situation for the better.

When they returned, the food was ready. They all sat and had a decent group meal. There was some talk, and even a couple of moments of laughter. Everyone started to reminisce about Sokolov. There were many stories to tell. Most had a theme of dislike due to the way Sokolov chose to manage the outpost, but there could be no doubt that there was respect present as well. Hamlin didn't have anything to add–besides, he felt it would be disrespectful to the men and women who had served with him much longer than he had. He was the rookie here.

After relaxing and listening to the stories as best he could (when they spoke English), he had a sudden thought flash through his mind. He couldn't be sure if it meant anything or not, but he thought it might. He didn't want to bring it up in front of the whole crew. He got up casually, strolled over and sat beside Lena.

"So, how are you now, Doctor?" she said. "Feeling all right?"

He nodded. "Yes. Not bad, all things considered. Say, could I steal a moment or two of your time?"

"Now?"

He nodded again.

"Very well. Your place or mine?"

"Sokolov's office, if you don't think it too inappropriate."

"It depends what you have in mind. But, yes, that is fine. I will follow you. Please."

He tried to walk casually, afraid everyone would be watching them go, but that only made his movements seem stiff and unnatural. Thankfully he didn't trip and fall over anything. No significant amount of attention seemed to be paid by the rest of the crew to the fact that they were about to enter the former boss's command post. That was good. Hamlin didn't want a riot or mutiny on his hands.

He stood aside and let Lena enter. He stepped in and closed the door gently.

"All right. What is this all about, Doctor?"

"When I was talking to Sokolov earlier, he said something that I now find strange. At the time, it seemed both casual and perfectly normal. But knowing what I know now, I am wondering if there was some hidden meaning."

"What did he say?"

"He said, '*why not join me later in my office for a drink and maybe a cigar.*'"

"That's it?"

"I'm not sure those were the exact words he used, but yes."

"I agree with your first assessment. It seems perfectly normal to me."

"But he was only minutes away from taking his own life. He must have known at that point. So why invite me back later?"

"I don't know," she said. "Do you think it is in some way important?"

"Maybe. I do kind of feel that way, but, I just don't know why."

"Well, let's start by assuming it was a message. Those aren't very many words. It shouldn't be that hard to decipher. Try to work it out and I will help as best I can."

Hamlin turned and let his eyes wander around the room. The words in question really meant nothing special to him. And yet...

"The first thing he said was to meet him later. So...was he referring to coming back into his office after he died?"

"Hmm. Either that or he was inviting you to kill yourself as well. That would be one way of meeting him later."

"In a manner of thinking. But then he also said for a drink."

"And maybe a smoke."

Hamlin walked around behind the massive desk. On one side was a beautiful wooden cabinet.

"This is the liquor cabinet. Maybe we should open it and look inside."

She didn't seem to be picking up much enthusiasm for Hamlin's quest.

"All right. I don't see any harm in that. I'm not sure I see anything good coming out of it either, but what the hell? Maybe we can find something nice to get drunk on, and then we can make out on his desk."

"I'm thinking the current atmosphere isn't exactly conducive to romance."

He reached for the ornate knobs on the two door adjoining doors. It took only minimal effort and they both swung open. The cabinet was jammed full of a variety of liquor, most of which Hamlin was totally unfamiliar with.

"He's got a nice stash in here."

"That makes me think of another issue," Lena said. "We should probably secure this room or it will get scavenged. And like you are thinking, there might be things of importance in here. His booze and Cuban cigars will attract a lot of attention from the crew."

Hamlin bent over to get a better view. So far, bottles were all he could see. He had been hoping for something more significant, although he had no idea what.

"Do you see anything else?"

"No. I wonder if I should take these bottles out before I give up?" On a whim, he slid his fingers along the inside of the top trim board. He felt a small item stuck to the wood. He was able to grab a corner. It pulled out with minimal effort.

Now Lena showed some interest.

"What is it?"

"It seems to be a small paper envelope. I think it might be handmade. I also think I might be a genius. There's something in it." He started to pull it apart.

"What is in there?"

Hamlin had it out by now. "It's a key. Just a small one."

"Oh." She didn't seem to know how to react.

He held it up and scrutinized it.

"It says *Savinelli*. Does that mean anything to you?"

"No." She spoke softly and seemed to be thinking it over. "Wait, how small is that key?"

Hamlin held it so she could see it.

"I might know what that is. You said he also suggested having a cigar, correct?"

"He did, yes."

"Where is his humidor? I bet the key will fit it."

Based on a previous visit to the room, Francis knew exactly where it was. He walked over to the shelf where the ornate box sat. The key slid smoothly into the small locking mechanism on the front.

"Bingo." He opened it carefully. "Wow. I'm not much of a smoker, but does that smell good."

She was walking toward him now. "It is lined with cedar, no doubt. Do you see anything?"

"Lots of big, expensive cigars. Oh, and a few smaller and only slightly less expensive cigars. Nothing else."

"Are you sure?"

She was beside him now, peering intensely into the box. For some reason, the quest had now taken on significance for her.

"Just stogies. Sorry."

"Wait. Doctor, do you smoke?"

"No. Just at stag parties or if someone at work has a baby with their actual spouse. Why?"

"You do not have a humidor, then."

"No."

"Empty the cigars out of it. Carefully, of course."

"Umm, okay. Why?"

"Just do it."

He complied. Each one was handled with the same care he would extend to a stick of dynamite.

"Oh come now, they won't break. Just dump it out."

"No, no," he said. "This will only take a few more seconds."

He removed the remaining smokes with care, then tipped and observed the box. "Sorry, I don't see anything in here. It appears to be a dead end."

"But there is something in there that shouldn't be. No one puts a felt liner in a humidor."

It looked natural enough in there. Hamlin never would have thought of it. He took his finger and tried to coax it out. The back corner lifted a little.

"I think you're right. It seems like it is just a little bit loose in there." With a renewed effort, he was able to get it to pull out completely. Its removal revealed a small, folded piece of paper. Lena reached it and carefully pulled it out.

"What have we here? What secrets were you hiding, Sokolov?"

She unfolded it.

Hamlin tried to see. "What does it say?"

She frowned. "It is a number."

"Just a number?"

"Yes." She seemed to be deep in thought.

He reached over and reclaimed possession of the paper.

"7846392001068375300." He read the digits slowly. "That's one hell of a big number. What does it mean?"

She was staring blankly off into space. "I don't know."

"But it must be important."

"It would seem so."

"Damn."

"Exactly." She seemed to break out of her paralysis. "I think we have been in here long enough. We will draw more attention and speculation the longer we are here. Let's put everything back exactly as it was and get out of here."

"What about the paper? Put it back as well?"

"No. We should take it."

"Good idea. I'll stash it someplace safe."

Lena was outwardly calm, but on the inside a bomb had gone off.

"I have an idea. Let me copy those numbers down. Then we can each hide them. If they end up being important, I wouldn't want to see them get lost. Besides, that way we can both study them when we're alone and try to figure out what they mean."

'Sure. I think Sokolov keeps a pad on his desk. I'll put the cigars back and close up the liquor cabinet."

"Good," she said. "Very good."

They got a few sidelong glances when they returned, but nothing too noticeable. The group met informally for some time, talking about issues of security and how to move forward. A loose structure was agreed upon for administrative purposes and immediate duties were assigned. Hamlin volunteered to go out on a hunting mission. He was getting antsy and feeling like he wasn't really contributing much.

The rotation for guard duty was reaffirmed. Also, a suggestion was made and accepted regarding daily checking and cleaning of the guns. Questions about ammunition and the status of the weapon stock in Sokolov's office came up. All eyes slowly turned toward Hamlin. He quickly agreed to go in and check, inviting Barinov to come in with him for independent confirmation. That seemed to relax the crew just a little. Francis got the distinct impression that if he started to lord it over them, there would be a quick mutiny. His questionable authority over the station would come to an abrupt end. And that was fine at least in one regard–he didn't want it anyway.

There were no surprises regarding the weapons. There were two handguns and two rifles, which corresponded with what Sokolov had said to Hamlin earlier. Barinov gave some indication that he would have liked to do some snooping, but Hamlin found the backbone to put a quick end to that. He ushered the slightly disgruntled driller back to the group.

The end of another long and disconcerting day was now fast approaching. A handful of the crew decided to play darts, while the rest gradually dispersed and headed for bed. Hamlin had guard duty starting at six in the morning. After that, he would catch the next hunting party and go out searching for trouble. It was more than enough to convince him that he needed to get some rest. He decided that he would meditate on the possible meaning of the numbers from the cigar case before falling asleep. It was a good plan. But as he lay down and released his mind to ponder the possibilities, sleep overtook him and all conscious thought disappeared. Dream filled slumber was the best he could do for this night.

CHAPTER FOURTEEN

The alarm woke Hamlin in the morning. He didn't feel as refreshed as he had hoped for. His body gave little sign of cooperation as he forced himself into motion. He just made it in time to start his allotted time for guard duty. Temporary control of the handgun was relinquished to him along with control of the pile of Russian magazines. He wasn't sure which one he wanted least.

Soon people began to gradually filter in for breakfast. There wasn't a lot of life in the group. Smells of tea, coffee, and toast soon filled the air. A good Samaritan asked Hamlin if he wanted anything and he was soon set up with a steaming mug of instant coffee and two pieces of toast with marmalade. His outlook on the day began to slowly improve. At least, that was, until the power failed.

Francis had just taken a bite of toast when the lights abruptly went out. The room was pitch black and silent except for a few mumbling complaints. The sound of drawers opening and closing gave indication that someone was searching for a source of light. Finally, the weak beam of a flashlight punched a small hole in the darkness.

"Wait, don't move. Somebody will get hurt." Hamlin matched the gruff voice to Barinov.

Then the lights flickered and came back on.

"Back-up generator kicked in." Barinov added.

The room went back to normal. Hamlin took another bite of toast and washed it down with strong coffee.

"Hey, Hamlin." Barinov had sought him out.

"What just happened?"

Barinov shrugged. "Hard to say. Probably something minor. But we absolutely cannot run on one generator. Without power, we're in big trouble. We can't take the risk of not having a back-up unit available all the time. I need to take a crew out to troubleshoot and make repairs."

Hamlin nodded. "Of course."

"I'll take Yedemsky and Kravchuk. Hopefully it can be fixed quickly. I suggest we get ready and go now."

"That's fine, and thank you by the way. We'll continue on here. Is there anything we can do to help?"

Barinov wasn't receptive. "No. Let me round up my crew and get tools. We'll need the Cat, so first patrol might have to wait."

"No problem. These repairs should be the priority."

"Good." He nodded and turned to make arrangements. Hamlin had to admit that it felt flattering to have someone seek his approval before committing to action. His feelings would no doubt change if the crew was disgruntled rather than accommodating. Of course, none of this changed his current situation. He looked at the magazines and wished he'd brought some from home. The idea occurred to him that he could spend some time trying to figure the numbers out for Sokolov's office. They weren't memorized in his mind, but he could at least think of hypothetical associations for what they could mean. That would be a good starting point. The first questions was…why so many digits?

Barinov and his crew were soon ready and left for the generator shed. It was located near the drilling facility and would take a few minutes by Cat to get there. Hamlin wished them well and resumed analyzing Sokolov's code.

It was a huge string of numbers; no doubt about that. Hamlin thought from memory that it was twelve or thirteen digits altogether. So what possible uses could it have? What could it possibly stand for? He decided to start by looking at usage of numbers in a general sense.

Numbers were commonly used in codes. But what kind of codes? If you ordered a parcel, you could track it on-line by entering the correct code. It was usually a very long string of numbers. Hamlin decided that thought was worth hanging on to. Maybe there was a parcel or package or piece of equipment somewhere here that had this number stamped on it or the box it was packaged in. He would run that past Lena later when they could be alone.

There were address codes. Zip codes, postal codes, street numbers, numbers associated with certain buildings. But how would that apply down here? And this number just seemed too large for that. So…rejected.

Stars and celestial bodies were sometimes identified by numbers. Nobody could come up with enough original names to cover them all. But again, how would that apply here? Rejected.

Licenses and government issues identifications usually had large numbers to identify them; although letters were also usually dispersed in them, like license plates on cars. Could it apply here in some way? Possibly, but it didn't really jump out at him. Rejected.

Serial numbers were commonly long strings of numbers and/or letters. The size might be just about right. So what would it mean? Again, could it be a certain piece of equipment that was here? Perhaps. He decided to hang on to that thought as well.

Suddenly he had a brain wave. Radio frequencies. They could be identified by their unique frequencies, commonly expressed in hertz. A typical radio station signal would be measured at over ten million hertz. The numbers could be a specific signal, or perhaps multiple signals. If that was the case, however, then how would they know when or how to split the number up? Francis didn't have an answer, but he still liked the possibility. He kept this idea filed.

There were phone numbers. Depending on the country code and area code, they could be quite long. Maybe it was a direct line to someone or something important. But phones didn't work down here. Sokolov could only communicate by shortwave radio. Now the light went on. Maybe the numbers were a shortwave frequency that went straight to Moscow or someone else of great significance. Yes, he liked that one. He wondered if Lena or any of the other crew members knew how to operate a shortwave. One step at a time, he reasoned.

"Hey, big fella," Lena said, trying to imitate an American accent.

Hamlin hadn't noticed her until the last possible second. He nearly jumped when she spoke, but fought off the impulse at the last possible moment.

"Hey yourself. Nice accent."

"I'm working on it. Speaking of which, what are you working on? It looks rather uneventful over here."

"Looks can be deceiving. It has been very exciting in my little corner of the station. Why, just a few minutes ago, I was drinking a coffee. Since then, I have been busy daydreaming. Can you see where I am going with this? It's just one thing after another."

"Okay, I am convinced. I envy your life. Congratulations."

"As well you should. So what's happening with you?"

"Well, I was having my shower when all the lights went off. That was an exciting moment, I can tell you."

"Hmm. Too bad you didn't have to come walking out naked. But I see you managed to dress yourself nicely."

"Perhaps congratulations are in order."

"Sorry. I would never say anything designed to encourage a woman to stay fully clothed. It's just not happening."

"I see. I feel that I should do nothing to contribute to your delinquency. No public nudity."

"How about private?"

"Open for debate. Say, why don't you come and find me when you're finished with security duty. I would like to talk to you about last night."

Hamlin nodded. "I've been thinking about that. We should talk."

She rose to go. "Until later. And do be careful not to fire that thing prematurely."

Hamlin absorbed the insinuation with good humor. "That hasn't been a problem."

Barinov pulled the Cat up as close as he could to the building that housed the generators. There was simply no reason to walk any further than necessary outside in the cold.

"I'm going to leave it running," Barinov said. "That way we don't have to worry about restarting it. I do not want to get stuck out here."

They all hopped out and started grabbing tools and equipment. Yedemsky reached the door first. He pushed on it and it swung open easily.

"Hey! Some stupid ass didn't shut the door tightly. It's amazing this place didn't drift full of snow."

As they stepped in, Barinov threw the light switch. The room lit up and to their mutual relief, everything looked to be in order.

"What's so hard about shutting a damn door?" Barinov growled. "These little mistakes always seem to bite us in the ass somehow. You'd think all these PhD's would never do anything wrong."

The generator that was still operating sounded fine. No unusual or disconcerting noises at all. That was a good start.

"Okay. Let's see what's wrong with this dead one. Start with the fuel line and pump."

The smell of diesel fuel soon permeated the air.

"No problem with fuel," Kravchuk said.

"Don't pour it all over you," Barinov growled. "It is flammable, remember."

"Shit! Found the problem."

The other two walked over to where Yedemsky was standing. By then, it was obvious to all of them. The wires from the starting motor and fuel pump will all just hanging there.

"Son of a bitch!" Barinov yelled in frustration.

Yedemsky leaned in close. "There are not too badly damaged. If this is all that is wrong, we can fix it quickly."

Kravchuk was subdued. "But how did it happen? This is not wear and tear. Somebody vandalized this machine."

"Well," Barinov snarled, "there's not too fucking many of us left to choose from. We're down to ten, so it shouldn't be hard to figure out. We can go through that when we get back to the barracks. The question I have is, why?"

They were all yelling to be heard over the sound of the second generator.

"At least they only damaged one of the two," Yedemsky said. "It could have been worse."

"You're right there. If I would have done this, I could have shut both of them down for at least a week. Then where would we all be?" Barinov almost looked proud of his potential to wreak havoc.

"You're forgetting Pechkin and Kuvayev," Kravchuk said.

They all stopped cold at that thought.

"Say, we did bring a gun, right?" Yedemsky looked for the reaction on Barinov's face. It wasn't encouraging.

"Shit. I never once thought of it."

Another awkward moment of silence.

"How about I go back and get it?" Kravchuk suggested. "It will only take a few minutes. You can get started on the repairs. We should have some protection, just in case. What do you think?"

Barinov frowned. "The hell with it. If these wires are the only problem, we'll have this fixed before you could get back here anyway. Let's just do it and get out of here."

Kravchuk wasn't thrilled. The vision of Konstantine's destroyed body was still fresh in his mind. "Are you sure?"

Yedemsky already had his gloves off and was separating the individual wires.

"Yes, I'm sure." Barinov was not a subtle negotiator. "If you're worried about it, then either try to help or look for something we could use as a weapon. Just don't stand there constantly whining."

Yedemsky was actually smiling. "This is not too bad. I can fix it in five minutes. Go get me some connectors."

Kravchuk was already moving. Anything to speed this process along was his top priority now. He knew exactly where the supplies they needed were kept. He reached the grey, metal shelving unit and opened one of the small drawers. The connectors were small, so he pulled his gloves off and stuffed them temporarily into his pockets.

He wasted no time in returning.

"Here. Are you ready for these yet?"

"Not yet. Hold on." Yedemsky had removed the damaged connectors and was stripping the wires to accept the new ones.

"Careful." Barinov recognized the effort to work quickly. "Don't cut yourself. You don't have to rush so much."

"Okay. Give me a connector."

Kravchuk was happy to comply. While Yedemsky attached it, he couldn't help but look toward the doorway. The door was still shut tightly. Good.

The shed was rather dimly lit by six incandescent bulbs. They cast shadows around the room and left various little pockets where there was little direct light at all. It created a rather somber atmosphere.

"Okay. Another connector, please."

It was still freezing, but at least there was some small amount of heat in the building. When designing it, the thought was that it wouldn't be good for the generators to operate in the ambient outdoor temperatures. Extreme cold wasn't just hard on living things. It could also cause a long list of mechanical problems.

"Another one, Kravchuk."

Barinov had sauntered over to the big tanks that held the fuel for the generators. There was a clear tube that allowed for a quick check of the remaining levels. It had to last through the winter until more reserves could be brought in once summer arrived. The levels were fine.

"Okay, another."

"How many more?"

"Umm, just three more."

Barinov was back. He checked the oil level in the now idle motor.

"Okay, another please." Yedemsky was really moving now.

From this distance, in the poor lighting, no one saw the door handle start to move.

"Fuel and oil levels are good. Let's finish up and get out of here."

"Won't you have to reset the controls?" Yedemsky asked while he worked. "This one is still the primary generator. Change it to back-up and we'll be good to go."

"Right. I forgot." Barinov headed for the controls.

The outside door opened just a sliver.

"Another connector, Kravchuk. Just one to go."

The door swung wide open. It was still unnoticed.

The sound of a heavy switch being thrown echoed through the shed.

"Okay, everything is set. Finish that fucking thing and let's go back in the heat."

"Last connector, please."

Kravchuk gave it over, and then started to put his gloves back on.

Kuvayev, or what now remained of him, moved slowly into the doorway.

"All right. That's it. Just let me make this last connection. There!"

Yedemsky stood upright. "Let's just fire it up as a test, and then we're good to go."

Kravchuk glanced toward the doorway. His blood immediately turned to ice.

"Oh God."

Yedemsky saw the look on his face and turned toward his line of sight.

"Shit. Hey, Barinov."

"What?"

"We've got company."

He too looked at the open door.

"Son of a bitch."

Kuvayev somehow had one boot still on. It was all he wore. And yet, the heat was still pouring off him. Wisps of evaporating moisture emanated from his bare skin. His hair and beard were pointing in every possible direction. His head was lowered, but his eyes were locked on them. He was swaying slightly from side to side. And his eyes were unnaturally washed out, the irises a pale greyish-white color. His mouth was moving but so sound was discernible. To them, he looked gigantic and unstoppable.

Barinov risked a sideways glance. "Kravchuk, did you see anything we could use as a weapon?"

Kravchuk was very close to soiling himself. "A hammer, a crowbar, and a propane cylinder."

Yedemsky was shaking visibly. Barinov knew things were hanging by a very fine thread.

"Okay. Let's all move back toward the workbench and try to find something to protect ourselves. Move very slowly."

Kravchuk whirled around too quickly and triggered an automatic response. Kuvayev roared like a crazed beast and ran toward them with unimaginable fury. He was fast as well. Faster than any of them.

Yedemsky raised his arm in a defensive posture and screamed. Kuvayev was going to reach him first.

Hamlin was once again surprised out of a deep thought by the close approach of another crew member.

"Oh, Dr. Zhabin." He remembered to smile. Manners still counted. "How are you?"

"Bored, I'm afraid. I'm next on the schedule so I came to relieve you."

Hamlin checked the clock. "I still have forty-five minutes to go. You're early."

"I don't mind. My laundry is finished and my sleeping quarters cleaned. I don't have time to get involved in anything else and frankly, there isn't anything else to get involved with. I'll grab one of those fine magazines and get started."

Francis stood; his legs and back showing the signs of being seated for a long period of time.

"Very well, then. And thank you. Perhaps laundry would be a good thing for me to do as well."

"I believe you westerners refer to this as *living the dream*. Enjoy what remains of your morning."

Hamlin took several tentative steps, not really committed to his next course of action. Laundry did make sense. But he had another thought as well. He turned and headed for the hallway that led to Sokolov's room. He walked with purpose, like he had every reason to be doing what he was doing. He reached it unchallenged, then opened the door in a businesslike manner and stepped inside. He immediately closed it and breathed a sigh of relief. He looked around and took stock.

"Okay," he whispered to himself. "Brilliant. Now what?"

He sauntered over to the bookshelves and looked at some of the titles. Most of them were Russian and meant nothing to him. There were some in English but none that caught his interest for any reason. So much for that.

He walked over and sat in Sokolov's chair. There were several drawers in the desk that he had never seen the insides of before. With a slight guilty feeling, he started to open them one by one. What he found was typical for any business person's desk. Pens, pencils and markers; writing pads, folders, various little pins and clips; nothing unusual or noteworthy. The larger drawers had hanging files, but they all appeared to be written in Russian and so were of no interest. He slid the last one shut, and then folded his hands behind his head and leaned back to get comfortable while he thought.

"Making yourself at home?"

Hamlin nearly fell off the chair.

"Lena! Don't do that! I could have fallen and broke my neck."

She smiled, seemingly quite happy with herself.

"Well, I wouldn't want that. Your services are badly needed at this station."

He was sitting quite upright and balanced now.

"Right. I'm a first rate researcher and we all know it."

She was walking slowly toward him.

"That's not what I meant."

He snickered out loud. "Lena, if being suggestive was a sport, you'd be Olympic class. You could write books on the subject and go on a lecture tour."

"Why, thank you. We all have our unique skills."

She grabbed the handles on his chair and spun it so he was facing her directly. Then she whirled around lithely and sat on his lap. She started to gyrate slowly but perceptively.

"Well now," Hamlin said. "This is professional behavior at its finest. I'm guessing Sokolov didn't do much of this. This chair is probably wondering what the hell is going on."

"I'm not worried about the chair." She had switched over to her husky voice.

"Well, to be honest, I'm getting less so myself. Our priorities do change over time."

"So, tell me, Doctor," she said as her hips continued to do their marvelous work, "what were you after in here? I fear you were being bad."

"Naughty seems like a better word currently."

"And what about those numbers? What has a smart man like you managed to figure out?"

Concentration was getting progressively harder. So was something else. He slid his hands up under her shirt and went exploring.

"I, umm, tried to, you know, uh, think about that. I did. I have some, oh my, ideas."

"Doctor, you seem to be having trouble formulating your thoughts. Are you under some sort of duress?" She increased her speed.

"Oh, I, umm, no. That's just, you know, we could always...just...get to the...ah. Give me a minute, will you?"

He looked up aimlessly at the chart on the wall over her shoulders. It was of Antarctica and showed the location of their station. But his mind was elsewhere. This was going to happen soon and he wanted it badly. There could be some collateral issues to resolve afterwards, but they seemed incredibly petty right now.

"Here is my best move." She made a minor alteration to her speed and pressure points. She was right. It was the best.

"How is this even possible?" Hamlin hissed through clenched teeth, knowing it was too late to stop the process. The inevitable was going to happen. He teetered on the edge for a few seconds before arching himself against her to create more pressure where he needed it the most, and then bucked and moaned while nature took its course.

"My, my. What is wrong, Doctor? It would seem you are having some sort of seizure. It seemed to come upon you rather quickly."

"Had," he corrected. "I had a seizure. Oh my. I think I made a mess. And I'm not sure I appreciate your *quickly* comment."

She smiled. "And that is your problem. I'm wondering how you're going to walk back through the station now."

He looked over her shoulder again. The same chart caught his attention again. Suddenly he knew why.

She looked at his expression and frowned. "I know how men are, but they don't always lose interest quite that fast."

A smile slowly spread over his face.

"Lena. I think know what the numbers might be."

CHAPTER FIFTEEN

Barinov lived the longest by simply doing nothing. He stood silently and motionless while first Kravchuk and then Yedemsky drew the attention of Kuvayev. They both died horribly, right before his eyes, and he had done nothing. *Blunt force trauma*, he had thought to himself quietly while trying to work out a plan for escape. Kuvayev was brutally strong. Kravchuk only lasted a few seconds, until he had been thrown against one of the generators, striking it head first. It didn't take a medical professional to see the obvious damage that the impact had on his skull, or what was now left of it. The sound it made was sickening.

Yedemsky had been pummeled by huge blows, one arm clearly and loudly broken by the onslaught. Unfortunately, he had still been alive when Kuvayev decided it was time to use his teeth and began to feed in a violent frenzy of torn flesh, clothing, and spurting blood. The screams were unlike anything Barinov had ever heard.

But the shock he felt had to be overcome by the realization that an opportunity was being presented. By now, Kuvayev was completely engrossed in his attack and never gave any indication that he even remembered that Barinov was there. So, he began to walk slowly but steadily toward the open door.

He stepped through the doorway. One last fleeting looked indicated that he had gone completely unnoticed. Barinov turned toward the idling Cat and literally walked head-on into the waiting teeth of Pechkin.

His shrieks were muffled as they travelled along the snowy ground and caused no one any consternation. He, unfortunately, had to live through the worst nightmare anyone could imagine. And this was going to take some time.

"What is it? Tell me!"
"Latitude and longitude."
She spun around and looked at the chart.
"My God, you may be right. Do you have the numbers on you?"
He pulled a piece of paper out of his pants pocket.
"Recite them to me."

He did as directed.

"78463920010068375300."

"Okay." She had scratched them down on a piece of paper. "Now we separate them like this."

Hamlin looked down at the paper. It was a subtle change.

784639200-1068375300

"That's not as impressive as you seem to think it is."

She smiled. "Watch this." She wrote them down again. Hamlin saw the transformation.

78°57'39200" 106°83'75300"

"Son of a bitch. So where exactly is that?"

She picked up the paper and looked at the chart.

"It is here. Or at least very close to here." She was pointing at the station.

Hamlin was amazed that he had solved it. "Awesome. So what does it mean in practical terms?"

"I have an idea. When the repair crew returns, you and I will go out. We will say we are hunting. We'll program in these coordinates in the GPS and drive out to see where and what it is. Then, hopefully, the mystery will be solved."

Hamlin nodded. "I like it. Good plan. Hopefully those guys won't be too long. Now I'm kind of excited."

"You were kind of excited five minutes ago. Don't you have some cleaning up to do anyway?"

"True enough. You run some sort of diversion and I'll sneak through."

She patted him on his shoulder. "Sorry, my good doctor. I have done enough for you. You are now on your own."

"Fine. What the hell. It's hard to get mad at you when you do things like this. I'll just walk right through like I own the place."

"Good luck. I'll follow from a safe distance to see if you make it or not."

An hour went by before anyone vocalized concerns about the repair crew. At that point, the worry was nothing more than that they could be having trouble making the repairs. But the lights were still on so the fears were small. How bad could it be?

As time ticked by, the stress level rose proportionately. People began to cast furtive glances toward the door. The old clock on the wall became a popular target for wandering eyes. Small groups formed and words were now whispered rather than spoken out loud.

All seven crew members congregated in the common area. Francis decided that seven people had never looked like so few. The room was noticeably empty.

Lena and Zoya had grouped together and had an extended but unrevealed conversation. Francis decided to join them. Lena had shown the most aptitude toward leadership of them all since Sokolov left them so abruptly.

"Hi." It wasn't much of an introductory remark, but Hamlin was running intellectually low.

"Hello Dr. Hamlin." Lena's face was neutral. Dr. Grekov was noticeably stressed.

He decided to cut through the preliminaries.

"Look, I'm not mechanic, but isn't it safe to say that this is a very long time for a repair of this nature?"

"We don't know what the extent of the repairs are," Lena said.

"Five hours is a long time," Zoya interjected.

Hamlin nodded. "That's what I thought. In that instance, is there anything we can do?"

Both of them stared openly at Dr. Sayanski.

"Are you asking me if it is time to panic? Because the answer to that, I believe, is no."

Francis was disappointed with her response. He felt like some sort of action was now required.

"Fine. I suppose that's what I was asking. It just feels like we should do something. Sitting around and speculating just isn't healthy down here."

Lena stared at a scratch in the surface of the table, and then traced it with her finger.

"For clarification purposes, we could run out there and check on them, I suppose. It is a waste of time and resources, in reality. But we could bring an end to this unproductive conjecture, if nothing else."

Now they were getting somewhere.

"Does that old Cat still run?"

There was a bulky, old Cat sitting off to the side of the barracks connected to an equally bulky old trailer. Hamlin had never seen it run, but had heard some of the crew members mention it before.

She shrugged. "I don't know any more than you do. I suspect it does. We can try to start it. It moves rather slowly if I remember correctly, but it will get us there; if it will run."

"You and me?" Hamlin figured it was his idea.

Zoya leaned in toward Lena. "What about me? Can I come too?"

Lena shook her head as if in rebellion against the decision making powers being given to her, then waved her hand.

"Fine. What do I care? Let's load up the entire crew."

Hamlin stood. "Seating is limited, I'm afraid."

Lena stood as well. She turned toward the two tables that held all the remaining crew members.

"Dr. Hamlin is concerned about the repair crew," she announced. "We're going to start the old Cat and see if there is anything we can do to help them along. We shouldn't be long."

The others simply sat and stared in response. No optimism was generated by the announcement. Nothing had been working out very well of late.

They gathered by the door and left as a group. Hamlin was surprised when Dr. Grekov climbed in the driver's seat. Lena carried two rifles with her. She handed one to Francis without any ado, and then directed him to sit in the middle.

"I want easy access if a shot presents itself. I do not want to miss any opportunity to put an end to this shit, once and for all."

Francis slid in, careful to keep the gun pointed away from them.

"Here we go," Zoya said.

The engine turned over freely and started immediately. That was a relief. Lena disconnected the cord for the electric block heater before she jumped in.

"All right, Dr. Grekov. Let's go find out what is taking them so long."

The machine was louder and slower than the other Cat, but it moved and they weren't out in the cold.

Francis had a thought come to him out of the blue.

"Hey, if we have both rifles and security at the barracks has one handgun...does that mean the repair crew has the other handgun?"

Lena looked grim. "I checked. They didn't take any guns with them. They are unarmed."

Hamlin decided not to comment further until he had decided if that was a bad thing or no big deal.

"Was that intentional," Zoya asked as she drove along, "or did they just forget?"

"I don't know. It could go either way. Let's just get this done so we can go back and give the others some good news. We're all getting dangerously low with our emotional state."

They creaked and rattled along, each left pondering their own thoughts. None were particularly good at this stage. There was nothing to see outside but snow, so there was no distraction there. Hamlin wondered what the landscape would present to them once the sun reappeared in the spring. Surely there must be something to break the monotony somewhere in the distance. He missed the sky. He missed grass. He missed trees and birds and barking dogs. He missed warmth. He missed walking outside in shorts and a tee shirt. He made a promise to steer clear of reactionary, knee-jerk decisions in the future. He also made a promise to get down and kiss the ground when he got off the plane at Logan.

"There it is." Zoya was paying attention by default. She had no choice.

The other Cat sat there idling. That seemed like a good sign. The shed door was hanging open. Hamlin felt mixed about that.

"Stop here!" Lena ordered sharply. "Give us some room to work with. Zoya, you stay in the Cat. Francis, come with me." She opened her door and slid out. Hamlin did the same.

"Wait." She pulled off a mitt, then reached over and made an adjustment to his rifle. "Now you're fully automatic. Be careful if you shoot. A lot is going to happen in a very short time."

He stared at the open door. "Let's hope I don't have to."

She reached out her hand and put it on his chest just as they were about to take their next step.

"What is that?"

He looked at the ground by the Cat. Drifting had occurred as was to be expected, but there was no doubt that a reddish tinge was present under the upper layer of white.

"Oh, fuck. Is that what I think it is?"

She nodded. "Brace yourself. Let's go in. If something moves and it's not one of us, give it hell. Don't hesitate."

She was already moving toward the door. She popped her head in and out quickly. Then she repeated the act at a slower pace. Finally, she started to step inside. Hamlin, not really feeling sure of himself, followed nonetheless, fulfilling his backup role.

They stood shoulder to shoulder just inside the doorway and took stock.

"Hey, Barinov! Anybody! Are you in here?"

No response.

"Look." Francis pointed toward the far generator. He could see a foot protruding into his line of sight.

"Follow me," Lena snapped. "Remember your weapon. If this goes bad, shoot the hell out of this place."

They stepped cautiously closer. It didn't take long.

"It's Kravchuk," she whispered, concentrating as much on her peripheral vision as much as what was before her. She was looking for any kind of movement.

His head had sustained some type of horrible injury. There was a huge puddle of blood and quite possibly other parts on the ground. Once again, Francis felt an unreal sensation of terrible disgust and revulsion. He pulled his glove off to get a better grip on the trigger. This was way beyond serious.

"Okay, he's obviously dead. Let's find the others."

Francis was looking off to his immediate right. "Good lord. There's somebody over there."

This scene was a mess. Similar to Konstantine, this body had been ripped apart and strew asunder. Hamlin fancied that a suicide bomber would end up looking a lot like this.

"Can you tell who it is?"

Hamlin wasn't feeling well. "Yedemsky by the boots. Come on. I need to get out of here."

She hesitated. "What about Barinov?"

"Remember the blood in the snow outside?"

"Okay. Yes, I see what you're saying. Very well, then. Let's go."

Francis shocked himself by being capable of rational thought.

"What about the generators?"

She shook her head. "I don't know about mechanical things.' She then seemed to change her mind. "Here, wait."

She stepped ever so slowly and carefully toward a control panel. She punched a switch and the second generator fired up, causing Hamlin to jump. After thirty seconds or so, the initially running generator switched off. The lights on the panel all appeared to be green.

"That's what they are supposed to do. Let's go."

Now acutely aware of the danger of an ambush attack, Hamlin looked side to side as he walked toward the door.

They stepped outside and Lena slammed the door shut. With the decrease in noise, she could immediately hear screaming. They both whirled toward the direction they had come in from.

Pechkin stood beside the Cat, his attention now turned toward them. Zoya was hysterical inside the vehicle. At least he hadn't been able to make entry yet.

Lena actually started walking toward him.

"You motherfucker. I've had enough of this."

Pechkin swayed and stared open mouthed.

"Die once and for all, you evil piece of shit!"

She unloaded on him with everything her weapon was capable of. The ear numbing cracks coincided with the holes that were quickly forming on Pechkin's chest and face. In full auto mode, her weapon was capable of firing at a six hundred round per minute rate. She wasn't holding anything back.

Pechkin simply fell over backwards. She finally released the trigger. The barrel of her rifle was smoking.

She marched right over and kicked what was left of him in the ribs with her boot.

"I guess you won't bother us any more, you filth!" She kicked him again.

Hamlin couldn't think of anything appropriate to say. He simply blurted out the first thing that came to mind.

"I guess we know what stops them now."

Lena was breathing quite heavily. "If we could just find Kuvayev."

He decided right then and there to never engage her in a gun fight.

"I think we should talk to Zoya. She seems quite upset."

"Yes. Let's get out of here. You ride with her and I'll drive the other Cat back. Give me a minute to reload."

Hamlin ended up driving. Dr. Grekov was in no condition. Pechkin had scared her good. But she had sustained no injuries. None of them had. And now there was only Kuvayev. Maybe they were getting somewhere.

There was numb resignation when they returned and told their story. Now they were seven. The life had gone out of them in more ways than one.

"Look," Lena said. They could all fit around one table now so communication was rather easy. "No one can deny that this is bad. But we must have a plan. We must prepare to move forward. We must, at the very least, survive. And we can. It might even be easier now.

"Our supplies will last with no problem. We don't have to leave the barracks if we choose not to. Both generators are working properly. We are armed and we now know that a gunshot can stop those suffering from whatever this illness is. Besides, only Kuvayev is left. And who knows how much longer he can survive in his condition.

"The doors and windows have been reinforced. We should probably continue to post a watch at least during the night. That way the rest of us can rest easy. We are, I believe, quite secure in here. The building is old, but it is well built. We can survive. We will survive. We know what we are up against and we have only one foe remaining. There should be no more spread of the disease."

She paused.

"The gun works well. I dropped Pechkin like a sack of potatoes."

Hamlin had to nod in agreement at this point.

"Just aim high. If anything, we should hope that Kuvayev comes here. One good shot and this will all be over. We will declare whoever takes him out to be Hero of the Russian Federation." Surprisingly to Hamlin, this caused some heads to nod.

"We are strong. We are secure. We are prepared. Does anyone else have anything they want to say?"

"What about the bodies?" Obolensky asked.

Lena paused before answering.

"I say we leave them. Why risk infection or give Kuvayev an opportunity for an ambush? Let the crew that comes in the spring take responsibility for them."

"There is some heat in the generator building."

Lena hadn't initially thought of that. Would preservation be compromised? She thought not. The meager heat source probably didn't push the temperature above the freezing mark.

"Here's an idea," Hamlin said. He had debated as to whether or not it was appropriate for him to participate in a very sensitive conversation. But then he thought, why not? He alone represented over ten percent of the entire crew. They were all in this together now.

"Why don't we think about it and sleep on it. We can vote tomorrow if you want. We don't have to abandon them if that's not what you want. But it will be a difficult job to properly dispose of them. If you decide as a group that's what you want to do, I'll go and help."

Lena agreed. And that was important. She was the one who seemed to be stepping into the role of leader.

"As will I. But know that it will not be easy. The scene isn't pleasant. Give it some thought. Anyone else?"

"What about Sokolov's office?" This from an older researcher named Vitsin. He was usually quiet and Hamlin really hadn't gotten to know him at all. "Might there be more weapons or other things that we can use in there? He won't mind if we use them."

Francis could sense Lena stiffen at the very suggestion of allowing uncontrolled looting of Sokolov's room. But neither did she seem willing to openly oppose it. She let the idea hang there for reflection before answering.

"Dr. Hamlin and I have gone through it once very quickly. Sokolov left some instructions that indicate Hamlin is the one with authority regarding the room. I support this. My suggestion is that you allow us to go through it one more time. Then Francis can make a decision on whether to allow open access or not. Anything else?"

It was quiet now. It stayed quiet.

"Very well. I would like to take Dr. Hamlin out one more time to ensure both generators are still working and the shed is secure. After that, I am open to suggestions. Supper might be nice."

Dr. Grekov seemed to be in the early stages of recovery from her shock.

"I will start working on it."

Normally Hamlin would have wanted nothing to do with going out again, but he was certain that Lena had plans beyond what she had just revealed, so he went along willingly enough. Getting dressed for Vostok weather was becoming tedious. Maybe he would stay indoors for a few days after this.

CHAPTER SIXTEEN

She met him at the door, rifle in hand. She acknowledged him with a nod, and then they exited toward the Cat.

"You drive. I'll keep an eye open for Kuvayev."

He slid behind the wheel and slammed the door shut. Lena wasted no time in removing her gloves and programming the GPS with the coordinates that Sokolov left them.

"Get moving. Nobody needs to see what we are doing. I will give you directions once we get started."

Hamlin got the Cat rolling. The skid steer took a bit of getting used to, but not much maneuvering was required, so that made it much easier.

"Turn right. I'll tell you how much. A little more...stop! More to the right. Now go straight."

That was easy enough. They rolled along without incident, and Francis found that he was a little excited by their quest. He couldn't imagine that there would be anything that could reverse the negatives they had experienced, but as long as they weren't sure what awaited them, Hamlin decided to imagine the best.

"A little more right. That's it."

Hamlin looked at the GPS screen but it told him nothing.

"Any idea where we're heading yet?"

She nodded.

"I think so. There isn't much down here that is unknown or hidden, at least as far as our camp is concerned. There's an old building that is basically abandoned out this way. Why he would want us to go out here is a mystery to me. But keep going—we are almost there."

That didn't sound too exciting. Surely Sokolov must have had some good reason in mind.

"Another two hundred meters. Steady on."

He strained through the gloom but couldn't see anything.

"One hundred meters."

Still nothing. But then, abruptly, a large, run-down building came into view.

"All right, stop. Right here is fine."

He was disappointed in its appearance. It looked like a piece of junk. "What now?"

She actually smiled. "We go in, what else? Surely some treasure awaits, don't you think?"

"Sure doesn't look like it. We're leaving this running, correct?"

"You'd better. It would be a long, cold walk back. And I wouldn't be happy. Keep in mind I am carrying a gun."

"And I've seen you shoot it." Hamlin opened his door and stepped into the deep freeze.

The wind was picking up and the wind chill was brutal.

"Come on," Lena yelled. "Let's get in there. At least it will block most of the wind."

Hamlin simply followed. Outdoor conversation moved too much cold air into his lungs.

The rickety door put up a surprising amount of resistant before they could force it open. They stepped inside. It was disconcertingly dark. Hamlin couldn't make out any details at all.

"Now what?"

A sharp click and two rows of lights started to flicker on. Lena had her hand on the wall mounted switch and was smiling like she had just pulled one over on him.

"Who would think it? Lights!"

"Very funny." He stepped into the structure. "Not much to see anyway."

Everything that initially caught his eye was either old or decrepit, or a combination of both in most cases.

Lena walked further in, looking all around as she went.

"We should be careful. I don't want to miss anything."

"What exactly are we looking for, anyway?"

"I have no idea. Anything that looks usable, valuable, new or newer…or perhaps something hidden."

Hamlin started walking. There were no sources of heat; the temperature seemed identical to the outside. His breath rose in great plumes of warm vapor. He had no idea why that still held some sort of fascination after all the time he had been down here. He stepped around a pile of rusty pipes.

"Anything yet, Francis?"

"Well, if there was a junk yard anywhere around here, we probably have a few hundred bucks worth of scrap. That would get us a nice night on the town."

"Hmm. That sounds nice. The night on the town, I mean."

"Oh yeah. A seafood platter, some warm cheesy biscuits, and nice bottle of chardonnay and who knows–I might even nibble on some Caesar salad."

"Stop it. You're killing me."

Hamlin stopped walking. He was in the middle of the structure, looking toward what he perceived as the back wall.

"Hey, what's that?"

Lena immediately started walking toward him.

"What is what?"

"Such great language skills." He pointed. "There, along the wall. It looks like an upright freezer. I would guess you don't have much use for anything like that down here, though."

A large metal cabinet-like container stood innocuously by the wall.

"Hmm, I'm not sure. Let's have a closer look."

As they approached, Hamlin grew excited. The surface was shiny brushed metal, and it looked quite new and modern. That was when he noticed the cord.

"Hey, it's plugged in. What the hell does that mean? Is it a freezer?"

She stared it. "Really, Francis? A freezer down here? That makes no sense." She continued to stare. "Do you notice anything strange about this 'freezer'?"

There was something that he couldn't immediately put his finger on.

"Oh, wait. There's no handles on the outside. How would you open it?" There was a seam down the middle and hinges on the sides. Clearly there were two doors that would give access. But how?

Lena glanced back toward where they came in. The door was still securely shut. She set the rifle down carefully and then started to pull off her gloves.

"I see something. Look here."

There appeared to be an outline of a small rectangular seam in the front of the right side door. She touched it gently. It didn't budge. Next she tried to get her nails under the seam for leverage to pull it open. Again no results.

"Strange. Tell me, Doctor Hamlin, what is your big American brain telling you about getting this open? You must have a better idea than what I've come up with so far."

"I'm surprised you aren't thinking about trying to shoot it open."

She smiled a bit. "Who says I'm not?"

"Try this first. Push in on the panel."

She frowned. "That seems counter-productive. I want it to swing open, not to get jammed in any tighter than it already is."

"Just try."

She complied. To her surprise, the small panel depressed about half an inch with virtually no resistance. It clicked softly, and when she released the pressure on it, the left side popped open. She grabbed it and swung it wide open. Inside was an illuminated keypad with the digits zero through nine displayed in a simple grid pattern.

"I can't believe it," she said.

"You see. I'm a genius."

"I'll believe that when you figure out what the code is."

That put out his fire very quickly.

"It could be anything."

Lena shook her head. "If it is a random number, we will never get in. There may even be a security program that will disable the keypad after so many incorrect attempts."

Hamlin sighed, creating another impressive plume. "You're a veritable fount of good news. So what you're saying is, if we're not confident that we know what the code is, we shouldn't even try to open it."

"Correct."

Hamlin was stumped.

"Maybe it's in Sokolov's room somewhere."

She filtered that thought.

"Maybe. He did lead us here. He must have thought that we could figure out the code somehow. Before we give up or freeze trying, let's just think this through. What possible number could be used as the code?"

Hamlin's brain was tired. They had just gone through a similar process to figure out what the numbers that made up the coordinates for this building meant.

"Hey, wait a minute."

"What is it?" Lena asked.

"The coordinates for the building. I don't suppose there's any way that could be the combination."

"Well, that would explain why he thought we could figure it out. But it is such a large number. I doubt this thing would accept that many digits."

"Surely it won't lock after one failed attempt. I say try it. Either that, or we go back empty handed and admit that this could take some time to figure out."

She dug in her pocket and came up with the paper.

"Here, read them off to me slowly and I will enter them. We'll try it once."

He took it in his gloved hand.

"Tell me when you're ready."

She positioned herself carefully. "I'm ready. Do this before my hand is frozen."

"Here we go. Seven, eight, four, six, three, nine, two, zero, zero, one..."

"Wait!" The doors clicked and swung partially open, hissing when they did so. The interior was lit up softly be several rows of small LED lights. Lena swung the doors wide open and revealed the contents.

"Oh my Lord."

It was a cache. There were all sorts of exotic looking weapons hanging on the back of the container. They all appeared to be both new and modern. Hamlin didn't know much about weapons but identified what he was certain was a rocket launcher.

"Awesome," he gasped. "Now if we get bored, we can start World War Three just for fun."

Lena didn't reply and when he looked at her expression, he was surprised how grim and even confused she looked.

"Francis, these are all American weapons."

Was that really important?

"Really? Are you sure?"

"Yes." She spoke like she was in a dream.

"So, does that change things somehow?"

"I'm not sure. Why would they be here? Why would Sokolov know about them?"

Hamlin saw something that caught his eye. He reached out for it. Lena grabbed his arm and stopped his momentum.

"Wait! This could have some sort of defense system built into it. Don't try to take anything out."

"But there's my old handgun!"

She saw it and nodded. "A Beretta 9mm semi-automatic, Model 92, I believe. This is a beautiful gun, but I don't think it is safe or even wise to take any of these out of here. At least not yet."

"You sure know a lot about weapons. Isn't the Beretta Italian made?"

She shook her head. "They are made in Europe, but also in the U.S.A. I'm sure that is where this one originated."

Hamlin really wanted to put that gun in his hands.

"Are you certain that we can't take some of these? I think Sokolov wanted us to have them."

"Francis, if we came upon a space ship sitting on the ice, would you immediately want to go inside of it and take it for a ride?"

"Well, no."

"And why not?"

"Too many unknown variables."

"My point exactly. This is the same thing. How did this get here? Who are these for? Why are they here? Are they safe or booby-trapped? Do they even function? And I'm just getting started."

"I get it. I'd sure feel safer carrying that thing around. But it if you want to think this over first, I guess I could live with that. I suppose we don't want the rest to know about this."

"Absolutely. They'd all want to have that rocket launcher in their hands. We'd end up killing ourselves before anything else."

A loud bang made both of them jump. They whirled around to see the door hanging open and Kuvayev blocking their exit. He was huge and creepy.

Lena slowly started to bring her rifle up to firing position.

"Francis," she said in a soft voice, "don't move. Just stand right where you are."

Hamlin was terrified. He knew what the huge, sick man was capable of doing. He had seen the aftermath. In retrospect, he didn't think he could move if he wanted to.

Kuvayev was gasping for breath or something. He was making noises that almost sounded like he was trying to talk.

Lena now held the gun steadily in firing position.

"Big mistake, mother fucker. We're armed. Let's see how you like a fair fight."

She fired a single shot and Francis could see Kuvayev's head snap back. She fired three more times in rapid succession and the big man fell over onto the ground.

"That's all you got?" she hissed through clenched teeth. She seemed disappointed.

"Is he dead?" Hamlin still wasn't ready to approach him.

She walked toward the door. "Let's find out."

He sure looked dead. After several kicks and prods with no response, she was ready to make it official.

"He's dead, all right. About fucking time."

"Do you know what this means?" Hamlin felt a weight lift from his shoulders. "It's over. Nobody is left that's infected. No more ambushes, no more posting guards, no more guessing what every strange noise at night is."

She nodded. "We're safe now."

"Thank God. Finally."

On impulse, he pushed his face through the restrictions of her hood and kissed her on the forehead.

She was smiling now. "You know, Francis, you really are a sweet man. Now back off before I shoot you in the foot."

Hamlin laughed. The release of stress allowed other thoughts to become prevalent.

"Who are you, really?"

She feigned surprise. "What are you talking about?"

"Oh, come on. I know in these surroundings I'm probably the dummy of the group, but it's pretty obvious by now. You shoot like a professional, you analyze proficiently, you make quick decisions under duress, and you took control over the station within minutes of Sokolov leaving us. You're absolutely fearless in the face of danger. And quite frankly, you make love like you've had professional training and I'm not even sure what that means."

"Okay. You caught me. I'm a hooker-spy. Now, let's re-secure that locker, drag this abomination outside to freeze solid, and go back to give everybody the good news."

Hamlin almost said *everybody that's left* but caught himself just in time. And he couldn't help but notice how she had avoided giving him any kind of real answer to his question. He decided not to push it. Now they had some time to work with and maybe he would also have time to get his own answers. At any rate, *never push the woman with the smoking rifle in her hands* seemed like a safe motto. Reluctantly, he reached down to grab Kuvayev by the wrist for dragging purposes.

There was joy and relief at the barracks. The night turned into a semi-party. It wasn't super wild and crazy–everyone was still subdued after the loss of so many crew members. But there were smiles and handshakes and lots of little conversations that no longer had to be grim by nature.

Lena brought out cigars from Sokolov's room for any who wished to partake. They all did, even the ones who had never smoked before. It was like a rite of passage somehow and everyone wanted to be in on it. Many didn't last long after the smokes were lit. Also, it was apparent most hadn't been sleeping well and now wanted to get caught up, with the promise of fewer nightmares to encourage them.

The party, such as it was, started to break up early. Hamlin knew all too well why that was. He felt a wave of exhaustion wash over him. The doors were still locked and the windows reinforced, but there would be no posted guard tonight. The danger had passed and they were secure once again. And he wanted to sleep without dreams or reservations of any sort. He ground out his cigar somewhat prematurely, and then excused himself from what was left of the group. He had an appointment with a comfortable bed.

He slept right through. When he awoke and checked his clock, he was surprised that it was mid-morning. He felt great.

Francis wandered into the mess hall and almost everyone was already there. Breakfast seemed like a great idea. Bacon and eggs were already under way. Once again, the atmosphere seemed lighter. Expressions on people's faces were pleasant. Most greeted him verbally or with a nod as he walked past. He meandered into the kitchen.

"Ah, Professor Hamlin. Make yourself a plate." Even Doctor Grekov seemed to be back to her normal self. "There is plenty for everyone. I think maybe I made too much."

"Well, let me see what I can do to help with that." He picked up and plate and some silverware. "It smells great."

"There is coffee too," she said with a smile.

"Count me in. I'll be right back to get some."

"I will bring it out for you, yes?"

"You don't have to do that. I'm not disabled."

"No, but you might be soon if you don't accept her hospitality." Lena had snuck up behind Hamlin and poked him in the ribs. "Take it out for him, Zoya. He will love you for it."

She smiled and maybe even blushed a little. "Nice choice of words. We will see."

Francis shook his head as she walked away toward the coffee pot. "Wow, what a change in atmosphere from yesterday."

Lena, careful to be sure nobody was able to see, grabbed Hamlin by the ass.

"Are you complaining, Dr. Hamlin?"

He was struggling not to drop his plate in surprise.

"Not at all. Let the orgy begin."

"Fine," she snickered. "You might want to keep your distance from Vitsin if that's the direction we're going. I think he kind of likes you."

"Yikes. Thanks for the warning."

"I'll see you at the table."

Hamlin found his spot and wasted no time in tucking into his steaming plateful. Lena showed up with a small bowl of oatmeal.

"That's not going to get you through the day," he said between bites.

"Francis, we are two hours from lunch. I think I'll make it."

"You have an answer for everything. That tends to take the fun out of giving you the gears."

"You know, in retrospect, I could have shot you last night and claimed it was an accident."

"Thanks for showing restraint. I really appreciate it."

She laughed. "This is fun. I missed it, you know–the way you joke around so naturally. Maybe we can actually make it through the winter now."

"I'm going to eat constantly. That's my new focus. I want them to have to fly me out separately and individually because of my weight."

"And then you can start a new career as a fashion model." She blew on a spoonful of cereal.

"There, you see. You catch on very quickly. You could be as sardonic as the best of them. All it would take is for me to be your trainer. You could be a contender."

"Sure I could. I contend with you every day."

He stopped eating long enough to grab a swallow of coffee.

"On a serious note, what are we all going to do now? We've gone from fourteen to eight. The lake samples are no longer in play."

Lena took another conservative mouthful.

"Hmm, I know. We really should re-evaluate everything; our priorities, our duties as researchers, our duties as crew members–everything."

"Sounds right. I volunteer to be thong inspector."

"Rumor has it that Vitsin wears one of those, you know."

"I withdraw my application."

"Well, you are the last dedicated biologist. So you might be the hardest one to place in a new position. The drilling crew is gone but doesn't need to be replaced at this point. The climatologists can carry on with their work, no problem.

"Zoya and I are geologists. We have been analysing meteor samples found in this region. We have enough samples to keep us working for the next month or so. Maybe your new task could be to do recognisance, scouting for new samples. That might work. Then everyone is accounted for as far as research is concerned."

"Very good."

"Yes. Our only problem would be if things start breaking down. We have lost the engineers and tradesmen. Let's hope the furnaces and generators keep running."

"And we no longer have a medical doctor."

She nodded sadly. "Yes. Kuvayev was an integral part of our crew. How sad that he was one of the ones we lost."

She hadn't shown any qualms when she had gunned him down the previous night, but Hamlin figured that was a different circumstance. He let the thought slide by unacknowledged.

"So, we'll eat. We'll clean up. Then we'll meet. We will make our plan and we will move on. This is good."

Hamlin finished his last bite.

"You're right."

The meeting was short and agreeable. Lena filled the role of leader easily and confidently. Jobs were confirmed and assigned as required. Not only was the crew quick to approve of Lena's suggestions, they all were relieved and even enthusiastic to get back to a normal routine. Many of the stronger personalities were no longer with them, so fewer challenges and complaints surfaced. They transitioned easily back into a relatively normal routine.

Watching people go back to their stations to resume working made Hamlin feel out of place. He knew full well how much he needed a focus and purpose.

"Ah, there you are. And looking lost, too." Lena waved him to follow. "Come with me. I have something for you."

She led him into the small lab where she and Zoya worked. There was a case on the counter that seemed to be her immediate focus. Once unzipped, a small electronic device of some sort was removed.

"Here you go. Take good care of this."

He regarded it doubtfully. "What is it?"

"It's a magnetic gradiometer, capable of detecting perturbations in the Earth's magnetic field induced by the presence of meteorites. It connects to this."

She lifted up what looked like a small antenna.

"I think I've seen those on the roofs of trailers back home."

"This one is subtly different and blatantly more expensive. There is a bracket for it on the back of the Cat. I'll help you with the installation."

"Great. Thank you. By the way, what's the likelihood of me having success? I assume this is a bit of a *needle in a haystack* process."

"Not so much. Tell him, Zoya."

She turned and smiled, accentuating her dimples.

"Antarctica is the richest source of meteorites, especially with the relative lack of space travel now. The ground is littered with them. Once they land here, they just sit in the snow. There is nothing here to hide or camouflage them, except the drifting. When the sun returns, it is possible to go out without equipment and find them just lying there."

"No kidding. That is kind of exciting, in a seriously nerdy way. So, I have a good chance of being successful. Excellent. I assume these will tend to be rather small."

Lena was checking the connection for the meter.

"Oh yes. Most pieces would fit in your pocket nicely. However, an American found a fifteen-kilo piece two summers ago. You could knock a door down with one that big. It was about the size of one of Zoya's boobs."

Zoya immediately blushed. "Don't say things like that."

Lena smiled. "I forgot. I'm not supposed to notice those things."

"You're not supposed to talk about them." Zoya turned back to her work.

"Right," Hamlin said. "You clearly have a lot of serious things to do here, what with getting caught up after the missed days, making earth-shattering discoveries, deciding whether or not to mention Zoya's boobs...all in all I think I should leave you to your work. So, can you take a few minutes to get me ready?"

"Yes, of course. You get your outside clothes on, and I'll do the same. First we'll install the antenna, and then I'll show you how this process works. Then we'll see how productive you can be out in the field."

"Awesome." Hamlin was truly stoked to have a purpose again. He thought there was a chance that this might even be fun.

CHAPTER SEVENTEEN

The cold still had its incessant, brutal bite. Fortunately, the antenna attached with ease. They didn't even have to remove their gloves. After that, it took fifteen minutes inside the cab of the Cat for Lena to explain how the equipment worked and what kind of a process he needed to follow. Francis, proud owner of a doctoral degree, caught on quickly. She was soon comfortable sending him out for the first time.

"You have no weapons, as there is no longer any need to be armed. The equipment is quite simple to use. Make sure you set a grid that makes sense to you, and record your results so that you will not be repetitive as you start to make multiple trips. Other than that, make sure your radio works so you can call in if you have any trouble. Be careful getting out when picking up a sample. Do not walk far. If the Cat gets out of sight, you are in big trouble. Take your time, be successful, and have fun. We'll expect you back in two hours. That is long enough for your first time out. Show me what you can do."

"Aye-aye, Captain. I won't let you down."

"Good-bye, Doctor smart-ass. Good hunting."

The door slammed shut. Hamlin was out on his own for the first time since arriving here–at least as far as the working portion of the trip was concerned. He was ecstatic.

The Cat responded easily to his commands and he rolled away from the barracks. The GPS was functioning perfectly. Lena had helped him to set a simple grid pattern and he wasted no time in following it. This was perfect. It was just what he needed.

The Cat held the line he wanted to follow with minimal correction required. At first he really watched the meter, but as time and distance passed, he became more comfortable with trusting it to do what it was designed to do. He relaxed and de-stressed.

He found one piece that day. It came after the first hour had passed. The meter clearly showed that there was something on the ground that was giving off an electromagnetic signal. Once outside, it had taken some time to find it. Once he did, he felt stupid. The meter had tried to give him good directions and he had just failed to follow them well.

Eventually he had stumbled upon a piece slightly larger than a golf ball. It had a number of sculpted grooves in its dark shiny surface. There was little doubt as to what it was. There was no other way for any other type of similar material to exist here.

Once back inside, he bagged the sample and carried on. He was shocked how fast the two hours went by. Not going back empty handed was a definite bonus. His confidence had been boosted. With the aid of the GPS, he set a course back to the barracks.

Lena and Zoya were still working in their lab when he returned. He showed off his meteorite with obvious pride.

"Well, look at this." Lena held it up and appraised it as if it was a gem. "This is nice. Not bad for a first trip out. You are showing some promise, my good doctor."

"Thank you." He couldn't think of anything smart to say. He was actually pleased with her response.

"So, with such a successful conclusion to a very nice day, I propose we *pack it in,* as you Americans say. I think we should make burgers for supper and have a movie night. What do you say, Zoya?"

"Da, sounds very nice. Do you have any movies that a lady might like, Dr. Hamlin?"

That was a problem. Hamlin like action, adventure, and goofy comedies.

"I can find something. I'm sure of it. It may take some digging through the menu."

Lena stretched as she prepared to finish her work.

"Zoya, I think it is time that the men made a meal. I'll go give them the good news."

Burgers weren't too challenging from a culinary perspective. Francis even volunteered to assist. The frozen and canned ingredients notwithstanding, once again the meal was surprisingly good. Everyone seemed to have their appetite back. They baked frozen fries to make the necessary side dish to the simple feast. Lena volunteered a couple bottles of red wine from Sokolov's private stock as an accompaniment. It was an excellent meal.

Hamlin found Casablanca on his memory stick and decided that it was a good compromise between a romance and something that guys would like. Response was immediately good. He had just nicely settled in when Lena brushed up against him and indicated that she wanted to talk to him outside the group setting. He discreetly followed her out of the room.

"What's up?"

"Keep walking. Let's go into Sokolov's office."

Curious, he followed her wordlessly. They went in and she shut the door behind them.

"Francis, I know you are a smart guy. You figured out the meaning of the numbers, and you also guessed the combination for the cabinet in the outer shed. So, I'm wondering; after having a little time to absorb and reflect, what are your thoughts about the weapons stored out there?"

"What do you mean?"

"I mean, why are they there in the first place? Why are they American? Why did Sokolov know about them and why did he want you to know about them? I cannot help but believe that there is some significance to the answers to these questions and I have no idea what they are."

Hamlin sat in Sokolov's chair. There was no longer any need to feel guilty about it, he figured. He drew in a lungful of air, held it, and then blew it out in an audible stream.

"Lena, I don't know. There's so much going on here that I don't understand. I came here based on the face value of a request to assist with some biological research. I knew almost nothing about this place when I got here."

"And now?"

"And now it seems to me that there are many undercurrents in play in Vostok. There is intrigue and treachery; deceit and politics. It feels like there are things going on just below the surface that I don't comprehend. And that makes it difficult for me to understand something as weird and unexpected as a locker full of high powered weapons made in the good old U.S.A. On my first day in the lab, Konstantine wrote a note to tell me that the room was bugged. That was because I was talking to him about Sokolov and he didn't want to participate. Why is that?"

"Are you being rhetorical?"

"Only if you don't have a meaningful response."

She looked around the room as if all the answers were sitting on a shelf or hanging on the wall.

"Sokolov was a type of puppet. He represented the government and had the task of keeping us productive, and keeping us in line. He could be supportive when it was beneficial for his purposes, but he would also sell any of us out in an instant. I have no doubt that there is a file on each of us somewhere in this room, either paper or electronic. Probably even for you."

"Me?"

"The rumor was that this was his last work term here. Once spring arrived, he was going back to Moscow, and then retiring to some sort of meaningless post in Cuba. Sandy beaches, year round warmth, and a limitless supply of great rum. Not a bad end for a Russian citizen. Periodically he would have to meet with and entertain some sort of government sanctioned VIP, but other than that, he would be free to conduct his life however he wanted."

"Really? Somehow Sokolov didn't strike me as the type that would be happy drinking Daiquiris on the beach while watching the girls walk by."

She smirked. "Believe it or not, he was an avid arborist. He probably would have been given a home with a backyard that he could transform into his own private tropical paradise. It is not the worst way to spend your declining years."

"Especially viewed from this deep freeze," Hamlin said. "So, what does that tell me that will help to figure out our little mystery?"

"I'm just giving you insight. Draw your own conclusions."

Hamlin made a decision.

"Listen. I'm going to tell you something. I meant to keep it to myself, but I think it plays a role here."

He could tell that he had her undivided attention.

"Oh," she said casually, "and what might that be?"

"Well, this is a bit shocking and whole lot disconcerting, but Sokolov said your government had surmised that it was likely that we would find unknown viruses in the lake water before the testing ever started. They wanted us to find them so they could be evaluated as potential biological weapons. As a species, mankind would have no natural resistance to a virus that we had never been exposed to before. He speculated about using them against terrorists. And…he specifically mentioned that my government was interested as well. I got the impression that might have been partially responsible for why I was selected to come here in the first place."

She looked to be deep in thought. "I see."

"Unfortunately, even with that knowledge in mind, I have no idea why the weapons are there."

Lena was deep in thought and didn't respond.

"Do you?"

She seemed to snap out of it.

"Do I what?"

"Do you have any idea, knowing what I just told you, why the weapons are there?"

She shook her head emphatically. "No. No idea at all."

"That's disappointing." Hamlin replied.

A smile creased her face. "But that information gives us both something to think about. It may be very helpful in the long run. Francis, I think we should go back and watch the movie. No point in having everyone suspicious about our actions. What do you say?"

Her original enthusiasm to get there was now matched by her desire to leave. It seemed equally strong and disconcertingly contradictory. He decided to ponder the implications of that later.

"Sure. I'd hate to miss a classic."

She pulled him up out of the chair.

"Then be a gentleman, and escort a lady back."

"Of course." He opened the door and waited for her to exit. "Right this way, ma'am."

He lay awake later in bed, meditating on his conversation with Lena. Clearly something he had said caught her attention. Equally clear was the fact that she did not want to discuss it with him. He let numerous scenarios play out in his imagination as he gradually slid into a dreamless state that would see him through the night. Answers would have to wait.

Barinov, as he used to be known before he was attacked and infected, shuffled along through the snow. His new operating temperature made it possible to survive in this extreme cold. It also destroyed his mind.

He didn't have conscious thoughts above and beyond the occasional flirting notion that flickered across his brain like a person running past a window–only visible for the briefest of moments. But a few baser instincts still survived, such as the one that motivated him now. He was hungry.

He wasn't capable of formulating a complex plan to find food. Somehow, he had a guidance system that determined his steps, although he had no understanding of it. After meandering in a rather unstructured manner for some time, he turned in the general direction of the base camp where he used to live and work. That was where he'd find food. And that was where his remaining instincts, flawed as they now were, would eventually take him.

Hamlin woke up quickly, the transition from sleep happening smoothly and swiftly. He felt good. He was also still rather excited to take the Cat out and go on meteorite patrol. And he was ready for breakfast.

It didn't take long to get the news that threatened to steal his good mood away. A storm had settled over them during the night, and high winds now buffeted the area. In the quieter moments, he could hear it blowing while he ate. He sought out Lena for advice.

"Francis, you cannot go out in this. It would be extremely dangerous. Visibility is non-existent and the wind chill in not survivable. Pieces of space rock can wait."

He really wanted to argue. Sitting around pointlessly for another day was not on his agenda.

"Look, I can take a lanyard and clip myself in if I find something. That way I stay attached to the Cat."

"You would freeze. Every square inch of your skin would have to be covered at all times or the wind would give you frostbite instantaneously."

"Well, I could just run the grid pattern. If I find anything, I could just mark it as a waypoint. Then tomorrow or whenever this breaks, I could drive straight to it. It's still a great way to be more productive."

"And it gets you out of the barracks for a while."

"There is that, too."

"Well, I'm not the boss. I'm not really sure who is. I guess if you're foolish enough to gamble your well-being for a rock, then nobody here will try to stop you."

That felt like a cop out to Hamlin.

"I'd like to have your blessings. It would make me feel better."

"Then go, you stupid ass. Just don't make us send out a search party. We've had enough trouble."

"I shall be more than happy to comply," he said. In truth, he couldn't wait to get back out there.

She leaned in closer. "Be careful, Francis. If something happens to you, how am I going to get laid when the desire strikes?"

"Oh, I'm quite certain you could find a solution to that problem."

She lowered her voice even more.

"If you say 'Vitsin,' I'm going to cut you off for the rest of the winter."

He chuckled and it felt good.

"I'm not saying a word. Besides, I now have things to do. So if you'll excuse me, I'll be on my way."

He stood up from the table and ferried his tray into the kitchen. The freedom of the great outdoors beckoned and he was ready to answer the call.

He marked two pieces on his morning foray. He had no idea if that was good or not, but it was something and he felt great. The weather was rather scary, but the Cat was engineered for this environment and it ran perfectly. The cab stayed fairly warm and that was more than enough with all the clothes he was wearing. He actually had to remove a few items as a remedy because he was slightly over-heating.

He now had fifteen minutes to return on schedule so as not to upset any of the other crew members. He was determined not to be late. The grid was easy to follow on the GPS and he was making good time. That was when a thought hit him so hard, he actually stopped the machine to absorb it.

"Shit."

Nobody heard the mild oath. Hamlin needed it for a release.

"Wait a minute.."

He had been thinking about the weapons cache. A few simple facts had started to align in his subconscious and were on their way to forming a theory. It was a very disturbing theory, which he was nowhere near ready to accept. Hence the time for re-evaluation.

"Okay, let's work this through." Thinking out loud helped when trying to organize his thoughts.

"First of all, why are the weapons American? If I know that, the rest of the puzzle starts to fall into place on its own."

He thought about it.

"Lots of heavy weapons in an area where there is no conceivable need for them. So the second question is–what is their purpose?"

A connection was made.

"American weapons must be for Americans. Surely the Russians make enough of their own that they could have stock piled them if they felt it was necessary. And obviously they didn't. So, why did my countrymen think it necessary and which Americans are they for? There's only me here now."

He pondered some more. Obviously they weren't initially meant to be discovered.

"Why did Sokolov know about them? He's not American by any stretch. And why would he give me a hint to help me find them?"

The answer that he thought was there started to fade into the mist.

"Nobody else here knew about them, including Lena who is pretty darn sharp and doesn't miss much. She seemed very surprised and perhaps I would say upset by the discovery. So that brings me back to my original point. They aren't for the people here. So who are they for?"

More rumination.

"There's an American base here in Antarctica somewhere. Did Sokolov say how far? I kind of think that it was quite a distance. Is it too far for anyone to travel if they really wanted to get here?"

There was no way to come up with an answer.

"Okay, let's move forward using conjecture. At least that way, I can still make progress. Assuming they could reach us from the nearest American base, and assuming further that those weapons are for whoever makes the trip, then what does that tell me?"

Part of the answer seemed all too obvious.

"No one coming for a friendly visit needs machine guns and rocket launchers."

So why would they pay them an unfriendly visit? And why wouldn't they bring weapons with them?

"Because it's too far. Maybe they would only have enough room for fuel and supplies to make the round trip. They would have to pick up the weapons here, and then..." He lowered his voice even though he was alone. "And then destroy the evidence."

Evidence worth destroying would have been associated with doing something bad. Perhaps even very bad. But would his government actually sanction what he was starting to imagine?

"And why would Sokolov know about it, and do nothing to prevent it?"

Lena had said that the rumor was that Sokolov was going to retire after this work term was over. He was going to Cuba to his just rewards. Or was he?

"What if he got a better deal? What if my country was willing to up the ante enough to make him change his mind?"

If he liked working with plants, maybe they would give him his own tropical island.

But why? Why all that trouble, and expense, and risk...and violation of international law? The only thing they had here was...

"The virus."

He was getting cold now and not from the heaters malfunctioning.

"Sokolov said we were interested in it too. I wonder how interested? Could it be enough to justify coming here and taking it from this station?"

This could be really bad, assuming he was right...and he still wasn't ready to say he was. Perhaps he was completely off his rocker.

"Perhaps."

But if he wasn't...then...

"Holy fuck."

What would happen to the remaining crew if an American Special Forces team swept down on them? More to the point, what would happen to him? Leaving witnesses to international espionage didn't seem like a very good idea.

"Not a good idea, at all."

Once again, his voice had dropped to a whisper. Was the crew expendable in all of this? Was he? Something else was forming in the fog of his mind.

"Why did Sokolov give me the combination and clue to where the locker was when he knew he was about to die?"

He had a thought. That's all it was. Farfetched, no doubt there. But he was just brain storming which meant no thought was off limits. What if...

"It's thin. Really thin."

What if Sokolov changed the combination on the locker for leverage? The Special Forces team arrives and finds out that they can't access the weapons because their code is bogus. Then what?

"They're smart. They're creative. So what would they do?"

If this scenario was true, then they would have already been briefed about the few weapons in the barracks. So, they couldn't chance showing up at the door unarmed and try to take them all out with hand to hand combat. All it would take was for one old geezer to have a pistol in his hand and the Special Forces team gets gunned down. So...

"So they send one or two of them to the door. They knock and give some bullshit story about why they're there. First chance that comes along, they get the combination from Sokolov and then they're in business. But first he reaffirms his status as coming with them unharmed with the weapons as leverage."

So in Sokolov's absence...

"I'm it. It's the only way I have a chance of getting out of this alive. That's why he told me."

Why? Faced with death, Sokolov wanted to somehow redeem himself? What about his countrymen? In the end, Hamlin decided he didn't care. He did want to survive, though. And he felt the same about the rest of the crew. Most of them were like friends to him now. Could he live with himself after watching Lena and Zoya get gunned down?

"No. I can't."

That could mean only one thing at this point. He would talk to Lena discreetly and see if she thought he was nuts. If not, maybe they could start to come up with a plan. It seemed like there were still some holes and inconsistencies with his reasoning. He needed constructive feedback to hone the finer points.

"Shit, and I thought the zombies were bad."
He started rolling back toward the barracks.

CHAPTER EIGHTEEN

Someone had made fresh bread from unthawed dough. It smelled and tasted astonishingly good. Previously frozen chicken was made into chicken salad for sandwiches and onion rings were cooked in hot oil to go with them. Hamlin ate like a linebacker.

"I think it's the olfactory input. You smell the baking bread and your appetite goes crazy," he said to Zhabin, a researcher and meteorologist who was sitting across from him at the table.

"It's so warm and soft," Zhabin replied, all the while stuffing his face with another bite.

"And that's just the way you like it, Francis, is that not so?"

Lena once again arrived just in time to make a play on words. She sat beside him, which was perfect. He really wanted to talk to her, but didn't want to make it obvious to anybody else. He concentrated on the excellent fare in front of him and decided to be patient. She was one of the last people to fill her plate, ergo she would be one of the last to leave the table. That should present him with the opportunity he was looking for. But he had to fire off some sort of retaliatory strike in the meantime.

"Nobody has ever accused me of having good taste."

She got the insinuation and kicked him under the table. He just kept eating.

In the end, Lena fooled him by only eating half a sandwich. She left the table before they could have a real conversation. Once he had finished and taken the time to inquire about who made the meal (Grebenshchikov) so that he could lavish praise on the effort and result, he cleaned up and wandered down to Lena's lab.

He tapped once on the door and swung it open. She was looking at him wide-eyed as he stepped in.

"Oh, it's you."

"And there it is. That's the greeting every man hopes for. "

"I am sorry. I made the possible mistake of imposing a quota on myself for what I was going to accomplish today and I am currently running behind schedule. What can I do for you, Francis?"

He thought about swinging the door shut for privacy, but when he turned to look over his shoulder, Zoya was walking in. Now what? He had to say something that wasn't going to come out as too incoherent.

He made up a question about signal strength when finding larger or multiple samples. She looked at him like she knew that was bogus, but answered seriously regardless. He thanked her, apologized for interrupting, and went back to his own outdoor version of research. Their talk would have to wait.

He had a great afternoon from a results point of view. Four more samples were marked on the GPS. That gave him a total of six to pick up the next day, not including any others that he might locate after that. He briefly pondered what the daily record might be.

For the most part, he continued to think over the situation they were all in. He started to cling tighter to the conclusions from his morning contemplations. No new revelations came to him, but one overriding fear began to take hold and gnaw.

When would it happen?

If it was true, how long did they have until the attack came? Today? Tonight? How could he possibly figure it out? What answer made sense?

"We have the virus on ice and we know it's virulent. If they knew, they could come anytime to take it."

He thought about Sokolov and his shortwave radio. They had assumed that he used it to talk to Moscow or someone back in Russia. What if he was talking to the strike team leader? Then they would have all the knowledge they needed for this to happen. There was nothing to say that this might happen soon.

"He must have called them before he died. He would have told them that he wasn't going to make it. He might have even told them to seek me out as the one with the combination. Maybe. I guess if I hadn't figured it out, they'd be on their own. But why would he care at that point?"

What a mess. Hamlin decided to ask Lena about alternative theories before he affected her thought pattern by sharing his. Maybe he was wrong about all of this. He sure was hoping so.

A new thought rocked him. They didn't have any samples on ice. After Sokolov died, they had burned the outer lab to the ground. All the virus related research was there. Or at least had been. That added yet another twist. If a team showed up looking for the virus, it just wouldn't be here. That would piss them off.

"Son of a bitch."

After supper, Hamlin decided not to try being too clever about it. He simply told Lena that he wanted a word alone and the two of them retired to Sokolov's room. That was much more realistic than coming up with some elaborate and bizarre cover story to get her alone.

As was now typical, Francis sat in Sokolov's comfortable chair. Lena moved a few items and sat on the corner of the huge desk, legs dangling short of reaching the floor.

"So, what do you want, Francis?"

He had rehearsed this part of the conversation while out in the Cat.

"I was wondering if you had come up with any theories about the weapons and why they're here."

She sighed.

"Results have been most unsatisfactory. Every time I think I have found a plausible reason, it collapses under my own internal cross-questioning. So far, nothing makes any sense to me. What about you? What ideas came into you head while you were driving around in the bleak Antarctic winter? Or were you thinking about me the whole time?"

That broke the spell a little bit. Hamlin smiled and shook his head.

"You were, weren't you? You were thinking about me naked, you bad boy."

"You really are twisted, you know that?"

"I don't think so," she said, slipping back easily into her husky voice. "You are a man, so you cannot help yourself. Is that not so?"

"Yeah, that imaginary pornographic video of you is pretty much playing in the background of my mind all the time. I've learned to work around it, though. Can you try to focus on the business at hand?"

"Are you sure? This could get interesting quite quickly."

"I thought of something today. I need you to tell me I'm crazy. I'd love you to convince me that I'm wrong. But before that can happen, you need to listen. But it may involve concentration on your part. Do you think you're capable of that?"

"Oh, I'm capable. I'm very capable. As a matter of fact, I can multitask nicely. For example, I am quite certain that I could listen to you talk while you were humping me on Sokolov's desk. Do you think you could speak coherently while doing me like that? Can you formulate thoughts under those conditions, or will you simply lose your mind?"

He figured based on the direction the conversation had turned that she wouldn't mind, so he put his hand on her knee and patted it gently.

"Just listen to me, okay? Hear me out. What happens after that between two consenting adults is another matter. Let's just not do anything to mare the finish on this excellent desk."

She smiled sweetly.

"No promises."

"Fine. I'm going to start talking. I hope you can find the discipline to listen."

He talked. It became more of a ramble once he got started. It took some time and he knew he had her attention. He told her all about his theory of the commandos that could swoop down on them at any moment to grab samples of the virus that no longer exist. She lost her desire to be flirty and settled in for a good listen. When he finished she merely sat and stared off into space. He almost wished that she would break out laughing at the ridiculousness of his idea.

"Well, what do you think? Am I crazy?"

That seemed to break the spell and just like that she was back in the moment again. Her eyes met his.

"I think you are a smart man. I think I was correct in bringing our issues to you to unravel. And I think we need to finish this conversation in your room."

Hamlin smiled. "Two out of three ain't bad. At least I somewhat captured your attention."

"Oh, you have my attention. Now let's go so you can have the rest of me."

Hamlin stood. "How can I say no to that?"

This one took some time. Lena was determined not to let him have a quick end to it. Every time things were going well enough to bring him to the brink, she would disengage and try a different approach. He was learning something new every time they made out. Finally his body started sending him the message that it was time and by the way, you cannot take no for an answer. *Get it done, and done now.*

Finally, once his exertions were spent, he couldn't hold himself up any longer and collapsed on top of her, panting and sweaty.

"So now you take control," she purred. "You have never been so forceful before. This is a side of you that I like."

"My God. You're turning me into a full blown, unadulterated pervert. Is there any possible way left to screw you that you haven't had me try?"

"Hmm. Maybe one or two minor variations. I think you have all the basics covered now."

"Do I get a certificate of some sort?"

She giggled.

"Do you want me to get off?"

"No. I like the feel of your weight pushing on me. And I like to let your little soldier retreat slowly, waiting for orders from command central, if you know what I mean."

"If he stays in there long enough, I'm not sure if he'll even do a complete retreat."

She nuzzled the side of his face and kissed his cheek. "If he snaps back to attention, that would be fine too."

"Stop talking dirty long enough to tell me what you think about my theory."

She grunted and not in a good way.

"All right." She sighed. "I'm not sure. But I wouldn't be quick to completely dismiss your ideas. It would definitely help to explain the presence of the weapons. But really? Is it possible that your government could sanction something like this?"

He lifted himself a little and kissed her on the forehead.

"I don't know. That's the question I keep asking myself over and over. I want to say no. But in truth, I'm not sure. Maybe it's a small faction that the president doesn't even know about. Maybe it's a rogue group that wants to sell it to the highest bidder. But you know what's really funny about this, don't you?"

"What could possibly be funny about this?"

"The samples are gone! We burned down the lab and everything in it. Until a full drilling crew is here and all the equipment brought back to running order, there won't be any virus for anybody. Sorry, better luck next year. The apocalypse starter kit you ordered is out of stock. Too bad that you'll have to wait to destroy the world. And oh, incidentally, I guess you don't have to machine gun all of us now, right?"

"It is a most unpleasant hypothesis, Francis."

"Yes. And the question is—what do we do? Anything? Nothing? Arm ourselves? Start posting a guard again? Tell the others? Hide it from the others?"

"Sokolov probably has your research results on his hard drive."

"True. But that won't give anybody the virus."

"Yes, I suppose you're right."

"What I would really like; what I was hoping you were going to provide, is a synopsis that excludes any conspiracy and evil intentions, especially to the extent that my own government is involved. You know, the worst thoughts I have ever had about my elected officials thus far have been about tax rates and road repairs. This opens a whole new and very disturbing list of possibilities. And it means I qualify to apply to be a card carrying member of the conspiracy theory association. I never thought that day would ever arrive."

Lena leaned up and kissed the side of his neck.

"It takes us to a very dark place, does it not?"

He lost his emotional grip for but an instant and his feelings boiled over.

"This whole experience has been dark! And I volunteered to come here! Everything here is dark, nasty, and unpleasant. It's been a truly evil place."

He paused to collect his thoughts and looked down at the nude form of his willing partner still pinned under his weight. She perceived his thoughts and smiled. At that, he twitched briefly.

"Everything is unpleasant? There is nothing good at all?"

"Well, maybe one thing."

"Hmm. Well, if I'm going to lay here naked with my legs spread apart, and you're going to straddle me, I think we might as well make the best of it. When you have finished your task, then we can think about this doomsday hypothesis and figure out what to do next."

"I do believe that you're disconcertingly addictive."

She grasped her breasts while she knew he was watching and started to play with them.

"You don't say?"

"Imagine if cocaine had a vagina. That's you."

She laughed. "Do your work before somebody starts to worry about why we've been in here so long."

He discovered that he could still follow orders nicely.

The next day arrived with the storm winds still howling. Once again, Hamlin chose to go out anyway. He could mark more locations and cover more of the grid. It was all good.

Things went well. He marked three more spots to add to those he had discovered the previous day. Once again, as he drove along and let his mind wander unstructured, a thought formed of its own accord and jumped out at him. This one got his heart racing. He wasn't certain of its validity, but the implication seemed to be profound. He turned around and headed back to the barracks early.

Nobody was there to see him come in, which was great as far as he was concerned. He slipped into the geology lab and shut the door behind himself.

Lena and Zoya both looked up in mild surprise. Suddenly he was no longer convinced that this couldn't have waited.

"Hi ladies. How are things going?" It came out artificially benign and awkward.

"Dr. Hamlin," Lena said formally. "To what do we owe the pleasure of your company? No problems with your search I hope."

He shook his head as he responded. "No. I found a few more sample sites. Hopefully I can reach them tomorrow and start collecting all this swag."

"Excellent." She stared at him expectantly.

"I, uh, was wondering if maybe I could have a word. Alone I guess. If you're not too busy."

She seemed hesitant on how she was going to respond.

"Francis, forgive me, but I made a unilateral executive decision earlier this morning."

"What do you mean?"

"I told Zoya about the weapons. And our theories."

"Oh." His response was subdued.

Zoya held up a hand as if trying to stop traffic before crossing a busy street.

"It's all right. We can trust each other. We all have the same goals, no?"

Lena smirked. "We three form a very exclusive club. I'll call it *The Loyal Order of Hamlin's Penis*. You either have to be wearing it or have had it in you. Let's hope nobody else at the station qualifies to be a member besides us."

Hamlin sneered. "Oh, very funny. I think that's safe to say."

"Even Vitsin?"

Zoya giggled.

"Especially Vitsin. Give me a break."

"Very well. In that instance, I believe we can bring this inaugural meeting to order. What do you have to say for yourself, Dr. Hamlin? You look like a child who just caught the tooth fairy."

"I had another epiphany while driving the Cat. It seems to bring out the thinker in me, by the way. You know how I speculated that Sokolov left us the code because he had changed the original one?"

"Yes. Make the American's ask for it when they arrive as leverage. I remember."

"I had a different thought. What if he didn't change the combination? Maybe he couldn't even if he wanted to. You would think somebody on the American side would have anticipated that and provided a cabinet where that wasn't an option. It would or could ruin everything for them, if the rest of our theory is correct."

"I'm not following. If he didn't change it, what would be the point of giving it to you? You could only mess things up even if you did figure it out."

"Which we did."

"Yes. Very impressive. Zoya, tell him how smart he is so we can proceed."

"You are very smart, Francis. A genius, really."

"Oh, thank you for those unsolicited and authentic sentiments."

"Francis, please proceed with your new and improved theory."

"Of course. Well, what if Sokolov, who knew he was on the way out, either by his own hand or the disease, stepped back and looked at the big picture. There was no rich reward in American dollars in his future now, nor was there a house in Cuba. The whole motivation for selling out his country and countrymen, if that was in fact what he was doing, was now gone. So, maybe he had a change of heart. Maybe he didn't want to exit to whatever eternity had in store for him with the guilt of a now pointless betrayal on his heart. Or maybe he just remembered that he was a human being like the rest of us."

"So he gave you the code because…?"

"So we could open the cabinet and remove the weapons before the hit team or whatever it is arrives. We would be heavily armed and they theoretically wouldn't be. Even a bunch of old farts like us could hold them off if we knew they were coming and stole their cache."

"My God," Lena said. "This might be even worse than your first theory. According to you, they could be out there arming up as we speak. Damn!"

He shrugged. "I don't know. It's all speculation. But there has to be a reason for that locker. It isn't there by mistake or coincidence. Somebody put a great deal of effort into getting that thing here at the end of the world without being seen, then setting it up with power and everything. I just can't imagine how the Russian government knew anything about it. Why would they agree to it? I can't come up with an answer to that question. So that leaves us with deep intrigue and the potential for espionage."

A deafening, uncomfortable silence fell over the room.

"What do we do?" Zoya asked. Hamlin was glad she verbalized his thoughts for him. He was tired of being the one to ask the questions that came out leaning toward dumb.

Lena supplied the answer, such as it was. "I don't know. I'm just not sure."

More silence ensued.

"If this is even close to being true," Hamlin said, "then when is it likely to happen? Soon? Or do we still have some time to work this out?"

Lena rolled her head around as if trying to work some kinks out before answering.

"I would think it would happen fairly soon. Why wait until near the time when the first flight from Moscow arrives here? That would be a totally unnecessary and easily avoidable risk. And an ambush works better now under the cover of darkness. Why wait for the sun to reappear? Who could absolutely guarantee that none of us wouldn't see them arriving?"

"Do you think," Hamlin asked, "that Sokolov gave them a status update shortly before he left us? Would they know we had confirmed samples of the virus? Would they know some of us contracted it and what the results were? Because if he did, then they would have no real reason to wait, would they?"

"What about the weather?" Zoya asked. "If they waited maybe a month or so, it would start improving."

"Would that matter to them?" Lena challenged.

Hamlin jumped on the bandwagon. "If they have to drive from the nearest station, they're going to be a long time on the ice. Maybe better weather would be a factor."

"It would be a long and perilous trek, no question about that. They would have to travel as fast as possible, and that would put them at risk for hitting or dropping into some unforeseen obstacle. If they went slow and cautious, it would take forever to get here. And then they still have to face the return journey."

"Maybe they'd use multiple vehicles. Otherwise, if they had only one and it broke down they'd be totally screwed."

Lena decided to turn a corner in her reasoning process. "We could go around in circles for some time with this. What if we just asked ourselves one question–are there any negative implications in taking the weapons right now and sharing our suspicions with the crew?"

"Ah, very good," Hamlin observed. "Now we have a simple yes or no question. We no longer have to be absolutely certain of anything, nor do we have to have all the answers to every question figured out."

Lena smiled. "As you would say, Francis, I'm a genius."

"I want to vote now," Zoya said. "I say we take them. What legitimate reason could there be for them being here? And is this station not considered sovereign Russian territory anyway? Would our government not support our actions? If anything, we would be heroes of the state for doing this."

"If our theory is correct," Hamlin lamented.

"I say do it." Zoya wasn't often this forceful.

They both looked at Lena.

"Well, it really doesn't hurt anything that I can see if we do. If we're completely wrong about all of this, then we return the weapons and smile sheepishly once it is all straightened out. That is better than getting gunned down by a team of foreign mercenaries. The only thing is, if we proceed, then we must tell the others about our potential folly and reintroduce them to the still fresh memory of what it's like to live constantly with the stress of having your very life threatened."

"They should know," Zoya said.

"I think we've reached the point where we have a responsibility to tell them. Anything else would border on negligence." Francis figured this was the time to speak his mind.

Lena stood up front her seat and stretched. "Well then, we have much to do. Just as things were starting to settle down, too."

The rest of the crew surprised Hamlin by immediately engaging in a spirited debate about the veracity of their theory. They split down each side, pro and con, and away they went. After an hour, they compromised on agreeing to get the weapons and store them in the barracks whether they agreed with the premise of international espionage or not. If they were wrong, it couldn't hurt much. If they were right, it could save their lives.

Lena suggested that the other researchers simply return to their duties, while she, Zoya and Hamlin fetched the weapons and brought them back. This was easily agreed upon.

So after a quick lunch, the three of them dressed in their heavy outdoor gear and piled into the Cat. Zoya drove, which didn't bother Francis much considering the amount of time he had spent behind the wheel in the last couple of days. Lena reached over and patted him on the knee through numerous layers of clothing.

"So, Mr. American researcher, is this the adventure that you thought it would be?"

"No, not really. I'm not exactly sure what I expected, but this ain't it. I guess I thought it would be quiet, predictable and cerebral. I pictured months of sitting quietly in front of a microscope or something like that. It was supposed to be therapeutic."

"And why did you need therapy, my darling?"

He really had tried to avoid rehashing this particular memory since arriving here. Did he want to talk about it now? What the hell.

"Because I had just split up with my live-in partner of nearly two years. I was a little traumatised."

Lena raised her eyebrows. "You have never spoken of this before. So, you dumped her?"

"Not exactly. I came home from work one day and she was gone. All she left was a cute little note on the kitchen table."

"What did she say, if you don't mind me asking."

He sighed. "She basically insinuated that I should have known this was going to be the inevitable end of our relationship right from the get-go, and please don't be a dick and call me to ask me about it. Have a good life. Ciao."

"Oh my."

"That's sort of what I thought."

"And what did you do?"

"I called her."

"How soon after?"

"About thirty seconds."

"Oh my."

"You just said that."

"What did you say?"

Now Hamlin had to smile. "I can remember the exact three words. She picked up and said hello, and I said, '*what the fuck*?'"

Lena actually gasped a little. "Oh my, oh my. How did she react to that?"

"Not very well, actually. I'm paraphrasing somewhat, but she basically told me to grow up and get lost."

"I see."

"So, after a brief stint training for the Olympic drinking team, I decided a dramatic change might not be a bad idea. In retrospect, I should have gone to a professional to have my head examined. But I didn't, so bingo-bango, here I am."

She patted his knee again. "Oh, Francis, I am so sorry. You come down here damaged and vulnerable, and the first female you run into is me, playing the role of station slut. And of course, you also get a visit from the slut and her sexually confused friend with the big boobs who both stripped down and jumped into your bed without so much as a '*would you like some company*?'. Oh Francis, we didn't do you any favors. I apologize."

"Are you kidding me? Have you forgotten I'm a man? Apologies for sexing me up are totally unnecessary."

Zoya was trying hard to concentrate on her driving so she would have a legitimate reason not to participate in the discussion.

"On the bright side, if I somehow survive this house of horrors at the end of the world, my life is going to look pretty darn awesome, girlfriend or not, when I finally get back. Also, I have plenty of fodder to use for writing an article that should be easily publishable in any number of gentlemen's magazines. So it's not all bad."

"Nice to see you looking on the bright side," Lena said.

"Names will be changed to protect the innocent. Anyway, I'm confident I'll have a different attitude and will be able to appreciate and enjoy my life once I return back to it."

"I hope so," Lena said. "For you and for all of us. I have decided that this will be my last trip down here. I fear the cumulative stress will follow me home and stay with me for a long time. I need to move on with my life. Enough is enough."

"And you, Zoya?" Hamlin asked, uncomfortable with how she was being excluded from the conversation.

She turned briefly and smiled. "Undecided."

The Cat rolled on, drawing ever closer to the outer shed.

Barinov had wandered incessantly until he stumbled upon the generator building. He eventually managed to figure out the door and walked in on unsteady legs. He smelled food and was desperate for it now, such as his limited consciousness could convey.

Inside he found two sources. He fell upon the first one. It was frozen quite hard, so instead of a frantic feast, it was more of a slow gnarl. But that was okay. It was food and he was not on any kind of a schedule. He settled in for the long haul, the nourishment stoking the furnace inside him that kept the brutal cold completely at bay.

CHAPTER NINETEEN

It took some time to get started. They had to figure out if Lena's concern over the cache being booby-trapped was legitimate or not. After thinking it through, she decided it was perhaps less likely than she had originally thought. It was already protected by an electronic combination lock and secured in an abandoned building that nobody had any reason to visit. Once that conclusion was shared, they looked for switches, wires or any signs of tampering in the cabinet. That came up negative. Finally, Lena rigged up an old wooden broom handle that she used to poke one of the guns loose while crouching beside the cabinet and reaching around from a semi-protected position. Nothing went bang, so they decided her fears were officially unfounded.

Things moved fairly quickly once they got started. The last item they moved was a rocket launcher. Hamlin carried it as if it was a newborn infant. He sure as hell didn't want to drop it. The weight surprised him. In the movies, a muscle bound hero would handle this thing as if it were a pistol. Could it be that Hollywood misrepresented reality? Surely not.

Setting it down safely in the back of the Cat was the pinnacle of stress. Lena had bunched up an old blanket for him to set it on, and in the end, he got it placed without blowing everyone to kingdom come. He decided to put that accomplishment in the *good stuff* category.

"Okay, which country should we invade first? We should probably start small and work our way up. How about China?"

Lena continued to enjoy his sense of humor. "And what have the Chinese ever done to you?"

"Hmm, I suppose you're right. We have to stock Wal-Mart with high quality merchandise from somewhere. What was I thinking?"

"Let's get in before we freeze, you lunatic."

They piled in and Zoya soon had them turning back toward the barracks.

"Try not to hit any big bumps or hydro poles," Hamlin requested.

"She knows how to drive, you stupid ass," Lena responded. "You know enough to ignore him, Zoya, correct?"

She turned and finally smiled, making her dimples pop. "Of course."

"Good. Now, what are we going to do with all these doomsday devices when we get back?"

"The oven seems like a secure enough place for the ammo," Hamlin said.

Lena just stared in response.

"Okay, okay. I'm in a weird mood right now, I admit it. It feels like we've made another proactive move to take some control back. I feel good that we did. In addition, I'd appreciate it if you'd get off my back about it."

Lena turned toward the driver.

"Zoya, what do you think? Let's leave our resident lunatic out of this until he regains some semblance of composure."

She chose to respond seriously. "Well, what if we are invaded in the night while we're sleeping? We should keep some of it distributed and accessible just in case."

Lena was quick to agree. "Yes. We can spread some of the smaller weapons around, based on need and skill levels of the people in the area. Some of the bigger, more complicated pieces should go into one of the storerooms. We can do a survey of the crew and see who has operated what in their past lives. We don't want to be shooting ourselves. And it shouldn't be necessary for each and every person to be armed unless they want to be."

Zoya returned to looking straight ahead. "Yes. That is a good plan."

Lena looked back toward Hamlin. "And you, Francis? What do you think?"

"Well, if you really want my opinion, a fact which is in doubt as far as I'm concerned, I think your plan is too radical. I propose we do something low key and safe, like putting the rocket launcher on the table, pointed toward the door, with a string running from the knob to the trigger. But suit yourself."

"Zoya," Lena said, "get us back before I shoot this idiot."

The dimples came into play again. "I can do that."

Out of the seven remaining members, six agreed to be in possession and control of a weapon for defensive purposes. All had either training or experience in handling firearms. They put together a protocol for how the weapons were to be carried, stored, and operated. Parameters for actual discharge were also established.

"Let us hope most sincerely that we never have to use these to defend ourselves. But at least now there can be no doubt. Anyone coming in here won't take us without a hell of a fight." Lena was addressing the group after the weapons had been distributed or stored.

The working portion of the day had expired and a simple meal was prepared with everyone pitching in. The problem came afterwards. For some reason, everyone seemed unusually bored and melancholy. None of the usual distractions seemed to generate any enthusiasm. Realising that this could be the straw that breaks the camel's back, Lena decided to fetch some of the cigars and booze from Sokolov's room. It was a start.

Hamlin had some video of several comedians performing and wondered if that might be a nice change of entertainment venue for the crew. Whether Russians would get all the jokes or not, he wasn't sure. After consulting Lena, they decided it was worth a try.

After that, a rather pleasant evening unfolded, involving smoking, drinking, and lots of laughter. It turned out to be the medicine they needed. It was like every guffaw and chuckle poked a hole through the cover of gloom that had been lying over them. By the time they all turned in, the mood was appreciably lighter. Hamlin considered it yet another accomplishment to a fairly productive day.

The next morning brought the news Hamlin had been hoping for. The storm had passed and the winds had died off completely. It was still ferociously cold, but without any hint of a breeze, it was manageable. Now he could collect all the samples he had identified. Beautiful.

He gobbled a breakfast that would have put him at risk for a heart attack back home–here his body burned off all sorts of calories and other junk to maintain his temperature in the always cold environment. He figured he'd be putting on some weight when he returned home until his dietary habits could be reformed back to a normal routine. But that was an issue for then, not now. Now he just wanted to get out and drive.

Since conditions for the job were as good as they were ever going to get down here, he refuelled the Cat before leaving, The incessant dark didn't seem to bother him like it had at first, he thought as the fuel gravity fed from the overhead tank into the idling machine. He wondered what kind of a reaction he was going to have when the sun finally peeked over the horizon for the first time.

"I'll probably fall on my knees and cry," he said to no one, hoping that the fact that he liked to hear his own voice wasn't a sign that he was losing his marbles.

He finished without spilling any or dripping the smelly stuff on his gloves. Diesel was the gift that kept on giving when it was in a position to emit its unique odor. Safe and thankfully stench-free, Hamlin hopped in and started his morning quest.

The search area was large, but the GPS technology made it child's play to re-find his previous discoveries. He started with the closest ones, and then gradually moved away from the barracks into the open Antarctic plain. Francis had brought a small box along and the samples started to pile up as he went. He felt he was doing quite well. That all came to a sudden and unfortunate end at the furthest identified piece.

He was out of the Cat, having trouble finding it. He knew where it was within a few feet, but somehow just could get it to appear under the piercing beam of the flashlight he gripped awkwardly in his bulky glove.

"Where are you, you little bastard? Cooperate a little and I'll get both of us out of the cold."

He actually felt the hardness of it through his boot. He had stepped right on it.

"Splendid. Not exactly traditional, but who cares? There you are."

It took a little effort to pry it loose from the snow.

"Aha. Perfect. Into the box with you, and then I can start fresh."

He turned to see two men standing beside the Cat. He almost fainted.

"Don't run," one of them said unnecessarily. "There's nowhere to go."

Hardly the first words you would want to hear under the circumstances. "No shit. You'd think I'd have figured that one out for myself." The greeting set an immediate ominous tone. Why would their first thought be that he was going to run away? "Who the hell are you guys?"

"Come on over here," the same one said. "Let's climb inside and talk. There's no need for anybody to freeze."

Francis, rather than being overjoyed with having fresh faces to see, felt immediately defensive and hostile. "Well, it's my Cat, but help yourself."

The men didn't budge, and to Francis' disconcertion, their current position blocked access to the door. Suddenly running away didn't seem like such an outrageous option.

"If you assholes move, I'll gladly climb in." He felt decidedly uncomfortable about getting any closer to them. A realization formed in his mind. They must be part of the hit squad that the weapons had been meant for. They came too soon and openly during the day. Also, they had caught him standing unarmed and unaware, out in the middle of nowhere all by himself. Shit. So much for the plans that had him feeling so secure just the night before.

"You get in the back; we'll sit in the front. Then we can be comfortable while we talk."

Every word this guy said fell like ice on his ears. There was something very wrong here and he felt it with every fibre of his being.

What could he do? They might as well have caught him with his pants down around his ankles for how defenseless and vulnerable he felt.

"Sorry, I'm the driver. Company rules."

The man smiled. "Sorry. Change of plans. My company rules. Now get in."

Options seemed non-existent. There was no way he could run off and then walk his way back to the barracks. It was way too far from here and he'd simply get lost. These guys seemed so quietly confident in the superiority of their position. Francis had no doubt that in the end he would be defenseless against them in any kind of physical confrontation.

"Well, move out of my way, for God's sake. How else I am going to get in?" He really didn't want to approach them anyway.

The man moved ever so slightly, giving him just enough space to get past. Somehow forcing Hamlin into close proximity seemed to be one of the goals. What else was there to do?

He took a deep breath and then stepped as confidently as possible up to the Cat. His suit literally brushing against the guy as he reached for the door. All sorts of internal alarms were going off, and he expected that he was about to get pushed, punched, stabbed, or shot at any second. It took every bit of effort he could muster not to flinch perceptively. It was a relief to get inside. He immediately slammed the door shut, creating a small buffer.

The other two climbed into the front and shut their doors as well. The idling of the motor provided some background noise.

"You must be Hamlin." So far the second man hadn't said a word.

He was still being torn apart between fear and rage. "Lucky guess. Who are you?"

"No luck involved. You have no accent."

"Okay. So there's one thing I haven't picked up yet."

"This is very fortunate. For all of us, really."

"Look, this is considered sovereign Russian territory. I'm here doing research sanctioned by both Russian and American governments. I still don't know who you arrogant fuckers are, but you're about to be in a position where you're doing something for which there could be serious negative consequences for you."

The driver's side man laughed. He turned to his partner. "He swears a lot for a doctor." The partner remained silent.

"Look, Hamlin. We're moving quickly. Time is important for us. We're going to ask you several questions. You need to provide answers. This all boils down to something very basic. Either you answer or you don't. What's it going to be?"

"I don't know where you walked from to get here, but you can walk right back. Get out of my fucking Cat."

The two men exchanged a glance.

"I'm going to tell you something you should already know. This is the end of the world. You are hundreds of miles from the nearest station and thousands of miles from civilization. Nobody else will ever know what is about to happen between us here. Nobody. Ever. So, I need a quick confirmation from you. Are you going to answer some questions, yes or no?"

"You know, I should be overjoyed to have some fresh faces appear. But whoever and whatever you are, I would like it very much if you would just piss off."

"If we can get our hands on some samples, then that's exactly what we're going to do. So why don't you help us, and facilitate the very thing you want most."

Hamlin was suddenly flooded with the idea that he was going to die very soon. Probably before the end of the day. He wasn't ready for that. And what about the others? Was there anything he could do now that could protect them in any way? He couldn't think of a single thing.

"Let's start with this. Where are the samples?"

Despite his fear, Hamlin actually laughed. "Jokes on you, assholes. We burned down the lab that was housing the samples. Everything was destroyed. There's nothing left. All we're working on currently is some geology and weather related stuff. So how are you feeling about the trip down here now?"

"Cut the crap. You wouldn't do that. So for the last time, where are the samples?"

"Oh, that's right. I forgot. We did that after Sokolov died, so you wouldn't know about it."

"Sokolov is dead? What are you talking about?"

"The precious virus that you all want to get your hands on got loose down here. We lost seven people because of it. The lab was horribly contaminated so we burned it to the ground. And quite frankly, I don't give a flying shit whether you believe me or not."

That led to a moment of silence.

"So he caught it?"

"No, it was genital herpes. The shame was more than he could bear."

"God, you're an ass. Are you sure there are no samples?"

"Yup."

"None anywhere."

"Nope."

"What about the bodies? You say you lost seven. Where are they now?"

"We burned two. The rest are…scattered."

"Where exactly?"

Hamlin shrugged. "I'm sure you could find them eventually, if you wandered around long enough."

He didn't see it coming until the last possible second and then it was too late. The passenger side man hit him in the face with a pistol. Hard.

He slumped over, his ears ringing and his eyes watering. The side of his face where impact occurred make a snapping sound and his right eye felt like it was going to pop right out of its socket. It was watering profusely. They were yelling something at him and he just couldn't make it out. He wanted to respond in kind, but his injury demanded all of his attention. It hurt like a bastard. He was afraid it could be serious enough that he might lose the eyesight on the damaged side. He was no medical doctor, but it felt all wrong, even factoring out the pain.

"I said, where are they exactly? No more bullshit or we're going to do something way worse than that to make you talk. Where are they?"

He tried to sit upright but a piercing sharp pain dropped him back down. He moaned involuntarily. He needed medical attention, no doubt.

"Talk!"

What could be worse than this anyway? Getting shot, he supposed. Couldn't hurt a lot more, but the results would be more severe and permanent. He hoped the result of this wouldn't be.

"They're in the genny shed." It hurt to talk, so his volume was subdued. The vibration of his voice felt like it was splitting his head apart.

"That's better. You see? Cooperation is the way to go. This ugliness could have been completely avoided. So why did you put them in there?"

"Didn't. That's where they died."

"And you just left them there. Why?"

"Frozen now."

"Oh. I suppose that makes sense. That would be a good as anything down here. They all died from the virus?"

The truth would have taken too long to tell. His face was killing him. "Yes."

"So what does it do? When you contract it, I mean."

"High fever."

"High fever–okay. Anything else?"

"Madness."

Another pause.

"What do you mean by that?"

"Violence."

"So...what? Like kicking and screaming?"

"Biting."

"Interesting. Then unconsciousness and death, I suppose."

Again the truth was discarded. "Yes."

"And transmission?"

"Not certain. Direct contact."

"That's not good. Not airborne at all?"

"Not sure."

"Damn. What kind of a sloppy research station is this? All you brainiacs stuck down here with nothing to do and you still couldn't figure this one out. Did it not occur to you that the answer to that question could be important?"

"Things went to hell."

"Okay. I might even buy that."

Hamlin wanted the pain to start fading. Really, really wanted it. No luck so far on that front.

"Your tank looks full on this thing. That's good. Since you're resting at the moment, I'm going to drive it back to the barracks for you. When we get there, you're going to walk us through the front door like we're in-laws stopping by for Sunday dinner. We'll handle it from there. You can get some Tylenol or something while we conduct a little business. If you can keep from making a total ass of yourself, we'll be taking you with us. You'll be back stateside before you know it. And we have an excellent infirmary, so we'll get you fixed right up. It is a shame you slipped and fell like that. Landed right on your face, too. Well, accidents happen, right?"

Hamlin tried to respond and came out with a moan instead.

"Okay, I get it. Try to get your shit together. We're going to need you when we arrive."

The Cat started with a jerk, and then picked up momentum quickly. Francis had never tried to go this speed before. He wasn't going to have much time before they arrived at this rate. It didn't matter anyway. The pain seemed to take away his ability to think. The bumps weren't helping either.

CHAPTER TWENTY

The door to the lab opened. Lena looked up to see Hamlin standing there. She was starting to think of something funny to say when she noticed the purple swelling on the side of his face. He was swaying slightly even as he stood.

"Francis, what happened to you?"

She started to get up. A strange man she had never seen before pushed Hamlin out of the way roughly and stepped into the room. He had a pistol in his hand.

"No, no. Just stay seated please."

By now Zoya had turned. She gasped at what she saw.

"Just relax, ladies. Let's do this the easy way. I will keep this as simple as I can. Just do what I tell you and all will be good."

"Who are you?" Lena asked, already guessing what the answer would be.

"Totally irrelevant." He looked at Zoya. She looked terrified. "You, chunky, get up off your stool slowly. Then turn away from me."

Fear made her movements awkward and she almost stumbled and fell just dismounting.

"Careful now. We don't want any more facial injuries. They hurt like hell, just ask Dr. Hamlin here. Now, put both your hands behind your back, the wrists touching each other."

She complied listlessly, like she was just emerging from a coma. He slipped a plastic tie of some sort over her hands and snugged it up tight.

"Excellent. Now you." He turned toward Lena. "Same routine exactly. Stand up slow, turn away, then both hands behind the back. Nice and easy."

She was clearly frustrated, but options were lacking. Slowly she complied. Soon she too was trussed up tightly.

"There we go. Now, let the raping begin!"

Both women stiffened noticeably.

"Oh, come on now. I'm just kidding. Where's your sense of humor? Do you really think we went to all this trouble to grab a piece of Russian tail? Honestly ladies, don't flatter yourself. We could do much better at home. Come on now, it's time for a short walk. Step around me and out into the other room. Let's go."

They walked out obediently. Lena was seething inside.

"You too, Hamlin. Let's go."

"You said Tylenol when we got here," he slurred.

"You know, I might have lied about that. With all the weapons you allegedly have, I think it is in my best interests to keep you in sight. March!"

He obeyed awkwardly. When they reached the common area, they were the only ones there.

"How's it going back there?" their captor yelled down the hallway.

"Good," came the return reply.

"In that case, you ladies stand over there together with your backs up against the wall. Hamlin, you don't look so good. Take a seat at the table with me. It's time you took a load off."

He sat with a groan. He looked toward Lena and she met his eyes. She looked strong and defiant. Weirdly, he felt proud of her at that moment.

Soon the other men came marching in the room, arms bound behind them.

"Very nice. Look at the excellent partner I have. Good job. All you men, stand beside the two ladies if you will. Backs to the wall, please."

The men, choices now non-existent, all complied.

The other man sat beside his partner, his silence still intact. He set his pistol on the table and it made a solid clunk.

"Can you believe this? Supposedly they have enough weapons to repel a platoon of marines but we just walk in like we own the place. Not so much as a single shot fired. Oh my. But I suppose you are researchers, not fighters."

The room fell silent.

"Okay, we need to establish some structure to this farce. Here it is. I'm going to ask questions…you're going to answer questions. That will keep things moving smoothly, and, much more importantly, it will keep me and my partner happy. Very important, that last part. And that's all there is too it. Couldn't be easier. Do you all understand?"

The group stared silently, unsure of how to respond.

"I said do you understand!" he screamed at the top of his lungs, causing them all to jump. Heads nodded and some mumbled an affirmative response.

"That's better. Just work with me. My partner and I simply want what we came for. And I'm sure you'd be happy to get rid of it. So cooperation should come easily, you see?"

More mumbling and head nods.

"Outstanding. Now for the first question. We'll start with an easy one. I want you to get your self-confidence in gear. That should help as we work our way through this. So here we go. Listen carefully. Are you seven the only people here at this station? Take your time. Think about it if you have to. Just don't give me the wrong answer. What do you think?"

They seemed confused about how to respond.

"Oh, I see what's happening here. You all want to cooperate so badly, but you also want to do it politely. So, in order to prevent you from interrupting each other's answers or cutting each other off, or God help you, contradicting each other, I will assign one person as spokesman for the group. Okay? But before we go any farther, I have to shed a layer. Excuse me." He stood up, pulled his arms out of his parka, and then laid it on the table.

"There. Much better. Now, let me see. You sir, what is your name?" He pointed at a short, dour-looking man.

"Grebenshchikov."

"Are you serious? Sorry, but that doesn't work for me. I'm going to call you Greg, okay?"

The man didn't know if he was actually supposed to respond.

"I said, okay?"

"Yes! Yes, of course."

"Good. Very good, as a matter of fact. Because now I need an answer. What do you say?"

"Yes. We seven are the only ones here. Now."

"Congratulations, I believe you got that one right. As a prize, there will be no beatings or other assorted forms of torture meted out. Very nice indeed. Now, we come to the all-important second question. Again, it is critical to answer both thoroughly and truthfully. Here we go. Where are all the weapons from the cabinet?"

Grebenshchikov cleared his throat.

"Can you answer this one on your own, Greg, or do you need help from the team?"

The secondary question seemed to confuse him. Finally he spoke. "They are under the beds in our room. Except the big ones. They are in the back storage room on the shelves."

"Well done. I complement you on your speed and accuracy. My partner is going to go and confirm your answer. If you please."

He was already up and moving.

"I'm so confident that you told the truth, I'm going to go on with the next question while my partner is checking. Everybody okay with that?

Are you sure? Great! Then here we go. Now this is a big one. Where are the samples?" He said it with a bit of a flourish to emphasize the importance.

Grebenshchikov looked like he was about to choke on his tongue. He had been there that night and watched the shed go up in flames.

"Which samples?"

"Oh, come on now." His voice took on a nasty edge. "This is a really important one. Don't mess up now."

"I…"

"Greg, you look like you could use some help from the others. Come on, team. Help him out, now."

"We burned the shed."

"Oh, Greg. I'm extremely sorry, and I appreciate the effort, I really do. But that is the wrong answer. Darn it all, that means we have to talk about the various negative consequences of a wrong answer. I was really hoping we could avoid all the unpleasantries, but now, here they are staring us all in the face." He took his pistol and played with it on the tabletop. His partner walked back into the room.

"Well?"

He nodded slightly. "I found them all but one pistol."

"Excellent. I can live with that. So, one problem resolved. One still remains. Perhaps this could be settled quicker if you all had some perspective. Let me give you some by telling you about myself. I am a military man. I have had extensive training in many different fields. Because of my affiliation with Special Forces, I was able to take a little side course on how to make people tell you what you wanted them to. Some would call it torture, I prefer to think of it as utilizing the benefits of duress. My instructor was very pleased with me. I don't like to brag, but he said I was a natural. Are you all following me so far?"

There was a smattering of nods.

"Wow. Where is the enthusiasm? Do you not get how important this is? I mean, please do an inventory. You're all physically intact. No injuries, mild or otherwise. No sharp, debilitating pain, with the possible exception of Hamlin over here. Lifespans most likely to carry you through this into the spring when you will get picked up and returned home to your families and your life. That could change in the next few minutes. So I ask you again, are you with me so far?"

They all nodded and mumbled in agreement.

"Terrible. Just terrible. I've interrogated people before and they all seemed to be in the moment. They had great enthusiasm and they really participated. I'm just disappointed, that's all. But hey, you've got one more chance. Things could still improve. It's not over until the fat lady sings. So, tell me my friends, where are the frigging samples?"

Grebenshchikov tried to talk but for a moment his mouth lost all ability to coordinate its movements. "We had samples, but they were in the shed. We burned it all. We thought they were dangerous."

"Of course they're dangerous, Greg. Why do you suppose I'm interested in them? To use them as a secret ingredient in my *best in the neighborhood* barbeque sauce?" He collected himself for a moment. "So, let me get this straight. You are all telling me that there are no more samples?" His voice had slowed and dropped noticeably lower.

"There are...I mean... the data for the research is on Sokolov's computer," Grebenshchikov stammered.

"The data for the research? On Sokolov's computer? Lovely. Wonderful. And I'm sure in some rudimentary way that would be helpful to me IF ONLY I HAD THE SAMPLES!"

He slammed his gun against the table again and they all cringed. He lowered his head, shaking it all the while. Inexplicably, he started to laugh softly.

"The god-damned fucking data is on the God-damned fucking computer." He looked over at his partner. "Would you be so good as to retrieve this data and put it on some sort of stick or disc or whatever is available?"

He stood and walked off with a word.

"There, now you see? My partner is helpful. My partner is cooperative. He's accomplishing positive goals that help both of us. He's a team player. Why can't you people be team players?"

He lifted his pistol as he sat casually at the table. He aimed and fired a quick shot. The pistol had a silencer and made an anaemic *phewt* sound.

The bullet smashed through Grebenshchikov's kneecap. He shrieked and fell to the floor, clutching his leg as if to keep it from coming apart. The veins in his neck and forehead bulged as he dealt with the pain. A bloody smear already appeared on the linoleum as he thrashed.

The man stood and began to approach them.

"You see this? This is what happens! Why can't you just cooperate? Hey, hey! Greg, you need to shut up! Keep it quiet. I need to be able to communicate with the others."

Grebenshchikov struggled to stop verbalizing his agony. He moaned softly while tears ran down his face.

"Greg, that is another half-hearted effort and frankly, that's the last thing this team needs."

He swung his shooting hand out straight until the shot was lined up. He put a bullet through Grebenshchikov's head. The moaning and thrashing immediately ceased.

The crew tried not to overreact, but there were gasps and moans.

"I hope you all realize that this was your fault. You let Greg down. You could have prevented this. And you know what else? Now that the precedent has been set, guess where we go from here? Haven't you fucking Russians learned that discipline is progressive? It has to be! It's the only way it works. And look at where the bar is now set."

He shook his head as if he felt sorry for what had just transpired.

"It is what it is. That's unfortunate but it's also reality. So, who's next? Let's see. We have three men, Hamlin, and two women. Sorry to exclude from the *man* count, Hamlin, but you're already damaged. I'm sure you're very studly and macho, and would fit in nicely with the male group under ideal circumstances. I hope you forgive me. So, how about you, sir? What is your name?"

"There are some samples."

His head whipped around and looked toward the other end of the line. It was Lena that had spoken, in her deep, sultry voice.

"I'm sorry, but could you please repeat that, darling?" He started to walk slowly toward the women.

"There are still some samples. I saved them."

He stopped as a huge smile creased his face.

"There, you see? I told you. Didn't I tell you? Now this is teamwork! Nicely done. I'm sorry, beautiful, what was your name?"

"Lena."

"Lena. That's a good name. Lena, could you give me some more details about these samples that you are referring to? Please."

"I thought it was a shame, even with all the terrible side effects, to just waste the effort and sacrifice. So, I hid some away before we burned the lab."

He actually did a fist pump. "Awesome! I love you! I love the way you think. That is forward thinking. That is independent thinking. That is using your intuition to its fullest advantage. Ha-ha! Now, sweetheart, I think I will address you exclusively since you are obviously the go-to person in this group. If you could just give me some idea as to where these samples are, I would be most grateful."

"I would like to negotiate."

He looked a little like he had just been slapped. His eyes blinked rapidly a few times, and then he seemed to settle back down.

"I'm sorry. You just said…"

"Negotiate."

He sported a strange looking, smile/frown combination expression on his face.

"Negotiate? Okay. That took a lot of nerve. You did just see me shoot Greg, correct?"

She remained stoned faced, nodding slightly.

He waved his pointing finger in the air, using it to emphasize a point. "I like you, you know that? You remind me of myself. I think we might be kindred spirits of a sort. Isn't that awesome."

He strolled down casually until he was directly in front of her. He stood just far enough away that he remained out of kicking distance. This was not his first rodeo.

"I think I can summarize this situation in two ways. I need it resolved and I need it resolved quickly. You, however, have me over a barrel. You know where they are, I don't. So, you have proposed a negotiation. Interesting. I'm just going over my various options. Here's what I have come up with.

"Firstly, I have to determine if you're telling the truth or not. This could just be a stalling tactic, could it not? But, if we negotiate successfully, it won't take very long to confirm your claim's viability. So, that leads me to believe that negotiation is, and should be, still on the table.

"Second, I need to know if any of these other weaker-minded folks also know about the alleged samples. If that is the case, I can change my approach significantly."

"They don't. Only me."

"But darling, the problem is–I don't know if I can trust you. Can I take you at your word? Or are you simply trying to protect our friends and colleagues? I have no way of knowing for certain which is which. So you see my dilemma. I think it would benefit me to torture them all to death first. Then, and only then, will I be certain that this negotiation is really necessary."

"That would waste a lot of time."

He laughed softly again. "You are a cold one. I really do like you. No emotionally charged grovelling, just the facts. That's good. It helps me, you see. We can keep this moving along. So, where was I? Oh yes, about to torture and kill all the others."

His partner returned and sat calmly at the table. "Got it."

"Very good. Thank you. If you could hand that stick to me while I'm organizing this mess, that would be great. And incidentally, since we're talking now, there have been some significant developments since you left us. Lena here says that there are samples and she knows where they are. But, she wants to negotiate. I'm still thinking about it. It seems reasonable. What do you think?"

The man gave a curt nod.

"There you have it. Negotiating it is. So, how about you initiate the give and take, Lena. What is it you want?"

"Take me with you when you go."

That shocked everybody in the room, including and, perhaps especially, her fellow researchers.

"Oh my. That was unexpected. Look at the expression on these faces. It was unexpected for them as well. Take you with us when we go. Why would you ask that?"

"I want a cut."

More shock and surprise. "Lena, you're really keeping me off balance here."

"You can afford it."

He shook his head and turned away. He started to walk slowly, reflectively around the room.

"You could make that argument. I can see how you could. To be completely honest, it was originally to be a five way split. My current partner and myself decided that a change in the numbers would be much more lucrative for us, so we made a staffing adjustment on the way here. We downsized, to use the current popular lingo. Oh my, weren't they surprised. It wasn't exactly a pink slip, it was more of a red splatter."

He turned and meandered along the far wall. His voice was still easily distinguishable in the otherwise silent environment.

"So we went from a five way split to a two way split. Now here you are proposing what…a three way split?"

"Yes."

"Three way. Hmm. Doesn't have the same nice ring to it as a two way split."

"What do you get without the samples?"

He was walking slowly back toward them now.

"You are brazen and bold, Lena. What do we get without the samples? We get zilch, zip, zero. Did you like what I did there? Those were all words that start with z. We get bupkis, diddly squat, jack shit. So, I do get your point. A three way split of a large amount is better than a two way split of nothing. I commend you on your negotiating skills and tactics. Let's just say, for the sake of argument, that I'm not absolutely opposed to the idea of taking you on and bringing you with us. Where do we go from here?"

"I leave with you. We do a split. And these people are left behind unharmed."

"Now there's your problem right there, Lena. The old morality thing. Really? Does that even seem feasible in the midst of a deal that is intended to give a deadly virus to someone who probably plans to use it? And now you worry about five researchers and put this whole negotiation in jeopardy? You're trying to balance the slate by saving five as opposed to the deaths of possibly millions? Sorry, even I know that won't come out in the wash. So why even bother?"

"Those are my terms. Also, I have a question, if I may? Would you come over here so I can whisper something in your ear? I don't want the others to hear."

He wagged his finger at her. "Oh, Lena. You're a saucy one. You wouldn't be planning on kicking or biting me, would you? Because that would definitely sour the negotiations."

"One way to find out." She was utilizing her husky voice now.

"Okay. My friend here can keep an eye on the proceedings while you distract me, I suppose. If you do anything inappropriate, I'm going to shoot your chunky friend in her gut. Just saying."

He sauntered over, got close, and then hesitated. "You're not going to put your tongue in my ear or anything like that, are you? Because I'd rather you didn't. Unless you really mean it, of course. I assume that this is simply you wanting to screw over your comrades here, and you don't want them to know." He leaned in close.

She pressed her lips in until they brushed his skin. She whispered softly for a moment. And then, in what she hoped was a well calculated move, she did, in fact, flick her tongue in and out of his ear.

He pulled away, looking puzzled.

"I asked you not to do that unless you meant it. So I'm going to assume you meant it. We can discuss the implications of that later. Now, back to your proposal."

He sauntered toward the table where his partner sat. He pointed toward him.

"So, would it be okay if I let my partner in on the secret proposal?"

Her eyes grew wide. She shook her head.

"Oh, come on. I can see why you didn't want your companions to hear, but my partner? Of course I have to tell him. So, partner, you'll never guess what she proposed."

"What?" He continued to be a man of few words. As he would forever be.

"She said the two-way split was still the best." He whipped up his pistol and shot the man in the back of the head. Parts sprayed across the table, and he jerked off the seat and flopped onto the floor.

"And I happen to agree. Besides, you never offered to put your tongue in my ear even once in all the time I knew you."

Francis was way too close to the action. It took every ounce of concentration and willpower he had not to throw up.

"Hamlin, I almost forgot you there in all this excitement. Hang tight, little buddy. I think we'll have this resolved fairly quickly." He looked at the table. "Oh my, what a mess. If this all ends well for the rest of you, I recommend you don't eat here at this table any more. And I'll tell you something else; I'm certainly not cleaning that up."

He started back toward the group.

"What's next, Lena? Lena, with the big, long legs. How do we wrap this up? We should be going as soon as possible. There is a schedule to maintain, my dear. So help me out."

"I could think better if your hand was in my shirt."

He laughed long and loud. "Oh, Lena. You're a hoot. I'm so glad I got to meet you. You've changed my life in some small ways already. But mixing business with pleasure, now you know better than that. And speaking of knowing better, who do you really work for?"

She maintained a blank look. The question came out of nowhere. "What do you mean?"

"Oh, don't give me that. You might have fooled these idiots, who are only smart when their nose is in a book or a microscope, but you're not fooling me. Come on, you can tell me. Think of it as an exercise in building trust between us. Besides, I really want to see the expression on all of their faces. I'm starting to enjoy that shocked look that they do so well. So what do you say?"

"I…"

"Wait, wait. Let me guess. This might help to jog your memory. Obviously KGB. Right?"

She had no response.

He looked up at the ceiling. "Spetsnaz, no doubt."

She remained silent.

"Okay, shot in the dark here. I'm swinging for the fences…I would say…Vega group. Right? Am I right?"

She gave him a hard look.

"I knew it. It's standard operating procedure. They put Sokolov in as the overt overseer, and sneak in you as the covert backup plan. And the shocking thing, children, is that if push came to shove, you really would be Sokolov's superior and boss. Again, don't make me say it, am I right?"

She smiled. "One of only three women to ever make the rank of Colonel."

His raised his eyebrows. "Oh, sweetie. I had no idea. I probably should be saluting you. You're a few steps ahead of me. Why would they jam somebody as high as you down here? Aha. For the same reason I'm here. Because of your friend and mine, Mr. Deadly Virus. Right? Wow, this is going to look really bad on your dossier. No more promotions for you. You bad, bad girl. You're going to get a good spanking when you get home. Or maybe that's why you don't want to go home. Hmm. Or maybe it is why you do want to go home. Maybe that's how you got this rank in the first place."

He started pacing again. "Okay, I'm talking too much. This happens sometimes when I get a little excited. We need to get back to basics. So, Colonel, would you be as good as to give me your proposal? All of it, please, with as much detail as possible."

"Certainly. You and I get dressed and go out to the Cat. You leave your pistol here on the table. It will take these people several minutes to get free, so they won't interfere. I will take you to the samples. You confirm what they are to your satisfaction, and then we drive together to wherever it is that you were planning to go. You cannot double-cross me about the lives of these people because by then they will be armed and you will not. It's just you and me and the samples, free and clear. I will take my chances with you, and you can take me in a fight, I'm sure, so you should be willing to take your chances with me. It might not be ideal for you, but it is the only sure way that you will get the samples you need. By the way, how much money are we talking about for selling our souls on the open market?"

"Fifty million, Colonel. Split two ways, and that still ain't bad. Or maybe we can stay together and pool our resources. I wouldn't lose any sleep over it, though. I plan to raise the price once I have the samples back safe and sound. These people are very desperate to get their hands on this stuff. I'm thinking they'd pay one hundred million without batting an eye. They probably are counting on a price raise, anyway. So how does that sound?"

"Like a mansion on a tropical beach. Like many young men attending to my every wish. Like I should go down on you from here to our final destination."

"Colonel, I'm shocked. I've never had sex with a superior officer before. Sounds interesting, though. But before we seal the deal, just let me think this through. If I leave all these folks here alive, what harm can they do to me? They don't know my name, rank, or serial number. They could describe me, but the folks back at my home base are going to be able to provide that and more once they figure that out what I've been up to." He stopped and sighed. "I was planning on going deep undercover anyway. My own government is going to come after me, and they're pretty darned good at that sort of stuff. So, I guess what little you folks know won't really hurt me in the long run. Okay. Colonel, you have a deal."

"I don't suppose my wrists can be untied."

"Let me think about that. I'll tell you what. Let me pat you down real good and make sure you don't have any surprises waiting for me. Assuming the results are negative for knives, guns, grenades, and that sort of thing, then I will release you. The deal is, the first sign, the first hint of bad behaviour, and I'm going to shoot dimples here. And then the rest. Okay?"

"Okay. I understand."

"Great." He approached her and then patted her down in a professional, business-like manner.

"Colonel, you are clean. Spin around and face away from me, please."

He found a small knife in his pocket and snapped it into the open position. In one quick motion, he sliced through the tie.

She moved her arms into a normal position and rubbed her wrists. "Thank you. That's much better."

"You can thank me later. In some twisted, carnal way, hopefully. For now, we have work to do."

"Let me get dressed. Then I'll take you to the samples."

"Great! I'll just hang out here and watch. And keep an eye on the kids, while I'm at it."

She when to the rack that held all the coats and one-piece snowmobile suits. She dressed briskly.

Hamlin watched this all unfold with amazement. Of course, the fact that he felt he was going to die at the hands of this lunatic or possibly from the injury he had already sustained buffered the impact of all these revelations significantly. But he was still shocked by it all. Lena, a Colonel in the KGB? And now she was throwing in with this morally devoid psychopath? Surely it was a ploy to say their lives. But what about hers? This guy had killed all the other 'partners' in this scheme already, so why would her fate be any different? That was as far as he could think. The rest of his mind was trying to cope with the pain shooting through the side of his face.

She walked over, her legs swishing as she stepped because of the bulky clothing she had on.

"Okay, there you are. All ready to go. Good deal." In one hand he held his pistol, the other was resting on the closest tabletop. The fingers on his free hand began to drum out a quiet rhythm.

"Problem?" Lena asked.

He seemed frustrated. "Yes. Damn it. Cold feet, Lena. I mean Colonel. Or…whatever. I have to work on what I'm going to call you."

She smiled pleasantly. "What about lover?"

"Enough with the seduction, okay? Just let me deal with my…cold feet. Just some last minute jitters. I need to work this out, to walk through it just one last time. What have I got myself into here? Let's keep this simple. So, on one hand, you are demanding the lives of these five be spared. That goes against the grain–it does, I have to admit it. But, in exchange, I get to split one hundred million dollars and enjoy an eight hundred and fourteen mile long blow job. Hmm, when you lay it out bare like that, it does seem like a no-brainer, doesn't it? Okay, the deal stands. Let's go get us some samples."

She stood unmoving. "The pistol?"

"Oh, right. Momentary mental lapse. Sorry." He looked at it longingly and then set it down with a clunk. "Hey, wait a minute. Hamlin here isn't tied up. That changes the agreed upon time line."

"He probably has multiple injuries. He's in no condition to cause us any trouble. It changes nothing."

"I'd like to tie him up, just in case. Hamlin, on your feet!"

Francis was able to stand but just barely. He wobbled and found that not falling over became his sole focus.

"Oh, never mind. Look at you. You're a mess. Don't forget that Tylenol I suggested earlier." He turned and looked toward the door. "All right, Colonel, let's go. Fame and fortune awaits."

"I'll settle for the fortune."

He let her exit through the door first, and then gave one last look at the group before departing.

"You kids behave yourselves now, you hear?" And with that, the door slammed shut and he was gone.

A brief silence ensued. Everyone fully expected him to barge back in and renege on the deal, laughing all the time. But the door remained shut. Eventually the sound of the Cat driving away reached their ears.

"Thank God!" someone cried and they all started to move away from the wall.

"There are knives in the kitchen that should cut these off," Zoya suggested. She walked over to the table where Hamlin was slumped over. "Francis, are you all right?"

"I'm alive." It was all he could manage.

"I'll take care of you. Just rest for a minute."

Hamlin would have been just as happy to fall asleep and never wake up again at that moment. He complied easily.

CHAPTER TWENTY-ONE

"Who's driving?" Lena asked as they trudged toward the idling Cat.

"You are, for now."

They both hopped in briskly, glad to be out of the cold.

"All right, take me to the samples."

She started rolling slowly. The Cat made a tight turn around the side of the barracks and followed along the back wall. It was here that she stopped the machine.

"All right, sweetheart, what gives?"

She pointed to a lean-to that had been built on to the back of the building. "The samples are in there. Shall I get them?"

"In there?"

"Yes."

He shook his head. "All this fuss about something that was only a few feet away. But, how could I have known? Yeah, by all means, grab those bad boys so we can be on our way."

She hopped out. He watched closely as she accessed the shed and quickly emerged with a military green metallic box in her hands. She fumbled with the door but eventually climbed back in.

"That's it?"

"Yes, there are three core samples, all confirmed to hold the virus."

"Well, let's just have a quick look, shall we? Pop that thing open."

She complied. Sure enough, inside lay three ice cores.

"Yup, those are core samples, all right. Listen, I don't want to be a bother, but I'm going to insist that we go back in and put enough of them under a microscope so that I can see the virus for myself. What do you say?"

That was the last thing she wanted but she couldn't say it. "I say you shouldn't have hit the microbiologist so hard that he won't be any help to you in finding the virus."

"Hamlin?"

She nodded.

"Oh no. Isn't that just the way it's been going for me lately. That's almost funny in a tragic kind of way. Lena, I'm confident that somebody in there knows enough about basic science that they can help me, even if he can't. Come on, let's go. The quicker the better."

"Are you sure?"

He raised his hand. Hamlin's recently acquired black Beretta was in it. Lena forgot that he had recently gotten in the habit of putting it under the seat when he went out. "I'm sure. Now move it before I decide to dissolve our partnership right here and now. Get us back in there and fast."

She had little choice but to comply.

The worst case scenario took all of five minutes to happen. The last crew member had just got their tie cut off when the door slammed open and Lena stepped back in, followed by their captor.

"Did you miss me?" he yelled happily. "What, nobody armed and ready to repel boarders? What is wrong with you people? You ruined your one and only chance. Everybody, in here now!"

Dejected, they came slowly.

"Awesome. Now, everybody sit down at the table with Hamlin. That includes you, Miss Lena. Hurry it up!" He picked up his pistol which still lay in the same place he had dropped it.

"Let's move it. You, chunky. Don't sit. I need you to do something for me."

Zoya looked terrified.

"Oh, relax. It's not that bad. I need you to go into the back storage room where the larger weapons were put. I need you to find one that looks a lot like a machine gun, but just a little bulkier with a funny canister on the bottom. Think you can manage that?"

"Yes." Her voice broke, but she walked off steadily.

Lena looked grim. She knew what the weapon was. "What the hell are you doing?"

"The same thing I was always planning to do, Colonel."

"But what about the samples?"

"Oh, I believe you. If they didn't have the virus in them, why would you have bothered to save them in the first place? It's not like there's a shortage of ice to sample. We're sitting on what, two miles of it as we speak? I have no doubt the samples are valid."

"But you said…"

"I needed a reason to get you back in here. I really didn't want to shoot you in the Cat. How boring would that have been?"

"You're a monster."

"No, no. When you have as much money as I'm going to have, you don't get called monster. Maybe socially maligned or morally lacking or something like that. Ah, here she comes. Good girl. Bring that right over here to me."

Zoya seemed unsure how to carry the bulky weapon.

"You're doing just fine. Here, let me help you. I'll just take that so you don't drop it."

He walked over and took it from her.

"Excellent. Now just go on over and get a comfortable spot at the table."

She obeyed quietly.

Lena's mind was racing. There had to be an option. What could she do?

"You didn't even shut the door," she complained. "It's freezing in here already."

"Oh, I wouldn't worry about that. Things are going to warm up right shortly. Being cold is going to be your fondest wish in just a moment. I'm just going to…make a quick check here…"

He looked down at the weapon he now cradled. A pop and hiss emanated from it.

"Great! We have a pilot light. We are in business. Say, I would love to see that look you all are so capable of just one more time before I go. Lena, could you tell them what I have in my hands here, so they can put two and two together."

"Why? Why do you have to do this?"

"It's been kind of a fantasy for me. And frankly, I don't really see another opportunity presenting itself anytime soon. There are not a lot of circumstances that lead to the chance to use a flamethrower, no matter how much money you have. Especially on people."

A number of gasps emitted from the people at the table. Zoya lost it completely and started to cry.

"Oh, now, now. It's not all that bad. This thing is so intense, you'll only actually feel it for a few seconds. Ten, maybe twenty tops. Then you'll pass out from the pain. After that…nothing. So you see, it could be worse. If some of you could jump up and run around the room screaming after I set you on fire, well, I'd like that. It would be kind of cool; just like in the movies."

He checked over his shoulder to confirm the path to the open doorway. He started stepping away, finger now on the trigger.

"Here's hoping you all enjoy barbeque as much as I do."

"You'll burn in hell for this," Lena snarled defiantly.

"Well, you're the ones on the receiving end of this thing, so…"

As his finger tightened, he made the last mistake of his life. He allowed himself to be distracted. Barinov was making no effort to conceal himself or to be stealthy as he stumbled up the stairs and into the barracks. The allure of fresh, warm meat drove what little mental capacity he had left. But he was not detected. He loomed behind the soldier, poised himself, and drove forward, teeth-first into the side of his face.

"Hey! What the...Jesus!"

They grappled for a moment. The soldier managed to use a leverage move to flip Barinov over his shoulder and onto the linoleum floor. Blood dripped from the gaping mouth as opaque, blank eyes rolled. The soldier reached back and felt the open wound on the side of his neck.

"What the fuck are you? Damn it!" He pulled the Beretta out of his pocket and shot Barinov in the head. He immediately slumped to the floor. He had forgotten momentarily about the others. It was an opportunity that did not get missed.

Lena hit him from the side, her foot driving with all her strength into the knee of his planted foot. It popped audibly and he fell to the floor shrieking.

"Ow! Dammit! What the fuck! My leg!"

She picked up the gun he had dropped in all the confusion and held it limply in her hand.

"Damn you! Fuck! What have you done to me?"

"Broke your leg."

"Fuck! Fuck you! Bitch!" He continued to writhe.

"I'd be more worried about what Barinov just did to you."

"Oh shit, oh shit. I've got to go."

She actually smiled. "It doesn't matter now. You just got what you wanted."

"Bullshit! Bullshit! What the fuck...what are you saying?"

"You've been infected. The virus is all yours. Poetic justice if I do say so myself."

"What? No! Shit, shit, shit." He struggled to regain some semblance of composure and control. "We've got to talk, Colonel. You and me. Right now. There's still a hundred million on the line."

"Not for you. You'll be a raving lunatic like Barinov in forty-eight hours. We have no immunity or cure, remember? That's what makes it so valuable. Asshole."

"What? Wait...no. We can work this out. We can."

"I already have." She turned so she could see him and still address the others. "Listen, I have a plan."

They all seemed very interested.

"Zoya, get some painkiller. Francis needs it right now. Go."

She nodded and headed for the storage room.

"I have had enough of this place and this virus. This guy came here in some sort of vehicle that travelled fast enough so that the trip was relatively short. It also has the capacity to carry five people, according to what he said earlier. I say we take the Cat, follow the GPS back to where these monsters first appeared, find their vehicle and head for McMurdo. Based on what this prick has said, the management of the station has no idea what he is really doing here. We can get medical attention there. And we can get out of this God-forsaken place sooner. I, for one, have no desire to be here for another two months. What do you say?"

There was quick, unanimous agreement. Except, of course, for Hamlin who had his head down on the table.

"Francis, are you up to answering me?"

"Yeah." It was all he could muster.

"Fuck! Shit! Damn, that hurts. Hey, you need me. You need to take me with you. You'll never make it without me."

"We'll never make it with you. You'll turn into a drooling, flesh eating monster long before we arrive."

"No. No. You said forty-eight hours. We'll be there before then. They can help me."

"Sorry. As I said before, there's no cure. You're going to stay here, by yourself, and enjoy the transformation. It's exactly what you deserve. The real fun is in knowing what's coming."

Zoya came back with a bottle and a syringe.

"Good. Give him the shot now."

She walked over to Hamlin and put her hand on his shoulder gently.

"No, wait! What is wrong with you? This is still all fixable. Look, I'm sorry about the flamethrower thing. Maybe I was a little out of line with that idea. I get a little high strung when things are unfolding. Ouch! Shit! This can all be overcome. So there's what...six of us left? Split one hundred million and guess what...we are still rich beyond our wildest dreams. I can still make it happen. And this knee, it's just minor surgery to fix if someone knows what they're doing. Come on!"

Lena walked toward him, gun in her hand.

"You are not listening. No matter what we agree to, you're dead now. You have been infected. There is no cure. You will be like the walking dead within two to three days. It's over for you. And from us, you will get no sympathy. The world will be a better place without you."

"Oh, sweetheart, come on. That just can't be. Let's talk. I'm open to negotiation."

"Unfortunately, mother nature is not. We're leaving. I'll put your pistol on the back table. If you want to crawl over to it, you can do whatever you think is right. Either way, we won't be here, and you will never leave this place alive."

"No." Of all things, he started crying. "No. I have plans. This isn't possible. You're lying. I have to leave. People are expecting me. Important people."

"And I truly hope they end up in the same place as you. And soon."

She turned and walked away. "Everybody, get dressed. Grab some water and basic food. Zoya, how are you doing?"

"I gave him a shot. He'll start feeling better soon. But then he'll probably fall asleep. We need to get moving."

"Okay. He may need help getting dressed. You and I can do it. The rest of you, get ready. We're leaving this place."

"Shit! Dammit all! Give me my gun! Let me kill myself now. It's mine...give it to me."

"Sorry," Lena said. "You'll have to crawl over to get it. And don't go too fast. If it looks like you're going to reach it before we leave, I might have to break something else."

"No! No, no, no! Fuck! Shit! Why didn't I meet you sooner? Come on! We'd make an awesome team."

"No," she said simply. "We would not. Come on everybody, let's get out of here."

They started filing for the door, Hamlin leaning on the shoulder of one Zhabin for stability.

"Oh no! No! NO!"

The screaming continued until they had all walked out and Lena shut the door behind them.

"Good riddance. And God rest those we left behind. With one exception."

The GPS took them back to the exact spot where the two men had ambushed Hamlin. With light winds and no drifting snow to impede visibility, they found the other vehicle easily. It was an enormous hovercraft, sleek and modern. It sat with engines idling, just waiting for someone to return and commandeer her. There was ample room for everyone. Hamlin found a bunk and almost immediately passed out in it.

There were supplies of all sorts–food, water, medical equipment, and pharmaceuticals–but no weapons. Lena supposed that these men would have raised flags if they had left McMurdo armed to the teeth. Perhaps that was the reason for the cache in the outer building.

It was comfortable and powerful. And it had the return course already plotted into its navigational system. Lena had to struggle with the controls momentarily, but they were soon scooting along at a fairly high rate of speed. As they were floating over the minor imperfections on the surface of the ground, the ride was extremely smooth and comfortable.

They were all so relieved to be away from Vostok. Although uncertain of exactly what kind of reception to expect at McMurdo when they arrived with their wild story of espionage and carnage, they all figured it had to be better than what they were leaving behind. And nobody felt guilty about *who* they left behind.

McMurdo was vastly different from Vostok. With a winter population of over two hundred people–a number that swelled to over one thousand in the summer–it was more of a town than a station. They received immediate and excellent medical care, especially Hamlin, when they arrived. The base commander and his staff had many questions to ask of them. The story they told was wild and unlikely, but each version recanted by each person was consistent in the end on all the major points. The ultimate response to what had happened at Vostok was never discussed or revealed in front of the survivors. Lena suspected that the Americans would pay a return trip just to see for themselves. She had insisted that Moscow be notified about what had happened and the Americans had agreed easily enough. Some details would be changed or left out, no doubt. The Russians really had no way to get there for some time, so opportunities to investigate would still exist.

Hamlin was in a hospital bed for a week, and had a minor surgical procedure done to ensure that the fractured facial bone he had suffered would heal properly. After seven days, with some carefully administered pain medication, he was determined to be able to leave and be on his own. The Russians were treated well, but had some minor restrictions imposed on their movement around McMurdo. Nobody complained.

Because of their location on the coast and the size and condition of the runway that serviced the base, a flight was thought to be possible within two weeks to return the Russians home. The next flight to the USA would happen the following week and Hamlin would be on it. He couldn't wait. He had easily had enough of Antarctica for one lifetime.

CHAPTER TWENTY-TWO

The soft knock on his door was just what he wanted to hear. He had no qualms about leaving it unlocked here at the station.

"Come in!"

Lena entered, made eye contact, and smiled. "There you are. You look so much better than the last time I saw you."

"Well, thank you–I think. That could be paraphrased to say something like, *wow you sure looked like crap before*."

She closed the door gently. "You did look like crap before."

He chuckled. An outright laugh might just jiggle his still sensitive face a little too much.

"I can't think of anything else irreverent to say. We've been through quite an adventure, haven't we?"

She walked in slowly, checking out his temporary apartment. "This is nice, Francis. Are you sure you won't want to stay?"

"Oh yeah. Quite sure."

"I thought so." She walked over and kissed him softly on his forehead. "That didn't hurt, did it?"

"No. Not at all. It felt wonderful, as a matter of fact."

"Really?" Her eyes lit on the big screen television on the wall. "Don't tell me. You have cable down here?"

"Yeah, baby. Nothing but the best. Want to watch a movie with me? I might even consider something romantic if you want."

"It is nice of you to make such a major concession."

"I missed you. I'm really happy you're here."

"You don't say. It's nice to know I'm having a positive impact."

Another chuckle. "You're getting progressively more sarcastic as you go."

"Hmm. We are very similar people, you and I. I haven't worked out if that is a good thing or not. Say, are you cleared for sex by the medical professionals here?"

"Oh man. You have no idea how great that idea sounds to me. But I suspect I'd probably split my head open from all the heart pounding exertion. So, sorry, not this time."

"Too bad." She sat on the sofa beside him.

"I hear you're leaving in a couple weeks. Me too, by the way. Back to America and all she has to offer."

"You must be happy."

"Yes. I am."

They both looked at the screen momentarily as some inane talk show discussed the merits of recreational marijuana use. The droning covered up the silence.

"Lena, can I ask you something?"

"Of course. Anything."

"A little while back, before I really knew you as well as I do now, we had a conversation. We were sort of joking around, but basically we talked about you coming back with me to America. Now I'm wondering–and before it's too late to ask–would you?"

"Would I?"

"Yes. Come back with me."

"To do what?"

"To live. And love. With me."

She smiled. "Francis, you are so sweet. What about my parents back in Russia? What about my military career? Would I be looked at as a defector? A traitor? Would I ever be allowed to go back to my homeland again? They would think I sold the virus to your government, you see."

"Well, there is that, I suppose."

"I would have no job, no way to support myself; I would know no one but you and I would be completely at the mercy of your immigration department. What if I tried this and they rejected my request? Then I return to Russia to what? Prison time? Or worse? After what I just went through?"

"You really are casting a negative light on this."

"Francis, can I talk? Can I tell you some things?"

"Yes."

"Very well. When you first came to the station, I already had it in my head that I was going to seduce you. I felt it would give me leverage, build trust, and make it easier to talk about sensitive things if they happened to come up."

"Such as the research I was doing on the virus?"

"Yes." She said it firmly, without hesitation. There was no deceit in her manner.

"All right. I figured that."

"Soon afterwards, it became clear to me that I really was starting to like you. You are smart, and sensitive; you're a decent lover…

"Decent?"

"Let me finish. You are honest, and good, and funny. That means a lot to me. You make me laugh. You make me feel good about myself and even life in general. You're fun to be around. I can't wait to hear what words come out of your mouth next. No other man has ever been able to make me feel that way about them before."

"I was hoping that you would mention something about my love-making prowess, even in passing."

"There, you see? That's what I am talking about. Francis, at the end of it all, it occurs to me that I have a problem. And I just don't know what to do about it."

"That's funny, because you're usually very decisive. What's the problem? Maybe I can help?"

She sighed. "Not likely, Francis. For you see, you are the problem." She leaned in close to his face with hers, careful not to bump it. To his shock, he saw tears forming in her blue eyes.

"What is it?"

"I love you," she whispered, and then her head was on his shoulder as she started to cry softly.

He put his arm around her shoulder and hugged. He knew what he had to say, and it was the pure, unadulterated truth.

"I love you too," he whispered softly, keeping with the moment.

"What are we going to do?" she sobbed into his sweatshirt.

"I wish I knew."

They clung to each other for a while, until she seemed ready to disengage from their embrace.

"We have two weeks," she said.

To Hamlin, that seemed a ridiculously short amount of time. But he couldn't bring himself to rain on her overly optimistic parade.

"That we do."

"Listen, I suddenly have an idea. I'm going to go now, but I'll be back soon. Let me cook supper for you. I will make a traditional Russian dish. You will love it. I need to get some supplies. So, relax and think good thoughts. Wish me well on my quest."

"Okay. Happy grocery shopping. Good luck. And don't be too long."

She almost ran out of the apartment. "I won't be long."

He frowned ever so slightly. "That was weird."

The base commander of McMurdo Station was willing to speak to Lena on short notice. Although there was always a steady schedule of work and issues to deal with, winter was much quieter than the busy summer months.

"Close the door, please."

Lena was good at reading people and already had a decent idea what this man was all about from the initial questioning that had happened when they showed up in the hovercraft. He seemed fair enough, but also gave the impression that he had no time or interest in peripheral issues. He was very businesslike.

"Have a seat, please. What can I do for your?"

"I hope we can do something for each other."

He didn't give any sort of response beyond verbal. "And what would that be?"

"I would like to go to America."

He processed her statement quickly and quietly. "For a visit?"

"To live. Permanently."

"I see. Have you done any of the standard procedures necessary yet?"

"I would like to bypass the procedures."

"The procedures are there for a very good reason. There is an expectation between our two countries that they will be followed."

"I will be persecuted if I return to Russia."

She received a hard look after that statement.

"That doesn't make any sense to me. Your initial statement places you as a trusted member of the research team and a decorated officer in the military. Why would you be persecuted?"

"They might find out what I did."

"And what did you do?"

"I gave you a sample of the virus."

She had to give him credit. His facial expression never flinched. She wondered what was going on inside.

"I'm sorry, but I'm not following you. Please explain about the virus."

"I can get you a sample."

"From Vostok?"

"Originally, of course. But not now."

"Where is it now?"

"Here."

Now his expression changed. He squirmed in his seat.

"It's here? At this station?"

"It's very close. I did not bring it in to the station itself."

"Damn it. Of all people, you should know how profoundly dangerous that could be." He had heard all the details of what happened at Vostok.

"It is safe enough. Trust me. I don't want to have anything to do with it. Ever again."

"Then why bring it with you?" He wasn't completely convinced she was telling the truth.

She sighed. "It is still there, in the lake. Somebody will drill down and get it again. Me bringing it here doesn't change that fact in any way."

"You still didn't answer my question. Why would you bring it with you?"

"For leverage."

"Oh? Leverage for what?"

"To negotiate."

"I would feel better about this if I knew where the virus was. I have a great concern about the safety of this station."

"Then negotiate and I will tell you."

He sighed. "What do you want?"

"I want to live in America."

He narrowed his eyes. "How much money?"

"I just want to live in America. No money."

That surprised him. "What you're asking for falls outside of my jurisdiction. I can't guarantee anything even if I wanted to."

"No, but you could call someone who can."

"You're playing a dangerous game. What if I make a call and get told that we won't negotiate with you? Then we both have a huge problem because you've already told me that you brought the virus here."

She smiled. "A dangerous game? Compared to what we just went through at Vostok, this is like playing Crazy Eights with pre-schoolers."

On the inside, he was a very unhappy man. He liked control and order. This had the potential to be a time bomb.

"Go out into the hallway. Turn right and have a seat there. Don't go anywhere else. Can I trust you to do that?"

"Yes." The answer was straight and firm.

"All right. Go. Shut the door as you exit. Let me make some calls."

She nodded. "Thank you."

For the second time, a soft knock came at the door. Hamlin had fallen asleep on the couch. He looked at the clock through blurry eyes. It was late.

It opened slowly. "Francis? Are you there?"

He pulled himself into a partial upright position. "Yeah. I'm here."

Lena walked in. "I'm sorry. I didn't think I would be so long."

He waved her over. "Looks like grocery shopping didn't go very well."

She walked over and sat on the floor in front of him, her face now at his level as he lay there. "Never mind the shopping. I had another quest. And things went very well indeed."

He grunted as he adjusted his position slightly. "I must be tired. I have no idea what you're trying to say just now."

She leaned in and kissed his forehead. Then she kissed the uninjured side of his face. Then she moved in and took possession of his lips. Gently, but firmly, she imposed her will. A full minute went by before they disengaged. His motor was definitely running by then.

"Francis, I love you. I want to come to America and live with you. Okay?"

His smile was a little lopsided as he favored the good side of his face. "Lena, it's more than okay. I would love that more than anything. I wish we could find a way to overcome your issues."

She was very close. Her lips sought and found his ear and pressed softly and sensuously against it. "I already have," she said in the deep voice that drove Hamlin crazy.

"What? What do you mean?"

"I made a deal. With your government."

He was absolutely baffled by what she was saying. "My government? How is that possible? You mean just now, in the last few hours?"

She went for his throat, her teeth and tongue alternating in an unusual partnership. He offered no resistance.

"I talked to the base commander. He made a call. A deal was made. I am going to go home with you, if you truly want me to." She immediately resumed her assault on his exposed neck.

A shiver went up his spine. Her efforts were having good results. "How is that possible?"

"Negotiating. It works well if you do it right."

His mind was starting to blur away from the conversation and more into what she was doing. "And you do it right."

"Hmm. I try."

"Yes," he said, "you do."

She wasn't quite ready to let him lapse into a sex induced coma just yet. "Francis, I am serious. I can come. If you want me to. I will miss the Moscow flight and leave with you when you go. Is that what you want?"

His eyes softened. "Yes. Oh, God yes. Please come with me. At this point it would be a dream come true. I have so much to show you. You'll love my country."

That was, of course, the right answer.

"For that, Professor Hamlin, I think you deserve a reward. A little prevue of what awaits you when you get healed up back in America."

Francis decided he was willing to risk a little facial pain. That kind of can-do attitude would make the remaining days in Antarctica go by in a much nicer fashion.

The house was perfectly silent. Sunlight fell in through the south facing windows and the warmth generated was readily noticeable. Earlier that day, the cleaning lady had been in. Everything was spotless, shiny, and straightened up. No plants had survived the hiatus, but that could be easily remedied. The sound of a key being inserted into the front door lock broke the silence of the past three months. Life was about to return to the spacious brick home.

A soft clicking sound announced the bolt retracting from the frame. The door swung open with a barely perceptible squeak.

"Oh my God!" Lena put a hand on each side of her face as if it was about to explode. "Francis, is this really your house? It's gorgeous!"

He was power grinning, facial injury notwithstanding. "It's your home now. You better take the tour and start getting accustomed to it."

The wooden floors shone from the polishing done earlier. "Oh, so beautiful. How can you afford a castle? Do they pay you a million dollars at your job?"

"No, but I bet if I let you talk to the chancellor, he might consider it."

She walked in, noting first the dining room on the left, then straight ahead to the kitchen.

"It's like a palace. I can't believe I get to cook in here."

"Why, yes. I'm going to be benevolent and let you cook for me. In here. Just to show what an outstanding kind of guy I am."

She walked into the den, noticing the patio doors and the deck beyond. "Oh! Is that a spa?"

"That is one fine, American-made hot tub. It has enough jets to place you temporarily at the gates of heaven itself. And check out that barbecue! Huh? Looks good, right?"

She nodded. "So it is true about American men and outdoor cooking."

"Yeah, baby. You know it. So, what's next? Basement or upstairs?"

"Francis, your house is as big as the barracks at Vostok. And we had fourteen people living there."

"Don't get any ideas."

She giggled. "Okay, basement next."

238

It impressed her as much as the main floor. It was half finished, with carpeting, sectional couch, and a big screen television on the good side. A small bar and a pool table finished it off. It was just as well that they saved the upstairs for last.

She ooed and awed her way through the four bedrooms. She walked through the master into the en-suite and her jaw dropped.

"Oh." Her voice dropped to a reverent level. She walked in slowly, reaching out to softly touch various surfaces as she went. Finally she stopped, staring at the walk in shower.

"Oh, Francis. Look at this thing. It is amazing."

"It has a steam feature. And I think it will almost accommodate the entire Dallas Cowboy's cheerleading squad. How's that for good clean fun?"

She gave him a look. "I think it will be you and I having fun in there."

"No cheerleaders?"

"Let me think about it."

"Can I get that in writing?"

Her mind drifted off. "Francis, we need food."

"Right." That was another part of the American experience that he couldn't wait to expose her to. "We'll go grocery shopping. Now. Then we'll come back here and I'll show you what outdoor cooking is all about. Tomorrow, my gorgeous dream girl, we're going clothes shopping. I have a few outfits that I can't help envisioning you in. Besides, you'll need something appropriate for the hot tub."

"Will I? Is clothing really necessary?"

"I'm not positive. Mr. and Mrs. Pritchard next door may like to weigh in on this matter, although it's possible they may have differing opinions. Do keep in mind how short the fence is in the backyard."

"Hmm. Perhaps somebody needs to liven up this beautiful neighborhood."

"Yeah…as much as you're kind of turning me on even as you speak, do also keep in mind that there are several other university employees living in the area. Let's approach the public nudity idea gradually."

"We'll see."

"As long as nobody else does, I'm all for it."

Lena had been smiling since they entered the house. She was still doing it. "With that in mind, I would like to propose that we both need some freshening up. What I'm thinking is this–you wash my back and I'll wash yours. Then we can see what else needs scrubbing. I just can't wait to get into this shower."

"Why wait? It's yours too. I'll grab some towels and show you how this thing works. I think we should both get steamed."

And amongst other things, they did just that.

To say that it had been an eventful day seemed like a gross understatement to Hamlin. Shopping, barbecuing, hot tubbing, and finally just relaxing had all gone spectacularly well. Night had fallen and the only reprieve from the darkness was from the soft glow of solar lights along the path leading up to the stairs. Some stars were visible in the night sky above. He lay on a reclining padded lounge chair on the back deck.

Lena lay on him, nestled between his legs, her shoulders against his chest. They had pulled a blanket over themselves to prolong this portion of the evening. Fall was arriving soon and the heat of the day was dissipating.

"Francis, do you miss your girlfriend?"

"Who?"

"Good answer."

Under the blanket, he tightened his grip on her. "You know, it hurt like hell at the time, but now I realize she was exactly right. It was fun, but I was being delusional about the whole thing. We're both better off in the long run. Or, at least, I know I am."

"And what are you being now?"

"Infatuated, I suppose. Being around you today was like Christmas, New Years, my first date, and every other good thing I can think of, all rolled into one. Is it possible to be addicted to another human being? It's like you're a drug that I can't stop taking."

"That is good. You can take all you want."

"I just hope my heart can take it." He lowered his voice as if the neighbors could hear. "You know, I think I had at least a partial erection for like the last eighteen hours straight. As soon as I'm near you, my body starts getting ideas. How can I survive that over the long run?"

"Are they good ideas?"

"You are always a good idea."

She snuggled in tighter. "You know what I missed in Vostok? Just being outside. There, outdoors was a dangerous ordeal. Here, you just breath in the fresh air and enjoy it."

"I know," he said. "Hey, here's a question. Do you like to walk?"

"Walk? What do you mean?"

There are some excellent trails through the park," Hamlin replied. "We should start walking. You know, for exercise."

"Okay. I would like to walk with you."

They stopped talking and let the peace of the evening envelope them. It was the most relaxed Francis had been in months.

"Francis?"

"Hmm?"

"May I make an observation?"

"Hmm."

"If you stop rubbing my breasts, your erection problem may lessen."

"Hmm. I'm pretty sure I don't want to do that."

"Suit yourself. But no more complaints."

"Hmm. Who's complaining?"

She laughed softly. "I'm just, as you say here, giving you a hard time."

"Yes you are."

Another peaceful interlude followed.

"Francis?"

"Hmm?"

"We...will have some problems to take care of. You know?"

"I know."

"Even in this palace, I will eventually get bored."

"You'll need a job. That way I can retire early."

"That wasn't really what I was thinking," she said.

"We can buy a little ranch out in Montana, and then raise free-range hamsters."

"For pet stores?"

"No, silly. For the barbecue."

She shook her head. "I think you lost your mind back in Antarctica."

"You know what it is? Seriously. Trust me on this–I know some psychology profs. It's a release of all the stress built up over the past three months. I feel so relaxed right now. It's just incredible. So, all the bad things are just pouring out of me. And that makes me almost giddy."

"I feel it too. It is like...how do I say it...like a week's vacation at a luxury resort–but this is my life now so it won't ever end. It will just go on and on. Incredible!"

"Listen, Lena. Don't fret about the details just yet. Let me work some of my magic. I know you'll need a purpose and a focus. With your brains and abilities, I'm sure we can find something that will make you very satisfied. In the meantime, I'll teach you everything you need to know about being an American."

"Can I drive a car?"

"I don't know. Do you know how?"

"I can drive anything. Even some light armored vehicles."

"Sounds like a BMW would be right down your alley. And why not? We could probably finance it over ten or twelve years–just one hundred and twenty easy payments."

She lifted her hips and readjusted her position. She settled back in.

"Make me a few more promises like that and this evening is going to end very well for you."

"Oh my. Well, if that's the direction the night has taken, I do have an idea. How about we put in a pool?"

"A swimming pool? Here?"

"Sure. Just more easy payments, that's all."

"Francis!" She had transformed back into her husky voice. "I might have to let you have the grand prize for that."

He was way past being intrigued. "And what's the grand prize?"

She turned sideways under the blanket, and whispered the answer into his ear. Then she settled back in and snuggled up close. "Just one thing before you slip into another sex induced coma. Francis?"

"Yes?"

She moved until her lips just touched his. Her eyes were open just a slit. She had assumed the dreamy look he liked so much.

"I love you," she said soft and sweet.

"I love you too." They kissed slowly. Hamlin marveling at the warmth pouring off her soft body. She felt like she could melt all the ice in Antarctica. And at that moment, he wouldn't have bet against it.

THE END

www.ingramcontent.com/pod-product-compliance
Lightning Source LLC
Chambersburg PA
CBHW020102180626
46812CB00006B/2443